# Cowboys and Crowns Collection

## PART 1

## LACY WILLIAMS

Once Upon a Cowboy

# Chapter One



## EARLY FEBRUARY

*JUST KEEP SMILING.*

Princess Alessandra, second in line for the throne of Glorvaird, meandered through the crush of bodies as the Who's-Who of New York City society mingled on the sidewalk outside a ritzy hotel. Inside the ballroom would be even worse, stuffy with the heat of so many people. The icy air chilled her skin where the slinky dress she wore didn't cover nearly enough beneath her designer coat, but inside she'd be grateful to shed her outerwear.

She detested events like these. But her royal duty demanded her presence. Her sister, the crown princess, had tasked her with forging alliances with two powerful dignitaries, which she would attempt when she could get inside. Two hours, and she could return to her own hotel, several blocks away. And rid herself of the awful, pinching heels her stylist had provided.

Paparazzi snapped pictures from behind a cordoned-off line, the flashes from their cameras whisking her to the present and out of her thoughts. Hired security milled around, looking bored. After years of being in the public eye, she was used to the presence of both.

It didn't mean the press weren't as annoying as gnats, constantly buzzing in her ear.

One misstep, one faux pas, could follow her around on the Internet for a year.

She smoothed her skirt unobtrusively and kept the smile fixed on her face.

A hand on her elbow made her pause amidst the crowd.

Her bodyguard. Tim was dark-haired and fair-complected, bulky, and more than a head taller than she. He usually faded into the background.

The fact that he'd moved in close had her pulse speeding.

"What's—" *wrong?*

She didn't get both words out before a *pop* echoed above the rumble of the crowd.

Tim's body jerked.

He fell into her. Knocked her off the precarious heels. They tumbled together. Her elbow scraped against the pavement.

The crowd rumbled. Feet shuffled in the periphery as the other high society types didn't seem to know whether to move closer or farther away.

Alessandra struggled to separate herself from Tim, but he weighed close to a hundred pounds more than she did, and his body was heavy and unmoving. Her coat had fallen open when he'd landed atop her, and they seemed to be tangled together.

Why wasn't he moving?

"Stay—down," he gasped.

Someone screamed.

And she realized the hot, sticky substance that covered her hand where she'd tried to push him off was blood. *His* blood.

"Tim!"

Blind panic added strength to her scrambling, and at last she was able to push him off. He rolled to his back, his suit coat falling open to reveal his white shirt stained red.

"Someone—" She looked up at the blur of faces surrounding her. There was no one she recognized.

She pressed her hands to Tim's chest to try and stop the flow of blood, but more seeped up between her fingers. *No!*

"Please, is there a doctor?" she called out. In the cacophony of voices, she couldn't make out a distinct answer. "Can someone call for help?"

But as she looked down on the man bleeding out beneath her hands, she realized it was too late. Tim's eyes had gone glassy and unfocused.

He was gone.

Someone had shot him.

He'd died protecting *her.*

Her fright didn't recede as she glanced at the faces surrounding her. Some sympathetic. Some crying, panicking now that they realized the nightmare was real. Two of the hired policemen edged through the crowd and knelt beside her.

They provided scant cover.

Was someone waiting to take another shot? A sniper? A killer in the crowd?

If she stood, would another bullet find her? Would she collapse beside Tim, her life dripping out onto the New York sidewalk?

She'd stayed crouched beside the man who'd given everything to protect her, shielded by the police who hovered near. People everywhere. Noises. The scent of blood.

She'd never felt so alone.

One thing was clear. She had to get away.

Far, far away.

GIDEON HALE WINCED as he stepped off the somewhat sheltered back porch and into the biting February wind. He'd already waved Apollo, a German Shepherd Dog, back inside to his bed in the mudroom. No use in both of them freezing their guts out here tonight.

It was after ten and the other cowhands were abed. Not him.

At least it wasn't snowing. Or sleeting. For now. The north Texas weather could change quickly, and often did.

He left the ranch house behind, his booted strides quickly eating up the distance across the yard. The moon shone above the row of elms that lined the gravel drive, casting eerie shadows. By rote, his eyes scanned for anything out of place. Until he shook himself out of it.

This wasn't Afghanistan. Or any of the top-secret locations he'd traveled to.

By the time he hit the barn, his hands were chilled inside his leather gloves. He slipped through the double doors and pulled them closed behind him.

The barn was split into two sections. One enclosed, one open to the elements. It provided shelter to the Angus cows that were his family's livelihood, allowing the mamas and babies free access to the paddock beyond.

He'd brought in two prospective mamas from the larger, western field earlier in the day, suspecting they were close to giving birth.

This was a critical time of year for the Triple-H. Calving season.

The next few weeks would determine how much of a profit they'd make this year. His family was counting on him.

And he knew it was Mother Nature, not a conscious choice, but it seemed as if the animals always gave birth on the most bitter nights of the year.

When he checked on the soon-to-be mamas, they were resting peacefully. No signs of agitation, no sign that they were close to giving birth.

Which made him suspicious. Running a herd of fifteen-hundred, they rarely went a day this time of year without several births.

So he bundled his work coat tighter around himself and went out the back of the barn, rounding the side of the structure to where the UTV was parked. It didn't want to crank, probably because of the bitter temperatures. He prayed it wasn't the battery, prayed he wouldn't get stranded out in the fields on a night like this and have to walk home.

The UTV started, and he threw it in gear, bumping his way out of the barnyard and into the field behind. The vehicle had a windshield but little else to shelter him from the open air, and he was frozen through by the time he reached the paddock where the rest of the mamas and expecting mamas were kept.

Sometimes, on nights like this, he wished he was back on the Teams. It had been blisteringly hot during their last covert mission in a place he wasn't supposed to talk about, and he'd lost several pounds of water weight. Two years ago, he'd been an integral part of the close-knit team. Had been armed and lying on his stomach on the sand next to Cash, too close to the Tangoes to whisper a joke or two, separated from the rest of their team by a few hundred yards as they waited for the order to infiltrate.

It hadn't been comfortable. And it wasn't the adrenaline rush that he missed now.

It was the camaraderie. Those guys knew him. They were like brothers.

Gideon had blown his knee out on that mission, injured himself so badly that he wasn't fit for duty anymore. And while he'd been in the hospital, his stepdad had died. Which meant his little brother and sister had needed him to run the Triple H.

So here he was. Missing his SEAL family and freezing his toes off on what might be a wild goose chase. He gritted his teeth against the thoughts. Shook them off. What he had been didn't matter now. His place was here.

He located the herd, tucked in a shallow gully. Between the UTV headlights and the fog lights rigged on the roof, he started counting.

One cow was missing. Or maybe he'd counted wrong.

Thoughts of his warm bed had him closing his eyes for a split second. Then, with a groan, he reversed the UTV and started making another pass. Hopeful he'd been wrong.

But a second count didn't turn up the cow. Gideon had worked the herd long enough to know their markings and ear tag numbers and realized this was one of the few heifers who'd been bred. This would be her first delivery.

She'd probably be fine. Cows had been giving birth since the beginning of time, right?

But the bitter cold and the fact that sometimes cows that hadn't delivered a baby before got into trouble had him stubbornly refusing to give up. A lost cow was lost money. More when you considered the calf too. His family depended on the Triple H's income. After what Carrie had been through, she deserved for him to give it his all, even if it wasn't what he dreamed about in the dark of night.

He'd take one last pass through the pasture and see if he couldn't find the heifer.

Maybe he'd get back to bed before one. If he was lucky.

*Chapter Two*

GIDEON DIDN'T MAKE IT TO BED AT ALL.

By the time he'd found her, the cow had been in labor and was very distressed. There'd been blood, and she'd been down. He'd had no way to get her back to the warm barn, so he'd stripped out of his shirt and done what he could to assist the birth.

Turned out there was a reason she'd been in trouble. She'd given birth to twins. With the mama so weak—although she'd quickly gotten to her feet—and two calves shivering and covered in fluid, he'd known he had to get them back to the barn.

Which was a trial-and-a-half, because the mama had turned protective, fast.

It'd been nearly four when he'd finally stumbled into the farmhouse. Only to find Nate, the foreman, scrambling two dozen eggs for the rest of the hands. He'd spent a half hour discussing the day's agenda and stressing the need for Nate to send one of the hands out to check for more newborn babies in the field.

If it'd been any other day, he might've caught a combat nap, but his brother Matt was flying in on an early-morning flight, and the website showed it was on-time, which left Gideon only time for a quick shower.

Now, after a two-and-a-half hour drive to Dallas and sitting an hour in traffic, he waited in the baggage claim for his little bro.

Little.

Matt was active duty Air Force and on leave from his tour overseas. Gideon was proud of him.

And maybe a bit jealous too.

His bum knee *panged* in sympathy, and he shifted his feet, trying to alleviate some of the pressure. His eyes flicked to a TV angled from the ceiling. It was hard to hear in the echoing cavern of the luggage claim, but he caught the words "assassination attempt," and he zoned in. Apparently some European princess had gone missing in New York City. He wondered if any military personnel would be called in to help, or if the Feds were handling it.

And then he didn't have time to wonder anymore, because passengers started trickling down the escalators. Then came a flood, complete with a large family of jostling teenaged boys and a smaller family with a squalling baby and a toddler clinging to mom's pant leg. Dad pushed an overloaded stroller and looked like he wanted to be anywhere else.

And there was Matt, his fatigues and crew cut instantly recognizable among the civilian clothing surrounding him. He looked exhausted and stressed, lines fanning from the corners of his eyes. When he caught sight of Gideon, he smiled, but it was rough.

Gideon's stomach clamped into a tight ball. Something was wrong. He watched his brother's approach closely but couldn't see any signs of injury.

Then Matt was beside him.

"Hey, man." He wasn't ashamed to pull his brother into a back-slapping hug. "Good to see you." And it was. Now that he was on the other side of the deployment, he'd realized how much worry he'd put his family through while he'd been off on missions.

They both backed off to a respectable, manly distance. "You're looking pasty, old man," Matt said.

"Long night." Gideon shoved the Stetson back on his forehead. "Little heifer gave birth to twins out in the field."

Matt squinted. "And you had to help?"

Gideon shrugged. She'd been in pretty bad situation when he'd arrived on the scene, with the first calf twisted up in the womb. "They survived the night."

"How's Carrie and the little booger?" Matt asked as they turned to follow the crowd.

"They're fine. Can't wait to see you at dinner tonight."

They moved closer to the carousel, which now spun. Luggage appeared in a slow trickle. When Matt grabbed his government-issued duffel, Gideon couldn't help looking over his brother again. Was Matt limping slightly? He couldn't be sure. His brother was saying all the right things, but something was off.

Gideon made his brother hand over the duffel—which Matt did with only a minimum of stink-eye—and slung it over his shoulder as he led the way to the parking garage.

"You hungry? Figured we could stop somewhere on the way back to the Triple H."

Matt shifted his nearer shoulder, and Gideon resisted the urge to narrow his eyes. Dislocated? Or was Gideon just being paranoid? Trying to see the worries that plagued him because he could guess what his brother had walked into over there?

"Sure, I could eat."

That was a good sign, at least.

They reached the right level in the parking garage and approached the truck. Gideon stowed Matt's duffel in the truck bed, where it landed next to the blue tarp he'd thrown over the tools he'd used two days ago to repair a section of broken fencing in one of the pastures. He'd meant to unload the tools in the barn yesterday but had never gotten around to it.

He was glad to hop in the truck and crank the heater. He rubbed his chapped hands together. If anything, it had gotten colder in the night, although he hadn't heard about a front moving through.

He felt the shift in the cargo as he backed out of the parking space and kicked the truck into *Drive*. Hadn't realized he'd used that many tools.

Matt slouched in his seat, long legs eating up the space beneath the dash.

"How long is your leave?"

"Three weeks. Maybe a month." He grunted. "Why, you need another hand for the spring cutting?"

Gideon grinned. Castrating bull calves, turning them into steers, had been his brother's least favorite task on the ranch during their growing up years. "If you're going to be a sissy about it, I'm sure the hands and I can handle it without you."

Matt leaned his head against the seat-back. "Trey still hanging around? Still mooning over Carrie?"

"I don't know about mooning. We've still got the same guys working for us. Nate, Brian, Trey, Dan, Chase. If cattle prices stay up, we'll make enough from the summer sale to buy out old man Cameron. Maybe add another hundred head."

Matt grunted again. He'd worked the ranch, same as Gideon, and left as soon as he was of age. Same as Gideon. Neither one of them had wanted to stay on and work the ranch long-term. Only now

Gideon was back, running the ranch for their family. Trying not to chafe under the small-town life.

Carrie needed him. He owed her.

"Think *Gerry's* will be too busy for breakfast?" Matt asked.

The mom-and-pop diner was halfway home, not too far off the interstate, and a popular eatery in three counties. Mama G, the proprietress, served a mean omelet.

"Might be too busy if I hadn't called Mama G on my way down and told her you were back home for awhile. She's reserving a table for you, soldier-boy."

Matt grinned, but there was something behind the smile that Gideon couldn't read, not when he needed to keep his eyes on the interstate traffic.

Over an hour later, they exited I-30. It'd be another fifteen minutes of two-lane highway to *Gerry's*. They'd covered all the small talk Gideon could stand in his exhausted state and fallen into a comfortable silence. It'd always been like that growing up. They'd understood each other, sometimes hadn't needed words.

A thump from the truck bed had Gideon glancing in the rearview mirror, then reaching up to tug the mirror down so he could see. He hadn't taken the last turn fast enough for the tools and duffel to shift. Not that much.

Was something moving back there? He hadn't seen any kind of bird come out of the sky. He'd checked that Apollo hadn't hopped up in the truck bed before he'd left the house this morning at oh-dark-hundred.

Matt had been staring out the window, but now came alert, sitting up straight. "What's the matter?" He twisted in his seat, glancing out the back window, then back at Gideon.

"Something moved in the back."

He felt Matt's skeptical stare. "Like what?"

Gideon shrugged, shifting his neck side to side. He'd been sitting in the truck for too long this morning after a long night, and his muscles were tight. "Something."

He spotted a turnout off the two-lane state highway and put on his blinker.

"Seriously?"

He glanced at his brother, brows raised. "You're that hungry for Mama G's cooking? Can't wait two minutes for me to tie down my tools?"

Matt just frowned.

Gideon stopped with a crunch of the tires on dirt and threw the truck into Park. "Just give me a minute."

Of course Matt followed him out of the truck.

He'd left it idling, but something rustled beneath the tarp even above the engine noise. Glancing at Matt over the truck bed, he reached in and rolled back the tarp to find a white-faced woman huddled beneath.

ALESSANDRA WAS FROZEN THROUGH. She couldn't feel her fingers or toes, and her teeth had stopped chattering an hour ago. She'd never been so cold her teeth ceased chattering. The irony of escaping an assassin only to die of hypothermia.

She barely registered that the truck had stopped before the darkness of her covering lifted and she came face-to-face with a grizzly bear. With a jolt she realized it was a man, but with a dark, shaggy beard covering his face and long hair that fell into his eyes, he might as well have been a bear. The look in his intense, dark eyes said he'd kill her.

"Who are you?" he growled.

She tried to answer, but her lips wouldn't form words.

"She's half-frozen," said another voice. Her neck twinged when she tried to turn her head, and she strained her eyes to the opposite side of the truck bed to see another man, this one clean cut and in a military uniform, although he shared the same dark eyes as the first. Related?

Her heart pounded with fear, but she still couldn't make her muscles move. She had no strength left, not after running for thirty-six hours. She'd passed through six airports, spent most of that time hiding in restrooms and freaking out over every glance another passenger sent her way.

The first man—the grizzly bear—grunted and reached for her. She was used to everyone carefully staying out of her personal space, but she couldn't form a protest when his hand clamped around her upper arm. He tugged, and she slid across the slippery metal truck bed.

And then he hauled her bodily over the side, lifting her easily, as if she were a bag of Glorvaird apples or one of the tools that had been poking her beneath the plastic tarp.

Military-man stayed on his side of the truck.

Her legs wobbled, but she didn't fall when he set her on her feet.

Who where they? Did they mean her harm?

"L-let g-go of me." There. She'd gotten the words out, and even with the wobble, she'd sounded almost imperial.

The grizzly bear did let go, and she had to clutch the side of the pickup and lock her knees to keep from tumbling to the ground.

She didn't like the way he looked her up and down. Not the way she was used to men looking at her. Usually they were assessing her figure, not her threat level.

*She* wasn't the threat. He was!

"Who are you?" he demanded. "Why were you stowed away in my truck?"

She stalled, looking away from the bear's narrow-eyed gaze and over his shoulder instead.

She'd hoped to escape the airport without being tracked by surveillance cameras, hoped that when the truck stopped, she'd be able to unobtrusively get out without anyone being the wiser.

She'd failed.

And it appeared she'd hitched a ride to the middle of nowhere. They'd stopped along a stretch of lonely two-lane road. Fields of red-brown dirt extended to the horizon in both directions. There was nothing else within eyesight. Just the two men and the truck.

No escape.

She should be worried, but right now, she felt only the same numbness that had stolen over her yesterday.

"How'd you get in my truck?" he demanded. His eyes glittered with what she assumed was anger.

"I c-climbed in. I n-needed to get o-out of the airport w-without being seen." She'd snuck down the escalators to the parking garage, hiding in a large group that seemed to be coming off a mission trip, judging by their colorful backpacks with patches sewn on. In the parking garage, the group had loaded up into two large vans, and she'd been left alone, creeping between vehicles and not sure what to do next.

Then, a scary-looking man with a shaved head had come off the elevator, and she'd panicked anew. Had he tracked her here from New York?

She'd seen the beat-up truck and the plastic blanket inside the bed and quickly jumped in and covered herself up. It could barely be called a plan. It evidently hadn't been a good one.

She was finding she wasn't very good at taking care of herself. Although at least when she'd been running, she hadn't had time to think about...

The bear must've said something else that she'd missed, lost in her thoughts. She was getting kind of foggy. She still wore the evening dress and long coat she'd had on for the benefit two evenings ago. The clothes were impractical and had done nothing to keep her warm, exposed as she was in the back of the truck.

"Gideon, get her in the truck."

The bear—Gideon—growled at the other man. Maybe he really was part-animal.

"Does she look dangerous?"

Gideon the Bear assessed her again with a long up-and-down glance. He muttered something under his breath and moved toward her, gripped her upper arm.

She tried to pull away. Too weak. He towed her to the cab, yanked open the door with his opposite hand, and practically shoved her inside.

The other man, the soldier, was getting in from the passenger side. "You need some help?" he asked, as she struggled to make her icy muscles move enough to slide in the truck.

She shook her head slightly.

There was no way to ignore the presence of Gideon the Bear behind her, and she soon found herself squished between the two broad-shouldered men. The soldier reached across and turned the knob for the heater. It was already much warmer, just being inside the truck, but the extra heat bled through her skin and into her extremities. And it felt so good.

Until her skin started to prickle. And then it didn't feel good at all.


GIDEON SHARED a look with Matt above the blonde's head as she began to shiver violently.

She was putting on a brave face, but he knew what it felt like to be so close to hypothermia—he'd been close once, on his very first mission with the teams.

When your body started warming up, it felt like tiny knives pricking all over your skin. It hurt.

Judging from the fancy dress and coat—was she even wearing stockings?—he guessed she had exposure, though the skin he could see wasn't the awful grayish-white that would indicate frostbite, or he'd be driving her to the nearest hospital.

He didn't think Matt's motives for getting her in the truck were entirely altruistic. His brother had to have known that the heat would be painful for her. No, Matt knew that now was the time to get some information out of her.

"Who are you?" Gideon asked again.

She glanced at him askance. "N-no one." Her teeth were chattering now, which he guessed was a good sign.

Matt stared at the woman.

Gideon could admit she was attractive. Striking, with her pale blue eyes and long blonde hair. She'd looked so frightened when he'd pulled back the tarp. Like a waif in need of rescuing.

Which just raised his suspicions higher. Something was really wrong here.

Why had she targeted *his* truck?

"What's your name?" Gideon pressed. "What're you running from?" Because it was obvious she was running from something. The evening gown and coat stunk of money. And those shoes... they were impractical, skinny heels and strappy—you'd break your ankle trying to make a quick getaway. Even the faint whiff of perfume she wore smelled of money.

And for a moment when he'd pulled her out of the truck, her coat had fallen open, and he'd thought he'd seen a dark stain inside. Dried blood?

Everything about her was setting off warning bells in his head.

And then Matt raised his eyes to meet Gideon's gaze above her head again, and this time he shook his head slightly.

Gideon shook his head right back. Matt might be a trained soldier, but Gideon was an operator and trusted his instincts. He didn't know what his little brother was thinking. Coddling her?

Matt didn't back down. *I know who she is*, he mouthed above her head.

What—how?

"Can you—take me somewhere with a telephone?" the woman asked.

"We aren't going anywhere until you give me some answers."

Matt frowned at him.

She looked past him, to the door.

Let her try.

She was trapped between the two of them. No way would a lightweight like her be able to get past a former SEAL and a soldier. And anyway, if she got out of the truck, where would she go? Only one stock-hauling semi had passed them since they'd pulled over. No way was she walking far in those shoes.

"You promised me *Gerry's*," Matt reminded him.

Gideon resisted the urge to roll his eyes. How could his brother be slave to his stomach right now? The fact that there had been a woman hiding in the back of his truck had derailed their breakfast plans.

"Let's take her with us," Matt continued, as if Gideon had already agreed. "We can figure out what to do from there."

*No way.*

Matt must've seen his refusal in the set of his jaw. He mouthed, *trust me*.

Gideon knew his little brother probably meant well, but Gideon was driving. He was in charge here.

But judging by the stubborn set of the woman's chin, she wasn't giving answers anytime soon. Could Matt really know who she was?

Gideon rested one wrist over the steering wheel and glanced at the land surrounding him. There was nothing here. They had another ten miles to go before they reached the small town where *Gerry's* was located.

What was he going to do, leave her to hitchhike? He might be suspicious, but he wasn't cruel.

No way was a cab or Uber driver from the city driving all the way out to *Gerry's* to pick her up, but if they left her with a hundred bucks, it didn't count as abandoning her, did it?

What other choice did they have? It's not like he'd invited her to hitch a ride in his truck.

"Fine." He put the truck in gear and hit the gas, pulling back onto the two-lane.

Matt yanked his phone from one of his cargo pockets and played with it. Seriously, his text couldn't wait until they got this mess figured out?

The woman remained silent, rocking slightly back and forth, though her shivers had lessened.

A few minutes later, they pulled in front of *Gerry's* and found a lucky parking spot at the back of the lot—lucky because they didn't have to park in the overflow lot across the street. The sleepy little town was mostly quiet, no traffic coming down Main Street, even though *Gerry's* lot was full. The feed store two doors down also boasted a few cars in the lot, but the church and bank across the street seemed virtually empty.

He got out, motioning for the woman to follow him. "C'mon."

He saw her glance around as she slid from the truck until her feet touched the ground.

"Don't even think about it." He took her upper arm, ensuring she wouldn't try to bolt. What had her so flighty?

"I'll thank you not to put your hands on me." Her voice wasn't wobbling anymore, and that tilt of her chin... was she seriously trying to order him around?

"When I start getting some answers, we can negotiate."

Matt shot him a look as he joined them in front of the truck, sandwiching the woman between them.

Inside, the restaurant was bustling. Mama G, slightly overweight and in her fifties, must've been watching for them, because she was out from behind the counter before the bell above the door had quit ringing, her arms thrown around Matt in an exuberant hug.

Several good 'ol boys took up seats at the counter—probably a few of them Vets. They started clapping, and soon the restaurant erupted in applause and "welcome homes," for his brother. Matt deserved it, even if they didn't know most of these folks.

And Gideon used the distraction to tow the woman to the booth against the wall with a small, handwritten *Reserved* card sitting on its edge.

The woman glared at him, but he was much bigger than she was, and she allowed herself to be nudged into one side of the booth.

He followed her in, blocking her way out.

The applause died out, and Matt approached, accepting several backslaps on his way. He slid into the opposite side of the booth and handed Gideon his phone.

The screen was lit with a picture that did look sort of like the woman sitting regally beside him, her back straight as a poker. Sort of. The phone picture showed a beautiful young woman with perfectly-styled hair and too much makeup smiling at the camera. The woman beside him looked bedraggled, her hair limp, her face pale. Definitely her.

She glared at him, and he glanced back at the phone. Read the photo caption. *Princess Alessandra of Glorvaird* at some fancy-pants reception last year.

A princess?

Suddenly, he remembered the newscast he'd caught only seconds of in the airport. This was the princess who'd been shot at in New York? Whose bodyguard had died?

How in the heck had she ended up here?

# Chapter Three

Alessandra watched in horror as Gideon the Bear glanced at the phone's screen. Her own picture looked back at her.

Her heart beat in her throat, threatening to choke her.

Any chance at anonymity she'd had was gone.

The question remained: what would they do now? The two strangers could hold her for ransom. Abandon her.

But the compassionate glance that the soldier sent her... Somehow, she knew the brother in military garb was on her side. Would he help her?

Gideon the Bear's head came up slowly. While he'd been suspicious and surly before, something clicked inside him as quickly as his posture changed. Where he'd been tense, now his shoulders had straightened, something tight and controlled in his actions.

"I guess you've had a hard couple of days, haven't you?" Military-man asked.

At his words, unbidden tears filled her eyes.

Tim.

She'd tried to keep him from her thoughts. but every time she closed her eyes or started to drift off, images of his blood flowing up between her fingers played behind her eyes. He was dead.

She blinked at the images now, working to erase them.

Gideon the Bear shifted closer to her—close enough for their thighs to brush—and she tensed.

"Easy," the soldier said, his voice a low rumble that barely carried across the table. He tilted his head, and she followed his glance to a young woman wearing an apron over her T-shirt and jeans, rapidly approaching their table.

Gideon's arm stretched across the back of the booth. Not quite touching, but close enough that she felt the heat radiating from him.

She wasn't used to the closeness, to someone else being in her space, and she wanted to curl into a ball in the corner of the booth, regardless of the soldier's assurance.

"Pull your coat closed," the Bear murmured, head tilted toward her, as if they were having an intimate conversation. "It stands out, but not as bad as your dress underneath."

She didn't have to look around to know it was true. On the way in, she'd seen the older men in overalls and worn flannel shirts, the young mother with her brood in stained discount-store clothing.

She stuck out like a sore thumb.

She might not trust Gideon the Bear, but she could admit he was right.

She pulled her coat closed and crossed her arms just as the waitress reached their table.

"So you're back." It was said to the soldier with a smile, but Alessandra had grown up around politicians, dignitaries and other royals, and she easily read the tension behind the woman's expression.

"So I am." The soldier's return smile was more genuine, but still, something underlying remained. "Life treating you right, Katie?"

"Just dandy." Only the words rang somehow false. Katie raised her order pad and pencil. "What can I get you?" While at first she'd only seemed to have eyes for the soldier, now her gaze widened to encompass Alessandra and Gideon as well.

Alessandra wanted to shrink beneath the table. If the two men had recognized her so easily, just how quickly would someone else discover her identity?

"Coffees all around," the soldier said easily. "And three of the house specials. Gideon said his girl has been begging him to bring her here for weeks. Right?"

Gideon's *what*?

Alessandra forced a trembling smile when the waitress's gaze darted back to her. She tried not to lean quite so far away from the hulking man at her side.

The man beside her didn't seem happy with the soldier's explanation either. She could see a muscle ticking beneath his eye.

Thankfully, the waitress didn't comment, only scratched something on her order pad before she turned away. A man in a worn ball cap with a green logo above the bill waved her down before she'd gone two steps.

"Way to act natural," the soldier scoffed.

"That was probably the worst thing you could've said," the Bear returned, leaning forward slightly, over the table. "If she wants to avoid people scrutinizing her. Everyone around here knows I haven't dated in"—his furious whisper broke off as he glanced at her briefly —"a long time."

The soldier shrugged, a smirk playing around the edges of his mouth. "It's about time," he said. "You're not getting any younger."

Gideon grunted.

The waitress reappeared at Gideon's elbow, efficiently setting three cups of coffee on the table, along with a small open carafe of creamer. "Sugar's on the table." She scurried away to buss a table that had just emptied.

The soldier's gaze stayed with Katie for longer than was really necessary.

Gideon scooted Alessandra's mug closer, and she wrapped her hands around it, grateful for the warmth that bled into her still-chilled body. He nudged the creamer her way, and she took it too.

"Thank you," she murmured.

"Ah, so you can talk."

She looked up sharply at his words. His dark eyes glittered, but it was almost impossible to read his expression behind the heavy, shaggy beard.

"Gid," the soldier chided. He sent an apologetic look to her. "I think we've got off on the wrong foot. I'm Matt Hale. Gideon is my big brother. My grumpy big brother. And you're—"

"Allie," Gideon interrupted. He didn't glance around furtively or do anything that might've brought attention to them, but he practically skewered his brother with a dark-eyed gaze. "It's better if you don't call her anything else."

Allie. She experienced a flash of memory from her childhood, when she'd wanted to be "just Allie," and live with the head housekeeper.

She blinked the memory away. She hadn't thought about that in years.

Had the shock of her ordeal caught up with her?

She let out a shaky breath. "If you recognized me," she nodded to Matt, "what's to stop someone else from doing so as well?" She sipped her doctored coffee, but the warmth didn't reach all the way inside, where she'd frozen solid when Tim had stepped in front of that bullet for her.

Matt smiled, an easy smile. Now that there was no sign of their waitress, his body language relaxed. He slouched in the bench seat, clearly at ease. "I spent all day yesterday in airports. They must've replayed the same news coverage every hour. But around here... most of the folks don't get cable or pay much attention to national news coverage. They maybe got a blip on the local nightly news."

She glanced at Gideon, who wasn't at all relaxed like his brother. But he nodded, confirming Matt's words.

"No one around here would expect to meet a"—he waved his hand her way—"someone like you. People see what they want to see."

Their confidence was something of a relief, but it didn't help with her current predicament.

"I'm U.S. Air Force," Matt said. "And Gideon is a former Navy SEAL. You might not have handpicked his truck before you climbed into it, but you've found two guys who are willing and able to help you."

Gideon mumbled something beneath his breath. He didn't seem happy to be sitting next to her.

Well, that made two of them.

The waitress made another appearance, this time delivering three steaming plates of omelets, bacon, sausage and toast.

Matt had already shoveled two bites into his mouth before the waitress had walked away.

The food smells, salty and meaty and hot, rose to Alessandra's nose. She had to be hungry.

But her body's response was off.

Alessandra stared down at her plate, wondering if she'd be able to eat at all. Yesterday, she'd been so focused on getting away from New York City, getting somewhere safe, that she had barely paid attention to her body's needs. When she'd bought a health bar from a vending machine in one of the airports she'd bounced around, she'd barely been able to stomach it, still reeling, grieving over Tim.

But now...her stomach gave an audible growl.

Matt seemed oblivious, his eyes closed as he savored the food.

But Gideon had to have heard it. He shifted slightly in the seat, his knee bumping hers in their close proximity. "It gets easier," he said in a low voice.

She glanced at him briefly, unsure how to take his meaning.

"To go on."

It didn't seem fair. She could go on eating. Go on living. When

Tim would never have the chance.

But she also didn't have a choice. She had a duty to her family. To her father. To her people.

She picked up a strip of bacon and bit into it. Salty, greasy goodness exploded over her tongue. Tears pricked her eyes at both the rightness and the wrongness of being able to enjoy it.

Thankfully, both men pretended not to notice as she raised her paper napkin to her face and dabbed at her tears.

A few moments passed in silence as the three of them ate.

"What happened after you left the—the scene of the shooting?" Gideon asked, his own fork clinking against his plate.

"Gid," Matt admonished through a mouthful of food.

"If she wants our help, we need to know what's going on. Have all the facts."

She hadn't said whether she would accept their help. Her gut told her she could trust the two men, but she didn't know whether she could risk putting someone else in danger. If what happened in New York had truly been an assassination attempt, what would keep the assassin from tracking her down?

She also didn't have any other choices, because after she'd maxed out the cash allowance on her cards back at the airport in Boston, she'd ditched her purse, cards and identification and everything, too afraid someone could track her movements.

"The police took me into a private room in the hotel," she said softly. She couldn't look at them, kept her gaze focused on her plate. "I made a phone call to the pal—to my sister." She'd almost blurted out that she'd called the *palace*. How stupid could she be? She was terrible at subterfuge. "There was—something was going on there as well."

The two men seemed to take her meaning without her having to explain everything—at least not for now. Gideon seemed the kind of person who left no secret unexplored. Pushy as he was.

She couldn't exactly say *bomb* aloud without risking someone overhearing and making the connection.

A bomb had been set off at the palace gates, nearly hitting a limousine that carried her younger sister, Mia. Just thinking about it made any remaining appetite vanish. Alessandra pushed her plate slightly away.

Her older sister Eloise had assured her that she and Mia and their father were fine, that most of the staff had been unharmed, but that they were on lockdown.

"I was told to go underground," she whispered. "Without Tim, I...did the best I could."

The visit to New York was only to last a few days, and the palace security team had deemed it completely safe. Tim had been her only guard.

How wrong they'd been.

Matt nodded, eyes sympathetic. She hesitated to turn her head and take in Gideon's expression. When she finally looked, his eyes were narrowed, assessing. Did he think she was *lying*?

"Any idea who wants—who would do something like this?"

She'd followed his first sentence before he'd cut himself off. *Any idea who wants you dead?*

"My aunt."

AN HOUR AND A HALF LATER, Gideon paced in the farmhouse kitchen, feeling caged.

He wanted to do more than pace. He wanted to put his fist through something.

He couldn't believe he'd agreed to Matt's farfetched plan. *Hide a princess on the Triple H?*

Matt had been right when he'd said they couldn't leave the princess to her own devices. She'd lucked out when she'd jumped in the back of his truck, finding help instead of someone who would do her harm. It was obvious she had no idea how to survive on her own. She hadn't even taken the time to purchase some cheap, touristy clothes in one of the airport shops, which might've given her some anonymity while she'd traveled. She'd still been wearing the slinky evening dress and heels she'd worn at the time of the shooting!

It would've been easy for Gideon to track her, if that had been his assignment.

He could only hope and pray that whoever had come after her in New York was a moron, or that their assignment had been to scare her off, not kill her.

He wanted answers from her so-called security team. He'd questioned her in-depth in the truck on the ride here, but she'd claimed they'd deemed her trip safe, kept the security light.

There could be someone on the inside. It was possible. That was one explanation for letting as assassin get so close to her.

Or else they were idiots.

He might be one too, because if someone was still after her, he'd just put his own family in danger. And that was something he couldn't live with.

With calving season upon them, he didn't have time to babysit a spoiled, rich princess who undoubtedly was used to a large staff catering to her every whim. He'd already reached out to one of his old SEAL teammates, Cash, asked for information about the investigation behind the shooting and bombing—he'd had to pry that out of her too—and gave him a heads up as to the princess's location. The other man had advised Gideon to lay low, keep her hidden.

This was a huge mistake. Gideon knew it, but he hadn't been able to talk Matt out of it or think of another solution on the fly. And looking down on the princess's wide, frightened eyes, he hadn't been able to tell her *no*, either.

He'd been shocked to feel compassion flare when she'd become visibly upset over the death of her bodyguard. That she'd felt such deep emotion over the loss of someone she employed made her seem...human. Almost.

He heard a tread on the stairs and stopped pacing. Faced the mission head-on, hands at his sides.

Her feet came into view first—bare—as she descended the steps from the second floor. Then a slender pair of legs encased in jeans. They were borrowed from a stash of clothes his sister had left behind and fit a little too snugly in the hips. A chambray work shirt over a faded T-shirt completed the outfit. With her hair pulled back in a braid behind her head, she looked the part of a working cowgirl.

He knew how badly appearances could deceive.

As she landed on the second-to-last step, her gaze lifted and their eyes met. Something in the soft blue depths hit him square in the chest.

It was uncomfortable. And he didn't like it. He flicked his gaze away, instead staring just over her right shoulder.

"You'll want to stay in the house," he said, voice a bit more gruff than he'd intended. "There's livestock roaming every pasture, and you're likely to get stepped on or scare them—and most of them are calving right now."

She nodded slowly.

He went on. "We're having supper tonight to celebrate my brother's leave—time off. You can stay out of sight, if you want. Or you can come down, meet all the hands. And my sister, Carrie."

She pressed her palms together, interlocking her fingers just in front of her midsection. A picture of calm. But he caught the slight tremble of her hands. "Is there anything I can do to help?"

He didn't figure someone who got waited on hand-and-foot knew her way around a kitchen, so the offer sounded pretty weak to him. "Nope. Just lay low."

He needed to get back out to the barn, get Dan on the radio and make sure the boys were making progress fencing off the far south pasture, but there was one more thing.

He approached the princess, bristling internally when she tensed. He knew she must be having a rough time of it, but he'd opened his home to her, offered his protection. Not something he did lightly. The least she could do was not flinch when he came near.

"Here," he gruffed. He held out his smartphone.

She just stared at him.

Finally, impatient, he waggled it. "Take it," he ordered. "It's mine. For emergencies. I've got a burner phone I can use for now. I've programmed numbers for me and Matt at the top of the contacts. I'd hold off calling or emailing your family for now—it's possible a hacker could intercept the signal and track where you are. Possible, not likely," he amended when her face paled.

She took the phone from him, her fingers a cool brush against his palm. "Thank you." She looked him directly, which bought her a modicum of respect. "For everything. I know I'm putting you out, and I hope to give you a more official thank you when I can get back to—to the palace."

He didn't need her thanks, but he nodded anyway. "I've got work to do."


ALESSANDRA STOOD in the hallway after Gideon the Bear had stalked past her and out through what appeared to be a mudroom, judging by the number of dirty boots piled on a rug next to the back door.

She should really stop thinking of him that way. He might look like a bear, might snarl and snuffle and grunt like one, but he'd shown her kindness by offering his home. Reluctant though the offer might have been.

She turned the phone over in her hands, at a loss.

Normally, every moment of her day was scheduled. Events for charities the palace supported. Keynote speeches. Time spent being updated on current events across the globe. Except for the scant, early-morning hours where she snuck "below-stairs," she rarely had time to herself.

Thus, the loss. She didn't know what to do with herself.

She turned a slow circle, taking in her surroundings. When they'd arrived, Matt had taken a phone call and wandered off toward the big, red barn that was situated on a slight hill above the house. Gideon had brought her inside and given her the change of clothes, but it was obvious he'd been in a hurry to get back to his work. She'd barely looked around when she'd come inside.

At the foot of the stairs, she stood in what appeared to be the heart of the home. The staircase landed in the center of the house, and all directions led somewhere else. The mudroom and back door were at the end of a short hallway, directly behind where she stood. Another offshoot led to—she peeked through a swinging door—the kitchen. She normally wasn't so nosy, but Gideon hadn't told her she couldn't look around.

She raised on the balls of her bare feet for long seconds before she committed herself. Then started off.

The kitchen was a mess. Someone had make breakfast, but the remains of eggs stuck in a pan on the stovetop, now brown. A biscuit pan was empty of bread, but had rings of cooked-on residue where it hadn't been scraped. A pile of plates sat next to the sink.

The countertops were littered with old mail, other assorted dishes and a...she didn't know what kind of farm implement it was, but the pronged tool looked dangerous. And like it belonged in the barn, not the kitchen. The cabinets were dated, the stain almost worn off in some places. The wallpaper was faded, and the fridge an old model.

The entire room was in need of an update and a thorough cleaning. Matt had said Gideon ran the ranch with several "hands"—cowboys, she thought. Did the mess really not bother the group of bachelors?

She wandered through the room and into a dining room. Only it was like no dining room she'd seen before. A rough-hewn wooden picnic table took up the center of the room. It would've been country charming if there had been any decoration to go with it. The table was bare, walls were bare, even the hardwood floor could've used a rug. And a good scrubbing.

Well, it was...functional. Certainly big enough to seat ten or so men. Maybe eight, if they were all as large as Gideon.

She edged past the table and back through the entryway she'd passed through earlier. This time, she kept going instead of turning back to the center staircase.

The family room had a lived-in look. The two low couches bookended a coffee table that had so many water rings that it almost seemed planned. A flat-screen TV took up one wall, and opposite that, a large rock fireplace appeared inviting. But there was no throw over the back of the couch, no homey touches anywhere.

She wandered through the entryway and past the staircase to the back corner of the house, the only place she hadn't explored. There were three doorways off the hall here. Bathroom. Linen closet. Bedroom.

She stood in the doorway, frozen for a long moment. The bed was made, a simple quilt thrown across it as bedspread. Curtains framed the window looking out on blue sky. A dresser was cluttered with a collection of spare change and, in the back corner, a huge, gold belt buckle.

On the side table stood two pictures. One was Matt, a woman that must be his sister, and... could that clean-shaven man be Gideon?

He was handsome. With his chiseled jaw and those sharp eyes, laugh lines fanning from his eyes... he would have caught her eye if they'd met in different circumstances.

Was this Gideon's room?

In the picture, a gray-haired man stood behind the three, his arms stretched to encompass them. Their father?

Behind the picture was another. She'd stepped into the room before she really meant to. Close enough to see the photo.

It was a candid shot of several men in camouflage sitting around in the desert. They were heavily armed with scary-looking black guns in hand. In this one, Gideon sported a shorter, trimmed beard and dark sunglasses.

He was laughing.

Something tugged deep in the pit of her stomach. A response to the man, even though he wasn't here.

She shouldn't be in his room. She backed up even as she realized she'd intruded into his personal domain.

She wouldn't like it if he'd invaded the inner sanctuary of her rooms back at the palace. He'd probably hate knowing she was in here.

She quickly ducked out of the room and regrouped in the hall-way, wrapping her arms around her middle.

What had happened to that smiling soldier? What had turned him into a surly grizzly bear?

Her thoughts dissipated.

Even though she stood in a patch of sunlight slanting in from the large picture windows in the living room, she didn't feel warm.

She was here, on a ranch in the middle of nowhere, Texas. She was safe.

But there was a part of her, a big part, that was also lost.

# Chapter Four



IF ALESSANDRA HAD EXPECTED GIDEON TO BE THE WORST-groomed of the cowhands, she would've been sorely disappointed that evening.

After the past, crazy forty-odd hours, she'd hit a wall sometime in the early afternoon. She'd dragged herself upstairs to lie down on the bed and only wakened when the noise level in the house below rose loud enough that it shook the rafters.

She was still mulling over Gideon's hesitant invitation. Should she go downstairs and join the party?

There was a small mirror on the tall chest of drawers next to the twin bed in the room she'd been given, and she squinted at her reflection in the fading light filtering through the curtains. Squinted her eyes more tightly together, so she wouldn't have to see the rat's nest that was her hair. The braid she'd put in earlier had come halfway apart, and one side of her hair stuck up in a matted mess where she'd slept on it.

This was one time she wouldn't have minded having her stylist on hand. She'd never had to worry about getting her hair right, because Anna was there to help her.

She untangled the rest of the braid and picked up the brush that Gideon had found for her somewhere. It pulled her hair when she began the first strokes. She'd showered earlier, and the conditioner was a cheap brand that made her hair feel rough between her fingers.

She didn't even have her own toiletries.

She stifled the whine that wanted to escape and set about

brushing her hair and then pulling it into a tight French braid that hopefully wouldn't look as messy as she felt inside.

A quick stop in the bathroom to splash her face and pinch her cheeks—neither did she have any makeup—and she forced herself to the head of the stairs.

Her stomach rumbled, making the decision for her.

Plus, there was no use hiding up here. She had a hunch Matt would come looking for her, even if the irascible Gideon wouldn't.

Downstairs, it was even louder. Men's voices and raucous laughter rang out through the house. The swinging door to the kitchen was closed, but she could hear the clanging of dishes and the movement of what might have been two people in there.

Most of the noise was coming from the living room.

She hesitated in the shadowed hall, looking in.

Gideon was closest to her, on the other side of the large open archway. He stood with feet slightly apart and arms crossed, what might be a scowl under his beard.

On the far couch, two men she didn't recognize lounged negligently, their dusty boots stretched out in front of them. She winced, thinking about the floor. One still wore a cowboy hat and let his head loll back on the couch. Both of them looked as if they'd been in their faded, dirty clothes for days. And both sported long, unkempt beards, like Gideon wore. Was this a Texas thing? Or a ranch hand thing? Did no one wash up for supper?

Matt perched on a barstool across the room, talking animatedly with another man, this one with a shock of short-cropped red hair. She couldn't see his face.

She must've moved, or maybe Gideon just sensed her presence, because his head turned toward her before she was ready to be spotted.

He cleared his throat and the room quieted instantly, everyone's attention on him.

"Guys, this is the little gal I was telling you about. Meet Allie."

She stepped into the light as three pairs of eyes—plus Matt's glinting gaze—swiveled toward her.

She'd keynoted enough that she was used to being the center of attention. Used to being in the spotlight, having cameras pointed at her. But this...she felt their attention acutely.

"Nate and Trey there on the couch," Gideon said with a nod.

She tried to smile, but it felt tremulous.

"And Brian," he motioned to the redhead near Matt. "Chase and Dan are putting the finishing touches on supper."

Often at public events, she had an aide nearby at all times to whisper a name in her ear or prompt her into conversation before she could make a mistake.

She floundered now.

"Thank you for opening your home to me," she said softly.

"It's Gideon's place," either Trey or Nate said from the couch with a big grin. "Interesting that he brought you out here. He usually keeps his distance from any pretty woman."

Trey-slash-Nate cut him off with an elbow to the ribs, eliciting a huff of air from the other man.

Gideon growled.

"It's my place too," Matt said easily, diverting attention from his brother.

"For now." Gideon said. "Not sure how long me'n Carrie will let you keep your shares, since you're pretty much career military."

She let her gaze slide to Gideon. Had he helped Matt avert the conversation from her purposely?

"He's never liked shoveling—" Brian started to say something crude but caught himself halfway through the word with a glance at Alessandra. Splotches of red climbed in his cheeks—he was clean shaven. "Sorry, ma'am."

She let it go with a shrug and a smile. She had no intention of coming in here and asking these men to change their lifestyles to suit her. They were doing *her* a favor.

But a glance at Gideon showed his face looked like a thundercloud.

Then someone knocked on the door. Matt jumped up from his stool.

She moved out of the way as Matt came toward her, heading for the door. He didn't quite get it open.

"Uncle Matt!"

The exuberant cry preceded a tornado of a small brunette girl who launched herself through the doorway at her uncle. Matt swept her up easily into his arms. A woman who must be Carrie, Gideon and Matt's sister, stepped over the threshold, and she too threw herself at Matt. He caught her too.

Alessandra caught the small sob that escaped the woman, even though her face was buried in Matt's shoulder.

Alessandra was intruding.

Her gaze connected with Gideon's where he stood opposite, behind the cluster of his family.

If she wasn't mistaken, his eyes had a sheen of moisture too.

. . .

GIDEON WAS INTENSELY aware of Alessandra at the dinner table, two seats away with his niece Scarlett between them.

Part of him really wanted to know what the princess thought of their gathering. This must be a lot different than what she was used to. The hands were in fine form, boisterous and loud as they showed off for both women. The one-course meal of hearty spaghetti and meatballs, salad and crusty garlic bread, was probably much simpler fare than she was used to. Their cutlery could never be called *silver*ware. And Apollo made a practice of crawling on the floor beneath the table, licking up any crumb that dared be dropped.

Although Scarlett had clung to Matt for a good ten minutes when his sister had arrived, she'd elected to sit next to Gideon at the supper table, and somehow wrangled Alessandra into the chair on her other side. With the shortie between them, he kept catching glances, finding himself in the laser sight of Alessandra's bright smile.

Although she was definitely out of place—quiet and unassuming —he caught the tail end of several of her smiles in response to something the guys or Scarlett had said. She was fresh, like a spring tulip. The diamond in a room full of coal lumps.

Once, when she'd laughed at something dumb Nate had said, Gideon had gotten a bite of meatball lodged in his esophagus. It stayed there, a hard lump that had him shifting uncomfortably in his seat.

He felt old. Out of place. Grumpy. Just like Matt had said earlier.

His brother was quieter than usual. Gideon still believed something had happened during his tour. Gideon had had one or two near-fatal incidents, and when you came home after something like that...well, it changed how you looked at things. How you treated the people you cared about.

He just wished his little brother hadn't had to go through it.

"Uncle Gid," Scarlett piped, distracting him from his thoughts.

"Yeah, squirt?" He never got tired of looking at the little upturned face.

Scarlett was four going on twenty-five, and he was a sucker for the freckles splashed across the bridge of her pert nose and those big, cornflower blue eyes.

Scarlett scooted close, her little shoulder brushing his elbow. She motioned for him to lean down. So he did, aware of Alessandra's attention on the two of them.

"I think Allie is a princess." Scarlett's breath was warm and smelled of garlic, and it distracted him long enough that he had to play her words over a second time before he grasped their meaning.

His stomach somersaulted. If his four-year-old niece could recognize Alessandra, they were in for a world of trouble. Had Carrie been playing the national news channel at home?

"What makes you think that, squirt?" Somehow he managed to get the words out evenly.

"Look how long her hair is," the pipsqueak whispered, her head bumping his chin as she turned to shoot a look at their guest and then quickly turned back when Alessandra caught her looking. "I think she's Rapunzel."

Reality intruded as his eyes focused on the long braid that hung down Alessandra's back and past her waist. Rapunzel, indeed.

"I don't know, squirt," he said softly. "She looks kinda regular to me."

Not really. Even wearing clothes that were similar to every one else's at the table, there was a different air to Alessandra. It wasn't entirely her posture—although she sat straighter than anyone he'd ever met, as if she balanced a book on her head at all times—and she hadn't tilted her nose up once. It was something else. Just *her*, maybe. She was too fine.

Whatever it was, she didn't belong here.

Tired of waiting on him or maybe dissatisfied with his answer, Scarlett turned to the princess. "Are you Rapunzel?"

"No, I'm not," Alessandra answered. "Is she your favorite princess?"

Scarlett shrugged. "I like the ice princess and her sister."

He didn't figure she was up on the latest animated princess movies, but Alessandra leaned closer to Scarlett. "Oh, I like her too. But really, the reindeer is my favorite character from that movie. Do you know the song he sings?"

She hummed a few bars until Scarlett belted out some words that sounded like gibberish to him, then both females dissolved into giggles.

Someone kicked his foot from beneath the table. He glared across to see his sister, squished in between Matt and Brian, watching him speculatively.

His ranch hands weren't as subtle.

"Boss, you planning on needing some time off?" Dan asked from the other end of the table. "Maybe doing some courting?"

Guffaws went around the room.

Fire flared in his cheeks, but hopefully the beard camouflaged it.

Scarlett was chattering to the princess, so maybe they'd missed the joke at his expense.

He wasn't sitting here mooning over the girl. He was listening in to make sure she didn't slip up and put his family in danger. Protecting Scarlett.

That was it.

If he did feel a bolt of attraction, he would never have an opportunity to act on it. Right. Imagine someone like *her* taking up with him. They'd rub each other the wrong way. What about him attending a palace function? They'd probably want to sprinkle glitter in his beard.

But an uncomfortable clutch of his chest remained.

THE GROUP SAT around the table, talking, for a long time after supper. Scarlett relocated to Matt's knee, regaling her uncle of tales about her preschool friends while Matt listened attentively. Gideon would have to get to the bottom of what was bugging his brother eventually.

Scarlett's desertion left a space between him and the princess, and he noticed Alessandra disappear from the table before too long. She'd probably gone upstairs to sleep. Or relax. Or whatever. Was probably bored with their simple talk of ranching and the folks in town. It was for the best, anyway. She'd be here a few days, maybe, then go back to her ritzy life.

The hands had accepted his explanation of a damsel in trouble without asking for a lot of details—but apparently they wanted to believe she was more to him than a mere acquaintance.

Ha.

When he carried his plate from the table into the kitchen, he found her elbow-deep in a sink full of sudsy water, scrubbing pots. Apollo lay at her feet, his black nose resting on brown paws.

Seeing her like this made that uncomfortable pinch in his chest return full bore.

Of all the things he'd imagined her doing, the dishes wasn't one of them. Had the noise of their conversations completed drowned out the clanking of pots and pans, the swish of the water?

"Everything okay?" he asked.

She startled and looked over her shoulder at him, their gazes connecting again. He easily read the shadows in her eyes.

"I'm fine." The firm set of her lips might indicate otherwise.

He wasn't going to push her, not now.

"We're kind of a rowdy bunch," he said. Not really apologizing. And stating the obvious.

She *hmmed*, but didn't agree or disagree.

"Sort of an acquired taste. Like black coffee. Or sushi."

This time, he won a small smile, seen only because she'd turned her head slightly toward him. He didn't know why it mattered, but seeing it made the tight knot in his chest loosen up, just slightly.

"Don't blame you at all for needing to take us in small doses."

She smiled again, just a small twitch of her mouth, but shook her head. Agreeing that his hands and his family were best a teaspoon at time? Or was she disagreeing?

She didn't explain.

"Nobody expects you to clean up after us, you know." He deposited his dirty plate and fork on the counter near her. It was conspicuously clean, as if it'd been freshly scrubbed—and the counter along the opposite side of the sink was laid out with clean dishes drying on towels. She'd been busy.

He moved to her other side. He picked up the last towel on the line she'd laid out and started drying the nearest item, the scrambled eggs skillet from this morning. It was spotless. He well knew how the egg residue cemented to the pan when it was left all day. And that was only one of the dishes that had littered the kitchen.

It even smelled cleaner in here. Like lemons.

He might've thought that Brian—on dinner duty—had cleaned up, if he didn't know his men so well. They preferred to leave the mess until there were no more dishes to use before anyone would take initiative.

"Inspecting my work?" she asked. Her attention remained on the pot she was vigorously scrubbing. He winced. Was it from yesterday? Or two days ago?

"No..."

But she must've heard the weak denial in his tone, because she frowned as she scrubbed even harder. "Maybe you think a pr—" She glanced over her shoulder. So did he. They were alone. "A person like me wouldn't know how to wash dishes."

That was exactly what he'd thought. Didn't being born a princess mean she'd grown up with a silver spoon in her mouth?


It shouldn't bother Alessandra that Gideon thought she was unable to perform a simple task, such as doing dishes. It wasn't exactly a skill she was known for.

She used the dishrag to scrub at one particular caked-on bit of gunk in the bottom corner of the pan. "When I was fourteen..." Soon after her father had started to seriously decline. "I started sneaking down to the kitchens in the wee hours of the morning. Our on-staff chef put me to work. Baking bread, helping with breakfast...and other things. He believed that anyone working in his kitchen should know how to clean up after themselves. Even me."

Chef Marco had become like a beloved uncle to her, though he was paid staff. Even as a teen, she'd known better than to air the family's private business to anyone. So even though she'd never talked about the overwhelming grief of watching her father decline, Marco had known. Had provided a steady presence, even as he put on a gruff outward act of not wanting the princess in his domain.

Marco and Krissy and Bella, two of the housemaids, had been more of a family to her than anyone else, but as her responsibilities to represent Glorvaird grew, she'd grown more distant from them.

Thinking about her sort-of-staff, sort-of-friends was why she'd eventually had to leave the group of boisterous cowboys and Carrie and Scarlett. She missed the familiar. Missed home.

More than anything, she'd wanted a family like this one. Oh, they didn't all have DNA ties, but it was clear that the cowhands had an affection for each other, even through the ribbing and teasing. It was also clear they respected Gideon and his leadership as he ran the place.

Her own family...well, her father and older sister were difficult. And Mia, her younger sister, was often gone, flitting around social events.

He hadn't responded to her story about helping in the kitchen, and she glanced at him to see his brow furrowed above the flat cookie tray he was drying.

She nudged his elbow with hers and tried for a smile. "It isn't as if I haven't made judgments about you, too."

She couldn't pinpoint what exactly made her spout the teasing statement. There was safety in being reserved, holding herself separate from someone she would likely only know for a matter of days. But something inside her wanted to erase the deep grooves in his forehead.

"What do you mean?"

"Just that." She was unable to prevent her lips from twitching with a smile at his frown.

She motioned to his face. "I spent the entire morning thinking of you as *Gideon the Bear*, because of how you go around growling and grunting at everyone. And, well...you seem sort of dangerous..." She trailed off. She'd meant to say something about his dark, overgrown beard and hair that needed a trim, even motioned in a halfhearted circle toward his head. She'd meant to make him smile. It hadn't worked.

His frown didn't lift. It deepened. Her stomach pitched.

"But," she continued quickly, "when you're with your niece, you're more of a teddy bear." She'd been shocked at first, to see him smiling with Scarlett, who obviously had him wrapped around her little finger.

She'd even heard him chuckle once. Seen the flash of white teeth behind his beard. His eyes had *sparkled*.

Those moments had been like looking at a totally different man. An attractive one, like the picture she'd stumbled upon in his bedroom.

"So my initial assessment was wrong," she said quickly, before her thoughts could get—more—out of control. "Or at least, not completely correct. You have a tough side that was probably necessary as an active-duty soldier. And you also have a...sweet side."

She snapped her mouth shut, realizing she was babbling. And blundering. She'd nearly scrubbed the finish off the pot and quickly moved to rinse it in the second sink.

There was no avoiding Gideon as she upended the damp pot on one of the drying towels. He set aside the towel and leaned one hip against the countertop. Crossed his arms over his chest.

Her face burned. She certainly hadn't meant to say so much. There was something about him that made her nervous.

She barely dared to look up into his eyes, afraid she'd offended him in some way. When she did, she couldn't read his expression. His eyes glittered slightly, but the masked emotion could be anger or humor or anything, really.

Finally, he spoke. "So you're saying you're a"—his eyes widened slightly—"*you-know-what*, who likes to do dishes."

His nostrils flared slightly, and one corner of his mouth tipped up. He was teasing her?

Movement from behind them broke the moment, and she flushed, quickly going back to the sink, though the mountain of dirty dishes had been reduced to a more manageable hill.

"Gideon, are you picking on your houseguest?" It was Carrie's strident voice. "You don't have to clean up after these pigs—I mean bachelors—honey."

The other woman touched Alessandra's shoulder, a gesture meant to convey solidarity, but the unexpected touch startled her. People usually weren't so familiar. Of course, Carrie didn't know her true identity either, or she might not get so close.

Alessandra hated the subterfuge, though she understood why it was necessary.

Gideon backed away, raising both hands in front of himself. "I didn't make her do anything. I walked in, and she was already halfway through the pile."

Carrie moved into the place beside Alessandra that he'd recently vacated, picking up the damp towel and twisting it into some kind of snapping weapon that she wielded to drive him out of the room. She joined Alessandra beside the sink and took up the task of drying, much more efficiently than Gideon had.

"I don't know what kind of trouble you're in," Carrie said, voice low, "and I don't need to know. Gideon and his boys will take care of you."

Alessandra didn't know whether the woman was gearing up for a warning, but she braced herself anyway.

"I just wanted you to know that if you need a woman to talk to, I'm not too far away. My place in town is only about a ten-minute drive from here. I work afternoons, while Scarlett is in school."

The offer was so unexpected that tears welled in Alessandra's eyes. She blinked them back. "Thank you."

"I'm planning on making a run out here in the morning, after I drop Scarlett at class. I doubt either of my brothers thought to provide you anything more than a bar of rough soap and a change of clothes. I've got some things you can borrow, and I'll stop by the drug store for the essentials."

Carrie's words were so true that Alessandra couldn't help the wet giggle that emerged. "Thank you. Very much."

Carrie shook her head in an exaggerated manner. "We grew up together, but I don't think I rubbed off on them all that much. They don't know an eyelash curler from a flat iron, and heaven forbid you start crying in front of them. Easiest way to get rid of them in a pinch, by the way. Of course, Mom was gone by the time we were teenagers."

Alessandra handed Carrie the next dish. They were down to the supper plates now, the water in the sink grown tepid. "My mother died when I was five."

They shared a glance. It was a unifying thing. Losing a mother was something you never quite got over.

They finished the rest of the dishes in no time at all, Gideon's sister carrying the conversation, mostly talking about Scarlett. There was no mention of Scarlett's father, and Alessandra couldn't help wondering what had happened to him, though she didn't get up the guts to ask.

They wiped off their hands on clean towels. Alessandra's were pruny from being in the water so long. Carrie kept her eyes down. "About Gideon... He's got a good heart, but...he won't open up. Don't expect too much from him."

Carrie raised her head, her eyes trying to impart the message that Alessandra was struggling to comprehend. "I-I won't," she said, because that's what Carrie seemed to expect.

Did everyone thing she and Gideon were involved? She remembered his earlier statement at the diner that he hadn't dated in a long while. Were his friends and family just seeing what they wanted to see?

Was there any use in telling the other woman that she had absolutely no expectations of Gideon? He'd offered her sanctuary while the royal security force worked with the Glorvaird and New York law enforcement teams to investigate the shooting and bombing. When the head of palace security was able to find her a secure way home, she'd return to the family duty that awaited her.

Carrie surprised her with a goodbye hug. Alessandra had to fight not to tighten up at the familiarity.

It made her nose sting.

When was the last time one of her own sisters had hugged her?

She couldn't remember.

# Chapter Five

THAT SAME NIGHT, GIDEON STAYED LATE IN THE BIRTHING barn. He watched a mama giving birth, just making sure everything went the way it was supposed to.

He was afraid to go back to the house. Afraid that, even though it was late, he would run into Alessandra again. That she'd start rambling in that adorable way that made him want to smile. Or hug her.

*Gideon the Bear.*

There was a little jagged piece of broken mirror nailed to one of the studs on the far wall, and he caught a bit of his scowling reflection.

*The Bear.*

It wasn't the worst thing he'd been called in his life.

He tilted his head slightly, catching sight of the unkempt hair and scraggly beard. He looked like a mountain man. A little like a real bear.

He jerked his chin up, and there was that scowl again in the reflection.

He didn't really growl and grunt all the time, did he? He ran his hand through his beard, a little ashamed of himself. Since when did he not care?

Sure, he had high expectations. He paid his hands better than any other ranch around, and if they slacked off on the job, it ticked him off. The Triple H ran a large herd and every cog had to operate.

And when someone hitched an unexpected ride in his truck,

something that could potentially put his family in danger, he might've come off a little grumpy...

Was that really how she saw him? How everybody saw him? She'd seemed to admire his interaction with Scarlett, but the rest hadn't been very complimentary.

And she'd been right. He'd judged her harshly, thinking she didn't have any experience with domestic chores.

He didn't know what to think about her story about hanging out in the kitchens with the royal chef. There had been a slight pause when she'd begun the story. One that made him think there was more behind the story than she'd told him.

Or was that just his suspicious, grizzly-like nature, rearing its head?

There was a computer in the tack room, in the area of the barn closed off to protect it from the elements. It was an old one, but it had Internet access.

He took one last look at the cow and decided she could work on her own for awhile before he pushed through the door toward the tack room.

It took longer than he would've liked for the old machine to boot up, but within a few minutes he was logged on to the Internet, searching for everything he could find about her family. Something he probably should've done earlier in the day, and would've if he hadn't lost time bringing the princess out here and then checking in with all the hands.

Her mom had passed away when she was little. He felt a sympathetic pang, because it was something they had in common. There were some old mentions of concerns over the King's health, but they seemed to taper off after a few years.

The crown princess, Alessandra's older sister, had been in a car accident as a preteen and bore scars across her face and torso. She had been basically out of public sight, no pictures or anything, until her coronation when she came of age at eighteen. He'd seen worse. She would never be a grand beauty, but he didn't think the scars detracted that much from her looks. The gossip rags, however, claimed she had a beastly personality. He couldn't find one picture of her smiling, and sure enough, in several paparazzi shots, she wore a nasty snarl across her face.

Alessandra's younger sister seemed to be in the media all the time. Her bubbly smile came through in pixels, and he could guess she enjoyed the attention. She was young but seemed to be on the arm of several handsome young men at different times. A social butterfly? Or did she enjoy toying with young men's affections? It was impossible to know.

Alessandra didn't get as much media coverage as either of her sisters. She appeared regularly at charity events and palace-sponsored occasions. Her smile was much more reserved than her younger sister's. After interacting with her today, he didn't think what he was studying on his screen was her real smile at all.

At breakfast, she'd claimed her aunt might be behind the bombing and assassination attempt. He searched for information on a possible family feud but didn't find much. The king's sister had been estranged since her eighteenth birthday. She'd married and had two sons, now about the same age as Alessandra and her sisters. The reason for the estrangement wasn't publicized. Nothing was mentioned anywhere about the aunt's relationship to the crown being revoked. Which meant the king's nephews were technically princes in their own right.

What could make a woman hate the king and his daughters so much that she tried to kill them?

It wasn't his job to find out. It wasn't even really his job to protect Alessandra, but he'd taken it on. He'd give Cash a couple of days for reconnaissance, and hopefully things would settle down enough for her to go home.

He couldn't wait for things to get back to normal.


ALESSANDRA COULDN'T SLEEP.

She'd gone to bed, even dozed a little, but nightmares quickly followed. Of those awful moments when Tim had surged toward her in the crowd. The muted *pop!* of the gun discharging. And Tim's blood after he'd knocked her to the ground.

Then the scene went a little fuzzy.

Her dream-self pressed harder on Tim's chest, trying to save him. Only something had changed. She looked closely at his face and realized her dream self was pressing on *Gideon's* chest. That it was *Gideon's* broken body beneath her hands.

She woke with a gasp.

She bolted up in the twin bed, breathed deeply.

The bed was safe. Lumpier than anything she was used to, but safe. She tucked the quilt over her knees and wrapped her arms around herself.

She couldn't deal with whatever part of her subconscious had put Gideon into the dream. Surely it was because he'd been kind to her, and he'd been one of the last people she'd seen before she'd gone to bed. And he was protecting her.

That was all there was to it, right?

She grieved for Tim, tears falling now as she thought about the man who'd given his life for her. Who would comfort his sister and mother back in Glorvaird?

Until now, she hadn't paid attention to the other thoughts that she'd shoved away after Tim's death. But questions swirled now. How had a killer gotten so close to her? Close enough that her bodyguard had barely had time to step into the line of fire? Although some events she attended were publicized on the palace website and in the media, her exact schedule was never confirmed. Tim had been her only body-guard, but there was a team of hired men and women who scouted each location, each function she attended beforehand. And everyone in that crowd was supposed to have been invited to the party.

She didn't have answers.

She also didn't think her aunt—if that's who'd initiated the bombing and the shooting—would give up. She didn't know the woman personally, and Father didn't talk about her much, but there were always whispers among the staff about her aunt's unhappiness with the way her father ruled the country. Helena wanted to rule.

But because of the bloodlines, she would have to kill all of them—the king and his three daughters—before she would be crowned. Would the people of Glorvaird even accept her if she was behind the killings? Perhaps that's why it was so hard to connect the attempted killings to anyone. Her aunt was covering her tracks, and well.

Or perhaps it hadn't been her aunt after all, though Alessandra couldn't think of another party with such violent intentions toward her family. Glorvaird was a small, peaceful country that relied on trade with its neighbors and worked to keep peaceful agreements in place.

Knowing her swirling thoughts weren't conducive to sleep, Alessandra got out of bed. The bedroom was bare and simple, with not even a television to distract her.

Because she had only the clothes that Gideon had given her, she'd gone to bed in just a T-shirt and undergarments. Now she pulled the jeans back on. Then she slipped into the hallway.

She paused on the top step, one hand covering the smile that bloomed. She hadn't heard it from inside her room, but heavy snores emanated from most of the upstairs bedrooms. She knew the ranch hands worked hard. Guessed they played hard. Apparently, they slept hard, too.

She crept downstairs, but there was no sign of anyone else awake.

The microwave clock in the kitchen read one a.m. and she guessed the crew had to be out working early.

But knowing that didn't get her any closer to a restful state. She needed something to *do*.

And she found it in the kitchen.

She'd finished the dishes earlier, but Carrie had shooed her out before she'd attacked any of the other cleaning issues. Not that she hadn't noticed and catalogued them.

The countertops and window needed a good washing. As did the microwave, stovetop, and oven. Even the shelves in the cabinets wore a layer of dust between where the dishes rested.

And the floor was desperately in need of a good mopping.

She turned on the soft light over the sink, not the full overhead light, hoping that she wouldn't wake Gideon in his back bedroom. She found a plethora of cleaning supplies beneath the sink. Mostly unopened.

And she set to work.


Gideon had slept hard after foolishly being out in the barn so late—for the second night in a row. He woke abruptly.

Something was wrong.

Light streamed through his window, which meant he'd overslept by at least an hour and a half. The clock read seven-thirty.

The hands were going to give him heck for sleeping in.

He emerged from his room minutes later, running one hand through his hair. And stopped cold.

Someone had baked. The sweet smell of cinnamon and sugar wafted through the house.

He found Dan and Trey standing in the foyer, a plate in each of their hands, shoveling food into their mouths. Judging from the crumbs on their plates, they'd enjoyed...were those cinnamon rolls? And some kind of pie made from eggs and vegetables. They were staring into the living room until he approached, and then Dan started to swivel away, defending the remaining eggs on his plate.

"What's going on?" Gideon asked.

"Shh," Trey shushed him with a scandalized look into the living room.

Gideon frowned and stepped forward so he could see.

Alessandra was curled up on the far couch. Sleeping. One hand was tucked beneath her face. Her hair was loose and wavy—probably from the braid she'd worn yesterday—and formed a cloud all around her.

Why wasn't she upstairs, in her own bed?

"She must've made breakfast," Dan murmured from behind him. "Sticky buns and quiche in the oven when I got up."

"Cleaned the whole kitchen too," Trey whispered.

Gideon hadn't been able to tear his gaze from the sleeping princess, but now he registered the spray bottle and dirty rag on the low table not far from where she lay.

He sniffed again, this time registering the scent of lemony soap beneath the food smells. *She'd cleaned?*

Sure enough, his boots didn't stick to the kitchen floor when he finally turned them that direction. The appliances were *shiny*. Even the sunlight seemed to sparkle through the window. Everything was spotless.

"Cleaning fairy got us in here, too," Matt called out from the dining room.

Gideon bypassed the tray of buns and the dish with eggs that sat on the stovetop—for now—to stick his head through the doorway. Matt, Nate, Brian and Chase all lounged around the table, stuffing their faces. The dog was under the table again.

"Why are you all not at work already?"

"Breakfast," Brian slurred, his mouth full. A piece of eggs zoomed out of his overly full mouth and landed on the table.

Gideon winced. "Do you think someone who spent the night cleaning up after you lot wants to do it all over again? Have a little respect."

Brian looked appropriately abashed and used his fingers to scoop the egg back onto his plate.

"You're gonna keep her around, aren't you?" Chase asked hopefully.

"Yeah," Nate chimed in. "She's a mighty good cook."

Brian swallowed the rest of his food. "Not sure what she sees in you, but you've got to turn on some kind of charm and keep her around."

"Yeah," chimed Trey, as he and Dan joined the crowd from the doorway off the front hall.

Matt's eyes glittered as he looked to Gideon, waiting for the answer like everyone else. Matt should know better than to wear that expression. The woman was a *princess*.

There was no way she could stay, but Gideon couldn't tell the boys that.

He sighed. "I told you yesterday, she's in trouble. Just needs a place to lay low for a few days." But he couldn't resist teasing them. "Besides, do you really think someone like her"—he jerked his finger over his shoulder—"would want to hang around a bunch of hands who think personal grooming is optional and don't even know how to clean up after themselves?"

Matt grinned, shoving another forkful of food into his mouth. The other hands looked down at themselves. They were a rough bunch. Other than Carrie, they didn't interact much with women. Didn't spend much time in town. There wasn't much need to trim a beard or get a haircut. Or buy new clothes.

Like he was one to talk, anyway. She'd called him *Gideon the Bear*. Not just for his personality.

It wasn't as if it mattered anyway, because she'd be leaving soon. They'd go back to their regular routines, and she'd go back to her palace. She wouldn't be around to appreciate it if they all up and decided to shave and wear clean clothes anyway.

But the thought remained lodged in his gut, a boulder.

Matt stood and headed toward the kitchen. Gideon followed, leaving the other hands muttering around the kitchen table.

"Thought I'd saddle up Rufus and do some fence line checking," Matt said as he moved to wash his plate and cup in the sink. Gideon was glad to see that his brother, at least, wouldn't leave more of a mess for Alessandra. "It's been awhile since I've had a good ride."

Gideon nodded slowly, mentally running over the list of things he'd planned to do today. He made a snap decision. "I'll ride with you. We can catch up. Scarlett and Carrie weren't the only ones who missed you, you know."

It would give him a chance to talk to Matt, see if he could figure out what was causing the shadows in his brother's eyes.

Two hours later, Gideon was enjoying the familiar feel of the horse beneath him and the sounds of the horses whickering to each other.

Even though sometimes he ached to be back with the Teams, this land was part of him.

But a chill wind blew through his coat, and he hadn't gotten any closer to answers about what was going on with Matt. He'd asked about his brother's tour and gotten deflected. Asked if Matt had any romantic prospects, wondering if maybe his brother was having woman problems, and gotten shut down. There was maybe something there, but his brother wasn't talking.

They had been close in high school, before Gideon had left for the

Navy. But that didn't necessarily mean they'd shared each other's confidences. Gideon had stood up for Matt once in a fistfight. Matt had covered for him when a prank had gone wrong.

But they didn't talk about their feelings. They were guys. They just didn't.

Which made it hard now to figure out how to help.

Gideon was left with a nagging feeling that something had happened on tour. But if Matt didn't want to talk about it, how could he get it out of him?

He was on the verge of giving up when he spotted a flash of white against a dark patch of mud, several yards away. He wheeled his horse closer.

Was that a cigarette butt? None of the hands smoked.

He hopped off the horse, bending to examine it. Picked it up. It *was* a butt.

He showed it to Matt, who didn't seem upset about it. "Could've been from someone who snuck on the place to visit the fishing pond."

"Or from someone scouting the place." Gideon didn't like the feel of it. Out of place. On the heels of the princess's arrival.

"Listen, Nate came to me last night, while you were in the barn."

Gideon looked up, still not convinced about the butt, but he flicked it back on the ground.

"He said you're treating him like a hand, not the foreman. You trying to edge him out of his job?"

"*What?*" *Bear.* How long would Alessandra's nickname haunt him?

"You've got to give a man room to do his job," Matt said.

"He's got plenty of room to do it, long as he and the hands get it right."

"You sure that's how he feels?"

Gideon didn't know. He did know he was frustrated at not knowing whether the cigarette butt was something to be worried about. Now this.

He wasn't a micro-manager, not really. Was that how the hands saw him?

He didn't know how much mental energy he could give to this, with a princess to watch out for. It was just one more thing for him to add to his never-ending list.

Chapter Six

Around lunchtime, Gideon got a call from Cash that there was some chatter about continuing plots against the Glorvaird royalty.

Which was exactly what he didn't want to hear.

According to Cash, there were no whispers of the princess's location, but after finding the cigarette butt that shouldn't have been there, he spent the afternoon scouting for any other signs that a stranger had been on the ranch.

Hours of riding and tracking didn't turn up anything else, but he couldn't get rid of the sense that someone with an agenda had been here. He'd learned to trust his gut, and his gut was hardly ever wrong.

He spent the next hour in the barn, making calls to locals, asking if they'd seen any suspicious activity. Probably they all thought he was nuts, but he couldn't help that.

The sun was setting and his stomach was growling when he headed across the yard for the house. He hated the feeling of blindness. Hated thinking someone could be watching the place, and he wouldn't know until it was too late.

As he crossed the yard, the back door opened, and the princess appeared, stepping out onto the back porch. Out in the open.

The hair on the back of his neck rose all at once, and he took the porch steps at a run. "Get back," he ordered, but either she didn't share his sense of urgency or she didn't realize anything was wrong, because instead of moving, she froze.

Which meant that he collided with her, full body, knocking her off her feet. He heard her gasp as he swept her along with him, quickly thumping her back against the clapboard siding. It wasn't enough to keep her out of sight, so he tucked her head into his shoulder, too.

"I told you to stay inside," he said harshly, breath sawing in and out of his chest. Adrenaline pulsed through his veins with every throb of his heart.

She said something, but it was muffled against his chest, and he couldn't make it out.

He shuffled the both of them two feet to the left and yanked open the screen door before he pushed her inside, careful to keep himself between her and any possible threat.

Only when he had slammed the interior door shut and bodily pushed her several feet into the mudroom did he take a deep breath.

"What's the matter? Gideon?" That was Carrie's voice, coming from the kitchen.

Alessandra watched him with eyes wide and dark with fear. All the color had leached from her face.

"Gideon, let go of her."

He still held both of the princess's shoulders, though now she was at arms' length and not pressed close to him. Her flowery scent was burned into his nostrils, into his brain.

"Gideon," Carrie said again.

He shook himself out of the moment, dropped his hands to his sides, realizing for the first time with some clarity that Alessandra was dressed up. Oh, not dressed up, per se, but differently than she had been yesterday. She wore some kind of fuzzy sweater over a pale yellow dress that flared around her knees. It made her look feminine and soft, and with her hair down and wavy...

He didn't know what to do with the attraction that welled almost violently inside him, riding the tide of his rioting adrenaline and blood pressure.

He backed up a step and used one hand to take off his hat; the other he swept through his hair, hoping the motion might hide any hint of the turmoil he was experiencing.

"What were you doing outside?" he barked.

"I was coming to look for you. Matt said he thought you were still in the barn. It's suppertime."

*Suppertime.* When was the last time someone had cared enough to make sure he came in for supper? Something twisted in his stomach.

But the fear he'd felt when he'd seen her out in the open remained.

His nostrils flared as he contemplated what he might do to his brother. "He should've told you to stay inside. Why didn't you just call my cell?"

Carrie was still approaching, waving a wooden spoon in his direction. "I was watching through the window and saw you barrel into Allie. Her head hit the wall pretty hard—I heard the *clunk* from inside."

Had he done that?

"Can you give us a minute?" he asked his sister, and if the words weren't completely polite, Carrie must've seen in his expression that he was shaken up, because she disappeared into the kitchen.

He moved in close to Alessandra again, tossing his hat on a nearby hook before he reached for her. One hand cupped her shoulder while he threaded his other hand through the hair at her nape, feeling for a bump.

*Crap.* The sweater was as soft as it looked. And her hair was even softer.

"I'm sorry if I hurt you." He said the words more to distract himself than anything else.

It didn't work.

"I'll be all right." From this close, her softly-spoken words were only a puff of air against his chin. "I thought I was safe here."

He didn't feel a bump or abrasion on the back of her head, but for some reason his hand got stuck there, cupping the back of her head like a boyfriend might hold a girlfriend.

He read the questions and lingering fear in her expressive eyes. "I got a call from one of my buddies and there's still some noise that your family remains a target. I don't have any evidence that someone is *here*, but..."

Her lip trembled, slightly. And for a prolonged moment, he really wanted to lean in and kiss her. Wanted it so bad that he let go of her completely and stepped back, so quickly that she wobbled and had to steady herself with one hand against the wall.

What was he even thinking? He was sweaty and smelled like horses from working out in the barn. He was probably the last person on earth that she'd be interested in kissing.

"I don't know..." He turned his back and ran a hand through his hair again. What was it about her that shook him up so badly? "It could be nothing, but I've got a feeling. Like something's coming."

He dared to look at her, hoping he wouldn't see an expression that meant she thought he was crazy.

She didn't. She looked slightly steadier than she had earlier, her eyes more clear.

"We don't know each other very well, but I trust you," she said. "If you want me to take more precautions, I will. Although I haven't stepped foot outside since yesterday. Until..." She nodded to the door, and he remembered the feeling of her pressed against him on the other side of that wall. Remembered too well.

And the fear that had caused it.

He nodded. "I appreciate it." He couldn't let himself think about something happening to her.

ALESSANDRA RELIED on every stitch of media training she'd ever had to present a calm facade as she preceded Gideon into the kitchen.

He'd been frightened when he'd barreled into her outside. She'd felt it in the intentionality of his compact movements.

It was hard to imagine what might frighten someone like Gideon, who was so very much a soldier, so sure of himself. That in itself was scary. That fear remained with her now.

Whether the danger was real or not, he'd shielded her completely. She'd been under a protective detail hundreds of times, but she'd never had she felt so totally safe.

And then, in the mudroom... She'd thought for a moment that he would kiss her.

She'd wanted him to. Wanted to know what it felt like to be kissed by someone as virile and alive as Gideon.

Oh, she'd had a few first kisses. The rare second one. The men her father would approve of were groomed and polished. Boring. She dealt with political and social issues on a daily basis. Didn't want her dating life to revolve around them.

Until now, she hadn't known what she'd been missing.

If she'd been braver, she might've used the opportunity to stretch up on tiptoes and kiss *him*. But she'd chickened out.

All Gideon had seen from her was a scared rabbit, one who knew how to clean. So what? He hadn't seen how eloquent she could be. Hadn't seen her passion for children—her mostly-secret passion, as she didn't have enough time to devote to the charities she really wanted to help.

He'd probably rebuff her if she got up the courage to kiss him.

He stopped short in the kitchen, hanging back where the bright lights changed from the mudroom and hallway to the kitchen proper.

Carrie was at the stove, stirring the pot of chili they'd worked on together earlier. Alessandra could hear Scarlett giving some of the hands a preschool lesson in the dining room.

But it was Dan and Trey that Gideon was staring at. As if he'd never seen them before. "What—?"

Both men were clean shaven, and Carrie had given them both haircuts before supper. They looked completely different—in fact, Alessandra had startled at first when she'd walked into the hall and spotted Trey earlier. They even wore button-up shirts over their jeans that seemed to be freshly laundered. In the dining room, she'd seen that Brian and Chase had done the same.

"I brought my shears out from the shop this afternoon. They clean up pretty good, don't they?" Carrie asked. She patted Trey—nearest her—on the shoulder.

Alessandra looked between the Trey and Gideon, who seemed to be having some kind of stare-off contest.

"Any reason you pokes decided to get all gussied up? Today?" There was a slightly menacing tone in Gideon's words, one that would have had her cowering in her shoes if it had been aimed at her.

But Trey's chin jerked even higher. "Pretty ladies coming around makes a man want to look his best, boss."

"Maybe the *ladies* won't be hanging around for long," Gideon growled.

Carrie crossed her arms over her chest, aiming a glance that was almost belligerent toward her brother. "*I* think it's about time."

Gideon made an incoherent sound beneath his breath, and Alessandra had to pinch her lips together to keep from smiling. Carrie had told her earlier that her big brother was overprotective, but Alessandra hadn't gotten to see it in action until now. She couldn't help but wonder at the interplay among Gideon, his sister, and Trey.

Dan had wisely slipped into the dining room when he'd seen Gideon's thunderous expression.

"What about you, Gideon?" Carrie asked, her words almost a taunt. She used the first two fingers of one hand to make a clipping motion. "How long has it been since you've had a cut?"

Gideon shot an inscrutable look in Alessandra's direction before he shook his head tightly at his sister. "Not tonight."

"Gideon's probably hungry," Alessandra put in, wanting to ease the strange tension that had built at Carrie's last comment. "He didn't come in for lunch."

She moved to dish him a deep bowl of chili, nudging Carrie out of the way. The other woman slipped her arm through Trey's, and they escaped into the front hall, bypassing the dining room. The cadence of their low conversation carried, but not the actual words.

"You don't have to cook for us," he said, shouldering in next to her and running water to scrub his hands in the sink.

The scent of sharp spices rose to her as she ladled out the meat and beans.

"And I don't have to clean for you," she returned, holding out the bowl and a spoon upright for him. "It makes me feel useful."

He finished drying his hands and tucked the towel back in its holder above the sink. One eyebrow quirked. "You have a hard time relaxing? Ever go on vacation?"

A slow blush burned her cheeks, but she met his gaze squarely. She was used to her life being scheduled. Tightly packed with activities. It wasn't anything to be ashamed of. "Sometimes it's easier to stay busy."

He couldn't know how true it was, especially when living with her father and older sister. The truth was, she'd felt more affection from the cowboys and Carrie here than she had in years with her own family. Being on the Triple H felt like *home*.

So cleaning up a little and cooking didn't feel like chores. It felt like giving back to the people who'd helped her, who'd made her feel welcome.


FOR THE SECOND night in a row, Alessandra couldn't sleep. Not only did she have to contend with the images of Tim's death, but now there was the worry of someone coming after her here, on Gideon's land. After the boisterous supper and some visiting with the cowboys before bedtime, once everything had quieted, she couldn't forget those moments with Gideon's on the back porch.

She'd run to save her life, but had she managed to put Gideon and his family's and employees' lives in danger?

She crept down to the first floor, once again to the cadence of snoring cowboys in the upstairs hallway.

But this time, when she hit the bottom step, an arm like an iron band wrapped around her waist, and a hand clamped over her mouth.

She panicked and a shriek rose in her throat. Would anyone even hear her with her mouth and nose blocked?

"Ssh."

The hand moved away from her mouth, while the arm remained.

She opened her mouth to scream when the man's scent and presence registered. *Gideon.*

Heart thrumming like a hummingbird's wings, she struggled to draw breath. Her knees weak from fright, the band of his arm was the only thing holding her upright.

He whispered a rough word. "I didn't mean to scare you. Matt's just outside the back door. I think he's on the phone. I was trying to hear his conversation."

She panted through the pounding of her heart but couldn't manage to catch her breath.

He seemed to realize exactly how shaken up she was, because he gently turned her toward him, though the embrace was loose, with space between their bodies. "Sorry," he murmured. "Sorry."

One of his hands came up to cup her cheek, his chapped skin warm against her chilled self.

"Alessandra..."

He breathed her name—her real name. It was the first time she'd heard it since she'd been on the ranch. And then, as if he couldn't help himself, he bent his head toward her and kissed her.

Earlier, she'd wondered what it would feel like to be kissed by Gideon. The reality was like being swept away in a tsunami. Blood rushed to her face at the first brush of his lips against hers. His mouth slanted gently but firmly against hers as his nose brushed her cheek. She'd expected his beard to feel stiff and bristly, but instead it was soft, his mustache tickling her upper lip. She smiled into the kiss, and he drew away slightly, leaving only a breath between their lips.

She brushed his upper lip with her index finger. Whispered, "I've never kissed a man with a beard before."

She was close enough to make out the slight flare of his nostrils before he lowered his head to hers once more. This time he deepened the kiss, and she was lost in a wave of swirling warmth.

Too soon, he drew away, pressing his cheek against hers.

"Sorry," this time he breathed the word against her cheek.

Sorry for scaring her, or for kissing her?

Her trembling had steadied, but now her body hummed with something else entirely. "I thought..." She tried to speak, but her voice emerged wobbly. "I thought someone had gotten inside."

He moved slightly away, holding her loosely now. He used one hand to brush a strand of hair out of her face. "No one's going to get inside. Apollo would sound an alert."

She heard the dog's snuffle of a snore from somewhere else in the house. Maybe from near the front door?

"He didn't bark when I came downstairs," she pointed out.

She sensed more than saw him smile in the dark. "I asked the hands to set up a watch. Someone'll be awake at all times during the night. Nobody's getting inside. Matt's on first."

She exhaled a breath that was slightly less shaky. "Why were you spying on your brother?"

She felt tension through the links of his arms still around her. She still couldn't see his face. There was a long pause before he answered. "I think something is wrong. Maybe it's a woman or maybe something happened just before he got sent home on leave."

"Have you asked him about it?" It was a terribly impertinent question, but it slipped out anyway.

"Tried," came the short answer. "He's not being real forthcoming."

"How sure are you?"

If anything, the tension in him increased. "It's nothing I can put my finger on. Just a..."

"Feeling." She waited for him to say something more, but he remained silent. So she offered, "Maybe he'll open up when he's ready."

She couldn't see Gideon's face, but could almost imagine the skeptical twist of his lips, though he didn't make a sound.

"He's an adult," she whispered, feeling as if she were stepping over the line with the statement. But it was true. It was admirable that Gideon cared what was going on with his brother, but Matt didn't have to tell his brother anything. It—whatever it was—was his burden to bear.

Gideon didn't respond, and she was afraid she *had* overstepped.

Then he shook her slightly. "There's nothing left for you to clean. You should be sleeping."

"I haven't tackled the living room windows yet," she teased softly. Then, in a whisper. "I...can't sleep. Every time I start to drift off, I see..." *Tim.*

His hands tightened infinitesimally where they rested on her waist.

She swallowed hard. "My...my mom died when I was young, but I don't really remember..."

A breath passed between them.

"This was different," he said, and his voice was rough. "It was violent. Traumatic."

She nodded, throat closing up.

"It will take some time. The memories will start to lose their power. You won't forget, but the sharpness of those moments will fade. You'll be able to divert your thoughts. Sleep better."

"Really?" She could barely fathom it.

"Yeah." He must've sensed that she needed extra reassurance because he went on. "One of the first missions I went on... We were sent in covertly to rescue this hostage. Our cover was blown."

She could tell from the deepening timber of his voice that it was hard for him to talk about this. She rested her palms gently against his muscled chest, wanting to offer comfort. She was more than a little impressed by the strength she felt beneath her hands.

"We got out, but the hostage was shot. He bled out in my hands. I didn't sleep for a week. Spent some time talking to the shrink assigned to the Teams. Still had trouble turning it off, but after awhile...it got easier."

His story ended, and she could hear the rough breaths as he exhaled. She couldn't see his face—no doubt he was thankful for that—but she still knew that re-telling these events had reopened the wound he felt. Because there was more to the man this his gruff, powerful demeanor.

"Thank you for telling me," she said. It seemed so inadequate for what he'd given her.

Knowing that a strong, powerful man like Gideon was, in fact, as human as she was a comfort. It likely wouldn't help her to sleep tonight, or tomorrow night, but she was glad he'd shared with her.

"Is that why you're worried about Matt? Are you afraid something like that happened to him?"

He exhaled, the puff of warm air brushing her forehead. "I guess. After what happened during my last tour—my stepdad died—now it's up to me to take care of the family."

It was a nice thought, but... Matt and Carrie were adults, each with their own lives. The ranch was well-run, with a foreman and plenty of hands. Was Gideon's sense of caretaking verging on overprotective?

She didn't know the whole situation. Had only known Gideon for two days. How could she make a judgment? She couldn't.

Suddenly the back door opened, and there was the sound of motion as Matt must have stepped inside. "Gid?"

Gideon cleared his throat. "Yeah."

The kitchen light flipped on, and Gideon stepped away from Alessandra, his arms finally falling away.

"Uh... am I interrupting something?" Matt's voice wasn't loud, but it carried a definite note of amusement.

"No," Gideon said firmly. Although if Matt had come in minutes earlier, he definitely would've been interrupting. "Allie can't sleep, and I thought I'd take her with me out to the barn."

Matt stared at his brother, an enigmatic expression crossing his face.

"Not for too long," Gideon insisted.

Matt shrugged. "This is your mission, brother. Do what you want."

Glad she'd pulled on a pair of jeans and warm, woolen socks with the long-sleeved T-shirt she'd worn to bed, Alessandra followed Gideon to the mudroom as Matt changed places with them, arms crossed over his chest as he watched from the hallway.

"You can borrow one of mine, even though it'll swallow you up." Gideon pulled a heavy brown corduroy coat from a hook on the wall and held it open for her. She stuffed her arms in the sleeves. Her hands didn't even poke through the ends, and the coat hung past her thighs.

He tugged, turning her back toward him, before he looped a scratchy knitted scarf over her neck and began tucking the front ends in a loose knot.

"Um..." She lifted her right foot to show the woolen socks.

His mouth quirked. "We've got an old pair of Carrie's boots here." He bent, rifling among the boots lined up against the wall, finally coming up with a pair of what looked like a cross between rain boots and work boots. "They might be a little big."

She had to hold onto his shoulder as he helped her step into the boots. And if she held on a moment too long, well...who could blame her?

Chapter Seven

Gideon knew this was a bad idea. Spending time alone with Alessandra. Getting close to her.

Definitely kissing her had been a bad idea.

But he couldn't seem to help himself, not when she'd been shaken by the memories of what had happened to her in New York. He knew what that was like.

And...okay. His motives weren't entirely altruistic.

The more time he spent with her, the more he liked her. She was a good listener. Didn't tell him he was foolish to be spying on his brother.

Getting involved with someone who was leaving felt like the most dangerous thing he'd done since he'd left the Teams.

But he couldn't seem to help himself.

He hustled her across the expanse of yard between the house and barn. *If* someone was watching the place, they probably wouldn't be expecting to see the princess coming outside at this time of night. And he'd bundled her up pretty good.

It only took seconds to jog across the space with Alessandra tucked under his arm, and then they reached the barn.

"You'll want to keep your coat on," he cautioned as he pulled the door closed. Although the building offered the protection from the cutting wind, only the office was heated, and not by much.

She followed him in, looking all around, her face open with curiosity and wonder. Her nose wrinkled adorably.

"You don't like the smell?" he teased.

"Now I understand why all the cowboys have been heading for the shower first thing before supper," she retorted. She smiled. *Smiled!* "It's the scent of your trade," she said with a little shrug. "It isn't disgusting."

He didn't know about that. "Glad you think so, but I'd still advise watching your step."

"What do you do out here at night?" she asked. "Aren't the animals sleeping?"

He led the way to the plank fence that separated them from the open part of the barn, where a mama and her new baby did, in fact, sleep. Opposite, a second cow circled in an agitated manner. Her belly was distended and judging by her movements, she was close.

"It's calving season." He motioned her to join him at the railing. "Right now we've got several new babies being born every day." He leveled a look at her. "And some at night. We track the cows that are close and try to get them into the barn, so we can watch them and make sure there aren't any complications with the birth."

"Are there often complications?"

He shrugged. "Sometimes. We help out if we can, get the vet out here if it turns into an emergency situation." He nodded to the cow who had now lain in the hay. "This little lady looks like she's close. If I'm right, you can watch a little miracle."

She leaned both elbows on the railing. Her hands weren't visible in the coat at all, it swallowed her up. But he'd felt a visceral *Mine!* when he'd tucked her into the coat a few minutes earlier.

"It seems like a lot of sleepless nights," she said with a sideways glance at him.

"For about a month. Maybe six weeks." He shrugged. "It's part of running a cattle operation."

"It must be vastly different than what you used to do—in the military."

He nodded. "It is. More cyclical. A lot less training required."

But she didn't seem to appreciate his humor. "Do you ever miss it? Being on assignment? Going into danger?"

Being on high alert this week had certainly reminded him of what he'd left behind. He missed being an important part of the team, having a critical assignment that meant the life or death of the mission.

"Doesn't matter. My knee blew out on my last mission. I wouldn't be fit for active duty anymore." And that killed him. He kept his focus on the cow, aware of Alessandra's gaze on his face. The cow was straining, obviously in the throes of labor, but nothing seemed to be happening.

"Besides," he said offhandedly, "someone's got to run this place. And Carrie and the squirt need me."

She slanted a look at him. "It seems as if Trey might be angling for the *she-needs-me* position in Carrie's life."

He grunted. "He'd better not be."

"Why not? He works for you. You've got to have some trust in him." Her statement was innocent, but it didn't help the acid churning in his gut.

"After what happened to her, Carrie needs someone..." He searched for the right word, but it wasn't coming to him easily.

"Who makes a better living than a cowhand?" she asked, turning to face him. "Who's more trustworthy? Good-looking? From a better background?"

He matched her stance, looking right down on her. "None of those."

Her head tilted to the side. "Then what?"

He ran a hand over his beard. "Two years ago, while I was on my last mission, my uncle died. Carrie's ex-husband had been gone since before Scarlett was born. But all of a sudden, he showed up. Thought she stood to get a big inheritance and tried to pound it out of her. By the time he was done, she had a concussion, broken arm, and two busted ribs."

It still made him sick to think about it. He'd been gone, and Carrie had been helpless.

Alessandra touched him, cupped his elbow in one hand. Brought him back from that dark place when he'd been laid up in the hospital, barely able to move for his knee, knowing nobody was there to take care of his sister.

"I think it's admirable that you want to be there for Carrie, but..." She bit her lip, looking down. "She is a grown woman. She can date— or marry—whomever she wants."

He knew that. He just wanted her to pick a winner this time. And while he'd known Trey for years, he wasn't sure the hand was the right guy for his sister.

He looked back to the cow, saw she was still in distress. "I've got to go in there and check her out."

ALESSANDRA WATCHED Gideon hop the fence and move to the cow lying prostrate in the hay.

"So now you've got the dish about Carrie. I want to know why your aunt is targeting your family."

She shivered, burrowing deeper into the coat. "I've never met my aunt, and my father doesn't like to talk about her."

"They don't get along?" He'd approached the cow's *derriere* and squatted there. From where she stood, she couldn't see exactly what he was doing.

"My father has...some challenges. It isn't publicized, but he's battled MS for years. It's terminal, and he's getting worse every day."

A few moments passed as he looked over the cow.

"That must be hard," he finally said.

It was. More so because she wanted things to be different. She'd hoped that being faced with his mortality would mean that her father would spend more time with her and her sisters. That she could get to know the *man* and not the *king*.

But instead, he'd pushed each of the three girls to work harder for the kingdom in the name of family duty. He'd insisted on carrying out his duties as much as possible. Because most of the burden of her father's illness fell on Eloise, Alessandra often felt invisible to her father.

There was a rush of fluid and blood and a little black body plopped into the hay near Gideon's feet. Gideon reached for clumps of hay and began rubbing, drying the little body.

The calf floundered in the hay for moments, and then mama and baby both managed their feet, and Gideon backed slowly away.

He returned to where she stood, hopping the fence again and standing elbow-to-elbow with her at the railing.

Although he watched as the mama licked her baby all over, she knew Gideon's attention was still focused on her.

"What about your security team?" Gideon asked. "Have there been any heightened threats lately? Phone calls to the palace? Letters?"

She was ashamed that she didn't know. "Not that I've been briefed on."

"No ex-boyfriends with an agenda?"

She turned her head to meet his sideways glance straight on. "No ex-boyfriends." She'd had dates, sometimes multiple dates, but no one serious enough to call a boyfriend.

Had he asked out of concern about the shooting, or was he fishing?

She raised her brows at him. "What about you? Did your last girl-friend break your heart? There's no one special for you?"

He frowned, eyes on the cow and calf. "I didn't date while on the

Teams. It's hard on girlfriends not to know where your man is or if he'll come back. Hang on."

He went back into the pen, approaching the mama and baby slowly.

The cow bellowed at him, and he froze a few feet in.

"What's wrong?" she whispered.

"The calf should be suckling by now," he answered over his shoulder. "She's not helping it out. And she doesn't seem to want to let me get close."

He didn't elaborate. He attempted to get close to the animals twice more, but the cow lowered its head when he neared, and he backed off, returned to the fence near Alessandra.

She'd seen that thundercloud expression on his face before.

"What will happen, then?" Alessandra worried aloud. "Will the calf—?"

"If she rejects it, we'll likely end up bottle-feeding the thing. Which is a huge pain."

His focus was still on the animals, and he didn't see the twitch of her lips.

He might be gruff, but she was learning to see beyond it. He was soft enough to care if the calf lived or died, and not just for the money. He might complain about having to feed the calf, but she knew he would do it.

He was just that kind of cowboy.

# Chapter Eight

Chapter note*

"C'MON, HONEY. LET TREY FINISH CLEANING UP," GIDEON was watching Alessandra in the reflection cast by the kitchen window against the darkened sky outside. He saw the flash of either annoyance or surprise pass over her expression before she turned on her heel.

She raised one royal eyebrow at him. "Honey?"

He was aware of the cowboy watching from the shadowed dining room as he tugged the dishtowel from her hands and tossed it over her shoulder. It landed on the counter next to the sink overflowing with soap suds.

He raised an imperious eyebrow at her. "Darlin'?"

This time, she wrinkled her nose.

He might as well have been sucker-punched. She was so adorable. "Sweetheart?" he teased.

She advanced on him one step at a time.

He upped his game. "Your highness sweetie pumpkin pie?"

She burst out in an unladylike snigger, quickly muffled behind the back of her wrist.

He found himself wearing an answering smile. He wasn't usually one to act the goofball, but it was worth it to see her eyes light up and to hear her laugh.

"What can I do for you?" she asked. "Shall I fetch you a cup of coffee? Or warm up one of the cinnamon rolls left from this morning? Or are you heading out to the barn?"

It was a good guess. He'd spent every night out there for a week.

But he was still aware of Trey watching from the dining room as Gideon edged closer and gently rested his hands on her hips. "I need you."

Surprise flared in her eyes, and he twitched his eyes to the side, the only indication he could give her that Trey was watching without giving the whole thing away.

Her gaze flicked over his shoulder for a brief second, the look so infinitesimal that he almost missed it, but she lost some of the openness to her expression.

She leaned into him and linked her hands behind his neck. "What did you have in mind, Honey Bear?"

He knew she'd only thrown out the nickname because he'd teased her with some of his own. And to remind him that she'd once thought him so unkempt and rude that he could've been a bear.

But it felt so real that he had to clear his throat. "I thought we could watch a movie."

"You want to watch a movie?" She sounded skeptical. Not surprising, since he didn't often relax long enough to sit through a two-hour flick.

And then she glanced behind her to those infernal dishes.

He hadn't had a relationship in recent memory, and this one was a hundred percent pretend.

But he couldn't even distract her from the *dishes*?

Now, feeling like he had something to prove, he leaned his head down to brush a kiss on her jaw.

He felt the shiver shimmy down her back. Hoped he wasn't offending her. She would probably have slugged him if he did. As he'd come to know her, he recognized she was made of stern stuff.

"Trey can handle the dishes," he said against her cheek. "I haven't gotten to talk to you in days."

He edged back.

Her eyes were soft and warm as she gazed at him. "All right."

He linked their hands together, but before he could move his feet, she was tugging him toward the pantry. "We can't watch a movie without popcorn."

It was embarrassing how long it took him to locate the box. More proof that he didn't spend enough time in the kitchen.

While the microwave made a racket popping the corn, Gideon went to the fridge. "You want a soda?"

"Sure."

Trey wandered into the kitchen, heading for the sink. Gideon knew the man well enough to know he was watching everything that happened between himself and Alessandra, who had turned away to fetch a bowl from one of the cabinets.

"Hey, sweetie…"

Alessandra turned to glare at him at the same moment he slipped his arm around her waist. He snuck his hand—and the ice-cold can he held—against her bare arm, and she jumped with a little shriek.

She turned in his arms, her palms raised to push him away. But he was crowding her into the corner where the cabinets met.

Her eyes flashed. "That was unnecessary."

"Couldn't help myself." He was close, leaning in. Ready to snatch a kiss or maybe touch her with the cold can again.

The look in her eyes dared him to try.

He dipped his head.

But the microwave timer beeped, and distracting him enough that Alessandra slipped under his outstretched arm.

She grabbed a bowl for the popcorn, and he carried two cans of Coke and a glass full of ice. He'd noticed her preference for drinking out of a glass and not a can. Too classy for that.

In the living room, he set the drinks on the coffee table.

"What was that all about?" Alessandra murmured. "The scene in the kitchen?"

"I overhead a couple of the boys speculating about whether we're really in a relationship."

She bit her lip, and he nodded to the built-in on the wall where a handful of DVDs were shelved.

He followed her over there, standing too close, with a hand on her lower back. "It's my fault. I haven't sold it enough."

After the kiss they'd shared, after watching her interact with his family and friends, after everything… It wouldn't take much for him to fall.

And then where would he be? She was a *princess*. He was the hired muscle.

There was no future for them.

So he'd been keeping his distance.

But she had no future, period, if one of his guys ran his mouth in town. Gossip spread like wildfire in these parts. He didn't need anyone wondering about the woman hiding on his ranch. Or asking questions.

Which was why he'd skipped the barn tonight and come up with this plan for movie night.

And then he'd been drawn in by the spell that was her.

He could do this. He could sit through one movie with her and keep his lips to himself.

"You pick."

She glanced over her shoulder as he moved away. "You like chick flicks?"

He didn't, but he wasn't going to argue.

He reached for the knitted afghan spread out over the couch. Moving it dislodged a clipboard that had been hidden beneath. It clattered to the floor.

Alessandra turned at the noise. He mumbled an apology and bent to grab it. The paper clipped to the board had several paragraphs written on it. In French. His gaze lingered a beat too long, caught on the words *accord commercial*. Trade agreement.

"Yours?" He flashed the clipboard at Alessandra before he nudged it onto the coffee table. As far as he knew, no one else in this house spoke or wrote French.

"My grocery list," she said brightly.

He lifted one eyebrow.

She shook her head. She either didn't want to talk about it—or couldn't. That was her right. She'd made notes in a place where she expected a modicum of privacy.

It wasn't his business.

He blindly took the disk she handed him and put it in the DVD player, then grabbed the remote.

She was hovering awkwardly in front of the couch.

He sat, tugging her hand so she came with him, then curled up close to his side.

While he stretched his arm over the back of the couch, she settled the popcorn in the scant space between them.

There.

He could do this.

Except he hadn't been prepared for the brush of her hair against his neck. The way her face tilted up toward his, seeking a reaction when the buddy cop flick began.

The feeling of rightness at having her beside him.

He'd never been that good at playacting.

His heart was in trouble.

———

*I overheard a couple of the boys speculating about whether we're really in a relationship.*

Back in the kitchen, Alessandra had forgotten for a moment, a breath. Or maybe she had started to believe in the story they'd been telling everyone else.

For a moment, while he'd flirted with her, they had simply been Gideon and Alessandra.

And she'd liked it.

If she ignored everything, squinted her eyes just right, and turned off all the voices in her brain, she could still pretend. The back of his hand brushed hers as they both reached into the popcorn bowl at the same moment. Her peripheral vision caught his glance at her. She smiled softly. If she were braver, she might hook her pinky through his. Might tug his hand over to her lap and hold it.

But she wasn't that brave.

And she could pretend all she wanted, but she felt their time together ticking away like a countdown clock. Someday, not too far in the future, the threat against her would be dispatched and she would go back to her life in Glorvaird.

Gideon was intelligent. He hadn't talked much about his work with the Navy SEALs, but she knew SEALs weren't ordinary soldiers.

SEALs had to understand the political situations of the countries they inserted into. They worked in teams, where communication was imperative. Gideon was probably an excellent negotiator.

And she was almost certain he could speak French. He'd hesitated over her notes on the trade agreement that she'd read on the royal jet as she'd traveled to New York. When she got back home, she would be expected to jump right back into the busy work of the royal family.

The movie continued, but her thoughts wandered.

Gideon was not the kind of man she'd ever expected she would be attracted to. The men she had dated before were poised, well-groomed, and arrogant. Though, they always deferred to her because of her status.

Gideon hadn't been shy about giving orders when her life was on the line. He was a protector. He cared deeply about his family.

He was the kind of man that she could see forever with.

Except he had deep roots here in Texas soil, tethering him to the Triple H.

This time he caught her looking. "You aren't watching the show."

"I'm just playing my part," she whispered. "If this were real, you would steal my focus from whatever was on that screen."

Maybe it was the dim lighting in the room, but she imagined she saw a flush rising in his cheeks.

He shifted on the couch, and his gaze swung back to the TV. "If this were real, you wouldn't even know my name. We would never have met. Or, if we did, you would've only known me as one of your hired bodyguards."

She turned her gaze back toward the movie, but she wasn't able to focus. Was Gideon right? They'd been thrown together in this unexpected situation. If it weren't for the assassination attempt, she never would have met him, never been thrown into his sphere. The man didn't even go to town if he could help it.

Had she been that shallow? That she wouldn't have recognized the connection with Gideon if they hadn't been isolated on the ranch?

She didn't have an answer for that. The attraction and connection she felt toward him were stronger than anything she had ever felt. It was as if her heart had seen his and somehow recognized it.

But what if they had never met?

And now that she knew the kind of man he was, how was she supposed to go back to her life without him in it?

Was she supposed to just forget about him? Forget about Scarlett, who had wormed her way into Alessandra's heart with her mischievous smiles and contagious giggles? Forget about the untamed Texas land, where she had begun to feel safe again?

She was so lost in her thoughts that it took her by surprise when she glanced over at Gideon and realized he'd fallen asleep. His head had lolled back against the cushion behind him.

With the overhead light off and the soft light from the TV casting colorful designs on his skin, she took a moment to study him.

Relaxed in sleep, the fine lines around his eyes and mouth had disappeared. He had a tiny scar, a white line that disappeared into his hairline just underneath his ear. She'd never noticed it before.

What would it be like to wake up next to Gideon every morning? To see him every day like this, vulnerable and relaxed? This was a side of him that no one else got to see.

And he trusted her with it.

Her heart lurched at the thought.

They could never forge a life together. It was impossible. It was foolish to allow such thoughts to linger. Hadn't she learned that from her life in the palace? It didn't matter what she wanted. She had a duty to her country, and she must fulfill it.

Her father had told her that for the first time when she'd been five and attempted to beg off from attending a state dinner. His voice had been cold and emotionless. He'd barely looked at her.

Gideon was her father's opposite.

When he looked at her, he saw the woman behind the crown.

As she watched him, something in his expression shifted. He grimaced and his hand resting on the cushion between them fisted. Was he dreaming? He must be. His eyes darted under his eyelids.

"Gideon."

She had barely whispered his name when he came fully alert. His gaze scanned the room as if he were looking for danger. And then it came to rest on her. His eyes softened.

"I think you've spent enough time *watching* this movie with me tonight," she said. "We should go to bed."

Gideon worked as hard as his hired cowboys. He should be resting on his night off.

"Don' need sleep. Just need you."

Her stomach did a slow flip, a similar feeling to what she felt in the moments before the royal jet lifted off from the runway.

She'd thought he was awake, but obviously he was still half-asleep. He would never have admitted it otherwise.

His eyes were warm. His arm slipped off the back of the couch to wrap around her shoulders.

*Just need you.*

Had he meant it?

His head tipped toward her, and she longed to close the distance between them. She wanted Gideon's real kiss, not one he gave her because they were trying to fool his friends. A true kiss between Gideon the man and Alessandra the woman. Not the soldier. Not the princess.

But she knew with crystal clarity that, if she kissed Gideon at this moment, her heart would never recover.

She stopped him with a hand against the breast pocket of his shirt. "We should go to bed before we make a mistake."

He stilled at the touch of her hand, and he seemed to wake up. He blinked. The soft expression was wiped from his face, replaced with one that was carefully blank.

"You're right." He stood, turning his back and rubbing the base of his neck.

She was used to seeing him self-assured, and the gesture revealed how unsettled he was.

It also made her stomach crackle with nerves.

She stood up, too, and the popcorn bowl toppled from her lap, forgotten.

The popcorn had gone everywhere, including underneath the

couch. She started to kneel, but Gideon touched her elbow. "I'll clean up. Go on to bed."

She straightened and, for a moment, they were face-to-face in the dim room. Oh, how she wanted to take back her words. Wanted to step closer and be folded in his strong arms.

But she didn't dare.

# Chapter Nine

Over the next few days, Gideon watched as Alessandra seem to thrive in ranch life.

With no further sign of anyone on their property, no noise from local law enforcement, and Cash assuring him that the reports they were getting didn't have Alessandra's whereabouts located anywhere near north Texas, he no longer kept her confined to the house.

She spent hours in the barn, bottle-feeding the calf she'd dubbed Valentine.

She cooked and cleaned up after the hands, no matter how much he chided her to do otherwise. Where, before her arrival, the hands had been rowdy and willing to let their appearance and behavior slide, they were more polite and cleaned up each night before supper. She'd changed them for the better.

Once, he caught her watching a national news broadcast with a pensive look on her face, but other than that, she seemed content.

He, however, was a boiling mess of emotions.

He couldn't seem to keep himself from sneaking kisses. In the barn. After supper, while she corralled him to dry dishes for her. He found her addictive, especially when she smiled a secret little smile after he'd kissed her—a smile he hadn't seen her give to anyone else.

He'd even trimmed his beard. He hadn't shaved it, because she seemed to like it.

But all the while, he reminded himself that she wasn't here to stay, no matter how well she seemed to fit into his life.

She was used to the jet-set lifestyle. Fancy parties. Events where she rubbed elbows with famous people.

She would eventually marry a prince.

Not an ex-Navy SEAL with a ruined knee and obligations that tied him to the family ranch.

Somehow, he'd become uncomfortable in his own life as well. He needed to keep Alessandra safe. He'd accepted it as his own personal mission. So he left Nate with more responsibility, so he could scout their land and the neighbors close by.

Though he'd relaxed a little, allowing Alessandra to the barn, he didn't trust that things had gone quiet. Every so often, he got that awful feeling down the back of his neck and shoulders, like someone was watching.

Waiting.

Biding their time.

Like he'd do, if he was tasked with taking out the princess.

It just made him more itchy, being out of the loop. Relying on the Glorvaird and New York enforcement agencies. Not being in on it.

And he wasn't a patient man.

Even through his distraction, the Triple H hadn't fallen down around their shoulders.

Was Matt right that Gideon had stunted Nate's potential by taking on too much responsibility for the ranch duties?

Worse, was Alessandra right that he'd done the same to Carrie? Had he kept his little sister from finding happiness because he'd been determined to fix every single thing that went wrong in her life?

He didn't know how to manage all of that.

He didn't know how to keep from getting hurt when Alessandra left. Where his place was, if it wasn't as the boss of the Triple H. Who needed him, if Carrie didn't? If he couldn't help Matt? If Nate could run the ranch without him?

He was anchorless. A SEAL without a team.

And then his phone rang.


ALESSANDRA FELT Gideon's heightened tension at supper. Almost as if he was pulling away from her.

After the meal, he drew her into the living room, leaving Matt and the hands behind at the dining table.

His expression was deadly serious as he said, "Your head of security called. They're ready for you to come home to Glorvaird."

She'd known it was coming, but the words were still unexpected.

She wasn't ready yet. Valentine was only a few days old. And she was supposed to have lunch with Carrie on Friday.

And Gideon...

He was already heading for the door. "You'll want to pack up tonight. We'll leave early in the morning for the airport. They're sending you a new passport, which we'll pick up on the way."

And then he was gone, banging through the mudroom and out the back door.

She sat for a moment, heart pounding. Should she follow him?

She'd give him until the dishes were done to clear his mind.

But he didn't come back, not after the last dish had been washed and put away.

She waited in the living room, curled beneath an afghan as the house darkened around her. She let her eyes roam, noting the changes. She and Carrie had made them together. Photos of the Hales: Gideon, Matt, Carrie, and Scarlett, now lined the walls. A pitcher with hothouse flowers from town claimed space on the end table.

It wasn't the empty dreary room it had been when she'd arrived.

She'd like to think she'd brought changes to the people, too.

She idly played with the phone Gideon had given her, scanning through the pictures on the high-tech device. She'd surreptitiously taken several candid photos of Gideon when he hadn't been watching. Him working with the cattle, actively shooing two mama cows and their days-old babies back out into the open pasture. Laughing from across the supper table at something Matt had said. She rarely saw those genuine smiles cross Gideon's face, much less his entire face lit and open with laughter. Mostly when he interacted with his family, though a few times his expression had been open and soft after they'd kissed.

She traced the line of his smile with the tip of her finger. She was falling in love with the irascible cowboy.

She'd thought something real was growing between them. Which was why his absence tonight confused and hurt her.

At ten, she decided not to wait any longer. She was a princess, wasn't she? Capable of standing up for herself. Facing hard things, not cowering. She'd find Gideon and tell him how she felt. They couldn't leave things like this. Unresolved.

All the cowhands were upstairs in bed, except for Nate, who nursed a cup of coffee as he stood in front of the kitchen window, looking out.

She'd already bundled up in the heaviest sweater Carrie had

loaned her and thick wool socks. "I'm going to run out to the barn," she told the hand, whose eyes twinkled with merriment.

"I'll keep an eye out," he promised.

She slipped into Carrie's old work boots and Gideon's coat, bundling up as best she could before she darted across the yard.

Something felt different tonight.

She was aware of Nate standing on the back porch, watching her cross to the barn. But somehow, without Gideon beside her, the darkness felt menacing. The cold felt threatening.

Was her mind making things up because of the anticipation of leaving tomorrow? She'd found safety, an inkling of peace on the ranch.

Wind rushed at her back, and she misjudged the final few feet, running into the door with a *thump*. She straightened, not hurt but a little shaken at the way she'd let her imagination take off. When she tugged on the door, it wouldn't budge.

And then it did, almost ripping from her hands. Gideon stood there, inches from her.

His face was dark as he pulled her inside the lit space, throwing a glare over her shoulder.

"What the—?" He mumbled what she thought was an expletive before releasing her. She reeled a few feet away. "You walked out here in the dark, alone?"

"I ran," she said. "And Nate was watching from the porch. Besides... aren't you taking the bodyguard thing a little far? I thought things were safe now."

He muttered something else beneath his breath. "Just because nothing's happened doesn't mean you're safe. It could mean the threat has gone underground."

It was a valid point. She'd had no sense that anything had been wrong in New York City, either. Gideon was the soldier.

"I'm sorry."

Her apology didn't seem to ease his tension. His Stetson was pulled low over his eyes, and he backed a few feet farther from her.

She wrapped her arms around her middle under the pretense of holding the coat together. "If you'd come inside earlier, I wouldn't have had to come looking for you."

"Shouldn't you be in bed by now?" he muttered.

"Shouldn't you?" she returned. Then, softer, "I need to talk to you."

"Why?" he asked, voice flat. "Why are we still pretending when you're going home tomorrow?"

His words stung. "Pretending?" It had all been real to her. Every moment with Gideon had brought a sense of belonging.

Until now.

"I can't do it anymore." The hardness in his voice was like being struck, and she clutched herself tighter. "Pretend that all of this is going to have a happy ending."

A muscle ticked away in his jaw, proving he wasn't as emotionless as he let on.

She took a deep breath, searching for the right words.

"I've been doing some thinking," she said, heart thrumming loudly in her ears. "We might come from different places, but that doesn't mean we can't be together—"

He laughed, a harsh sound. "Are you going to ditch your family and stay on the ranch? I know you've been enjoying yourself, but what about Dear Old Dad? What about your *obligations*?" His words were a verbal punch. She'd confided in him that she often felt stifled by her royal duties. That she wished for a closer relationship with her father. And now he was throwing her words back at her.

She shivered at the twist of his lips. Why was he being this way?

"You know I wouldn't be able to stay on all time. But if we split our time—"

"Split our time?"

She jerked her chin up. "You are more than the Triple H. You're well spoken and intelligent. Well-traveled. You could hold your own with any of the dignitaries I've met."

He looked dumbfounded. "You want me to go with you?"

"Like I said, we could split our time—"

But he was already shaking his head. "I can't leave. I've got to be here to look after the ranch—"

"That's Nate's job," she reminded him softly. She could see from the set of his shoulders that she wasn't getting through.

"What if something happened to Carrie again, and I was half the globe away?"

And she could see the guilt eating him up, still.

"What if you were half the globe away, and *nothing happened*?" she asked gently. "What if you're giving up your chance at a different life for a hypothetical?"

He took off his hat and ran his hand through his hair, a gesture she knew meant he was upset.

"My whole life has been planned out for me, up until now," she said, wishing, praying that he could understand. "I never had a reason to fight for anything different, until now. Until you."

Hat still clutched in one hand, he looked at her. She could see the torment in his eyes. "I just don't see how it would work, long-term."

"But..." *She loved him.* The words stuck in her throat at the resigned look on his face.

"It makes sense that the ranch has been a place of rest for you. Something totally different than what you're used to. And a place that's kept you safe. But in six months, or next year during calving season... the newness will wear off. Even if you split your time..."

She noticed he didn't use the word *we*.

"You'll figure out this place is all work, work, and more *work*. *We*"—he pointed back and forth between them—"won't work. Not for long."

She didn't know how he'd become so defeated. Did he really think they were that different, after all she'd tried to do to prove to him that she could be a cowgirl, too?

Tears rose, and she valiantly fought them back. Her heart might be breaking, but she didn't want him to see, not now that he'd rejected her.

"I'll see you home," he said, and she couldn't look at him. "But that's it. That's all it can be."

GIDEON WASN'T his best self the next morning, not after tossing and turning for hours.

He couldn't erase the image of Alessandra holding herself together last night, her hands shaking as she clutched her elbows.

As if, by denying that they could have something lasting together, he'd broken her.

The SEALs had taught him the value of considering every angle, every scenario, every possible ending. He couldn't see a way forward that didn't end with one of them in heartbreak—most likely him.

He feared his heart might be breaking now. He felt nauseated, like something he'd eaten last night hadn't set well with him.

She'd been quiet on the ride to Dallas, once again sandwiched between him and Matt in the truck. He'd spent the entire drive watching for a tail, unconvinced she was safe, and fighting the icy roads.

There was no tail, but he still had that awful feeling down the back of his neck.

The airport was bustling as he pulled into the underground parking lot where this had all started. She slid out of the truck after him, and when as he helped her to the ground, he got his first good look at her of the morning. She wore a long, elegant coat similar to the one she'd worn that very first day. It fell open, revealing a slim pantsuit and heels—though not as unwieldy as the stone-encrusted ones they'd found her in. She looked night-and-day different from the farm girl who'd worn her hair in a braid and donned one of his flannel shirts when she fed the undernourished calf. Carrie must've gone shopping on her behalf, though they still hadn't let his sister in on "Allie's" secret identity.

He and Matt flanked her as they walked inside.

"Keep your eyes open," he told his brother, though it wasn't necessary. At least Matt seemed to be taking this seriously, scanning the crowds as they passed through the lower-level corridor and then arrived at the passenger check-in. Because Gideon had printed her boarding pass at home, they were able to move directly to the Security line. He'd coordinated with the royal security team and planned to accompany her to New York, then hop a flight right back home. Matt would kill time around here, and they'd drive back to the Triple H together.

This was the end of his time with Alessandra.

She hugged Matt at the Security line, then walked through, that princess-grace evident in her posture, her calm exterior.

Gideon stayed close, silent, like a bodyguard would. Which felt appropriate, since she still wasn't speaking to him.

She clutched his cell phone between her hands, though he didn't know why.

Inside the terminal, they discovered the flight had been delayed as the airport personnel de-iced the runway. He growled quietly. It was only an hour's delay, but it meant more time out in the open.

The hair on the back of his neck was tingling again, this time the pit of his stomach carried a knot the size of a boulder.

The gate attendant confirmed the delay, and he stifled the urge to punch someone.

"Can we get something to eat?" the princess asked.

He agreed reluctantly.

Everyone else seemed to have the same idea, because the few food places that were open on their end of the terminal were packed. Alessandra stood in line for a bakery kiosk, him beside her.

The feeling on the back of his neck got worse. He kept Alessandra close to his side, noticing and hating it when she unobtrusively put a few inches between them.

He craned his neck, trying to see in all directions. Could someone have snuck a gun inside the airport, where security was tight? Or a knife? He knew it could happen, but...

There. Near the restrooms, a man in a long trench coat was darting looks in all directions, one hand tucked beneath his coat. Gideon lost focus on the crowd around them as he zeroed in on the suspicious guy.

"Sorry the lines are so long," an older, feminine voice said from nearby. "Would you like to try one of our apple fritters? It's a free sample."

Gideon turned back to the princess, just in time to see her take a paper-wrapped pastry from a uniformed woman. He didn't get a good look at the woman's face, only the dingy gray ponytail hanging from the back of her ballcap.

Focus now split between Trench-coat Guy and the woman who'd approached Alessandra, Gideon lost a half-second of reaction time.

"Wait—"

But he was too late to stop the princess from raising the tissue-wrapped pastry to her mouth. She ate a bite.

Still distracted by Trench-coat Guy, he put his hand beneath Alessandra's elbow. "Can we sit down now?" He didn't wait for an answer.

They didn't make it back.

"Gideon, I'm—"

Alessandra faltered mid-step, and the only reason he was able to catch her around the waist was because he'd been so close to her.

*What was happening?*

Her eyelids fluttered rapidly, and her cheeks were reddening as he watched. She collapsed, and the pastry she'd held dropped to the floor.

Panic threading through his veins, he knelt, cradling her head. "Alessandra. Honey?"

He searched for a pulse even as she lost consciousness.

"Help!" he called out, waving down the gate attendant. "I need medical help!"

He touched her beneath the coat, feeling for any sign of a bullet entry, though there was no blood blooming, and he'd heard no *pop*, even from a gunshot that had been silenced.

Had she been poisoned? The thought was absurd, but what else could've happened?

Fear clawed through him at her weak, fluttering pulse.

He was supposed to have protected her.

How could he have let this happen?

# Chapter Ten

Hours later, Gideon sat beside Alessandra's hospital bed in the secure ICU wing of the university hospital, head in his hands.

He'd been praying, frantic wordless prayers, since the princess had been poisoned at the airport. He'd believed the royal security team when they'd said the danger was past. Hadn't given enough credence to his gut.

Someone had gotten close enough to *poison* her.

And Gideon had let it happen.

The doctors had praised his quick thinking as he'd scooped up the remainder of the apple pastry into a plastic baggie before they'd rushed Alessandra out of the airport on a medevac helicopter. First, they'd pumped her stomach. Initial testing of the pastry had identified large doses of cyanide, and the doctors had quickly given her an anti-cyanide antidote kit.

She'd remained unconscious since the airport. It was probably a blessing for her not to be awake to feel the poison ravaging her body, but Gideon wished and prayed for nothing more than her to open those bright blue eyes and look at him.

He pinched the bridge of his nose, hoping to stem the tears that burned behind his nose.

In all the chaos, with his adrenaline pumping, he'd felt the same clarity he had back when he was with the Teams on a mission. The high-octane situation had burned away all his excuses, all the worries that had once seemed so important that they'd clouded his judgment. And his true feelings.

He loved her.

And all the rest of it didn't matter.

She'd been right. They could figure things out with their schedules, the ranch, his siblings.

None of that mattered when all he could see was her closed eyes, her motionless body.

He just wanted to *be* with her. For any time they could carve out to spend together, for now, forever.

But first, she had to wake up. The doctors and nurses were monitoring her closely, but they wouldn't be able to fully evaluate how much damage the cyanide had done until she regained consciousness.

A knock at the door brought his head up, though it felt as if it weighed a thousand pounds.

While the ER doctors had been working to save her life, he'd coordinated with local law enforcement and the nearest high-clearance security team he could find to set up this secure wing in the hospital. Where before he'd been content to let the royal security team manage things from offsite, he refused to risk her life again, not when he could do something about it.

Carrie stuck her head around the door, and he stood, surprise overcoming the lethargy in his limbs. "What're you doing here?"

"Matt called." She stepped inside as he reached for her, and her arms came around him in a hug that had him blinking against his burning eyes. "The guys are here, too, out in the waiting room."

He hugged her tightly, unable to find words. Alessandra had been right. He hadn't been able to protect her from right beside her. He needed to learn to let go and trust God and Carrie. She could handle her own life.

Even if it wasn't entirely comfortable right now.

"How is she?" Carrie asked.

"Unconscious." He ran a hand through his hair, missing his hat. It'd been lost somewhere in the melee. "It takes hours to run the full test on the poison she ingested, but the doctors think they've at least stopped it from doing further damage."

Carrie sniffled a little as she looked at Alessandra's pale face against the pillow, hair mussed and IVs trailing from Alessandra's arm.

Gideon's chest felt so full and hot that he wanted to howl.

Suddenly, more bodies were crowding inside. The ranch hands were led by Trey, who had his chin hitched in the air and a stubborn glint in his eyes. "Figured if y'all are holding a prayer vigil, we'd better all get in on it." He moved next to Carrie, one hand resting at her waist.

Gideon nodded once, letting the cowboy—and his friend—know that he couldn't protest a friendship or relationship anymore.

Matt came near, clapping him on the shoulder.

"The nurse know you're all in here? Probably against protocol." But for the moment, Gideon's will was too weak to protest more.

And then, Carrie and all the ranch hands had slung their arms around each other, circling the bed in one big man-hug as they bowed heads. On the end of the chain, Gideon gently laid his free hand on Alessandra's shoulder.

Each man shared a special prayer on Alessandra's behalf, beseeching God to heal her and bring her back to them.

By the time Dan had finished, every one of them was clearing his throat or surreptitiously wiping his eyes. They moved slightly away from each other and the brotherly intimacy of the moment, some of them shuffling their feet. Dan and Nate shoved their hats back on their heads.

"Is she really a princess?" Chase hooked his thumb over his shoulder.

Gideon glared at Matt, who raised his hands helplessly. "Sorry, man. Some reporter got shots while she was getting loaded into the helicopter."

Gideon winced.

"Got *pictures*," Matt corrected himself. "And by the time we got to the hospital, it was all over social media and local news stations."

That was a nightmare for another time. At least he'd had the foresight to secure this wing of the hospital.

"So she really is?" Chase pressed.

Gideon nodded. "Yeah."

Brian whistled low. "And we had her cleaning up after us like a maid."

Carrie's eyes were shining. "Scarlett will be thrilled. She's claimed this whole time that Allie was a princess."

Gideon rubbed the back of his neck with one hand. "She's not coming back to the Triple H. When she wakes up"—he almost choked on the words, but he had to believe she was going to wake up—"she's going back to Glorvaird."

Carrie looked at him with a glint of mischief in her eyes. "Maybe. I guess we'll see."

He clung to his sister's hope. Right now, it was all he had.

• • •

ALESSANDRA WAS TRAPPED IN COLD, terrifying darkness, unable to move. Barely able to think.

Voices came. Someone stuck something nasty down her throat and she gagged. The contents of her stomach emptied.

Oh, she *hated* being sick.

She was so hot.

No, *cold*.

And then came the voice of the man she loved. Gideon.

She even thought she heard Carrie, Matt, and the other hands. Were they...praying for her?

Peace and warmth stole over her. Snatches of conversation wafted to her, as if from far away.

"...she really a princess?"

"...she's going back to Glorvaird."

"Maybe..."

She couldn't go back. Not yet. There was still something undone. Something she hadn't told Gideon.

Why couldn't she wake up?

She needed...

She went cold again. Started shaking uncontrollably. Couldn't find her tongue.

And then there were voices again—strange ones. "She's seizing!"

Where had Gideon gone? Her friends?

She needed them.

Needed him.

Was lost.


IT WAS AFTER MIDNIGHT, but Gideon couldn't sleep. The ICU room allowed for one uncomfortable chair, and the cowboys and his siblings had agreed to stay in the waiting room for now.

Why hadn't Alessandra woken?

Earlier, after the impromptu prayer vigil, she'd shown signs of improving.

And then she'd had some kind of seizure, her body reacting to the poison. The doctors had been able to help her ride it out, but since then, there'd been no sign of awareness behind her eyes. He imagined her lost in a deep pool. Maybe the seizure had brought her close to the surface. Since then, though, she seemed to have sunk all the way at the bottom, her beautiful heart hidden beneath the murky waves. Would she ever make it to the surface again?

Was he losing her? Was she drifting away even now as he watched her pale face?

This waiting...he was dying a slow death.

If she died, he would never be the same. He couldn't bear to think of a world where he wouldn't hear her laugh, see the flash of her teeth in that secret smile she'd only given to him.

He took her hand. Shook it gently. "Wake up, Allie-girl."

Nothing. No blip on the machines monitoring her. No catch of her breath.

"I need you—" His voice broke on the words. She'd never know how devastated he was at this moment, how very badly he'd realized he needed her.

"I was wrong. You were right." If ever there were words to wake a woman up...

And it was true. He'd been wrong to push her away. He should've been pulling her closer. They were a team, the two of them.

He waited. Still no change.

The clock ticked. The monitors proved she was still here, still with him. But still not.

"Please." He bowed his head over her hand, squeezed his eyes against the tears that were so close.

"Please." He didn't know what he was pleading for. For God not to take her, maybe. For her to come back to him.

*Right now, thank you very much.*

He rose from the chair, unable to contain the nervous energy that buzzed through him. He rested his hands against the railing and leaned over her, so pale and still in the bed. At least the awful red had faded from her skin, one of the signs of the cyanide poisoning.

"Alessandra," he breathed.

He leaned closer. Didn't even know what he was doing, but he had to do something.

He brushed one soft kiss, a feather kiss, again her mouth. One against her forehead. He let his chin rest against her temple.

And whispered, "I love you."


Alessandra felt Gideon's presence nearby, felt the brush of his whiskers against her temple.

*"I love you."*

She opened her eyes.

He froze. He backed slightly away, enough so she could see his dear face.

His hands were clamped around the hospital bed railing, close enough that she barely had to move to reach for him. He met her grasp, his fingers tangling with hers.

"Alessandra." His breath caught, and there was no missing the sheen of tears in his eyes. Her sensitive *Bear*.

"Hi," she whispered, the word burning her throat. Tears stung her eyes.

He breathed out a shaky exhale, squeezed her hand once. He let go only to move away momentarily, and then he was back with a cup of water and a straw. He held it to her lips, and she drank greedily, feeling echoes of fever—or something—that had overwhelmed while she'd been lost in the darkness.

When she'd had her fill, he put away the cup. "I should call the nurse. There are a lot of people waiting for you to wake up."

He took her hand again and stared at her.

Long enough that she began to wonder what had happened. Had her hair been all shaved off? "What is it?"

He narrowed his eyes slightly. "For a bit there, I thought I might never see you looking back at me again."

"Was I sick?" she asked. "I remember feeling feverish, and cold. Choking. Throwing up."

"You were poisoned," he said. "You collapsed at the airport. The woman gave you that pastry... Remember?"

She did, barely.

"Mostly I remember you were going to let me walk away."

His eyes darkened, and he leaned close to touch his temple against hers. "That's because I was doing what my sex often does. Being an idiot."

Relief and love flowed through her. "So you've changed your mind, then? About us not *working* in the long-term?"

"Well, for one thing, your royal security team needs a massive overhaul. I can't trust them to get you back to Glorvaird safely, so it seems I'll be forced to accompany you at least that far."

He brushed a kiss against her upper cheek. "There's no telling how long it will take before they can be whipped into shape, and I can't leave you unprotected. You're too important." Though most of his words held a teasing note, those last were spoken with an intense seriousness.

"And then there's the fact that I've fallen in love with you," he said softly. "And I can't live without you. So I suppose the roundabout answer is: yes, I've changed my mind."

She raised her other hand, the first real movement she'd made since waking. Everything seemed to be in working order, though she felt as weak as a baby. She cupped his cheek, his trimmed beard rough against her palm. "I'm in love with you, too."

His eyes squeezed shut, but not before she saw the depths of emotion that overwhelmed him.

"*That* seems like the second miracle of the day," he whispered. He brushed another gentle kiss against her lips. He drew away slightly, and her hand fell to the bed. "But if God wants to heap blessings on my head..."

She smiled. "You won't argue?"

"Not today."

He was forced to move back as a nurse and doctor bustled in, surprised to see her awake.

They began asking questions immediately, prodding her with a thermometer and stethoscope, but she held Gideon's gaze throughout.

It was a little bit astounding.

She'd never expected to be running for her life, then stranded on a working ranch for days on end. If not for New York, she never would have met Gideon.

Although he hadn't admitted to it, she guessed that if it hadn't been for Gideon's training and quick thinking, she could've died in the airport.

And then, he'd declared his love for her.

Miracles, indeed.

# Epilogue



*"THE KISSING PRINCESS"*

Mia, third in line to the Glorvaird crown, crumpled the newsprint between both hands.

She considered throwing it in the fire burning on the nearby hearth, but ultimately smoothed it out on the table. The headline shouted up at her again, making her lose any appetite for the breakfast spread laid out on a silver tray before her.

Is that what they really thought of her? All the public could see of her?

Beneath the headline was a photograph of her—yes, kissing—the young duke of Regis, a neighboring kingdom.

The long-range, slightly grainy photo didn't show the moments that followed, when she'd discovered his infidelity. The photograph didn't show the resounding slap she'd delivered.

The press liked to paint her as someone who hopped from boyfriend to boyfriend, who liked to play with men's hearts and give kisses freely, but it wasn't the truth. Not at all.

She fell in love easily. Too easily, as the line of jerks that had left her with a broken heart could attest to.

But the media didn't care about that.

Voices intruded, and she slouched in the wingback chair in the palace's blue parlor.

It sounded like her sister and her new—American—beau. She'd welcomed her sister back to the palace last night and met the handsome, dark-bearded man, but she didn't want company now. Maybe if she was quiet enough, still enough, they wouldn't find her here, and she could continue her sulk in private.

"You're having brunch with Eloise?" Gideon asked.

"Mm hmm. Worried about being left to your own devices?"

There was a quiet moment, and Mia squeezed her eyes closed, imagining her sister locking lips with the handsome American.

"Not too worried," came Gideon's voice, amused and warm. "I might sneak down and talk with your head of security while you're busy."

"Again?"

"There were a couple of recent email threats that they should look into."

Mia's pulse sped momentarily. She'd been a part of the motorcade that the bombing had narrowly missed just three months ago. It had been the most frightening thing she'd ever experienced, and for brief seconds she'd thought she wouldn't survive. Since then, palace life had returned to a normal, if more vigilant, state.

She'd hoped that the threat was past, but it seemed Gideon didn't think so. Did he know something she didn't, or was his suspicion because of his former role as a soldier and the near-misses Alessandra had had?

"Stop *worrying* so much," Alessandra said to her beau. "You'll start to go prematurely gray, and then my people will think I'm dating a much older man."

"I'll stop *taking precautions* when I'm certain there are no threats against the woman I love."

It was a swoon-worthy statement. Mia's stomach twisted. Some of it was happiness for her sister. Some of it, she hated to admit, was envy. She wanted that kind of love for herself. Was desperate for it.

Her eyes fell to the front page again, as Alessandra and Gideon's voices faded to murmurs. Was it her imagination, or did her desperation show in the grainy photograph?

She couldn't go on like this. It wasn't healthy.

She needed to prove to herself—and to the kingdom—that she wasn't just the *kissing princess*.

And that's when she promised she would not kiss another man unless he was the man she would marry.


GIDEON WATCHED Alessandra disappear down the hall to meet her sister. He stood with both hands in the front pockets of his slacks, posture relaxed, just in case she turned around.

*"I'll stop taking precautions when I'm certain there are no real threats against the woman I love."*

He was fairly sure he'd convinced her that all he was thinking about was her security. Right now, nothing could be further from the truth.

When she turned the corner at the end of the opulent, marble-floored hall, he swiveled on his heel and marched back to the quarters he'd been assigned, in a different hall than where the princesses resided. He unrolled his shirt sleeves as he walked, pushing the cuffs back down and buttoning them.

He had another mission in mind today. And one didn't have an audience with the king in shirtsleeves. Inside the richly-appointed bedroom, he checked his black leather shoes for scuffs—none—and pulled the tie out of the top pocket of his suitcase, laid out on the foot of the bed.

Carrie had helped him pick it out. He'd confided in his sister before he and Alessandra had left the United States. She thought his plan to ask the king for Alessandra's hand before planning an extravagant proposal was romantic and perfect.

He wished he was as certain.

He stood before the bureau mirror, tucking the tie around his neck and knotting it.

In the past three months, he and Alessandra had been almost inseparable. He'd escorted her home a week after her near-fatal poisoning and met her older sister, Eloise. The king had been home, but the recent events had laid him up with an "episode," and Gideon hadn't had a chance to meet the man.

Gideon had stayed with Alessandra for nearly two months as the kingdom reeled from the attempts on their royal family. Had worked extensively with the security team, and although they hadn't discovered an inside man, their procedures had been sloppy, and the head of security had been happy to have Gideon as an advisor.

Then, they'd returned to the United States to the ranch. This time, with two of Alessandra's staff members as she worked on a proposal for a children's program that she'd been dreaming about for years. He'd had a few weeks to work with Nate and make some decisions about the ranch. Matt was back on active duty, and Gideon only had contact with him an occasional email and even rarer phone calls.

He and Alessandra had grown closer than ever. She'd been right that they could fit into each other's lives. He'd seen her nurturing spirit in the projects for which she chose to wield her influence. She made him laugh, made him notice the little things that he was often too busy to care about.

But there was still a part of him that worried things would fall apart. Something had happened between Carrie and Trey while he'd been in Glorvaird the first time, and although his sister had insisted that things were fine, he'd noticed the tension between them.

And while his feelings for Alessandra had deepened and grown...what if she wasn't ready for an engagement? What if she loved him, but she didn't want to marry him?

He knew there was protocol. That's why he was going to talk to her father first. But what if the man didn't approve? Gideon had no royal bloodlines. Although the ranch made a small profit most years, the real asset was their land. In no way was he considered rich.

Why in the world would the king agree?

But Gideon wasn't a coward, and he wasn't going to back down from this. He straightened the lapel of his suit jacket in the mirror and ran his comb through his hair once more—Alessandra had insisted he keep the beard—before gritting a frown and then turning for the door.

But before he left... He went to the suitcase once more and dug out the small, square jeweler's box he'd stowed beneath his drawers. For luck.

He'd had to work to convince the king's aide to give him the meeting, trusting the man with the real reason. Now he met the aide in the hall and followed the serious-faced fellow down another long hallway to a set of double-doors decorated with swirls of what might be real gold.

Gideon took one last deep breath as the doors swung open.

"You'll have a quarter hour," the assistant said in low tones as Gideon passed by him to enter the room.

The doors closed behind him.

The king sat behind a large cherry-wood desk ensconced in a fancy wheelchair. Alessandra had told Gideon what to expect when he eventually met her father—not knowing this was planned for today—but the man's wasted muscles and thinning white hair were still a shock. Gideon hid his reaction by bowing from the waist, the way he'd been instructed.

"Your Highness. Thank you for taking this meeting with me."

He straightened, meeting the King's stare. Though the man's body was failing him, there was no weakness in his shrewd gaze.

. . .

ALESSANDRA SAT across a small tea table from her older sister. Fine china and an elegant spread of pastries and fruit covered the white lacy tablecloth.

"So you're set on the American cowboy?"

Eloise wasn't one to mince words. Her sister's eyes met Alessandra's briefly and then skittered away. She didn't like to look at anyone in the face for very long. After years of being around her sister, Alessandra was used to it, though it still hurt.

Her sister's scars had never bothered Alessandra, not even when they'd been fresh and bright red, slashing across her cheek and neck, down into the shoulder of her blouses. But Eloise was incredibly sensitive about them.

She could also be incredibly rude.

"I love Gideon, yes," Alessandra answered.

Eloise picked apart the flaky pastry on her plate. "And I suppose you'll be spending a large amount of time in the States."

Alessandra frowned. She'd spoken to Eloise at-length after she'd arrived back in Glorvaird about her future plans. Eloise had agreed that she could cut back on some of her other events and take on some charity projects for children, ones that were close to her heart.

Was Eloise now thinking Alessandra would shirk her duties?

"We'll be spending some time at Gideon's home. His ranch has busy seasons where he's needed there."

Instead of acting upset, like Alessandra expected, Eloise nodded slowly. "Good. I have a project I need you to take on for me. It's very...sensitive."

Interest piqued, Alessandra leaned forward. "What kind of project?"

Eloise looked almost pained, if Alessandra had pegged her expression correctly. "This..." She shifted uncomfortably in her seat, and Alessandra had a moment of uncertainty. "Father recently confided in me that there was an infidelity when we were young."

Alessandra sat back in her seat, stunned. Of all the things she might've guessed, that wasn't one of them.

"There was a child. A daughter. Not legitimized, of course." Eloise looked down at the napkin in her lap. Alessandra still couldn't find words.

A sister. A half-sister.

"Her mother moved to America after the birth, and Father kept tabs on them for some time, but then the private investigator he'd hired lost them. Now, Father wants to find the girl. Before..."

*Before he died.* Alessandra's throat closed up. "I didn't think it was that close."

Eloise shrugged, her eyes on the window across. "The doctors say it might be as little as a year."

It wasn't nearly long enough. Being with Gideon had showed her that she could be brave enough to seek a deeper, reconciled relationship with her father, but... To only have such a limited time left brought a physical pain.

"Of course I'll help in whatever way I can," she said, a little hoarsely.

"I've two different investigators looking into finding her, but perhaps your man might have other contacts that would help."

Alessandra nodded. *Her man.* Yes, she'd enlist Gideon's help.

She wanted to get back to him now. To tell him of this new development. Talk through her muddled feelings about this revelation.

A sister.

When she found Gideon in the gardens, he seemed subdued. He glanced over his shoulder from where he stood near a stone bench in the rose arbor, and she saw his face was dark and brows were drawn. As she neared, she saw his suit jacket lying folded across one corner of the bench. And when he turned all the way around, she saw the tie he'd loosened around his neck.

She went to him and wrapped her arms around his waist. "What's the matter?"

She could feel the tension coiled in him, the tightness of his muscles.

"Nothing." His arms came around her upper back. He leaned back slightly, to better look into her face. "How was your sister?"

"Fine. I've got something to talk to you about." She squeezed his waist. "Later." And raised her face for his kiss.

He obliged her for a sweet kiss, but pulled away too soon.

"Something *is* the matter," she said with a slightly exaggerated moue. She reached up with one hand to touch his face, resting her palm against his cheek gently brushing with her thumb.

"No. I'm just...nervous."

"Nervous?" Her Gideon? Not likely. He broke their embrace and motioned for her to sit on the bench.

She humored him, perching on the edge of the cool stone. The scent of roses surrounded them and made the moment impossibly romantic. He stood tall, and she craned her neck to look up at him. One hand rested in his trouser pocket.

"I had everything planned perfectly for tonight, but...I don't think I can wait."

Then he dropped to one knee, and her stomach dipped. He reached for her with his empty hand, as his opposite hand brought a small black box out of his pocket. All her swirling thoughts stopped.

So did her breath.

"Alessandra, I love you. I can't imagine my life without you in it. Would you do me the honor of marrying me?"

She squeezed his hand tightly as tears blurred her vision. She blinked them back. "I love you, too. And...I'm so sorry to ruin your moment, but have you spoken to my father?"

One corner of his mouth tilted up. "Just this morning."

Her breathing eased. "And...? What did he say?"

"He gave his blessing."

She threw her arms around Gideon's neck, almost toppling them both. "Thank God."

She peppered his face with kisses until he took her lips in a breath-stealing kiss. When they were both breathing hard, he pulled away and settled on the bench next to her.

"So that's a *yes*." It wasn't really a question, not the way he said it, slightly arrogant and more than a little relieved.

She leaned into his shoulder, watching as he pried open the black jeweler's box. "I would've married you anyway, without Father's blessing, but this makes it better..." Her thoughts, her words cut off as she caught sight of the ring. "Gideon..."

A large, sparkling diamond winked up at her, sunlight casting rainbows around it on Gideon's hands.

"It's too much." She didn't know the exact price tag, but a diamond like that must've cost his last two years' profits.

He cleared his throat. "I know we come from very different worlds, and I may never fit completely into yours, but I wanted to give you something fit for a princess."

He slipped it onto her finger, the metal cool against her skin. And because she was watching so closely, she noticed that his fingers were trembling.

She laced their fingers together, twisting the tangle of fingers to admire the darker tan of his skin against hers, and the sparkle of the ring.

"I love you," she said, looking into his dear face. "And *I'm* honored to be able to spend the rest of my life with you."

He steadied himself with a minute straightening of his shoulders, and she knew she'd said the right thing. Gideon might show the world a tough soldier, but she was the one who got to see the real man behind the facade.

*That* was the real treasure she valued. Gideon's heart.

92

*Note*

Originally published in 2016, Chapter 8 didn't exist at that time. It was added in 2022 as a special bonus chapter. I hope you enjoyed it!

Back to the story.

# Cowboy Charming

<h1 style="text-align:center">Prologue</h1>

Fourteen-year-old Ethan Townsend stood next to his dad's hospital bed, shaking.

*Terminal.*

His thoughts circled like the wheels on his bike when he rode really fast. Wasn't a terminal part of the airport? Somewhere you went to check in for your flight? Not a diagnosis.

His dad was dying.

He nervously picked at the sheet that covered Dad's lower half. Dad reached out and clasped Ethan's hand.

How long had it been since Dad held his hand? His thoughts spun faster. The last time he could remember, he'd been ten, and his best friend had snubbed him in Cub Scouts.

Back then, Dad's hand was warm and rough, calloused from the work he did on the family-owned dairy farm.

Now Dad's skin was cool and clammy.

"I know it's hard, but I need you to be brave."

He couldn't look at his father, not yet. He stared through the half-open hospital-room door. His stepmother, Carol, stood in the hall-way, sobbing silently into her hands.

How could Dad expect him to be brave? He was just a kid.

His jaw wobbled, and he clamped it tight, trying to keep the emotion he was bottling from spilling over.

"It's okay to cry, Ethan."

Dad tugged him closer, and he climbed into bed, curling up

against his father the same way he had when he'd been five and they'd lost Mom.

"Don't ever let anyone tell you it's not okay to cry."

And he felt Dad's tears fall on his head.

Later, when they'd both cried themselves out, Dad let Ethan stay next to him in the bed.

"The dairy will provide for you and Carol and the boys. But with me gone, Robbie and Sam will need you to show them how to be real men."

He could barely think about his stepbrothers. Could barely think about the lessons Dad had taught him, usually when tossing a football around in the backyard.

Dad was supposed to be here to watch him start on the JV football team this fall.

He wasn't supposed to *die*.

Dad ruffled Ethan's hair when tears threatened again. "You've got your mother's courage." Dad's voice was rough, like he was close to tears, too. "Don't ever lose it."

NINETEEN-YEAR-OLD ETHAN CLUTCHED the envelope in his hand, making the half-mile walk from the mailbox to the single-wide mobile home on the dairy farm. Two years ago, Carol had sold the house in town, and they'd been forced to move into this little trailer. He'd been born in that house. It held his memories of Mom and Dad.

Now, he slept on the living-room sofa while Robbie and Sam shared one of the two bedrooms. Carol had the other.

He'd been waiting for weeks for this envelope. It was going to be his ticket out of here.

The envelope was made from thick paper. Nice paper. *Embossed* with the university crest. And inside was his acceptance letter. He'd gotten in, even though he'd had to delay a year to help Carol make ends meet on the dairy.

She wasn't going to be happy he was leaving. But this was his chance to get the education he'd dreamed of since before his dad had died. He'd even been awarded a scholarship.

As he crested the slight rise leading up to the trailer and barn, shouts met his ears and drew his head up.

Eleven-year-old Robbie ran toward him, shouting. His expression was panic-stricken.

Ethan would've dismissed it as one of his stepbrothers' many pranks—always at his expense—except for the tears streaming down Robbie's face.

"It's Mom!"

Two hours later, Ethan sat in the hospital waiting room between his stepbrothers. The same numbness he'd felt after his dad's death had stolen over him, though to a lesser degree. He hadn't loved Carol. She'd given him a roof over his head and—most of the time—three meals a day. But she'd also expected a lot of him. He'd been running the dairy since he was sixteen. He'd never gotten to play JV football, or varsity. When he wasn't working the dairy, she'd expected him to maintain the trailer and the yard—though Robbie was old enough now to run the push mower.

Before he'd turned sixteen, she'd fired two managers, run up her credit card bills, and lost so much revenue that she'd been forced to sell off most of the land and a number of the producing cows. Which meant that no matter what he did, they barely eked out a living. If they ever had extra, she spent it on new clothes for her and the boys.

Ethan wore secondhand clothes from the Goodwill store. Just as well, since he was usually up to his knees in muck.

College was supposed to be his ticket out, but the doctor had just delivered the worst news possible.

Carol was gone.

The boys had no other relatives.

Which meant there was no one else to look after them. *He* was their closest relative.

Looking down at them now, Robbie at eleven, and Sam at ten, Ethan remembered what it had felt like when Dad died. How could he abandon them to the system?

He couldn't.

# *Chapter One*



*SIX YEARS LATER*

Princess Mia, third in line for the crown of Glorvaird, stood in the shade of a big, red Texas barn and watched a real cattle operation.

The October sun warmed everything, baking the brown grasses in the fields and the cowboys working there. But the wind carried a distinct chill that had her shivering in her jean jacket. She was used to mild, rainy weather in the coastal kingdom of Glorvaird, but this dry wind was new and made her nose itch.

She'd traveled to the States a few times before on royal business, but always to one of the bigger cities. New York. L.A. This was her first experience with country life.

So far she had to admit the view wasn't bad. Cowboys prowled everywhere, all of them busy bringing a long line of cows through a series of pens and then chutes where a cowboy shoved some kind of tube into the cow's mouth and medication was dispensed down their throat.

It was disgusting work.

Her sister, Princess Alessandra, sat atop a rail fence, avidly watching. It was smelly, loud work as the cattle bawled and milled, stirring up dust. She couldn't imagine what her sister found so fascinating.

Or maybe she could. Alessandra was likely watching the love of her life, ranch owner Gideon Hale, who worked amid the other cowboys. The sunlight sparkled off the diamond ring she wore on her left hand.

Mia was only a little jealous.

She was aware of the admiring glances she kept receiving from the men as they moved around the yard. Gideon and Alessandra had introduced her to a few of the hands, but there were several others whom she hadn't met yet.

Texas had its fair share of handsome cowboys.

And all of them seemed to enjoy looking at her.

Except one.

The auburn-haired cowboy—at least what she could see of his hair beneath the tan cowboy hat he wore—hadn't glanced at her once.

It shouldn't bother her. She shouldn't be curious about him. It wasn't that he was withdrawn, because he spoke several times to the men he was working with, and she saw him smile more than once. It was that he was the only man on the place, other than Gideon, who hadn't looked at her once.

And so what if she was used to attention, admiring glances? She couldn't forget the promise she'd made herself back in Glorvaird. She wasn't going to kiss another man until she was sure he was the one she'd marry.

Which meant she really shouldn't even be looking at the cowboy. At any cowboy.

She was only twenty-three and had five failed relationships behind her. One for each year since her eighteenth birthday.

Was she so wrong to long for true love?

She was glad to have been included in this trip with Alessandra and Gideon. Her sister had asked for her help with final preparations for the big engagement ball that she and Gideon were throwing in three weeks. There would be a similar ball in Glorvaird, but Alessandra wanted this party to celebrate with their American friends, for whom it wouldn't be cost effective to travel so far for a party, though some would come to the royal wedding in her home country.

And Mia had wanted to get away from the media storm still raging after her last, very public, breakup.

She'd thought being here would be a distraction.

She just hadn't planned on the distraction being a handsome cowboy who refused to look in her direction.


ETHAN COULDN'T HELP but be aware of the beautiful blonde.

He'd first noticed her mid-morning, when she and another

blonde had emerged from the ranch house to watch the chaos ensuing near the barn.

Their appearances were similar enough that he thought they must be sisters, though he didn't know either of them. The blonde, who he guessed was the older sister, wore jeans and a man's work coat. Her boots had seen their fair share of farm work. He guessed the coat must belong to Gideon because at one point, she'd stopped him, and they'd shared a warm kiss.

But the younger sister... she wore skinny jeans that hugged her slender curves, and a white blouse beneath a rhinestone-studded denim jacket.

Nobody who worked on a ranch wore white around farm chores. And her high-heeled boots were more appropriate for a fashion event than the barnyard.

Regardless, he couldn't keep from sneaking glances at her. At first, she hung back, perching on an ice chest closer to the barn than the corrals where they ran cows through.

But soon enough, she was moving among the guys, distributing cold bottles of water out of the ice chest. She made it a point to speak to the different hands.

The October weather couldn't be called brisk, and the work was grueling. He'd sweated through the T-shirt he wore beneath a flannel overshirt. The sweat was downright refreshing compared to the cow drool and medication that had been slung onto him by the ornery beasts. He was sure he smelled worse than the bovines they were drenching with worming medication.

Finally, it was his turn to take a break from the drenching position —sticking the elongated tube down the cows' throats and squeezing de-worming medication down their gullets.

He'd take five and then climb back in and start driving cows into the chute. Another hour and a half, and he could take a short break in the AC in his truck before heading home to start the afternoon milking. Taking on this extra job would make for a couple of eighteen hour days, but the extra cash was needed at home. Like always. His stepbrothers were demanding new *kicks*.

He leaned on the railing, not holding his breath for the beautiful young woman to head his way with one of those water bottles.

He'd learned early on that girls like *her* never gave the time of day to guys like *him*. He hadn't seen her around town before, and there was no doubt she was related to the beautiful blonde that was Gideon Hale's girlfriend, but somehow he knew that *she'd* know just by looking at him that he was hired help. *Dirt poor* hired help.

"Thirsty?"

The lilting female voice shocked him into looking up before he'd thought better of it. She was *right there*, extending a bottle still dripping from the ice water in the chest.

He pushed his hat back slightly on his head and took it. "Thank you, ma'am. Miss."

His face went hot as he stumbled—didn't younger women hate to be called ma'am?—and he cursed his fair coloring, knowing he was probably blushing.

She was even more beautiful up close, with dancing, ice-blue eyes and the lightest splash of freckles across her nose and high cheekbones. Her long, blonde hair was pulled behind her head in a curly ponytail.

"You can call me Mia." Her smile had him noticing her shapely lips. "No, 'miss' required."

He swallowed hard. "I'm Ethan Townsend."

Her flowery, feminine scent was noticeable, probably because he stank so badly. That realization just made him blush harder.

He expected her to walk away, having done the polite thing by not leaving him out as she was handing out cold drinks. To his surprise, she propped her pretty, pointy-toed boot on the bottom railing and leaned her elbows on the fence next to him.

"So, Ethan. How long have you worked on the Triple H?"

He'd taken a gulp of the cold water, and now swallowed it wrong. It burned all the way down. He cleared his throat.

"I'm just extra help for a couple of days."

"Oh, I didn't realize."

There was a short, awkward pause, and then she asked, "What do you do?"

"I run a dairy farm on the opposite side of town." He didn't like to say he owned the farm, because really, the bank owned it. Carol had mortgaged it to the hilt, and he was lucky to make the payments and keep enough cash for himself and the boys to eat. Teenaged boys weren't cheap to feed.

"That must be a fun job."

Fun. Said the woman who'd obviously never had to be on the clock at four a.m. She'd probably never even thought about cleaning machinery and shoveling cow patties until your eyes crossed, and then doing it all over again in the afternoon.

And repeating it. Every single day.

He didn't nod, couldn't lie, though he softened it with what smile he could dredge up. "It's something." Hopefully only for another three years, but he couldn't focus too hard on that. Couldn't afford to jinx himself.

He was no expert in holding his own in a conversation with a beautiful woman, but it seemed like it was his turn to say something. "Are you just visiting our part of Texas?"

She tilted her head to one side, her brows furrowed slightly in a way that shouldn't be so adorable. Like she couldn't figure him out. She glanced over to where Gideon's girlfriend sat and then back to him. "Yes, for a few weeks."

And then Brian, one of the Triple H hands, rode by inside the temp fence they'd constructed early that morning, his horse kicking up dust. "Townsend, you about done flirting with the princess? I know it's a treat having a real royal highness around, but you ain't getting paid to stand there."

He was used to the ribbing from the Triple H hands. They were a tight-knit group, and when he got hired on for the most unpleasant tasks, like today's drenching and springtime steer cutting, they made him a part of the pack.

But this joke hit him right in the solar plexus. Princess? This gal was a princess?

Brian laughed. "You didn't know? How could you not know, man?"

Most days, he barely had time to eat. His stepbrothers had the only TV in the house in their bedroom, and they couldn't afford to take the paper.

And ever since last summer, he'd blocked his ears from all town gossip.

He could barely glance at her, but when he did, he noticed the color high on her cheeks. "I think it's refreshing," she called out to Brian, who was already spreading Ethan's humiliation to the next closest cowhand.

She slid a glance to him, offered a smile. "My sister is engaged to Gideon."

There must be a story there, but his throat had closed up. He wouldn't have asked anyway.

He'd been standing here next to a real, live princess and probably making himself look a fool. As if he needed any help with that.

He'd grabbed the water and now forced it down his gullet, twisting the cap back on the empty bottle. He tossed it in a nearby barrel and nodded at the beautiful princess who'd given him the time of day. "Thank you."

He didn't dare glance at her as he ducked through the railing and back into the corral.

He was such a dunce.

ALESSANDRA RUBBED HER EYE SOCKETS, blinking away the after-glare from staring at her laptop screen for too long. She was curled up on the couch in Gideon's living room, only one lamp lighting the space. Gideon's German Shepherd Dog Apollo snored softly from his cushion near the front door.

Though she was frustrated with her self-assigned task, she was glad to be on the Triple H. It felt like home, maybe more so than her suite of rooms at the castle in Glorvaird. Her kingdom was part bustling metropolis and part seaside village, but when she was there, she missed the wide-open spaces of Gideon's north Texas ranch.

"You still up?"

Gideon stood in the doorway, leaning one broad shoulder against the jamb. He'd told her he needed to work on the ranch's books for a while, but that had been... she checked the clock on her laptop's screen. Nearly three hours ago. He'd untucked his shirt and now stood in sock feet, apparently ready to go to bed.

"I thought this would be easier," she admitted, closing the laptop's screen and pushing it away on the couch cushion. Before she'd left Glorvaird, her older sister Eloise had delivered a piece of unexpected news—that the princesses had a half-sister from an affair their father'd had years ago—and tasked Alessandra with finding the lost princess.

Gideon came closer, and Alessandra stood, stretching her stiff muscles. She'd been so zoned-in to her search on the computer, following rabbit trail after rabbit trail.

Gideon's hands closed over her elbows, sliding slowly up her arms as he held her close.

"It'll take time," he said into her hair.

She knew he'd put out feelers with his contacts in the military—Gideon was a former Navy SEAL. She also knew her older sister had hired two private investigators to try and find the girl—woman now—who'd fallen off the map several years ago.

Her father wanted to see his long-lost daughter before he died. And though the doctor could only estimate when that might be, the clock was ticking. Alessandra felt the unknown deadline pressing down on her, and with it, a desire to return to Glorvaird to try and build the closer relationship with her father that she'd always wanted.

If Father was willing. When he'd first been diagnosed with MS, he hadn't wanted to make any changes to his lifestyle, hadn't wanted to spend more time with his daughters, even though his time on earth was limited.

That still hurt, but she was determined not to let her father go without fighting for a closer relationship.

Now that loving Gideon had shown her what a real relationship, built from true love, could look like.

Just being close to her fiancé like this made her frustration start to fall away. She leaned her head against his shoulder. His hands moved up even more, rubbing gentle circles into her shoulders and the back of her neck, loosening muscles gone tight from inactivity.

"You tell Mia yet?"

"No." As Gideon would say, that was the other *burr under her saddle*. Eloise had told Alessandra about their lost sister, and it had been a total shock. Eloise *hadn't* told Mia. She'd left it up to Alessandra when to break the news.

Alessandra was still coming to terms with it herself. Her mother had died when she was small, just five years old. Mia had been even smaller at three. She had no memories of their mother. If Alessandra had felt betrayed at hearing this news about their father, what would Mia feel? Father had been the only parent she'd known.

Plus, she was still trying to navigate the changing relationship with her younger sister. It wasn't until Alessandra's life had been threatened by an assassination attempt that she'd faced the reality of how broken their family had become. With Father caught up in his royal duties and now pushing many of those duties onto the crown princess, there was no real family structure.

And Alessandra wanted a real family. When she'd come to Gideon's ranch, lost and alone, she'd found the family she'd been looking for. And she wanted to rebuild what *could be* with her own family.

If Mia found out she'd been keeping this secret—for over two weeks now—she'd be hurt. It might put a wedge between the tentative friendship they'd been expanding since Alessandra had returned to Glorvaird after the assassination attempt.

Gideon's magic fingers relaxed her so much that her head fell back.

Which must've been what he wanted, because it gave him access to her face. His calloused hands moved to cup her jaw, and he lowered his mouth to hers, kissing her with a gentle intensity that had her tingling all the way down to her toes.

Her hands rested on his muscled chest, amazed at the power harnessed there, amazed that this virile, powerful man loved her back.

He pressed kisses against her temple and cheek, finally pressing his jaw to her ear.

Her racing heart still hadn't slowed.

"What about you?" she asked. "Did you get your books balanced?" She didn't know anything about the ranch's accounting, but Gideon carried a heavy load with managing the ranch, which his stepfather had left to the three Hales, Gideon, his brother Matt, and his sister Carrie. When Gideon had declared his love for Alessandra, he'd also given up some of the rigid control, leaving more of running the ranch in the foreman's hands. The ranch also employed four other hands to care for the large spread and keep it running smoothly.

It wasn't easy for Gideon to be away for long periods of time. But he'd done it because he loved her.

Now she felt the tension coiled in him. She realized he hadn't answered her question. "What?" she whispered.

"Something's going on," he said. "There's a discrepancy in the accounting. I haven't found what it is yet, but it wasn't there before we left for Glorvaird."

Her stomach pitched. "What does that mean? Someone's stealing from the Triple H?"

He shrugged slightly, his chest moving beneath her hands. "I don't know yet. It could be an honest mistake." She knew Gideon though, knew he'd seen some of the worst things human beings could do to each other during his missions. He had to be suspicious that it *wasn't* a mistake. "If one of the hands is responsible, I don't want them to know I've figured anything out yet. Can you keep this is a secret?"

"Of course." She stretched up slightly on her toes and pressed a kiss against his bearded cheek.

"If I'm tied up with this, I'll have to take some time away from the details of the engagement party."

She loved that he called it a party when it was really a full-fledged ball.

"That's all right. I've got Mia here to help, and the event coordinator has handled most of the details." The time they split between Glorvaird and Texas necessitated that they utilized one of the premiere party planners in Dallas. "Since we've already found the venue, it's more about coordinating with the florist and decorators. And finding my dress."

"And managing the security team," he reminded her. "I'll make time for that."

She couldn't help smiling. "And the security team." Since her near-assassination, Gideon had been overprotective. Not that she minded having him close, and protecting was in his nature.

But how would his protective nature react if he discovered someone was stealing from the Triple H?

Chapter Two

ETHAN WAS ELBOW-DEEP SCRUBBING DOG POOP OUT OF THE kennels when he was paged to the front of the veterinarian's office.

In addition to the odd jobs he picked up, he worked three days a week as a kennel assistant. Mostly cleaning cages. Sometimes clipping a dog's or cat's nails or exercising the dogs who were boarding.

And occasionally, if there was a difficult animal, usually a large dog, the vet would ask for his help when the technicians—most of them vets in training—needed it.

Turned out, he was good with difficult animals.

Just not difficult brothers.

Without the education he'd given up his one shot at, this work was the closest he could get to his dream job.

He joined the vet, Suzanne, and the tech in the larger of the two exam rooms, surprised into hesitating in the doorway when he caught sight of the blonde head bent over a good-sized German Shepherd Dog he recognized. The animal must be edging close to eighty pounds, all muscle.

It wasn't the dog that had his stomach clenching. It was the woman holding its leash.

She looked up, her hair falling in a golden cascade over her shoulder. His initial guess had been correct. It *was* the princess. Mia.

He hadn't been able to stop thinking about her in the three days since he'd seen her at the Triple H. Today she wore slim slacks with dressy flat shoes and a fuzzy pale green sweater.

Movement caught his eye, and he remembered there were others in the room. Suzanne stood beside the exam table but hadn't approached the dog yet. The usual tech, Candy, was at the vet's elbow, also not approaching the dog.

"Good old Apollo," he said because he didn't know whether it was appropriate to say hello to a princess, or even if he should.

He smelled like dog poop and probably looked like it too. Not that it mattered when Mia was so far out of his realm.

Her expression eased into a smile. "Hi, Ethan."

She remembered his name.

And he didn't miss the vet's sideways look.

"This guy giving you ladies trouble?" He stepped right up to the dog, pushing away the hesitancy he'd felt moments ago. He had to provide a steady presence for the dog, so it would calm down and endure the exam. "I'm a little surprised one of the guys didn't bring him in."

"Trey is outside," Mia explained. "I caught a ride to town with him and Apollo, but he had to take an important phone call." Mia surrendered the leash to Ethan, and their fingers brushed. He worked at schooling his face into a neutral expression, not wanting to show the *zing* that'd traveled up his arm and straight to his gut.

Candy ducked out of the room, apparently content to let Ethan handle the dog. He'd seen Apollo for the last two annual exams. The big guy did not appreciate the rectal thermometer or the needles that delivered his shots.

Mia stepped back, and Ethan ran his hands down the dog's back and shoulders. Apollo's ears relaxed a little, and Ethan nodded to the vet, who approached with a confident gait.

"Ethan is our resident dog whisperer," Suzanne said, and he felt Mia's curious gaze on him. He kept his focus on the dog.

"He can calm down any unruly animal," the vet continued. "Even this guy."

He was aware of Mia slightly behind him and at his elbow but kept his face angled toward the dog. Maybe she wouldn't see him blushing this time.

"Apollo isn't so bad," he said, with a scratch of the dog's chest. He kept his hand there while the vet manipulated the dog's back legs and feet, checking his joints and muscle movement.

"Is this another of your odd jobs?" Mia asked curiously.

Suzanne answered before he could. "Ethan started volunteering here when he was ten. We had high hopes that he'd join the practice."

The vet moved to Apollo's head, and Ethan moved back a bit,

allowing her the room she needed to check the dog's teeth, eyes, and ears.

Suzanne couldn't know how much of a blow her words were, casual as they were spoken. He'd wanted it too, so very badly.

"You know there's still scholarship money earmarked with your name," Suzanne said.

Okay, maybe she did know.

She brought it up every few months, as if he could ever forget it. What did she hope to accomplish now, bringing it up in front of the princess?

He'd tried to keep up with his education that first year after Carol passed. Enrolled in six hours of online classes. It had been impossible to keep up while caring for a ten- and eleven-year-old and running the dairy.

He smiled stiffly at Suzanne, who went on with the exam as if she'd been talking about the weather, not his life. She engaged the princess in conversation about her impressions of Texas.

At four years old, Apollo was in the prime of his life, and it didn't take much longer to give him his vaccinations.

Ethan's heart rate came down after the princess had left the room. The vet was paged for an urgent phone call, and he found himself alone in the exam room. He took out the industrial-strength cleaner beneath the cabinets and wiped down the floor where Apollo had stood for his examination, then disposed of the needles properly.

He was on his way back to the kennels when the front desk paged him to take a phone call. He ducked into the small employee lunch room, heart pounding. In his experience, surprise phone calls were usually bad news.

He was right.

The high school office asked him to come down. He had just enough time before the afternoon milking.

He met his stepbrothers in the hallway just outside the principal's office. They sat on hard plastic chairs, both wearing sullen expressions.

"It wasn't our fault," Sam muttered.

It never was.

No matter what he said or did, the boys seemed to have a problem with authority. Unlike his dad with him, Carol hadn't instilled any respect in them at all.

Maybe it was because she hadn't respected Ethan, no matter what he'd done for the family, what he'd sacrificed.

Things had come to a head last winter, when his brothers had been picked up by the sheriff's office for defacing one of the buildings on Main Street with spray paint. And the half-empty twelve-pack of beer cans they'd been caught with hadn't won them any brownie points. The business owner had pressed charges, and Robbie and Sam had had to go in front of the county judge. They'd been sentenced to forty hours of community service each.

Ethan had hoped the event had scared them straight, and it had, for a few months.

But then, the boys' behavior had become increasingly worse. He'd had two calls from their teachers in the past month.

The principal, a woman in her mid-fifties with slate-gray hair, stuck her head out the office door. "Coach wants you boys at football practice. I'd like to see you again in the morning, before your first class."

Robbie rolled his eyes.

Ethan nudged his foot, and both boys heaved aggravated sighs.

"Fine," Robbie muttered.

They scooted down the hall toward the locker rooms, leaving Ethan to enter the principal's office alone.

He'd never visited when he'd been in high school.

She steepled her fingers on the edge of her desk after they'd both sat down. "There's been another incident."

He took the chair across from her, praying he wasn't getting anything nasty on the upholstery. "I'm sorry."

It was his standard answer. They both knew it. They both knew he *was* sorry. He just didn't know how to make his stepbrothers feel regret.

Somehow, Carol had made them believe they could get away with whatever they wanted. No matter how many times he grounded them or took away their video games, they couldn't seem to understand that their actions had consequences.

In two more years, Robbie had a chance to get out of this town. To go to college and *be* something.

"Both boys were in Sam's classroom before the bell rang and were cutting up with some friends. The teacher overheard some inappropriate things and asked the boys to quit the conversation. But Robbie and Sam shouted at the teacher. They cursed at him and were threatening bodily harm before another teacher and myself diffused the situation. They've both received detentions after football practice for a week."

Ethan nodded, stunned. How could his stepbrothers do something like this?

"There's another issue that we need to discuss. Both your step-brothers are failing their French classes. If they can't get their grades up by mid-term, they won't be eligible to finish the football season."

Now Ethan felt as if he'd been sucker-punched. "How bad is it? Is there make up work they can do?"

"I've talked to the French teacher, and unless they put some real work into it, they're going to be so far behind that they'll never catch up. He's offered two make-up tests. *Verbal* tests."

She reached a piece of paper over the desk, and he took it with a sense of doom. He knew the boys had to have two foreign-language credits to get into college. Sam was enrolled in the basic-level French, while Robbie was taking his second year. And that with their mediocre grades, football scholarships were the only way they were going to be able to afford tuition.

He stared at the paper in his hand. He'd barely passed his own high school foreign language classes because he'd been working so many hours outside of school. And that had been years ago. There was no way could he tutor them himself. And with their budget so tight, how could he afford to pay someone?

The principal sighed. She stood and came around the desk, leaning her hip against its edge.

"Ethan." She sighed, and he braced himself.

"Have you thought about just... letting the boys go?"

That was totally unexpected.

Letting them go?

"Everyone in town admired what you did when your stepmother died. God knows you didn't have to take on the care of two minors when you were that young."

At the time, he hadn't felt as if he'd had a choice. The boys had needed him, and he'd had those memories of his father's death burned into his mind.

"You've nearly killed yourself since you were sixteen to keep that farm going, and none of your family appreciated you. Robbie and Sam are old enough now to understand consequences. I don't think anybody would blame you if you let them go into the system."

He couldn't find words. His gut reaction was denial. How could he turn his back on his stepbrothers? When they'd lost so much, just like he had. He was the only family they had left.

He shoved to his feet, the turmoil in his gut causing enough agitation that he couldn't remain seated. "Thanks for your concern. I'll talk to them about—" He waved the paper still clutched in his hand.

"Ethan."

He was enough of a rule-follower that he stopped in the doorway.

"I didn't mean to cause offense." Her voice and expression conveyed apology, but he wasn't offended. Just shocked.

"You've given so much...first to your stepmother, and now to the boys. But what about yourself? When do you get to live?"

Heat burned his face. He didn't have an answer. If he didn't work the dairy, they didn't eat. Just making their bills left him no time for anything else—much less figuring out a plan.

He excused himself, making his way out of the quiet school while the principal's words clattered in his mind.

The visitors' lot was adjacent to the football field, and he stopped near the chain-link fence that separated the field from the sidewalk. He rested his palm on the cool metal bar at the top of the fence.

Let them go? All the years he'd cared for his brothers, he'd never considered sending them into the system. Foster care.

It felt horrible to think it, but the idea was appealing. They'd never appreciated all he'd done for them, no more than their mother had. He could relinquish his ornery stepbrothers to the state and get on with his life.

But they were family—sort of. Hadn't he promised his father he'd show them how to be real men? He hadn't done that yet. And even though they were more trouble than a stall full of cow dung, they were his brothers.

Stepbrothers who, at the rate they were going, wouldn't make it into college, scholarship or not. He'd staked everything, his entire future, on the fact that the boys would leave for college after graduation.

Today's news was especially painful after the vet's reminder of what he'd given up.

One of the coaches shouted, and the offensive line, including Robbie and Sam, rushed forward, smashing their bodies against a series of weighted sleds with dummies atop them. Ethan's brothers rammed into those dummies like they rammed through life, destroying everything in their path without as much as a glance to see the damage they left in their wake.

What was he supposed to do if they lost their chance to go to college? He wouldn't continue to support them past their eighteenth birthdays. College was their chance to make something of themselves. A chance he hadn't had.

How could he convince them not to squander it?

From further down the field, the quarterback threw a long, spiral pass to one of the receivers under the watchful eyes of the assistant coach.

Ethan would have given anything to have played. He'd started on peewee teams at five. He and his dad had loved playing catch. Making plans for JV and varsity. If his dad had lived, Ethan knew he would've been at every game. They'd even talked a little about what colleges Ethan might go to on a football scholarship, when it was time.

But all those dreams had died with Dad.

This was Ethan's reality now. He needed to find a way to convince Robbie and Sam to straighten up for these last two years of school. To move on. Then, when they were both gone, he could start making plans for himself.


Trey's mysterious phone call had led to a mysterious errand, which left Mia and Apollo at loose ends.

Today's crisp autumn weather was lovely, and she didn't mind taking the dog for a walk, though she was aware of the two royal security team members following not far behind. She was more aware of them than ever, after the limousine she'd been riding in had nearly been the victim of a bombing a few months ago in Glorvaird.

Apollo had relaxed since his exam, since they'd left the veterinarian's office. Now he walked jauntily at her side.

She'd turned off of quaint Main Street and onto a more residential road, and before she knew it, they'd stumbled upon the local high school.

Curious, mostly because she'd never had any typical high school experiences, only tutors, she let herself and Apollo wander in that direction.

She was rounding a lush, green exercise field of some sort when she caught sight of a familiar figure, standing alone at the fence.

Ethan.

Perhaps it was her day to run into the cowboy-farmer-jack-of-all-trades. He'd been professional and polite in the vet's office earlier. No sign of the blushing young man that had ducked his head shyly at the Triple H. She didn't know why, but she was surprised to have discovered that at one time he'd had bigger dreams.

What had stopped him from chasing them?

Now he appeared pensive. Maybe upset. What was he doing at the school anyway? He was too young to have high school-aged children.

She should leave it alone. Leave him alone, but she found her feet carrying her in that direction anyway.

She hadn't been paying attention to the activity on the field beyond the cowboy, but as she moved to join him, several young men wearing padding and helmets crashed into each other, tackling one another to the ground.

She jumped, Apollo lunged, and she squeaked as she gripped his leash tighter. Ethan turned toward her.

She didn't know what expression he wore, if he were surprised to see here, because she couldn't tear her eyes from the players who were... it looked like they were lining up to get ready to tackle each other again!

The hand that wasn't holding Apollo's leash came up to cover her mouth.

"I guess you've never seen American football before," Ethan said dryly, finally pulling her gaze to him.

He'd lost the pensive look he'd worn before he'd known she was there, but instead of smiling, he wore a slightly-guarded look. Or maybe haunted.

Whatever it was, it bothered her.

She didn't know him from Adam, but from that first day, there'd been something that drew her to him. And while she knew she couldn't make everyone happy, she could usually draw a smile from most people.

"This would be my first taste of American football," she agreed, stepping slightly closer.

Ethan bent to greet Apollo, and the dog gave him a happy smile and a wag of his tail, not holding against Ethan what had happened in the vet's office earlier.

"They're practicing...?" she guessed of the football players.

"Yeah." He scratched Apollo's ears and straightened to his full height, his Stetson throwing shadows across his face. "Not as much now that season is here, but twice a day in the early fall."

Something in his expression... a wistfulness as he watched the players, prompted her to ask, "Did you play?"

Now a shadow passed behind his eyes. "No."

He didn't offer more of an explanation, but somehow she knew there was something he wasn't saying.

He nodded to the field. "My stepbrothers are out there. Robbie and Sam."

She looked but couldn't differentiate one boy from another with their identical, unnumbered training jerseys and helmets.

"So they just...keep crashing into each other?" she asked.

She wasn't looking directly at him but had enough of a view of his face to see the side of his mouth quirk up. "No. In a real game, the goal is to get the ball into the other team's end zone. That's the other end of the field. It's how you score points."

"And the other team wants to stop you?" she asked. "Thus, the...crashing?"

"Tackling. Yeah, you've got it." He had a nice smile, when he'd relaxed enough to show it. "Football is pretty intense around here. The whole town gets into it. You should take in a game while you're in town."

"Oh, that'd be fun! When?"

She watched in fascination as his face filled with color in a wave from his chin to the place where his forehead disappeared into his hat. He coughed a little into his fist.

"Erm, there's a game on Friday night." His voice sounded a little as if he'd swallowed a frog.

"Lovely! You could pick me up. What time should I be ready?"

His face had gone an even deeper shade of red, and she wondered if he'd spend the whole of Friday night looking as if he'd choked something down the wrong pipe.

"Six, I guess."

One of her security team cleared his throat, and she looked behind to see him jerking his chin, like they needed to be going. She sighed and turned back to the cowboy. "Here, let me borrow your phone."

He looked flummoxed, and she couldn't help the smile that pulled at her lips. "I'll input my number, in case you need to reach me."

He dug in his front pocket and came up with an older model flip-phone. She schooled her reaction, because she hadn't seen one in years. Tilted her head. "You know what, why don't you add your number to mine?"

She drew her metallic, thin smart phone, from her pocket, and with a few flicks of her fingers, pulled up her contacts list.

He fumbled it when she handed him the phone. "Sorry," he muttered.

She couldn't help noticing his calloused hands as he input the digits and wondered what it would feel like to have one of them holding hers. Of all the men she'd dated—royals and businessmen and the one soccer player—none of them had been anything like Ethan.

Maybe that was why she was so drawn to him.

She pondered it as she took her phone back, said a quick goodbye, and turned her steps back toward the street where Trey had parked the Triple H's farm truck. She couldn't help looking over her shoulder as she walked away.

Ethan had returned to leaning on the fence, his posture once again slightly withdrawn.

She had to remember her promise. No matter how much she was attracted to the shy cowboy, she wasn't kissing *anyone*. Not until she met *the* one.

But that didn't mean she couldn't enjoy the company of one handsome cowboy.

$$Chapter\ Three$$

Ethan wasn't sure exactly how this had happened as he turned his truck down the Triple H's drive just after six on Friday night.

Somehow, he'd been wrangled into a date with Princess Mia.

*Him.*

On a date.

With a princess.

He'd cleaned out most of the junk that regularly accumulated in his truck, but he'd hoped to have time to run it through the car wash and vacuum it. Unfortunately, an issue with one of the milking machines had delayed him by an hour this afternoon, and he'd barely gotten a shower.

So he'd stuck one of those air fresheners on the heating vent and hoped for the best.

There wasn't any use in pretending to be something he wasn't. His truck was fifteen years old, the same one that Dad had bought for the dairy before he'd passed.

If she hadn't already figured out that Ethan wasn't made of money, she would soon.

Surprisingly, they'd texted a couple of times since Wednesday. The first time her name had popped up his phone's screen, he'd stared for a good minute before he'd decided to answer.

*Mia: what does one wear to a high school football game?*

He was twenty-six and had never dated before. No one that he'd been interested in had been interested in him, for obvious reasons.

He'd fumbled his way through a response.

*Ethan: jeans.*

*Mia: I won't be out of place without a team sweatshirt or something?*

*Ethan: No.*

The next day, she'd texted him mid-morning, but when he'd expected another query about the football game, instead she'd asked whether he could teach her to ride a horse. When he'd agreed, she'd sent:

*Mia: Good, then we need to schedule date #2.*

He'd stared at that one for even longer than her first, unexpected message. *Date #2?* That meant she thought of the football game as Date #1, didn't it?

No idea what to do with that.

So here he was, a moron who didn't know quite what to expect going on a date with someone so out of his stratosphere. Out of his galaxy, even.

One at a time, he rubbed his sweaty hands on his jeans.

He pulled into the Triple H drive, as always, unable to keep from enjoying the rolling pastures as the old truck slowly rolled toward the house. Being here always reminded him of what he'd lost with Dad's passing. Land. Home. Security.

When he reached the ranch house, two guys in dark suits and even darker glasses strode off the porch. They met him as he got out of the truck. While he hadn't known Mia was a princess that very first day, he'd certainly gotten a crash course. This must be her security team.

"You got anything on you? Weapons, drugs?" One of the guys asked the questions as the other one cranked open the truck door and leaned inside. Without permission.

"No," Ethan said.

Apparently they weren't taking his word for it. The guy forcibly turned Ethan around and started patting him down. Ethan wore a long-sleeved T-shirt beneath his corduroy jacket and jeans. There wasn't any place to hide anything interesting, and the security guy was done in moments.

It didn't stop Ethan from being embarrassed as the goon backed off, leaving Ethan to turn and face the house.

"Gideon!" He thought that was Mia's voice calling out from inside, though it might've been her sister.

What had he gotten himself into? He left the security guys to search his truck and headed for the house. When he hit the porch steps, he could see inside the half-open front door. Mia had her hands on her hips and was staring down the rancher, though she was a head shorter. "You promised your goons wouldn't harass Ethan."

That she'd used the same word to describe them as Ethan had cheered him.

"Just because we're in Texas, and just because Ethan's done some jobs for me, doesn't mean I can forgo basic safety precautions. There's still a real threat against the Glorvaird crown and I have to—"

"Is there *really*?" she demanded, and he had to admire the fire blazing from her eyes. He was a little glad it wasn't directed at him. "Because *nothing has happened* in months."

"That doesn't mean that nothing will happen," Gideon returned.

She hesitated, her shoulders heaving with breath as if she'd been about to blast him again.

"Um, knock knock?" Ethan said through the open door.

Mia turned to him immediately, her blonde hair billowing in a curtain behind her. He got a look at the slim black pants and that rhinestone-encrusted jean jacket she'd worn the day they'd met. She looked relieved to have an out from the conversation with her soon-to-be brother-in-law.

She motioned him in, and he stepped over the threshold.

"I'm really sorry," she said quietly, looking up into his eyes with a sincerity that couldn't be faked.

He got tongue-tied in the face of her beauty and had to settle for a shrug. "It's okay," he finally managed.

She looked over his shoulder, frowning, and he followed her gaze to see the security guys sweeping beneath his truck with a mirror on a stick. Were they seriously looking for a bomb or something?

He shook his head slightly. "They won't find anything."

"Good." Gideon moved forward and clapped Ethan on the shoulder. "What time you do expect to have her back?"

"All right, Dad," Mia said with an exaggerated elbow to Gideon's gut, edging him back and out of the conversation. "I'm not a teenager, and I'll be back when I feel like it."

Gideon frowned, but Mia didn't wait for him to say anything else. She slipped her hand into Ethan's and tugged him toward the door.

The shock of having her soft, slender fingers wrapped in his rendered him speechless.

"I'm really sorry," she said again. "Alessandra says Gideon's been overreacting ever since someone targeted her... She nearly died."

She had?

When they reached his truck, the two security guys moved off. Instead of going around to the passenger side, like he expected, she yanked open the driver's side door and climbed inside, sliding across the bench seat.

He followed her in.

She took a breath, looking out the window. "There was also a bomb, back in Glorvaird. I was in a limo, and the bomb exploded pretty close to where we were driving past. Shattered my window."

She glanced back at him, tried for a smile, but he saw the shadows in her eyes. "Things have been quiet ever since."

"That must've been scary," he said slowly. "I guess I can understand why Gideon's so protective."

Her smile turned a little wry. "Good. Because we'll have an escort."

He cranked the engine and then followed her gaze to the black sedan that was edging out from beside the ranch house. So her security would come with them.

How frightening must it have been to live through that? He could deal with the security if it kept Mia safe.

She seemed to breathe easier as they turned out of the ranch drive and onto the two-lane highway that would take them back to town.

He hid a wince as she looked around the interior of his truck. She didn't wrinkle her nose or make any outward sign that riding in the older vehicle bothered her, but he figured she was good at hiding her emotions.

Once again, he reminded himself there wasn't any use in pretending to be something he wasn't.

But it didn't stop him from wishing, just a little, that he could've been someone different. Someone who deserved to be on a date with a princess.


MIA WALKED NEXT TO ETHAN, trying not to feel out of place. Trying not to be conspicuous with the two hulking bodyguards following a pace behind them. She hadn't realized her designer jeans and jacket would be so out of place. Everyone else wore what looked like faded work jeans and sweatshirts, though Ethan had texted her that a team sweatshirt wasn't necessary.

She'd meant to talk to Gideon and Alessandra about the level of security. Most days she vacillated between feeling the goon guards were overkill and feeling edgy, like someone could be watching her. But she certainly hadn't meant to lose her temper in front of Ethan.

Something was going on with Gideon and Alessandra. She didn't know what, whether it was something in their relationship or something else, but there had been more than one time that they'd broken off their conversation when she'd entered the room.

She hated feeling like they were keeping secrets from her. But maybe she was being overly sensitive. Maybe it wasn't about her at all.

The crowd entering the outdoor football stadium was a mix of families with moms and dads with kids and teenagers in pairs and threesomes. It was noisy and chaotic, and she loved the energy.

It was also completely different from the last date she'd been on. She and Richard had been at a quiet, private table in an expensive restaurant back home. And look how that had turned out.

She slipped her hand into Ethan's for the second time, partly to keep from getting separated from him in the crowd, but partly to see the slow blush that climbed into his cheeks. He carried a folded fleece blanket in his other arm.

He paid the admission charge, and they continued, swept along with the crowd toward a set of metal bleachers. Her detail followed right behind.

Several people greeted Ethan, one the veterinarian Mia recognized, who was walking beside a teenage girl. Mia noticed the woman's eyebrows go up toward her hairline.

They found a space on the bleachers, and Goon One and Goon Two settled in two rows behind them. She looked around eagerly, taking in the players on the field—lots of them— the bright lights, and the crowd.

"You'll have to explain what's going on to me," she said. "I don't know the rules."

They let go of each other's hands to get settled, and he stuck the blanket between his feet.

"Right now they're just warming up."

Her eyes caught on the cheerleading squad, already pumping up the crowd from below. Several rows of bleachers near the front were filled with uniformed band members, each holding different instruments.

"This is so fun. Thank you for bringing me."

He looked at her askance. "You're serious?"

"Why wouldn't I be?"

He rubbed both hands over his thighs. "This is a high school football game," he said as if she'd somehow missed that fact. "You probably attend events like Wimbledon and the Olympics and—"

"Water polo?" She leaned one elbow on her knee and rested her cheek on her fist. She raised her brows at him. "So I can't be interested in a high school sport?"

He had the good grace to look embarrassed. But then seemed to recover. "What was your last date?"

She wrinkled her nose. "It was a dinner date. And it wasn't a particularly good one."

He didn't ask for more details.

So she went back to the original topic. "Or maybe you think I was looking for any reason to get out from under my sister and Gideon's noses for a few hours?"

He slanted a glance at her, his mouth tight, though not quite a frown. "Were you?"

"Only a little." She nudged his boot with the toe of her shoe. "Is it really so farfetched that I might want to spend time with you?"

He murmured something under his breath and rubbed the back of his neck, expression chagrined.

"What?" she pressed.

He shook his head.

"What was your last date?"

"I haven't dated much. At all." That color was rising in his face again, and she tried not to let it distract her.

"Which is it?" she asked. "Much? Or at all?"

He kept his gaze on the field. A whistle blew, and he let out a small exhale. "That's the referee's whistle. They're starting."

She turned to face the field, aware of the man at her elbow. How could someone like Ethan not have dated? He was handsome, young. She didn't know anything about dairy farming, but it seemed as if he had a strong work ethic.

On the field, players from each team lined up, bent low and forward. One player jogged back and forth behind the line.

The crowd didn't go completely silent, but it seemed to hold its breath. She could hear one of the players, standing behind the line, shouting. She couldn't make out the words.

And then both lines seemed to break at the same moment and rush toward each other. The guy from behind the line somehow had a brown ball in hand and, before she could even register everything that was happening on the field, he threw it to the ground in an empty spot.

The crowd groaned.

"Was that bad?" She glanced at Ethan. His blush had tamed somewhat, but he still kept his eyes on the field, not on her.

"Incomplete pass," Ethan said. "They'll have four downs—it's like four attempts—to get the ball ten or more yards down the field. If they don't make the yards they need, the other team gets the ball."

"Hmm." She watched as the teams lined up again. The sequence started out the same, with both teams rushing at each other, but this time when she expected the guy behind the line to have the ball, it had disappeared.

The crowd cheered, and Ethan pointed to a young man sprinting down the field just before he was smashed by another, larger player.

She leaned close, her shoulder bumping Ethan's. "Much?" she whispered. "Or at all?"

He shot her a resigned look, one that read, *are you happy now?* "At all."

"Why not?"


MIA'S frank question had Ethan stumped. He was getting a little more used to her directness and had—thankfully—stopped blushing so much.

Had he given up on dating too easily? He'd always believed he was too busy, that any girl he was attracted to would reject him because of his financial and family situation.

"I've had custody of my brothers since I was nineteen," he said. "Since my stepmother died."

"Oh. I didn't realize." She bumped his shoulder again, this time a gesture of solidarity. Not that he'd minded the flirtatious way she'd done it before. "That must've been hard for you, taking on all that responsibility at such a young age."

He looked back to the field, where the home team had fumbled the ball and the visitors were setting up offense. Carol had pushed him to run the dairy, to take care of the family like Dad would've wanted, often manipulating him with guilt and tears.

"It wasn't that bad," he said. There had been moments—sometimes very few and far between—where he'd felt close to his stepbrothers. Like the time when the boys had been twelve and thirteen, and the three of them had snuck away for a morning of fishing in the creek.

Those moments had grown much more rare in the last few years. Now...this might be the last time he watched them play, if they couldn't get their grades up. It was a sobering thought.

When he looked back to Mia, she was considering him with what almost looked like admiration.

He averted his eyes. Surely he was imagining that. Seeing what he wanted to see.

"They're going to try a big pass," he said, nodding to the field, hoping to divert her attention.

"How can you tell?"

Okay, he wasn't imagining that she'd edged slightly closer. Where there'd been a couple of inches between their legs, now her jean-clad thigh rested next to his.

"Uhh... See the formation? The way the players are lined up?" He glanced at her, but she just looked more confused. "When they're lined up like that, it usually means they're going to try a long pass."

Maybe she'd moved closer because she was cold. With the sun going down, the breeze was starting to get chilly. That's why he'd brought the blanket.

"Do you come to all your stepbrothers' games?"

He shook his head, trying to clear the fuzz that came from being so close to her. "Just the home games. And I don't always stay until the end. The ladies—the cows—have to be milked twice a day. The first time early in the morning, so it makes for a short night."

"How early?"

"I'm usually in the barn by four."

Her mouth fell open. "But that's still the middle of the night."

"It's technically morning."

She shook her head emphatically. "That's...torture!"

He couldn't help smiling at her emphatic words. "It isn't so bad. You get used to it, after a while." He'd been doing it for so long he couldn't remember anything else.

"Well, I hope your brothers appreciate what you're sacrificing for them."

She'd meant it as a joke, meant the lost sleep he'd never get back. He knew she did, and yet, the words penetrated the careful wall he'd built. He always tried not to think about his brothers and the many ways they'd taken advantage.

*What about living your life?* The principal's words from earlier in the week echoed in his subconscious and reared their heads at inopportune times. Like now. Did he even have a right to think like that?

"Wow, look at that frown. I'm sorry I brought it up." Mia leaned into him again, her concerned expression drawing him from his funk.

"It's okay." He shrugged, tried to shrug it away, like he usually did. Lately, it was harder to lock those thoughts away where they belonged.

"I guess everybody has difficult family."

He grabbed on to the subject change with both hands. "You too?"

The easy smile faded, and he instantly missed it. She glanced around them, as if just registering the crowd on all sides.

And he realized she was probably worried that what she told him could be overheard and might be spilled to social media or tabloid magazines.

He might tire of the small town grapevine, but he couldn't imagine feeling under a microscope all the time.

"It's okay," he said quickly. "You can tell me later." Or not at all. He'd already experienced so much on this date, he couldn't expect a second one.

She looked slightly relieved. "I'll owe you a favor."

"Do you speak French?" he joked.

"*Mais oui.*"

# Chapter Four

GIDEON RAN THROUGH THE EXCEL SPREADSHEET ONCE more. He'd been scrolling up and down the screen, staring at columns of numbers for hours, and his head was pounding.

He was trained for combat, could speak six languages, and could build a bomb. But he was no accountant.

Leaning back from where he'd been hunched over the laptop keyboard at the dining room table, he realized evening was falling. He'd been so focused on the computer that he'd missed the entire afternoon.

But after two days of meticulously combing through bank statements and the monthly accounting ledgers, he'd finally found the discrepancy.

Three months ago, while he and Alessandra had been in Glorvaird, there'd been a ten-thousand-dollar withdrawal from the bank. Since then, multiple transactions for expenses had been adjusted, increasing the expense amounts by different amounts, from a hundred dollars to several hundred at a time.

If the adjustments had been a one-time error, or maybe had occurred twice, he could've chalked it up to a mistake. But the mysterious bank withdrawal and the adjustments to numerous expenditures meant someone was trying to cover their tracks. Someone had stolen from the Triple H.

They'd almost gotten away with it too, since the difference between the bank balance and the transaction register was almost non-existent now. If he hadn't noticed it last week, he could've missed it entirely. That might've opened the door for the thief to steal *more* from his family.

Had the person done it simply because Gideon had been distracted by his new relationship with Alessandra? Because he was traveling part-time with his fiancée?

He didn't want to consider it, but other than his brother and sister, Nate was the only person on the ranch who had access to the bank account. As the foreman, he had to be able to make purchases to run the Triple H. Gideon hated to think that a man he trusted so deeply would do something like this.

But there was also the fact that something had happened between his sister and a hand named Trey. When Gideon and Alessandra had declared their love for each other and decided to make a go of things, it had seemed as if Trey and Carrie had been beginning a relationship. Sometime while Gideon and Alessandra had been in Glorvaird, Trey and Carrie had cooled things off. Gideon didn't know why, and neither the ranch hand nor Carrie was talking. Was there any chance Trey had either conned his sister out of the money or had somehow used her to facilitate the transaction?

With Gideon's brother Matt overseas, that left hands Dan, Brian and Chase as the other suspects. Could any of them have pulled this off?

Until this point, everyone on the Triple H had felt like family. Been trusted as such.

Gideon rubbed his forehead, but it didn't ease the pounding behind his eyes.

"Gideon?" Alessandra said his name, and he looked up, blinking.

She came up behind him, and he blanked the screen, more out of habit than wanting to keep it from her. Her arms came around his shoulders, her cheek pressed into his. "Isn't it about time for a break?"

He nodded, enjoying the rasp of his beard against her cheek, but he couldn't shake the disappointment and anger that weighted him down.

She bussed his cheek with a kiss. "Find something?"

She must've felt him tense up, because she put a few inches between them, no longer teasing and flirty, though she still held on to his shoulders. "You did," she whispered.

"Part of it. I'm waiting on the bank to provide photocopies of the transaction. The manager thought he could pull digital copies of the surveillance cameras, too. I won't know for sure which one of the guys it was until then."

She fell silent. Emotion radiated off of her, and when she spoke, her voice was quiet but brimming with hurt. "One of the guys? I can't believe any of the cowboys would do that to you."

He was almost one hundred percent sure it was Nate. Nate was the only one with bank access, though the other hands could access the ranch's computer at any time.

He knew Alessandra had found peace and solace here when she'd been on the run from the assassins who'd tried to kill her. The cowboys had been a big part of that. And he felt just the same about the guys. They'd been together a long time. Dan had come to them most recently, and he'd been on the payroll for five years. It wasn't a pleasant feeling to think that someone you counted as family had stabbed you in the back.

He rubbed his fists into his eye sockets but didn't quite dislodge her hands from his shoulders. "Are we making a mistake here?"

She went perfectly still, and he regretted the words as soon as he'd said them. But just because he regretted them didn't mean the thought hadn't been rolling around his head since he'd first discovered there might be a theft.

She let go of him and took several steps away from his chair. She wrapped her arms around her middle in a pose that reminded him of when he'd rejected their relationship—when he'd thought they'd be better off going their separate ways.

This time, the diamond engagement ring sparkled from her left hand.

"What, exactly, do you mean by that?" Her voice was low and even, but he could hear the undertone of hurt.

He stood up, bad knee cracking as he straightened to his full height.

How could he explain this in a way that wouldn't hurt her more? "When someone commits a crime, there's usually this conflagration of three things." He used his index finger to draw a triangle in the air in front of himself. "Need," he ticked off the first side of the triangle. "Rationalization." Ticked the second. "And opportunity." He glanced at her, but it was clear from her puzzled expression that she didn't see where he was going with this. "Me being gone for months at a time opened a door. Whoever did this took advantage."

She nodded slowly, her mouth a flat line that he hated. "Opportunity. I get it. So you think if you'd been here, this wouldn't have happened?"

He shrugged, looked away.

They'd talked before, at length, about his protective tendencies, especially where his sister was concerned. His fears that Carrie and her daughter Scarlett could be hurt or in danger while he was gone overseas were part of the struggle he'd had when he'd wrestled with being with Alessandra in the first place.

He thought he'd overcome the need to be here, on the Triple H. But this situation had brought those fears right back. He couldn't help feeling that if he'd been on the premises, this wouldn't have happened.

Alessandra uncrossed her arms, paced several steps toward him with arms akimbo. "You weren't on a top secret mission, Gideon. Whoever did this could have picked up the phone and gotten you on your cell at any time. If they were in trouble, they should've asked you for help. Not taken the cash and tried to cover it up. This is *not your fault.*"

He looked at her, forced himself to let go of the stress and guilt and betrayal he'd felt all afternoon, and really looked at the fiery princess, riled up on his behalf. He reached for her, and she came into his arms easily.

He could let go of his tension—some of it at least—but he still couldn't help feeling that this was at least partly his fault. His responsibility. And he'd been gone.

But holding Alessandra close, burying his face in her hair... He couldn't imagine pushing her away a second time, especially not when they were supposed to be celebrating their engagement. She was *his*. She'd agreed to be his wife.

He couldn't let her go, but he also had a responsibility to his family and to the Triple H.

What was he supposed to do now?

"WHAT IS THAT SMELL?" Robbie asked from his slouched seat at the small kitchen table.

Ethan knew what the smell was. Skunk.

He moved past the boys at the cramped kitchen table in their single-wide and headed for the back door. He only had to crack it to see their golden Labrador, Peanut, sitting at attention just outside, wanting to come in.

And just cracking the door let in more of the awful stink.

He shut the door quickly.

"Did you let Peanut out?" he asked the boy, turning back to the table.

Sam didn't look up from the comic book he had spread across the other end of the table. "I did a while ago."

The boys had an open bag of potato chips and Oreos between them on the tabletop. With both of them and their football bulk slouched there, there was only room left at the very corner.

Ethan was having a hard time picturing Princess Mia seated there.

And an even harder time imagining his brothers behaving politely while she tutored them.

Was this tutoring session just asking for trouble?

When he'd made the teasing comment at the football game last weekend, he'd never expected her to agree to help. He'd even tried to dissuade her, but it seemed once she'd set her mind on it, he wouldn't be able to talk her out of it.

He'd planned to stick close and make sure his brothers showed the proper respect, but with their golden lab smelling up the entire trailer just by sitting on the back porch, he didn't see how he could do that. He could lock Peanut in the dairy barn, but that'd cause him no end of trouble in the morning when the cows revolted against the smell.

"Did you check the back gate?" Ethan pressed Sam. The gate had a faulty latch, and if it didn't get closed tightly, it came open. Now it appeared the dog had gotten out and found a disaster. His brothers' irresponsibility was nothing new, but this timing was the worst.

He could just picture the princess holding a handkerchief over her nose and mouth and trying not to gag as she helped his brothers.

This was a disaster.

A knock sounded at the front door. Crap.

He threw an encompassing glance at them. "Behave. I mean it. Remember, you playing football depends on your grades."

They'd been argumentative and defensive about the incident with their teacher and the subsequent detention. And he'd spoken to them at-length over the past days about what it would mean for their college careers if they didn't get football scholarships, and if they didn't get these grades up.

But now Robbie made a face, as if mimicking Ethan. Sam snorted softly.

Ethan suppressed a sigh. What could he do but open the front door?

It was only a matter of steps in their fifteen-by-seventy-two foot trailer. He'd tried not to think about the disparity between what Mia was used to and what she'd find here. He didn't want to be ashamed of his circumstances, not when he'd fought tooth and nail to provide for his family.

But that didn't stop heat from burning his face as he pulled open the door.

"Hey," he greeted her. One of her security goons was on the step just behind her. At least with someone burly like that on the premises, his stepbrothers weren't likely to get in real trouble.

"I've got a small problem. You can probably smell it."

Her nose scrunched, obscuring her freckles and creating an adorable crinkle between her eyes. "What is it?"

"Skunk. My stepbrothers... My dog got out of the yard and apparently met up with one. Let me introduce you to the boys, then I'll disappear out back to give her a bath. I didn't mean to leave you on your own."

She reached out and touched his forearm, stopping his rushed words. "No worries. Can I come in?"

His face went even hotter as he moved to let her pass. He made quick work of the introductions in the kitchen and then left Mia and her bodyguard inside with his stepbrothers and walked out the back door. He was a little afraid to read in her expression what she really thought of the tiny trailer.

Peanut lay on the edge of the small back deck, her chin on her front paws. When he walked over to her, she looked up at him with morose eyes.

"You're a mess, girl," he said with a sigh.

And then he left the porch behind, casting one last look at the trailer. "And so am I. C'mon."

A half hour later, he wasn't sure who'd gotten the bigger bath, him or Peanut. After a tomato juice rinse and two shampoos, she smelled moderately better. Of course, she'd shaken excess shampoo and water all over him numerous times, when his reflexes hadn't been fast enough to stop her.

Now *he* smelled like wet dog.

He'd taken off the worn chambray over-shirt that had borne the brunt of most of the soaking and now wore a T-shirt and jeans that were only *mostly damp*.

Half of the deck was bathed in late afternoon sunlight, and Peanut lay stretched out on her side, soaking up its warmth. He stood nearby, leaning against the railing with his arms crossed.

Should he go inside? There would be no sneaking past his stepbrothers or the princess. The place was too small for them not to notice when he opened the back door. But at least he could clean up a little in his bedroom, get a clean, dry shirt.

Before he'd had time to think a decision all the way through, the back door opened and Robbie's head poked out. "Hank's here. Sam and me're going to hang with the guys for a while."

"Wait!" Their friends were here? This tutoring session had been planned for three days! Ethan squared off toward the door. "What about your tutoring? Mia came out here to help you two. You can't just run off."

"It's been like a half hour, Ethan. We're bored, and we're going."

Before Ethan could take more than a half-step toward the house, Robbie had slammed the door closed, leaving Ethan outside, alone.

Frustrated. And embarrassed by his stepbrothers' actions.

He ran one hand through his hair, bracing himself to go inside and apologize.

He was reaching out for the door when it opened again, this time Mia danced outside and almost right into his arms.

He jerked back up a step. Didn't know if she saw his fumble as she turned to make sure the door latched.

"I guess they're already gone?" He didn't really have much hope that they'd stayed, not since she'd come outside.

"Yes."

He rubbed the back of his neck with one hand. "I'm sorry if they were rude to you."

"They weren't really," she said, and he narrowed his eyes, trying to gauge whether she was stretching the truth. "They weren't all that attentive."

He exhaled, frustration with his brothers and embarrassment warring in him. "I'm sorry," he said again.

She shrugged, and smiled. "It's all right. I really came to see you, anyway." She rendered him speechless and open-mouthed as she turned to look at Peanut. With her back turned, he could admire her knee-length skirt, the tights, and the slate-colored sweater that hugged her curves.

"Is this the guy—"

"Gal," he managed in a strangled voice.

She gave him a sassy *look* over her shoulder. "The *lady* that got attacked by a mean old skunk?"

Peanut raised her head, tail thumping the wood deck beneath her. When she realized Mia was approaching, the dog got to her feet.

He cleared his throat, tried to find some shred of dignity. "She probably hunted it down. That one has a nose for getting into trouble."

"Aw, she seems sweet."

Peanut sat obligingly to be petted, almost as regal as Mia was as the princess scratched behind her ears and beneath her chin.

"She is," he agreed. "Mostly."

"Hmm." This time when she glanced over her shoulder, an ornery smile lit her eyes. "Like her owner."

MIA KNEW she shouldn't take such pleasure in seeing that blush climb in Ethan's cheeks, but she couldn't help herself.

The dog's fur was soft and damp beneath her hands, and she gave the animal one last pat before she turned to Ethan. She'd already asked her security detail to wait in the car.

"I believe I promised you some of my secrets," she said.

She didn't really want to divulge her family's drama to Ethan, but fair was fair, and she wasn't ready to head back to the Triple H yet. Something had happened between Gideon and Alessandra two days ago. They were still engaged, still apparently happy, but there was some tension between them, and Alessandra wasn't talking.

It made for long, quiet evenings on her own.

"You don't owe me anything," Ethan said. He settled against the railing in a loose-limbed, relaxed pose.

And that was just another thing to like about the dairy farmer. He didn't keep count of favors owed. There was no scale to balance, like her former boyfriend, the duke of Regis, who'd always expected something from her.

Ethan was like no one she'd ever met before. Last Friday night, when the wind had turned cold, he'd tucked her into the fleece blanket he'd brought along.

It had taken her ten minutes to talk him into sharing the blanket, when his hands had been white with cold as he'd tried to tuck them into his jacket pockets. And when the blanket had been wrapped around both of their shoulders, enclosing them in warmth, she'd waited.

He hadn't tried anything. Hadn't put his arm around her. Hadn't held her hand. Hadn't tried to sneak a kiss.

None of the men she knew would've missed a chance like that.

His hesitation had made her lean into him on Friday, blaming the blanket for the need to be close, when really, it had been all her.

She knew he was attracted to her. At least, she thought so. Even if she discounted the blushes as something else—embarrassment or humility—every once in a while, she caught him looking at her with an intensity that could only be attraction.

Was he really that honorable? Or did something else hold him back?

She settled next to him at the railing, close enough that their shoulders brushed, but she faced outward.

"This is really pretty," she said, getting her first long look at his property. A long, low white barn was nestled into the landscape across the way. A white rail fence spread back onto the property, and black and white cows dotted green fields beyond.

"Thank you." He turned to match her stance, though he stood straight while she leaned against the railing. "But it's nothing like it used to be when my dad was alive."

His words were even, but she heard the underlying emotion.

"My stepmother was forced to sell off quite a bit of our land. Which means we don't have enough grazing pasture for full capacity. Which means it's hard to make a profit. You can see there are repairs that need to be made but..." *We can't afford it.* She heard the words he didn't say.

She saw that the barn needed to be painted. And some of the fence drooped, as if it needed to be replaced.

Ethan sounded defeated. It was slight, but there. The inside of his family's trailer was older, out of date. Tiny. The entire thing was smaller than many hotel rooms she'd stayed in before.

But everything was neat and tidy. She remembered herself as a teen—all right, and sometimes now—how her clothes ended up all over the place. Of course the palace had staff that cooked and cleaned up after the royal family. Ethan managed it all himself. Without, it seemed, much help from his stepbrothers.

"I think it's amazing what you've done for your family, all on your own."

He shook his head slightly, but she persisted. "It *is*."

He didn't make another denial, but she saw the twist of his lips that said he didn't think he was amazing at all.

They stood in comfortable silence for a few moments. She sighed. "My family can also be...difficult."

She didn't like to talk about it. Had barely broached the subject with the men she'd dated before. But somehow, Ethan's patience as he waited for her to elaborate made it easier to keep going.

She told him all of it. Father's MS diagnosis when she'd been ten and feeling that she didn't really know the man, only the crown. Eloise's near-fatal car accident years ago and how it had turned her sister into a beastly person. That she and Alessandra didn't have the close relationship that she wanted.

The only thing she didn't tell him was her dating past. She was a little ashamed of how easily she'd let herself fall in love with those other men.

Though in the face of her deepening feelings for Ethan, she wasn't sure she could call those old flings love. Not really. Now, her previous feelings seemed more like infatuation.

Somehow, while she'd been talking, Ethan's hand had closed over hers on the railing. She'd been the one to link their fingers together, wanting the closeness of that more intimate clasp.

He didn't offer her platitudes, just held on.

Alessandra's engagement ball was ten days away. At Eloise's prodding, Mia had promised she would come home soon after.

But how could she just walk away from someone as special as Ethan? She wanted to see him again.

Now she leaned toward him, pressing into his shoulder and looking up at him. Their hands remained linked.

"Are you planning to come to the engagement ball?' she asked softly.

He exhaled what might've been a bit of a laugh, his lips twisting until he looked down on her and must've realized she was serious.

"Me?" He seemed incredulous.

"Yes, you." She bumped him with her hip. "Everyone's invited."

"Everyone like the *governor* of Texas and *Brad Pitt* and..." He raised his eyebrows as if daring her to contradict him. Or to go on with the list, she wasn't sure.

And she realized she desperately wanted him there. He would be the only real friend in a sea of people who wanted things from her. There'd be press, who'd already started sniffing around town, looking for more news about *the kissing princess*.

"I think Brad declined the invitation. Which is really too bad." Her lips quirked. She turned toward him, still clinging to his hand, which forced him to face her as well.

"Please, will you come? For me?"

He stared down at her, and she couldn't decipher his expression. Uncertainty? Confusion?

"There'll be dancing, right? The fancy kind, like...waltzing?" He asked it as if he didn't even know if waltz was the right term. He shrugged slightly, almost helplessly. "I don't know how to dance like that."

"Well, then. I'll show you."

. . .

Ethan had only meant to find an excuse—any excuse—for Mia to rescind her invitation to her sister's engagement ball, but instead he found himself with his arms full of slender woman.

This was...uncomfortable. She was too close, and he was afraid he still smelled like wet dog.

It was also heaven.

The sun had set while she'd talked about her family, sharing with him in a way that no one had since his dad had died. Now only a sliver of light showed on the western horizon, and the flood light halfway between the barn and house was the only other illumination. Every once in a while a car passed on the two-lane road out front.

It made things feel more intimate than they probably should have. He breathed shallowly, wondering if he should call this off completely.

She stepped back slightly and touched his shoulders, then ran her small hands along his upper arms, positioning them the way she wanted. Then she pushed down.

He lowered his arms, thinking that's what she wanted, but she *tsked* at him. "No, no. You've got to have strong arms to lead your partner. Not noodle arms. Try again."

He raised his arms back to where she'd had them, and this time when she pushed down against him, he resisted her and kept his arms in place.

"Good." When she smiled up at him like that, he felt about ten feet tall.

And then she stepped forward, into the circle of his arms, and his brain and ability to speak floated right out of the top of his head.

She tucked his right hand around the curve of her waist before resting her left hand on his shoulder. Her other hand came up to clasp his.

His mouth was so dry he couldn't tell her that this was a recipe for disaster and that they'd better stop now.

They were so close that her temple brushed his chin as she settled fully into his arms. He swallowed hard.

"The waltz is a simple pattern," she said softly, as if she sensed the intimacy of the moment as well. "One, two, three. One, two, three. Pretend we're standing in a box. You're the man, you'll lead. That means you'll move forward, and I'll follow you."

"And you're just going to trust me not to let you run into anything?" It seemed dangerous to let a man guide her backwards.

"I said 'pretend we're in a box.' We won't be moving that much.

Let's try it. Your left foot first. One, two, three. One, two—" *Oof.* She stifled the sound.

He froze.

He'd stepped on her foot.

He winced. "Sorry." He glanced down to see what kind of shoes she was wearing, what kind of damage he might've done to her toes.

"I'm fine." Her hand came off his shoulder, and he thought she might step away, but she chucked him beneath his jaw. "Chin up. Eyes up. Again. One, two, three."

He didn't step on her foot this time, moving slowly to prevent it from happening.

She stopped him with a hand to his chest. "You're a half step behind the count, now. You have to follow the music—"

"What music?"

She thumped him on the chest, a silent reprimand. "Don't worry that you're going to step on me. Trust that I'll follow your lead."

She looked up at him fiercely, and the stubborn tilt of her chin made his stomach flip and his heart pound. *I'll follow your lead.* Surely, she'd meant the words literally. He was the only one reading into this. He had to be.

This time when she counted the beats off, he squinted his eyes almost closed, not wanting to see her face if he did step on her again. He did as she asked, trusted her count, and this time, they completed the square with no mishaps.

She made him do it again, smiling up at him like he'd accomplished something fantastic, instead of a simple dance step. He'd started to relax infinitesimally when she said, "Good. Now let's add a turn."

He didn't fumble it too badly. She made him do it again.

The moon started to come up, lending a silver glimmer to her skin and a luminescence to her eyes as she gazed up at him.

"At the ball I'll be wearing a gown with a huge skirt," she said. "So it will make it slightly more difficult to maneuver. But you'll also have less chance of stepping on my feet."

She spoke as if he'd already agreed to go. As if she'd actually want to dance with him if he did go. He hadn't been joking about the caliber of the other guests. No way would he fit in there. But if she wanted him there...

She let go of his shoulder and spun out in a turn beneath his upraised arm, laughing. The spirited, free sound went straight to his heart. When she twirled back to him, he went still.

She met him there, resting her free hand on his chest. He still had her other hand clasped in his. He drew it to his chest, just above his heart.

She was bright, like a diamond shining up at him from his arms.

He couldn't breathe.

Her eyes were large, and he thought maybe he should let her go, except then her gaze flicked down to his mouth and held there for a protracted moment.

*Did she want him to kiss her?*

The outrageous thought twirled through his mind in the same way she'd spun in his arms. It made him just as wobbly.

Then she leaned toward him slightly. Maybe raised up on her tiptoes.

He only had instinct to go on and lowered his head. His pulse pounded in his temples and he was really going to kiss—

Suddenly, she pushed away from his embrace, and he released her instantly.

Cool autumn air rushed into the space between their bodies, and as she turned from him, the flood light illuminated the stricken expression on her face.

Heat and humiliation pounded through him with every beat of his heart. "I'm sorry," he said.

"No, it wasn't—" *You.*

Wasn't that something people said when it *was* you? His inexperience hampered him, but it stood to reason he'd misread all of her cues. He'd only imagined her leaning toward him, imagined her glance at his lips.

She tucked a lock of hair behind her ear. "I need to go."

He cleared his throat. "Yes, all right."

He trailed her around the trailer and through the chain-link gate, mind grasping for what to say. Should he apologize again?

Then she got in the car with her security goon, offering only a subdued goodbye before the door clunked closed.

He was afraid of what she'd think if he stood there watching her drive away, so he gave a lame wave and turned to climb the trailer steps.

Inside, he leaned his shoulder against the closed door, breaths harsh and loud in the stillness.

Had he just ruined the first real friendship he'd had since his dad?

# Chapter Five

"Do you like how this looks?"

Alessandra's question drew Mia's head up from her phone. She'd been trying to decide whether she should text Ethan or not.

She gazed at her sister in the triplicate mirrors of the trendy, upscale Dallas boutique. Alessandra wore a floor-length, pale pink gown with a ruched skirt and an off-the-shoulders design.

They were the only ones in the dressing room this afternoon. At Gideon's insistence, they'd paid well for privacy, and the shop had closed to other customers for a few hours. Several smaller doors led off the mirrored main area, where multiple women could dress at the same time and then come out to admire themselves. Mia sat on one of the two small sofas that bracketed the wood floor and made it more welcoming.

"It's beautiful," Mia told her sister.

"That's a cop-out answer." Alessandra twirled to stare at her hips in the mirror. "It makes me look huge here." She motioned with both hands to her *derrière*.

"It's the way the skirt fits, it's not you. Anyone can see that." This was the sixth gown Alessandra had rejected.

And maybe Mia was a little distracted. It had been two days since she'd practically run out of Ethan's arms, and she was still spooked.

She'd almost kissed the man. Completely forgotten about her promise until the very last second.

She'd *wanted* his kiss. Desperately. Ardently.

"What is with you?" Alessandra complained as she slipped out of the dress. The stylist quickly and quietly took it from her, leaving Mia's sister in her slip and underwear as she waited for the next in line.

Mia blinked back the hot feeling in her eyes. "Nothing."

Alessandra crossed her arms. "Now you're lying to me. If you don't want to talk about your farmer-boy, fine, but you don't have to lie."

Mia's chin went up. "I don't want to talk about Ethan."

She didn't want to keep remembering the hurt that had pierced his eyes just before he'd shuttered his entire expression. Or how quick he'd been to say, *I'm sorry*.

The whole thing had been her fault.

She couldn't face the swirling thoughts. She stood up abruptly. "And if you want to talk about lying, why don't you let me in on the big secret that you've been holding onto since Glorvaird?"

Color leached out of Alessandra's face. "What?"

Mia was shaking now, but she couldn't stop the words from spewing forth. "You and Gideon keep having conversations that stop when I walk in the room. You haven't looked me in the eye since we left the palace."

Alessandra's gaze skittered away. The stylist started to come back into the room, her arms full of tulle, but Alessandra waved her off. She ducked away.

Alessandra pressed her hands together in front of her waist, a sign of tension that Mia knew and recognized. She waited her sister out.

After a long exhale, Alessandra looked her in the eye. "Father told Eloise about an—an affair. From when we were small. We have a half-sister somewhere in the states. Eloise asked me to find her. She dropped off the grid years ago."

Mia sat back down, stunned. That was the last thing she'd expected. She'd known there was a secret, but she hadn't given real thought to what it was.

An affair? A missing half-sister?

"When were you going to tell me?" She forced the words out past lips that felt numb.

Alessandra shrugged, her hands pressing together so hard her knuckles were white. "I was trying to figure out the best time."

Mia stood up, unable to keep looking at her sister. Betrayal fired through her veins and tears threatened. "I'll wait in the car."

"Mia—"

But she didn't wait to hear whatever else Alessandra was going to say.

. . .

Two days after the kiss that wasn't, Ethan was worn slick. The one thing he wanted most was to fall into bed and forget the last three days had happened.

He still couldn't reconcile what had happened those last few minutes he and Mia had been together.

But he also couldn't forget the look on her face when she'd asked him to go to the ball.

Was he crazy to even consider going? He knew he'd stick out like a mutt in a room full of Persian cats, but even so, he'd dug to the very back of his closet, to the box of his dad's things that Carol hadn't thrown away or sold. There wasn't much. A ball glove. A handful of baseball cards that had sentimental value.

And his dad's suit.

Ethan had shrugged into the charcoal-gray suit coat to test the fit and found that he must have the same body shape as Dad, because it fit perfectly.

Now he sat on the end of his bed and looked at the suit that he'd hung up in the doorway to his closet.

It was a timeless style, a simple cut, but even so, it looked dated. But Ethan had paid the electric bill and water bill earlier today and knew there was no money for a frivolous expense like a tuxedo rental, not if he and the boys wanted to eat.

It would do, and hopefully it wouldn't shame Mia too much if he wore it.

It wasn't as if he expected her to stay by his side during the fancy event. No doubt there would be expectations of her, since her sister was the guest of honor, and he knew she was helping manage the event.

Besides, she'd been completely silent on text messages since she'd run off the property Tuesday night. He'd gotten used to receiving one or two texts from her a day, little messages that were more friendly than anything.

That she hadn't texted him in two days was telling.

Maybe she regretted inviting him. Maybe she didn't want him to attend at all.

"Ethan!" Sam's voice rang out from the hallway.

Ethan wanted to ignore him, wanted to throw his arm over his eyes and lie down on the bed, but Sam burst in the door without waiting for an invitation to come in.

"There's nothing to eat."

He took a breath before answering. "Where's Robbie? You guys can borrow the truck and head to the store."

Sam shrugged. "Somewhere off with Hank and his buddies. I'm dying here."

Ethan knew that his brother would keep whining if he didn't get what he wanted. Maybe it was taking the easy way out, but he got in his truck and headed to the grocery store.

An hour later, he'd worked his way through the shopping and was finally on the home stretch. The checkout stand.

Of course, there were only two checkers and three people in both lines, and so he was barely holding on to his patience as he inched up to the conveyor belt.

And his eyes caught on a familiar face on the cover of one of the tabloids in the checkout stand rack.

Mia.

He looked away immediately, forcing his eyes to the bright afternoon sunlight streaming through the front window panes. Someone had painted an ad on the large glass, but it was faded and chipped off.

He didn't want to know why Mia was featured on a tabloid cover. He didn't.

But he couldn't keep his gaze from drifting back to the magazine.

It was a grainy picture, but he could clearly make out her features as she sat across a small table from a man in a suit and tie. They were holding hands. His eyes went to the caption.

*The Kissing Princess.*

*That* was her nickname? He felt as if ice trickled down his spine. *The kissing princess?* Really? When she'd pushed away from him the moment he'd even thought about kissing her?

Heart thumping, he knew he should look away from the magazine, but he couldn't. He edged slightly closer so he could read the print beneath the caption.

*Two former beaus fight to win the princess back—who will win her heart at the upcoming engagement ball?*

Two who? Men she'd dated? Men she'd been in love with? The tabloid seemed to indicate these men would be at the big engagement ball. One was a...he squinted at the small print...duke. The other one was a popular international soccer player.

Ethan closed his eyes.

Who was he kidding, thinking she could be attracted to him? These guys were... There was no competition. He wasn't even in the same stadium—the same hemisphere as a duke or a pro soccer player.

"Hon, you ready?" The checker's voice cut through his mental fog, and he started loading his groceries onto the conveyor belt. He moved numbly, kept his eyes downcast on the food, on giving his hands something to do.

He'd tried to stay realistic about being Mia's friend, done his best not to read anything other than friendship into her desire to spend time with him.

Where exactly would things go, even if she were interested in him romantically? She was a *princess*! He was stuck here taking care of his stepbrothers for at least another two years. Even after that, what could he offer her? A piddling living operating a dairy?

What a laugh.

He paid for his groceries and pushed his cart into the parking lot.

And his cell phone dinged the text message chime from his pocket.

*Mia: I need to see you.*

His hands shook as he stuffed the phone back into his jeans' pocket. He was still raw from the other night, from her withdrawal.

And what he'd read in the tabloid somehow made things worse.

He didn't know whether he could answer her or not. He loaded the groceries in his truck and drove home.

WHEN ETHAN PULLED into the drive, his headlights swept across the front of the trailer, and he spotted a small figure huddled on the front step.

Mia.

Her arms were wrapped around her knees, and her hair cascaded down her shoulders in a golden stream.

His stomach flipped, and he scrambled to find some sense of equilibrium. He hadn't answered her text, so hadn't expected to see her.

Where was her security escort? He craned his neck to see a head-light and part of the bumper of what looked like a farm truck hidden near the barn, further down his drive. Had she somehow ditched them?

What was going on?

He stepped out of the vehicle and filled his arms with two bags of groceries from the truck bed. Maybe if he kept things short, she'd leave. He was exhausted. Had already dealt with his stepbrothers enough for one day. He didn't know whether he could face more rejection from her.

But when he reached the step and got a good look at her in the twilight, he saw the silver tear tracks down her cheeks.

And the tension he'd been holding slid away in a wave of worry.

He set the grocery bags on the top step and reached for her. "Mia. What's wrong?"

She came off the steps and into his arms. She shook, still crying. Tucked her face into his chest.

Whatever had happened, it had obviously hurt her badly.

And he was man enough to push aside his own hurts.

He held her, letting her get the emotion out.

After a moment, she moved back slightly, using both hands to wipe moisture from her face.

He let her lead. When she sat on the step again, he sat next to her, leaving the groceries on the ground. His frozen foods would last, for now. He didn't hear Sam moving around inside. Maybe his step-brother was into a video game or something. If he was that hungry, he could come outside and unload the groceries himself.

Mia inhaled, her breath shaky, still unsteady. "Sorry."

His own throat was thick from emotion. "My dad told me it was okay to cry."

She smiled a watery small smile.

Remembering those last days was still painful, though muted now by the years.

"What's going on?" he asked.

And then words burst from her like another flood. A half-sister she'd never known about, her older sisters keeping secrets.

She was hurt. Felt betrayed.

And even if he couldn't identify with her feelings exactly, he could remember the emotions he'd experienced when Dad had died. He put his arm around her shoulders, wanting to comfort.

And that seemed to set her off again. Her sniffle turned into a soft sob. Her face crumpled, and she turned into his shoulder.

"I-I don't even d-deserve for you to be s-so nice to me!" she wailed, her words muffled in his shirt.

This time her sobs abated more quickly, and she sat back again, though still tucked into his arm.

"I'd like to explain," she said after a hiccough.

He shook his head, and his chin brushed her hair. "You don't owe me anything." And he meant it.

"Well, I'm going to anyway." The stubborn tilt of her chin told him she was on her way to recovering from her shock. "You've been a good friend to me. Better than anyone else."

She breathed in deeply, a little steadier now. "About a month ago, I made a promise to myself."

She looked down, her hair falling over her cheek and blocking his view of her eyes.

He waited.

"I promised I wasn't going to kiss anyone again until I was sure it was the man I would marry. You see, I have this habit of falling in love too easily. With the wrong guys."

The bottom dropped out of his stomach. What was she saying? Was she admitting he was a wrong guy?

He forced himself to listen.

"My sisters have always been close to each other. And my father has always been distant. Since I was a teenager and started realizing what love could be, I wanted it. Wanted someone to love me just for me, not for my crown or for what benefits a relationship could bring them. I wanted someone who just wanted me," she finished in a whisper.

The depth of her desire was evident, though she wouldn't look at him, and he couldn't see her eyes.

"And every time I thought I'd fallen for someone who was right, it turned out not to be all wrong. They all just wanted something from me."

What a horrible feeling, to believe the person you loved was using you.

"And every time it happened, I realized I'd given too much of myself to those—to the men I thought I loved. So I promised myself, no more kissing."

Now it made sense why she'd pulled away. She had this vow to uphold.

He swallowed hard. He didn't know if Mia lumped him in the category with those other jerks, but he did know one thing. None of them deserved her. And he would never push for what she wasn't ready to give.

He squeezed her shoulders lightly. She tipped her head and tucked into the space between his neck and shoulder, apparently spent.

He just held her, trying to ignore the pounding of his heart.

Mia might put off a joyful, vivacious personality, but there were hurts beneath that he'd never expected.

He'd been wrong to want something from her. All she needed was a friend.

*I promised I wouldn't kiss anyone... Unless it was the man I planned to marry.*

He would never be that man. A princess would never marry someone as dirt poor as he, someone with no prospects.

But he could be the friend she thought he already was.

ALESSANDRA SAT in the darkened living room, curled into the couch.

Mia had refused to speak to her on the long ride home from Dallas, ignoring every overture and only looking out the window.

After a few tries, Alessandra had given up.

She'd messed things up with Mia.

The awful thing was, she probably felt a lot of the same things her sister felt. Betrayed by her father. Hurt.

And then there were the questions. Had her mother known, before she'd died? Why hadn't they been enough for Father?

What was their sister like? Did she know about them?

Mostly, Alessandra felt guilty. She blamed herself for not telling Mia sooner. She should've told her sister back in Glorvaird, or even better, forced Eloise to bring her into their chat when Alessandra had found out.

Weren't their relationships fractured enough? She'd known keeping secrets wouldn't be healthy for them, but she'd done it anyway.

She was so stupid.

The light went on in the hall, and she shrank even further into the couch, hoping that whoever it was—one of the cowboys, probably— would pass on by without seeing her.

"Alessandra?"

No luck. Gideon strode into the room, as if he'd sensed her hiding there. Should've gone up to her bedroom while she'd had the chance.

Things had been strained between them since the other night.

*Are we making a mistake here?* he'd asked.

And it had broken something inside her, hearing those words. She'd been blissfully happy.

Ignorant maybe. Hadn't had an inkling that Gideon continued to struggle with leaving his family behind for months at a time.

Again, she felt stupid. How could she not have realized?

Gideon's protective nature had been one of the things about him she'd first fallen for. He'd made her feel safe, even when she'd been running for her life.

It wasn't realistic to think he'd be able to just turn it off, even though he'd made a huge sacrifice to be a part of her life.

She didn't think she'd made a noise, but he rounded the couch and came right to her.

He sat next to her, not quite touching.

She stretched the sleeves of her long-sleeved T-shirt to cover her hands and used the material to wipe beneath her eyes.

"Allie-girl," he said roughly, the nickname he rarely used.

"I'm okay." She tried to put on a brave face. She went for a smile, but she felt it wobble a bit.

She knew Gideon had put enormous pressure on himself to find the thief. He was worried about Carrie, too. She didn't want to add to his burden.

But his big, warm palm came to rest at her lower back. He exerted gentle pressure, pulling her to him and, weak as she was, she crawled into his embrace.

"I heard from one of the security detail that you and Mia had a fight," he said into the crown of her head. "She found out about the missing princess?"

She nodded, misery leaching over her anew.

He held her for a long time, not speaking. Then, finally, "I'm sorry for how all this played out."

Her stomach clenched into a tight little ball. Was he going to say that being with her wasn't worth all the trouble? Had be given up on them?

"This theft really hit me hard, and I've handled things all wrong. Especially with you. I'm sorry."

She couldn't help the tears that welled in her eyes, though she wished she could stem them.

She swallowed back a sob. "I'm sorry I didn't realize you were still struggling with the reality of being with me."

"I'm not." He said the words instantly, as if it were his gut reaction. It made her feel marginally better.

He exhaled, his breath ruffling the fine hair at her temple. "If I'd had my head on straight in the beginning... If I hadn't made excuses when you told me you wanted to be together, you wouldn't have a question in your mind right now. I don't regret choosing you, Allie-girl. I love you."

Hearing his words made her tear up again. "I love you too," she said through a tight throat.

"We'll get things figured out here," he said. "Maybe make some changes about how things are run. Everything will settle down."

She should be reassuring him, but he was doing that for her.

"Whatever you need from me," she told him, "I'm here."

He squeezed her lightly. "Mia will come around."

She hoped so. She needed to heal the rift with her sister.

## Chapter Six

Late afternoon, the day of the ball, Ethan wrapped up with the dairy cows. He was filthy and in desperate need of a shower.

And there was a small part of him that was excited. Anticipating seeing Mia in her fine ball gown.

Over the past week, the couple of texts they'd shared each day had escalated into phone calls. Sometimes hours-long calls that had him staying up past his usually-early bedtime.

He found he didn't miss the sleep.

After her revelation about the vow she'd made, they'd kept things carefully in the *Friend Zone*. There had been no more practice dances. No more embraces.

She'd told him all about her life in Glorvaird. About her passion for working with battered women. That she couldn't cook a bit. He'd told her everything he remembered about his dad. About how difficult it had been to give up his college dreams. That he'd always wanted to be a veterinarian, but probably never would.

She was the best friend he'd ever had.

And he hadn't been able to keep from falling in love with her. He never planned to tell her. It just was. Part of him, intrinsic to his being.

He loved Princess Mia.

He made his way from the dairy barn to the trailer, pausing to give Peanut a belly rub at the back porch.

He could hear the boys tussling inside before he opened the back door. They'd been edgy and difficult all week. He'd tried talking to them. Tried to bring up the tutoring again with no results.

He sighed, hand on the doorknob. He'd told them he'd be gone for the evening, and they'd had their laugh at his expense. Like everyone else in town, they'd seen the tabloids and knew that Mia had rich, famous suitors at her neck and call. They couldn't understand his friendship with the princess, but that didn't matter to him.

Mia had asked him to go tonight, so he would.

He opened the door to see Robbie take down Sam in a combination football tackle and chokehold—except Sam was wearing a familiar gray suit coat.

Was that—?

"No!" Ethan shouted as he watched in horror. Amidst his brothers wrestling, one sleeve ripped completely off of his father's suit coat.

Robbie and Sam straightened. Neither had the good grace to look abashed. From where he stood, Ethan could see the inside lining of the jacket hanging loose, torn in two places.

The suit pants were crumpled on the floor, a discarded chocolate bar melting atop them, no doubt staining the material irrevocably.

"Are you—? What the—?" He couldn't even get a fell sentence out past the knot of anger lodged in his throat.

"What did you do?" he finally managed.

"Aw, Eeth," Sam said. "We saw this hanging in your closet and thought it would be fun to try it on."

He fisted his hands at his sides, shaking from the rush of adrenaline and anger and despair. "You knew I was planning to go to Mia's ball tonight."

Robbie laughed. Actually laughed. "You were planning to wear that old junk suit?"

"It was my dad's," Ethan said.

"Uh, yeah," Robbie said, "and it's way outta style."

Ethan was unable to find words. No matter if they disagreed with the style or would laugh at him all day long, the suit was *his*. Not theirs. What right did they have to touch it? None.

"After everything I've done for you, everything I've given you —*this* is how you repay me?"

Robbie laughed again, a cruel sound. "Everything you've given us? Like what? This dingy trailer and rice and beans five times a week? Like how you can't even afford to get us a truck of our own? And how you constantly nag us to clean up and do our homework? You call that taking care of us?"

The words hit Ethan like a physical punch. Before he could respond, Robbie said, "C'mon Sam."

He jerked his thumb to the door, and Sam followed him, discarding the ruined suit coat on the floor as he did so.

They left, and the silence that remained seemed deafening.

Ethan moved on numb legs to pick up the pants and suit coat. He knew before looking that there was no way they could be repaired, even if he had more than the two hours before the ball was scheduled to start.

He laid them out on the worn sofa anyway.

And felt like crying. This suit was one of the last things he had of his father, and it was utterly ruined. Completely demolished.

It wasn't just the suit, it was losing his dad. Losing the dream of the life he'd wanted.

Suddenly, the unfairness of it all pressed down on him. No matter Robbie's rude, ungrateful words, Ethan knew he'd done his best by the boys. So what if they ate simple meals? At least they ate. They had a roof over their heads, even if it was a mobile home and not a fancy brick house.

Still shaking with anger and hurt, he made his way out of the front door and sat on the stoop, where he'd sat with Mia a week ago, where he'd promised himself to be her friend and not to expect more.

If he didn't show up at the ball, she was going to be disappointed. Maybe even hate him a little, since he'd promised to be there. He'd be just as bad as the other men who'd let her down.

She was heading back to Glorvaird in a couple of days. Tonight was one of his last chances to see her. Who knew when she'd come back again.

His stepbrothers had ruined everything.

He clutched his head in his hands, pressed his elbows to his knees. Stared at the step between his work boots, trying to figure out some kind of solution.

The sound of tires on gravel drew his gaze up. Whoever it was, he wasn't in the mood for company.

He was shocked to recognize the veterinarian's work truck.

She met him near the steps. "Doesn't look like you're getting all gussied up for that fancy party."

He shrugged helplessly. "You heard about that, huh?"

"You left your phone on the back counter in the office earlier in the week. I might've seen a text from your princess about it. What's keeping you from it?"

*His princess.* Oh, how he wished.

He went inside and brought the ripped jacket and soiled pants out, held them up for her to see.

"Wow. Your stepbrothers?"

He nodded miserably.

But there was a suspicious twinkle in her eyes as she went back to her truck and ducked inside the driver's side door. "I had my suspicions that those two might try to ruin this for you," she called over her shoulder.

She had? He hadn't seen it coming at all.

And then, "That's why I brought this."

She turned and lifted a garment hanging inside transparent plastic. A tuxedo.

His heart starting beating again. "What's this?"

"James"—her adult son—"bought it for his wedding and hasn't used it since. I borrowed it. And these." She held up a pair of black dress boots, slicked and shiny in the afternoon light. "Y'all are about the same size."

His throat tightened. "I can't—"

"It's on *loan*." She moved forward and thrust the garment bag into his hands, leaving him no choice but to take it.

"Thank you." She couldn't know how much this meant to him. That someone had noticed. That she'd gone out of her way to make this kind gesture.

She'd saved his day.

Maybe she did know, because her eyes now held a twinkle that looked suspiciously like unshed tears. "And Ethan? Comb your hair."


GIDEON WAITED with Alessandra in a small dressing room upstairs in the McMansion they'd rented out for the ball.

An engagement ball. He'd known better than to argue about it, knew that because of his fiancée's royal blood, there would be expectations.

He'd just as soon have gotten together with their closest friends and had a party over a pile of wings or grilled hamburgers.

"It's packed out there." Alessandra turned from where she'd been peeking through a crack in the outer door, closing it softly behind her. The huge skirt of her royal blue dress swished softly as she moved toward him. She smoothed it nervously, her long white gloves contrasting with the dark fabric.

He'd only seen her in a tiara once before, but she wore one tonight, with her hair swept up in a complicated twist high on her head. Her shoulders were bare and showed off a glittering sapphire necklace that probably cost more than his entire spread.

"That's good, right?" He'd bulked up the event security with a team he'd assembled from local law enforcement and some SEAL friends who were on leave and able to help him out.

He couldn't resist checking his phone. No new messages, which should mean everything was running like it should be. No one had tried to hop the security fence. Nothing suspicious was showing up on the series of security cameras he'd spent the week installing.

He slipped the phone back into the inside breast pocket of his jacket, but not before he caught Alessandra's frown. "Sorry," he said, with an unrepentant grin. Maybe he'd gone overboard, but he refused to take chances, not after what'd happened to Alessandra before.

"Do you remember the steps to our dance?" she pressed.

He moved forward, pant legs brushing against the hem of her dress as he got close enough to take her gloved hand.

"Stop worrying." He gave her hand a squeeze.

They'd had a private instructor visit the Triple H, and he'd learned a complicated waltz over the past two weeks. Here in a bit, when all the guests had arrived, Mia would announce them as a couple, and they'd make a grand entrance down a wide, curving staircase that led to the ground floor of the mansion. Three large ballrooms emptied into the grand foyer, every surface covered with marble. He and Alessandra would have a special dance together and then, according to his future bride, all he had to do was stand in a receiving line with her and greet their guests. Maybe mingle a bit later. Shake hands and smile.

He wasn't sure he believed it would be that easy, but he'd worked difficult missions and intended to see this one through.

Alessandra smiled tremulously at him. "Are you sure—really sure —you don't want to back out? We haven't been seen together publicly before now, so if there's any chance you want to call it off—"

"I don't." He cursed himself for the abrupt words he'd spoken two weeks ago that had made her believe he might not be in this for the long haul. "I love you, and we're getting married next spring."

Her lips trembled minutely. She sniffed delicately. He knew the stylist had taken a long time—over a half hour—to get her makeup just right. She wouldn't want to ruin it by crying.

He squeezed her hand again. "I'd kiss you if I weren't worried about messing up your lipstick. Your stylist is a little frightening. All those little metal tools..."

She smiled, like he'd hoped she would, the tense moment past.

They still had to find out who the thief was. There'd been some issue with the digital video, and the bank had had to request a backup copy. It was supposed to arrive first thing Monday morning.

Then there was going to be a reckoning on the ranch.

ETHAN STOOD at the top of a secondary staircase in the huge mansion that someone called home. He'd arrived early enough to check in with the scary security dude at the front door—thank God Mia had gotten his name on the list—and to witness Mia announce the happy couple, who'd proceeded down the large main staircase like royalty—which Alessandra was—and then danced a complicated dance to the live violin and cello music playing from the center of the house.

From across the room, he'd only been able to catch a glimpse of Mia, who wore a powder-blue gown. Separated by probably a hundred and fifty guests in their fancy tuxedos and long dresses, he hadn't been able to get the crowd to part for him to make his way over to her. Then she'd disappeared completely.

So he'd climbed these stairs to see if he could spot her from above.

He'd checked his cell phone several times, in case she was trying to locate him. Then he figured she might not have her phone on her with that fancy, frilly dress. Did something like that even have pockets?

One ugly whisper that sounded suspiciously like his stepmother's voice reverberated in his mind. *She doesn't really want you here.*

He tried his best to ignore the insidious voice, but it was difficult. Especially in light of his stepbrothers' actions from earlier in the day.

Then he spotted her. She moved effortlessly through the crowd, greeting those around her with the smile that never failed to make him weak in the knees.

She looked up, caught sight of him. She was still halfway across the room, but he clearly saw the way her smile changed. Became more real somehow. A special smile, just for him.

He saw her lips form his name as she started toward the staircase.

Heart pounding in his ears, he made his way down the steps to meet her. The unfamiliar boots were a size too small and pinched his feet, but the cut of the borrowed tuxedo fit well, just enough room for his shoulders in the jacket.

He'd had to stop someone in the parking lot and get help with the bowtie.

But neither pinching shoes or tie issues mattered as he took in the light shining from Mia's eyes as she closed the last few feet between them.

Her dress was something else. The pale blue made her skin luminescent, and she hadn't been joking when she'd mentioned the layer of fabric that he could easily see himself tripping on or stepping on if they really did try to dance. She was almost like a planet of her own.

He was definitely trapped in her gravitational field.

He stopped short, not wanting to muss her dress or the way her hair was perfectly styled, partly up and partly cascading down her back in soft curls.

She seemed to have no such compunction, because she threw herself the last two feet toward him, leaving him no choice but to catch her. He held her trim waist loosely between his hands, breathed in the sweet flowery perfume and just *Mia* beneath. Her huge skirt pressed against his legs, and he locked his limbs, afraid to move an inch and risk stepping on it.

He heard conversations cease nearby. Probably the who's who that was here wondered who he was to get a hug from the princess.

"You came," she whispered.

"You look... beautiful," he returned, his voice catching. This amazing creature counted him—*him!*—as a friend. Someone she wanted by her side. He still couldn't fathom it.

Her eyes shone at the compliment, and he was stunned all over again by her beauty. Inside and out.

"They're starting another waltz next," she said, "and I'd really like to dance with you."

"Are you sure?" he asked. "That might be a recipe for disaster."

She slid him a glance as she finally moved slightly away from him. "I'm sure. Come on."

He followed her.

Couples had arranged themselves on the marble dance floor in one of the huge ballrooms. Mia's dress was definitely the widest, but he glanced side to side, taking in the countless floor-length skirts. There were a lot of people, especially considering they represented obstacles that he needed to watch out for.

The last thing he wanted to do was embarrass Mia by bumping into someone else or tripping her in that infernal skirt.

She seemed to read his mind as the musicians drew out a long note. "Keep it simple. Trust the music," she said softly, her chin tilting up. "I trust you."

And when she said something like that, he'd willingly throw himself off the cliff. The music started in earnest, and he followed the count. He found that if he kept to the small square that Mia had taught him and threw in a quarter turn every so often, it wasn't that hard.

He didn't step on her skirt. They didn't run into any of the other couples.

And he might be sweating through his undershirt, but having her smile up at him like he was worth something made him feel like he was flying.


WITH THE HAPPY couple busy greeting their guests and the party going smoothly, Mia didn't want to waste another minute she could be spending with Ethan. After all, the palace had already scheduled her flight home for Monday morning.

So she dragged him out to the terrace, where a beautiful rose garden was putting out its final blooms of the season. She knew Gideon's security team had a presence out here, but they'd leave her and Ethan alone, if they knew what was good for them.

"That wasn't so bad, was it?" she teased. He'd done remarkably well with the simple waltz, and she'd been proud to be on his arm.

These past two weeks had been the happiest days of her life. Oh, there'd been bumps. She and Alessandra still hadn't patched things up, and she'd avoided two calls from Eloise.

But spending time with Ethan...discovering the kind of man he was...had been incredible.

She'd fallen for him. Hard. Her feelings were deeper than anything she'd experienced with anyone else.

He looked back to where the light spilled from the French doors that opened onto the terrace. Most of the partygoers remained inside, hoping to speak to Alessandra and Gideon, or to catch a glimpse of the other rich and famous guests, but some couples had meandered into the quiet darkness. Hopefully none of the invited press was out here, though she'd learned she could never be too careful.

"Are you sure you shouldn't be mingling? I don't want to keep you from your..." He made an uncertain gesture with one hand.

"Brad Pitt? I told you he declined the invite."

He smiled, but it faded too quickly. "I don't want to monopolize your time, if you're needed elsewhere."

And *that* was one of the reasons she'd fallen for him. Because he put her needs—and everyone else's—above his own.

"If you're worried about the duke and the soccer player," she said carefully, aware of what the tabloids had reported. "I said my *hellos* earlier. I would rather spend this time with you. I want to be with you." She finished with an honesty that would have been hard for her in the past.

Something intense flared in the depths of his eyes.

His selflessness was also why she hadn't spoken of the future. She wanted Ethan in her life, but she knew he was committed to raising his stepbrothers through their high school graduations. He'd told her some of his past, and people from town had been more than happy to fill in the rest. His stepmother's insistence that he devote all his spare time outside of schooling to maintaining the dairy. How *she* was the one who'd mishandled the property and sold it off to pay for her own extravagances.

Mia refused to add to his responsibilities or complicate his life. Surely, she could find reasons to visit the states—and Ethan—as often as possible. Which meant she needed to get over herself and talk to Alessandra and Eloise. Her sisters could smooth things over for her with travel plans and the international royal agenda.

But she also wanted tonight.

ETHAN TRIED NOT to feel the magic of the night. He really did.

But he was already in love with Mia. And when she looked at him like that...

He knew that whatever was happening between them was just for tonight. It had to be.

He shifted his feet, his toes pinching.

"What's the matter?" Mia asked.

"Borrowed these boots." He shrugged. "Might have a blister in the morning, but it was worth it to dance with you."

She glowed in the moonlight. "We can do it again. Just take off your boots. No one will see your sock feet out here."

He made a face, but the boots were really starting to hurt, so he took them off and placed them on a nearby stone bench.

The music was low as it filtered through the open French doors.

And when she came into his arms, it wasn't in the waltz hold they'd practiced before. She was much closer. Both her arms came around his neck, leaving him to hold her waist between his hands. Beneath his palms, the material of her dress was soft and smooth.

He still couldn't fathom that she'd rather be out here with him than inside with her old beaus.

"I've been thinking," she said. "That I'd like to stay in contact after all this."

She would?

She seemed to sense his incredulity, because she smiled softly up at him. "It won't be quite the same, but we can still talk on the phone. Send texts. And I'll be back in the states eventually."

He nodded, stunned and running her words through his mind. She wanted to continue their friendship.

He knew that eventually she'd be distracted by her royal life. Or the man she'd eventually fell in love with.

Just thinking about that gave him heartburn.

And then suddenly his jacket pocket was buzzing. Or rather, his phone.

He ignored it, focusing on Mia's dear face, trying to soak her in for the long days when she was gone.

But it rang again, and she moved slightly back, letting go. "It might be important."

When the screen lit, he saw it was straight up midnight. He didn't recognize the number. He connected the call.

"This is the county sheriff," the voice on the line said. "I've got your brothers in custody. They're drunk. We picked them up for breaking into the feed store in town. They did quite a bit of damage."

He couldn't find words.

Mia watched him from too close, and he turned his back to her, not wanting her to overhear, to be tainted by his family drama. He knew there was press attending the event tonight, and knew that Mia wanted to stay out of the limelight.

Finally, he got his voice to work, though it was rough. "I ll be there as soon as I can."

He still couldn't think straight as he turned back to Mia. She wore a concerned expression and reached out one hand to him, but he pulled back before she could touch him.

"I have to go," he said, the words wooden. His stepbrothers had ruined this night not once, but twice.

"Ethan, can I help you—?"

He shook his head violently, not wanting her to become a part of this. "I just—I have to go."

He gathered his boots from the bench, not bothering to put them on. Urgency surged through him. His stepbrothers were in jail.

Mia was close behind him, wanting to help, but he couldn't face her right now.

Before she could stop him, before she could say something that would make everything hurt worse, he walked off, brushing past a buff guy in a suit who had to be security. Ethan rounded the house instead of going inside, hitting the parking lot and then his truck in his sock feet. He tossed the boots to the floorboard and cranked the engine.

His brothers had ruined his night, but that wasn't the worst of it.

What if they'd ruined their chances for a new future?

What did that mean for *Ethan's* future?

Chapter Seven

At seven the next morning, Ethan sat in the county judge's chambers. His elbows rested on his knees, and he stared at his feet. It was Saturday, so the courthouse was empty and quiet, but the judge had made an emergency exception and allowed Ethan to come in so he could plead on his stepbrothers' behalf.

He hadn't slept all night. He'd started at the county sheriff's office, where they'd told him the judge wouldn't be in until Monday. He'd gone home to make phone calls and change out of the borrowed tuxedo, only then realizing he was missing one of the fancy black dress boots. Which meant he'd have to go back to the mansion where the ball had been held and find it later. And if he didn't, then maybe he'd have to call Mia, if the book wasn't lying in the gardens or parking lot.

He hadn't slept at all. Had stayed awake praying and worrying and trying to figure out a way to get his stepbrothers out of this mess.

Apparently, the idiots had gotten drunk with some of their friends and decided it would be fun to ride the tractor mowers parked in front of the feed store. He couldn't imagine where they'd gotten the keys. But they'd turned on at least one mower and driven it through the front windows of the store, destroying thousands of dollars' worth of merchandise.

He didn't know if he could fix this. There was no money in the budget to retain an attorney. How would the boys even make restitution? What would this do for their college plans? School?

"Back again, young man?" The judge, in his fifties with a balding head and hard-to-read eyes, entered the room. His long black robe flowed around him as he moved to sit behind a huge, old-looking wooden desk.

"Hello, your honor." Ethan had hoped never to see him again after last summer when the boys had been charged with vandalism.

The judge shuffled some papers on his desk and flipped open a manila folder. He didn't speak to Ethan again as he read whatever was in that document.

"Your brothers—excuse me, your stepbrothers—appear to be in a mess of trouble. We talked last summer about them getting a second chance, but it sure seems as if they've squandered it."

Ethan nodded miserably. "I'm really sorry, sir. They'd been a little more responsible since last summer..." He let the words trail off, because what they'd done last night obviously belied the statement. He glanced at the door behind him. "Shouldn't they be in here?"

The judge flipped the folder closed and leaned back in his chair, which protested with a metallic squeak. "I wanted to talk with you first, before I see your stepbrothers."

Ethan's stomach tightened into a little ball of misery. This didn't sound good.

"They were what, ten and eleven when you were granted custody of them?"

"Yes, sir." Ethan wiped sweaty palms on his jean-clad thighs.

"Did you know that last summer, after their arrest, I got several phone calls and two letters from your neighbors and friends?"

What? That was news to Ethan. "No, sir."

"They all wanted me to know how much you were sacrificing for those boys and how you'd tried your best not only to provide for them, but to teach them how to be good citizens."

He had tried to impart the lessons Dad had taught him, but somehow it'd gone all wrong. He didn't know how, couldn't see where he'd missed a crucial element, but clearly he had, because Robbie and Sam didn't get it. Ethan rubbed the bridge of his nose, behind which an ache built that he couldn't seem to get rid of.

"You've got good friends," the judge said.

Ethan nodded dumbly. He knew it. Just like the vet who'd watched out for him yesterday evening. But what did that have to do with his stepbrothers?

"And you've done your best to influence those boys. But I've been doing this a long time, and do you know what I see?"

The question didn't seem to require an answer. Ethan kept quiet.

"I see two young men who've been given every chance. Been taught right from wrong. Been loved on. And they still make bad choices. It's not your fault," the judge said quickly when Ethan squeezed his eyes shut. "You've given six years of your life to caring for and providing for these boys."

Longer, if one counted the time he'd spend working for his stepmother before his eighteenth birthday.

"It's my decision that your influence alone, as good as it's been, isn't enough to keep those two on the straight and narrow. They are removed from your custody and will become wards of the state. They'll likely have to serve some time in a youth detention facility for what they've done. They're not first-time offenders. And they're old enough to know better."

He sat dumbly in the chair. Not knowing what to feel. He would no longer have charge of his stepbrothers. He'd failed them.

Or they'd failed themselves.

His mind whirled with hurt, despair, fears for his stepbrothers.

He stood up, not sure what he should say. *Thank you* didn't seem quite right.

The older man stood too, then rounded his desk before clapping a hand on Ethan's shoulder. "This isn't your fault. You understand?"

How could it not be? When Ethan was supposed to have taught Robbie and Sam right from wrong?

"A lot of people care about you—as evidenced by their phone calls and letters from last summer. You've done your best. But your stepbrothers haven't. That's all this is."

Ethan walked out of the office feeling sick to his stomach. He didn't know where to turn. Whether he should try to see his stepbrothers and say goodbye.

The last time he'd spoken to them, Robbie had thrown Ethan's actions in his face. They'd destroyed his dad's suit, one of his few reminders of his father. He could still see his dad in that suit—wore it to church every Sunday.

But Robbie and Sam—they'd been ungrateful and rude.

Would saying goodbye provide closure or just pour gasoline on the fire of his stepbrothers' hatred?

MONDAY MORNING, Gideon had wanted to come to the bank by himself, but Alessandra had parked herself in the passenger seat of his truck with arms crossed and refused to move.

So here they were, seated side-by-side at a desk in the manager's office, with the county sheriff behind them as digital video played over a large computer monitor.

The bank manager stood nervously behind Gideon's shoulder. Gideon knew the man was worried about liability being placed on his bank or his employees, but as far as Gideon was concerned, whoever had perpetrated this theft was to blame. Not the bank.

"The time stamp was for 10:50 a.m.," the bank manager said nervously.

The video feed on the computer monitor showed that the digital film was approaching that time, and Gideon found himself squinting at the screen, waiting to see a grainy image of Nate cross into the footage.

But when it came, it wasn't Nate.

"That's Dan," Alessandra whispered.

It sure was. The ball cap pulled low over his face wasn't enough to shield him from the cameras, and they watched as the cowhand presented a piece of paper to the cashier. They watched as ten grand was counted out to him by the bank teller.

A half hour later, Dan sat with head in hands in the Triple H dining room. The sheriff read him his rights, and he sat silently, unmoving.

Dan didn't fight the arrest, though Gideon stood nearby as backup, just in case. The sheriff was armed, though, and Dan seemed more resigned than anything else. Nate had followed them up from the barn and stood in the doorway, watching in horror.

When the sheriff had finished, he looked to Gideon, maybe silently asking whether he wanted to confront the man or not.

But it was Nate who burst out with a question.

"If you needed money, why didn't you come to me?" Nate's words emerged angry, but Gideon knew his foreman must feel the same betrayal and hurt beneath that Gideon did.

Dan shook his head, not raising his gaze from the table. "You'd already bailed me out once, man."

That was news to Gideon, who cut his gaze to the foreman.

Nate ignored him, his entire focus on Dan. "So you just *stole* it? Stole from Gideon, who gave you a job outta high school, when you had nowhere else to turn?"

He sounded like he wanted to smack the other man upside the head, but Gideon shook his head in warning as the sheriff ushered Dan out of the room.

Alessandra perched at the long table as if all the air had been sucked out of her entire body. Gideon reached for her, and she met his hand, linking their fingers together. "Now we know," she said.

"Yeah." It didn't quite cure the bitter taste that had been lingering in the back of his throat these past weeks. But at least they could close the case. Move forward, if he could figure out how to do that now.

"Any reason you didn't tell me about missing *ten grand*?" Nate asked, drawing Gideon's gaze away from his woman.

Nate stood with feet spread and arms crossed, looking like he wanted to do battle. He stared at Gideon for a long moment before realization dawned on his face. "You thought *I* took it?"

Guilt flushed into Gideon's face, but he didn't back down. "I thought whoever had the easiest access to the bank account and the computerized ledgers did it. I'm sorry." He was man enough to apologize when he'd been so very, very wrong.

Nate took off his Stetson and slapped it against his thigh, sending a little puff of dust flying from his jeans. "I've been with you for ten years, man. How could you think I'd steal from you?"

Alessandra started to speak up, but Gideon cut her off with a wave of his hand. This was his mess to deal with. "You want to tell me why you loaned Dan a chunk of cash to pay off his...what, gambling debts?"

He must've hit right on the money, because Nate flushed a dull red through his neck and jaw.

"You knew one of the hands had a problem and didn't tell me?" Gideon pressed.

Nate's lips firmed into a white line.

Gideon didn't want to fight and he didn't want to lose their friendship. He purposely relaxed his stance, let his arms hang loose at his sides. "It seems like we both made mistakes." He let that sink in for a moment. "You know I don't trust easy."

Nate snorted, but his frown relaxed slightly.

"Understatement," Alessandra whispered.

Gideon cut a glance at her to let her know she'd pay for that dig later.

"This whole situation," Gideon circled his hand between the three of them. "Me being gone, laying more on your shoulders, *trusting you more*. It's going to take some getting used to. For all of us," he said with an eye-squint at Alessandra. "So we didn't get it right on the first try. The Triple H needs you. I need you." The words weren't easy for Gideon to say. Alessandra squeezed his hand in support.

Nate's frown disappeared almost completely. "We might not be blood, but we're family." He stuck out his hand.

Gideon shook it.

# Chapter Eight

On Sunday, Mia had tagged along with Gideon and Alessandra to their small church. She'd been enjoying a cup of coffee in the lobby when she'd overheard two women discussing Ethan and what had happened to his brothers over the weekend.

That afternoon, she hadn't wasted any time in enlisting Alessandra's help and making an impromptu video call to Eloise.

Now Monday morning, the sun was rising, and she was camped out on Ethan's back porch, waiting for him to come in from milking the cows.

Even though his world might be imploding, she knew he wouldn't be shirking his responsibilities.

Hearing secondhand about what he'd been through over the weekend, she'd realized he'd pushed her away the night of the ball at least partly because he'd known there was press in attendance and even more camped out in the parking lot. If she'd run off with him to the county jail, they'd have had a field day.

He'd wanted to protect her.

She wasn't *falling* in love with him. She *loved* him. Real love. True love.

The kind of love that made sacrifices. The kind of love she'd been waiting for all her life.

She wasn't waiting any longer.

She was going to be here for Ethan, for as long as he needed her. Hopefully for life.

There was a rush of cows exiting the back of the barn into the pasture. Then, a few minutes later, Ethan emerged from the front of the barn. He had his head down, and his shoulders were low, as if he carried a weight too heavy to bear.

She was ready to come beside him and bear some of it, too.

He must've sensed her presence, because his head came up as he entered the backyard gate. He stood stock still for a moment, staring at her. Peanut had had her head snuggled into Mia's lap, but she raised her chin and gave one happy bark to welcome him. The dog's tail thumped on the wood deck.

Ethan turned to carefully latch the gate closed. He took off his gloves as he approached, stopping at the bottom of the stairs. Too far away for Mia's purposes.

"Hey."


"HEY."

Ethan couldn't stop staring at Mia. Part of him was sure this was a dream, that he'd missed his three-thirty alarm and was fantasizing the entire thing.

She stood up, dislodging his dog and straightening to reveal the worn jeans and flannel shirt she had on. He'd never seen her in something so casual. She was even wearing worn-out boots.

Had he conjured up his perfect fantasy? A Mia who was his to keep?

"Seems you dropped this when you rushed out of the ball the other night." She held up something black. The dress boot he'd been missing.

He took it from her, the leather cool against his fingers.

He cleared his throat. "I thought you'd be packing for your flight."

An awful ache spread through him, just saying the words. He'd tried not to think about it all weekend, the fact that she was leaving. That he'd probably never see her again, even though she'd said otherwise the other night.

She moved down one step, which still put her a head above him. Two porch steps still separated them. "I made up with Alessandra."

He nodded, not sure what that had to do with her leaving.

"Turns out that family is one of the more important things in life, and between the both of us, we decided not to let our father's secrets and lies ruin our relationship."

He was glad for her. But the wounds his stepbrothers had inflicted over the weekend hadn't even formed a scab yet, and he felt a great gaping hole where he'd failed them.

Mia descended another stair, but in his hurt, he couldn't look at her. Instead, he averted his gaze over her shoulder.

"Alessandra also helped facilitate a conversation with my older sister." She descended the final step, which put her close enough to touch, though he didn't. "Basically, I told them both that I'm not leaving Texas."

At her words, his gaze flew to her face. "What?" *She wasn't leaving?*

She didn't answer with words. Instead, her arms came around his neck, and she stood on tiptoe as she leaned into him.

His hand that wasn't holding the borrowed boot came around her waist by reflex.

This time, she didn't give him room to question whether he was imagining her intent. She slid her hands into the hair at the nape of his neck and gave a gentle tug, bringing his head down.

She kissed him.

There was no room for thought as her lips feathered over his. She pressed in closer, and he dropped the boot, which fell with a soft *thunk*. His other hand slid around her waist.

He hadn't kissed anyone since Sarah Myers in the fifth grade, and this was nothing like that.

He moved wrong, and their chins bumped, breaking the kiss. But Mia only smiled and reached up to kiss him again. Her lips were incredibly soft, and she tasted like coffee and mint, and he never wanted to stop kissing her.

But of course, they eventually had to stop to catch their breath.

She didn't let go of him, and he was no fool. He pressed her close to his thudding heart, mind and adrenaline racing.

"Mia?"

She hummed from where she was tucked against his chest.

He didn't know quite how to get the question out. "You said— you said that the next time you kissed someone, it was going to be the man you wanted to marry." Okay, that wasn't a question at all, but who could think after those passionate kisses?

She didn't tease him. She moved slightly away, just enough that she could tilt her face up and see his.

He felt vulnerable even putting the suggestion out there. It seemed ludicrous. That someone like *her* would want to marry someone like *him*.

She reached up with one hand to cup his jaw. "I think you can safely consider that kiss my proposal."

Her *proposal*.

A hot burn started behind his nose. He had to be sure. "You want to marry *me*?"

She nodded, her eyes taking on a shine that might be happiness or might be tears.

He squeezed her close again, burying his face in her hair just in case some of the emotion overwhelming him snuck out as tears.

He didn't even realize he was shaking until he felt her hands brush calming strokes down his back. Never in a million years had he imagined this happening.

After she'd kissed him again, just to make sure he understood exactly what she was proposing, they sat side-by-side on the top step with their hands linked and her head on his shoulder.

Somehow she'd found out about his custody issue. Or non-issue. "If you want to fight for custody of your stepbrothers, the palace can help with obtaining the best attorneys."

He exhaled. And finally admitted to some of what had been running through his head all weekend. Or maybe for weeks, since he'd met with the principal. "It feels wrong to say this, but...maybe it's time to let them go. Robbie and Sam don't want to be with me. They've proved that over and over."

It felt a little like giving up, but with Mia looking at him like he hung the stars, it soothed the wound somewhat.

She reached up and bussed his cheek with a kiss, leaving a cinnamon-burn sensation behind as she nestled back against his shoulder. "So what do you want to do? Rebuild your dad's legacy here? Or...there *are* universities in Glorvaird. I know we could find the best veterinary program for you there."

Possibilities stretched before him. Limitless, with Mia at his side. He didn't even know what to think, what to start dreaming about first.

He had the best dream, the brightest star, right here with him.

She seemed to understand, because she grinned up at him, a smile both mischievous and light. "You don't have to decide right now."

And she kissed him again.

Epilogue

## ONE WEEK LATER

"ARE YOU SURE YOU REALLY WANT TO DO THIS?" Alessandra's teasing question turned Mia's head from where she'd been staring at the flower-adorned front of the small Las Vegas wedding chapel.

But her sister wasn't asking her. She was asking Ethan, who stood tall and handsome at Mia's side in his borrowed tux—and the new pair of dress boots she'd made him purchase to wear with it.

"Mia is notoriously grumpy in the mornings," Alessandra went on. "And you don't even want to know about her shopping habits."

Ethan looked to Mia, and his gaze didn't waver. "I'm sure I'll never find another woman as special as Mia."

Her heart thudded, and she shared a quick glance with Alessandra that expressed *aw!*

From slightly behind and to one side of her sister, Gideon made a face. Mia forgave him for it, because she knew he could be just as romantic as Ethan—after all, she'd overheard his romantic sentiments to her sister even before she'd met the man.

"I'm a little less certain that this is the kind of wedding Mia deserves," Ethan said.

Mia slipped her hand into his, edging closer. "We could do a fancy wedding in Glorvaird with five hundred in attendance—people you don't know and who'd only be there to be seen. It would take months to plan, and there'd be a million little details."

Over Alessandra's shoulder, Gideon groaned.

Mia didn't look away from Ethan's face. "But I don't want to wait."

His gaze crackled with intensity, and he smiled a slow smile. "I don't want to wait, either. If you're sure."

She was.

With Alessandra on her side, she'd talked to Eloise at length about Ethan's situation. She technically didn't need permission to get married, but she also didn't want to make things more difficult with father, considering he might not be with them for much longer.

Finally, her sister had agreed that because of the media storm that always followed Mia around, a Vegas wedding wouldn't do irreparable harm to the royal family's reputation or diplomatic connections.

Ethan had made peace with losing custody of his brothers, though Mia knew he still felt guilty, as if he'd let them down—which she found ridiculous. She kept that opinion to herself.

After much thought and prayer, Ethan had decided that while the dairy farm was his dad's legacy, it wasn't his dream to rebuild. They'd already begun looking for a buyer. Once the transaction closed, they would relocate—with Peanut—to Glorvaird.

Mia knew Ethan would make a fine prince. His finer qualities, his loyalty and goodness, would win over the hearts of her people, just as he'd won her over.

She couldn't wait to take him home. But first...

The rented minister beckoned them to the front of the small chapel. Gideon, who wore a suit, and Alessandra, who wore a simple wine-colored shift, walked arm-in-arm down the aisle first, leaving Mia and Ethan to follow.

She'd chosen an off-the-shoulder floor-length satin sheath and held a simple bouquet of roses in a deep red that matched Alessandra's dress.

She could see what Ethan thought of her in his eyes as he looked at her as if he couldn't tear his gaze away.

There was no doubt in her mind that this was right. Ethan was her one true love, and she knew they'd be blissfully happy together. For life.



"THEY LOOK HAPPY," Gideon whispered in Alessandra's ear as they witnessed Mia and Ethan speak their vows. They'd foregone the typical maid of honor and best man placement to stand together near the bride and groom.

And Ethan and Mia did look happy. He hadn't known Mia well before this trip—still didn't consider himself close with her—but Alessandra had expressed several times that she'd never seen her sister more settled and at peace.

Love did that for you.

For those few tense days when he'd been in the midst of investigating the Triple H theft, he'd questioned whether his and Alessandra's love would be enough to hold them together. When he should've been holding on to her. After the dust up with Dan, he and Nate had sat down and worked out some security measures for the ranch's finances and worked through some of the communication issues they'd had when Gideon had been gone to Glorvaird for weeks on end.

He hoped they could still make the transition work, for both his and Alessandra's sake, and for the Triple H.

There was still the issue of the royal family's overall security. Although nothing had happened in several months, and the threats they had received had been garden-variety and harmless, he wasn't convinced that the threat was over. If Alessandra's aunt was truly unhinged, danger could lurk around the next bend.

And he'd just gotten an email this morning from one of his contacts regarding Alessandra and Mia's half-sister. His guy had found a last known alias and an address. The information was several years old. It wasn't much to go on, but it was better than the nothing he'd had before.

Alessandra had been sequestered with her sister in their shared hotel room all morning, so Gideon hadn't had a chance to tell her yet. He could only hope this led to something positive.

What if the missing half-sister wasn't what Alessandra was building her up in her mind to be?

He wouldn't let his girl get hurt, but how did he protect her from this family issue that had been years in the making, since Alessandra had been a little girl?

All he could do was be there for her.

She glanced over her shoulder at him, eyes moist and shiny.

He leaned slightly closer, so he could whisper to her again. "Do we really have to invite five hundred people to ours?"

Her smile widened.

He'd go through the circus act of a big wedding. Heck, he'd walk through fire if she would just keep smiling at him like that, for the rest of their lives.

•  •  •

Pieter might technically be a prince, but he'd never met his royal cousins. The crown princess and her two sisters lived in the royal palace in the heart of Glorvaird, while Pieter, his mother, and his older brother Henri had been forced out of the kingdom. They resided in a villa in nearby Regis, a small territory close to Glorvaird.

It was a comfortable living, at least financially. The king of Glorvaird had been unable to sever his mother's inheritance, though he'd done everything in his power to ruin their lives.

Pieter and Henri had been dealing with their mother's eccentricities alone, ever since they'd been young boys.

But lately, things had grown worse.

Pieter had one love—bicycle racing. He wasn't good enough to ride in the Tour de France, but he'd hired on as a driver to follow and assist the team. In the weeks he'd been absent, apparently his mother had hired assassins in some hare-brained attempt that made sense only to her to claim the crown. Henri had gone incommunicado. Disappeared.

His mother's plot had been a mess to clean up and had cost more to keep quiet than he'd like to think about.

He was tired. Tired of dealing with his mom's mental health problems on his own. Tired of being rejected by a country that was in his blood.

He wanted to be acknowledged by the royal family. And a small part of him wanted to hurt them like he'd been hurt by the abandonment he'd suffered his whole life.

He just had to discover the best way to enact revenge.

It wasn't hard to follow his cousins' movements via the American media. Except for Eloise, who never seemed to leave the palace.

Could he insert himself in his cousins' life, without revealing his true identity? He'd need to be close to find out what could truly cause them pain.

After all, he'd learned from his mother, the master of pain.

# The Toad Prince

# Chapter One



FIVE-POINT-TWO MILES FROM HOME.

She'd been planning her big escape from her small life for twelve months and two days, and she'd only made it five-point-two miles from her home in north-central Texas.

All her careful planning, all the scrimping and saving, down the drain.

McKenna Hastings took two steps back from the open hood of her battered twenty-year-old pickup and stared at the steam rising from the engine. The truck made an ugly roadside decoration against the bright blue sky and fields green with their spring growth.

She'd spent years working on the truck. Changed the oil, the spark plugs, the battery, even the alternator, once.

She knew her truck. And she knew this had been coming, had hoped and prayed that the truck's last legs would hold for just a while longer.

Apparently, she'd long ago used up her last wish.

She'd already checked on Maximus. Her horse seemed content standing in the trailer attached to the truck. He wasn't shaken at all, not like she was when she'd seen the steam pouring from beneath the hood. The April weather was mild, and he'd be fine in the trailer until she came up with a solution.

Tears threatened and she valiantly sniffed, trying to stem them.

A few slipped free, and she swiped at them with the backs of her hands.

Her three cousins were going to laugh so hard when she had to call them to tow Maximus back home.

They'd already made every joke they could think of about her quest to become a rodeo queen.

This was supposed to be the first leg of her journey. The first event was tonight. She'd imagined Mama and Daddy looking down from heaven, watching and smiling on her. She was going to redeem Daddy's tragedy, live up to Mama's legacy on the circuit.

She touched the locket beneath the neck of her T-shirt. How could she give up now, when she was so close?

An engine revved and then idled. She swiped at her tears again, in case it was someone she knew—no doubt the small town grapevine would quickly catch wind of her failed adventure.

She turned to see an unfamiliar black truck, a current-year model if she wasn't mistaken. With boosted wheels and silver rims that sparkled in the midmorning light.

It rolled to a stop on the two-lane road beside her broken-down pickup.

The passenger side window lowered with a smooth electric slide— she was hit with a little pang of jealousy for her truck's crank windows —to reveal a handsome dark-haired man she'd never seen before.

"Need some help?" he asked in a barely-there accent she didn't recognize.

"Maybe."

She might only be nineteen, but she knew better than to get in a vehicle with a total stranger. On the other hand, she had grown up with three male cousins and knew how to fight her way out of almost any situation.

And a huge part of her was trying to find a way—any way—to keep her dream from going up in a puff of smoke.

Maybe it was foolish, but she stepped closer to the truck and stood on tiptoe to see inside. "I don't suppose you have a spare six-cylinder in here anywhere."

She used the moment to get a good look at her would-be hero. Wow, he was handsome. He had piercing blue eyes and a patrician nose. She'd read that in a book once but had never seen anyone who fit the description, until now. His strong jaw was covered in a day's worth of dark stubble.

Broad, muscled shoulders stretched beneath a plaid-patterned shirt complete with silver snaps up the front and on the pockets. The shirt didn't appear to have ever been worn before, and neither did the dark stonewashed Wranglers that encased a muscled pair of thighs.

She couldn't see his feet but would almost bet that his boots would be brand-new, too.

His outfit made her think he was some kind of would-be cowboy. The interior of his truck was spotless. No signs of anything a real cowboy would have on hand. Not a pair of leather gloves, a horse's hoof pick, or a coil of rope or anything else.

Maybe he was a serial killer posing as a cowboy, out looking for unsuspecting young women. Ones who wouldn't know any better.

"Are you quite finished checking me out?"

Her head snapped up, and she caught the end of his smile, one that invited all kinds of trouble.

And that was enough to make her step back from the truck.

A shadow moved deep in his eyes. Then he slid on a pair of designer sunglasses with dark lenses, hiding the nuances of his expression from her.

"Do you need a ride to town? Isn't there a little hamlet just up ahead?"

"A hamlet?" she repeated. She'd never heard anybody use that term outside of a romance novel.

Who was this guy?

No one could call the podunk hole she was trying to crawl out of a "hamlet."

"Town's three miles that way." She jerked her thumb over her shoulder. "But I'm not going there. I'm on my way to Austin." She slanted a look back at the rusted white trailer. "I can't leave my horse. Maximus is worth ten times more than my truck was."

———

PRINCE PIETER of Glorvaird couldn't believe the girl he'd stumbled upon.

Oh, he could easily agree that the horse she claimed was worth more than the truck would be without even seeing the animal—the pile of junk that still had steam rising from beneath its hood had obviously seen better days. Probably during Pieter's childhood.

But what he couldn't understand was why a beautiful woman like her was out here towing a horse trailer alone. With her sandy-colored long hair streaming down her back and dancing hazel eyes, and those features... She could easily be a fashion model.

And she was *young*. She couldn't be more than twenty. Her fresh-faced demeanor and the naivety coming off her in waves made him want to warn her off. She might as well wear a target on her back for unsavory people.

People like him.

Not that he had the time or the head space to devote to anything else right now. He was on a mission.

He wasn't even sure why he'd stopped.

Or why the sight of the silvery tears she'd tried to wipe away affected him. He wasn't one to be affected by a woman's manipulations—not after dealing with his mother since his childhood.

The girl seemed suspicious of him, which he supposed was a good thing. It was novel that she didn't recognize him as a prince. In Regis, where he and his mother made their home, he was well known and recognized often.

Was it providence that she was stranded here when he, too, was driving to Austin?

He'd landed in Dallas and traveled to the small town where the newspapers reported his cousin, Alessandra, lived while in the United States with her fiancé, a rancher. He'd arrived only to find his cousin gone to some cowboy competition—a rodeo—several hours away. Too far away to enact the revenge that drove him.

His mother spoke often and fondly of her growing-up years spent in Glorvaird, but she spoke even more of being betrayed by his uncle, the king, and forced out of her beloved homeland.

Wasn't Pieter a son of Glorvaird? Didn't he deserve to be embraced by the homeland he'd never visited? He didn't hold out hope for any kind of reconciliation with the royal family. He'd come to Texas with a vague idea of finding the one thing that would hurt his cousin the most.

The crown had abandoned him. The king was his uncle, yet he'd never met the man. Certainly he and Henri could've used some guidance over the years on how to deal with his mentally ill mother.

As far as he was concerned, his cousins and the king deserved what was coming to them. He just had to find the perfect vehicle for delivering the revenge he desired.

He'd never met his cousin. The papers reported she'd almost died, thanks to his mother's assassination attempt. The stories of her devoted fiancé, a former solider, claimed he was very protective of his soon-to-be bride.

Would it be easier to approach Alessandra if Pieter arrived at the rodeo grounds with this young woman? Who would ever suspect someone as innocent-looking as she?

He didn't know what her business was in Austin. Perhaps there was a chance she was going to the rodeo, as well, since she was towing her horse. Not that it mattered. He knew how to woo a woman to his way of thinking, and they'd have several hours in the truck together for him to win her over.

"It happens that I am also on my way to Austin," he said. "To meet my cousin."

A shadow of something—perhaps suspicion—flitted through her eyes, though she hid it quickly. Good girl.

"Perhaps we could strike a bargain."

She looked over her shoulder to the trailer. He saw the fine lines at the corner of her eyes as she considered his offer.

It wasn't as if there was much traffic on this two-lane road. No one had driven past during the several minutes he'd been stopped here.

She bit her lip, and he knew he'd won. She was going to agree.

"I'll tow your trailer and your horse to Austin. But what will you give me?"

She leveled a flat gaze on him, mouth firmed in a line. "Not what you're thinking, I'm sure. I'd rather call my cousins"—the deep frown she wore when she mentioned them told him how much she didn't like the idea—"than get physical with you."

He laughed at her unexpected words. Usually women were content to ply their wiles on him, try to charm him. But not this country girl, with her jeans and T-shirt and hair in a braid down her back.

Her frank words were such a complete departure from what he was accustomed to that his smile lingered.

And only seemed to increase her suspicion.

"I'm serious," she said.

He leaned his elbow on the steering wheel, body turned almost completely toward her now. "I can tell."

"So you... aren't interested?" He couldn't get an accurate read on her expression. Was she relieved or disappointed?

He couldn't say it without lying, not after what she'd just stirred in him. "I didn't say that," he returned. "But I think I can control myself for the four or five hours it takes to get you to Austin. Will you come along, then?"

"You said we'd strike a bargain." Her chin came up, and he clamped his lips against the urge to smile again. She might give a good show of trying to be tough, but he'd had so many hours of reading his mother that it was really more adorable than anything else.

"A boon then," he said. "To be redeemed later." It was almost too easy. He'd find a way to use this girl to get close to Alessandra.

She looked back again, and this time he realized she wasn't looking at the trailer, but at the road. Was she running away from something?

He reminded himself that he didn't care.

"It's a deal." She stuck her hand through the open truck window, and he stretched out to shake it. He was surprised by how calloused it was—almost what he might expect from a working *man's* hand.

"I'm McKenna Hastings."

"Pieter." He didn't give his title. Didn't want it getting out who he really was and what he was doing here, not until he'd formulated a better plan.

"I'll get Maximus out of the trailer," she said. "It'll be easier to unhitch that way."

He pulled his truck into the drainage ditch in front of hers, just in case someone did meander down this road. The truck was a rental and a high-dollar one at that.

By the time he'd gotten out of the truck, she'd fitted a ramp to the back of the open trailer and was backing out a magnificent solid black gelding.

He wasn't a horseman, didn't know much about conformation or the value of the animal, but he could see she'd been right about the animal's worth. It was almost comical, the juxtaposition between the quality of the animal and that of her vehicle.

It certainly made him curious.

The shiny black boots he'd purchased at a store in Dallas pinched his toes as he crunched through the grass at the road's edge.

He peered down at the connector where the trailer was hooked to her truck. He had staff that usually made sure his bicycle was attached to his sports utility vehicle when he went riding. And no idea how to disconnect this.

Then McKenna was beside him. "Here," she said.

He backed out of her way as she made quick work of untangling a chain and some wires and then lifting the trailer above the ball.

She was a slight thing, but she put her shoulder into the trailer and started pushing before he realized what she was doing.

"Hey!"

The trailer had already shifted by a foot or more before he joined her on the opposite side of the hitch and put his back into it.

The stupid boots slipped on the grass and gravel, and he almost lost his footing, but thankfully McKenna didn't seem to notice.

When they'd moved it several feet away from her truck and angled it so that he could back up to it, she straightened. She didn't even seem winded, so he tried to stifle his labored breathing.

"You move trailers by yourself often, Supergirl? I thought you said you had cousins to help you."

She shrugged, flicking a strand of hair that had fallen out of her braid and into her eyes. "A girl's gotta do what a girl's gotta do."

It was an answer designed to put him off, and he let it, for now. There'd be plenty of time to talk on the road.

———

AFTER SHE'D HITCHED the horse trailer to Pieter's truck and loaded Maximus back inside, McKenna ducked into her pickup to grab her bags.

The canvas duffel and well-used garment bag might not look like much, but they held her dreams.

She looked around the inside of the truck she'd bought second-hand at seventeen. The county might tow it by the time she returned after the weekend was over.

Then she spent several moments sending a text to her best friend, Kylie. Her friend might be off having the time of her life at Oklahoma University, but they talked every day. McKenna raised the phone to snap a photo of Pieter's truck, another of the man himself, and typed in his license plate number, since she'd been up close and personal with it while she'd hooked up the trailer.

She might be taking a chance accepting a ride from a total stranger, but she couldn't let this setback ruin her one chance at scholarship money that could change her life. And there was no way she was going with Pieter without leaving a trail of breadcrumbs for her friend, just in case.

Then she took a deep breath and got out of her truck. She was going to be in a world of trouble when one of her cousins drove to town and saw the abandoned truck. Would they think she'd been abducted?

But she still didn't text or call them. She would later. *Much* later.

She couldn't risk them coming after her and ruining her chance. They'd already done enough with their jeering and joking.

Duffel in hand and the garment bag slung over her shoulder, McKenna approached the black truck.

She'd known Pieter was a city boy pretending to be a cowboy based on his clothing, and his actions since he'd stepped out of the truck only confirmed her initial impression.

A real cowboy would've known how to unhitch a trailer. Would've known not to wear dress boots to work outside—or in her case, push a trailer. And a real cowboy would've followed her to her truck, asking if he could carry her bags.

There weren't cowboy *rules* so much as a code of honor.

And Pieter most definitely didn't have it.

Which made her wonder just why he'd stopped to help. She'd seen the calculation in his eyes. Knew that his "boon" might be painful when it came due. But she really had no choice, now did she?

Her new friend sat in the driver's seat adjusting the stereo as she opened the passenger door and then the rear door so she could load her bags into the backseat. It really was a nice truck, lots of legroom back there.

"You okay?" he asked, shooting a glance at her.

"Fine." She didn't need a man to open doors for her or unhitch her trailer. After her mom's death when she was three, she and her dad had made due. He'd taught her independence early on, told her Mama'd had an independent spirit.

Then when he'd passed, too, in the middle of a storm of disasters, she'd been thrown into life with her aunt and uncle and cousins. She'd had to lean on that independent spirit often, just to survive her abrasive, often rude and bullying cousins.

She'd learned fast to keep quiet and stay out of the way. She could do for herself.

All she had to do was prove herself.

Pieter put the truck in gear and eased onto the road.

She felt the slight rocking of the truck that meant Maximus had shifted in his trailer. In her truck with its bad shocks, she could feel every movement the horse made, but in this new model truck, the thousand-pound animal shifting barely caused a blip.

Her new friend glanced in the rearview mirror. "Anything I should know about pulling a horse trailer?"

"Max is a seasoned traveler," she said. "But horses sometimes move around. You shouldn't have any issues with this baby and its towing capacity, though." She patted the leather seat next to her thigh. The car even smelled new.

She couldn't help watching his hands flex and move on the steering wheel. He had nice hands. Powerful hands. Even if they were a bit soft, like she imagined a banker or stockbroker would have. Someone who worked inside, at a desk job.

Her cell phone pinged a message tone, and she glanced at it as unobtrusively as she could.

. . .

*KYLIE: OMG girl you're crazy! At least he's a hot stranger...*

PIETER GLANCED OVER AT HER. "Your family?"

"A friend. I sent her your picture and your license plate number. Just in case you're a crazy serial killer."

He grinned, eyes back on the road.

Was it her, or was his grin particularly feral-looking?

He tapped his index finger against the top of the steering wheel. "So...what's your story? Runaway?"

She wrinkled her nose, turning to stare out the window. "No," she said smartly. "I'm a competitor."

"Traveling alone?"

She shrugged. "My family is busy." And they weren't invited anyway.

"What event? Tub racing?"

Brows furrowed, she glanced at him. "Oh, you mean barrel racing? I'm guessing you've never been to a rodeo before..."

"Good guess. Then barrel racing, is it?"

"No." Her face heated and the words stuck in her throat. She had to clear it once before speaking again. "I'm competing to be rodeo queen."

She waited for his chuckle or even a smirk. She'd gotten enough of that from her cousins. But it didn't come, only a curious sidelong glance. "That's more like a pageant, isn't it?"

"Yes."

She'd won the local rodeo queen title last summer. That's when her plans had really started taking shape. How many times had her cousins told her that she was only good for her appearance?

So why shouldn't she use her looks?

Kylie had supported her plans to enter this larger competition in Austin, though McKenna's best friend didn't know the depths of desperation she felt to escape her life.

But McKenna had a niggling worry that the hometown title had been a fluke. What did she really have to offer to the larger rodeo community?

She needed the scholarship money if she was going to get out of her minimum wage job as a grocery store checker. Since her tenth birthday, she'd dreamed of being an attorney, a better one than her father's.

She couldn't give up now.

Chapter Two

GIDEON HALE STRODE THROUGH THE OUTDOOR RODEO grounds in full mission-planning mode. Early afternoon sunlight warmed his head and shoulders, though a brisk breeze ruffled his hair.

The former Navy SEAL had agreed to this plan of Alessandra's, but that was before he'd seen this venue.

His contacts had turned up a lead on the lost princess of Glorvaird, Alessandra's half sister, and they'd come to Austin to try and meet up with her at the rodeo.

The fairgrounds were a nightmare. Right now, they were fairly empty. The rodeo queen competition would begin tonight, and several RVs and horse trailers had parked in the venue's large lot, but the dirt-packed arena and other fairground buildings were empty and quiet.

He imagined them filled with cowboys and cowgirls, moms and dads and kids. Most of the people attending the rodeo would be here for the fun and the competition.

But if somewhere were here with evil intentions... Well, there were too many places to hide. Nooks and crannies between buildings. Even rooftops, where a sniper could have easy access.

The fairgrounds were impossible to secure, even with a larger force than the hired security team he'd assembled.

And he was dreading going back to the upscale Austin hotel and telling Alessandra that he didn't want her out here in the open.

After the huge engagement ball they'd hosted back home had gone off without a hitch, and after five months with no further credible threats, Alessandra seemed to believe that the target was off her back.

He wished he could be so sure, but his time in the military had taught him that threats rarely ever just *went away*. They might go dormant for a period.

But they always came back.

And it was his job to protect her. She'd nearly died on his watch, and he'd vowed never to let that happen again.

The problem was that Alessandra had recently learned about her half sister, the product of an illicit affair of her father's, and she was determined to meet the girl and bring her back to Glorvaird before the king died. With their upcoming wedding—a huge shindig that would take place in a Glorvaird cathedral with five hundred attendees—only six weeks away, Alessandra seemed even more determined to locate the princess *now*.

The missing princess had a last known residence in the States but had dropped off the map until recently. His contacts had turned up a barrel racer on the rodeo circuit who matched the age and birth date of the missing princess.

They still weren't one hundred percent sure this Tara Ballard was the princess they were looking for. It would take a DNA test to confirm her true identity, but Alessandra refused to be placated or to let Gideon handle the issue.

Alessandra had some kind of idea that if she saw this girl, she'd instantly know whether or not it was her long-lost sister.

He'd tried to caution her about getting her hopes up. Tried to tell her that the other woman might not want to connect, that there might be a reason she'd fallen off the map.

But nothing would stop his fiancée's optimistic hopes.

He'd promised to try. And he would.

But his first priority would always be Alessandra's safety. So how could he convince her to stay away from the rodeo over the next week?

———

PIETER COULDN'T CONTAIN his curiosity about his passenger as he drove the truck southwest along a flat, straight two-lane highway.

A rodeo queen.

He'd met plenty of models and actresses, had even dated a couple.

McKenna just didn't seem the type. Oh, she was pretty enough. Striking even, with her elfin features and bright eyes.

In his experience, women who were interested in pageants and modeling were usually vapid, extremely interested in fashion and money—his money—and self-absorbed.

And yeah, he'd only just met her, but he sensed that McKenna was more hometown girl than anything else.

So what was her deal?

"How'd you get into pageanting?" he asked. "Was your mother a rodeo queen or something?"

She was still staring out her window, and he couldn't take his eyes off the road for very long, but a sidelong glance at her revealed a wistful expression crossing her face.

"Yes. A long time ago. Last summer one of my cousins entered me in a local queen competition as a joke. But I went through with it and won. So...now I'm here."

There had to be more to it than that. He knew there must be. But she didn't seem to want to say more.

She set her chin again and looked his way. "What about you? What business do you have in Austin? You're obviously not a native Texan."

His shoulders wanted to tense, but he'd had many years of practice in hiding his true feelings, so he merely tightened his grip on the steering wheel and forced a smile he didn't feel. "I'm actually heading to the rodeo, as well. I'm meeting someone."

From the corner of his eye, he saw the tilt of her head. Felt her glance. "Hmm."

That was it. She *hmmed*.

"Is it a surprise? For the person you're meeting?" she asked.

He shrugged. "Sort of." Alessandra wouldn't be expecting him. He couldn't be sure whether she even knew he existed.

"Then you might want to reconsider your clothes."

He looked down at himself briefly. "What's wrong with them?"

"You don't look anything like a genuine cowboy. You'll stand out for sure when surrounded by real Texas good 'ol boys."

"How does a real cowboy dress?" he asked wryly. They'd only just met and she was critiquing his attire?

"Mostly T-shirts and jeans. But your jeans are so starched and clean, they've obviously never been worn before. And your boots..."

The continuous pinch of his toes made him cranky as he asked, "The boots?"

"They're dress boots. For Sunday church or maybe a fancy date night. Not for every day."

He stifled the growl that wanted to rise from his throat. She was dressed much like she'd described, her braid flipped over one shoulder of her T-shirt. Her boots were worn leather and caked with dirt and he didn't want to know what else.

"You should've asked the salesperson for help," she said. A small smirk played around the corners of her lips.

"I was in a hurry"

"To meet your cousin." She slanted a glance at him.

She was ether too nosy or too smart for her own good.

"Tell me more about this pageant of yours." He gave her a charming smile, one that usually worked to distract or disarm.

Before she could answer, her phone rang.

She sighed deeply but clicked the line open and held the phone to her ear.

"Where the heck are you?" came a belligerent male voice, loud in the quiet cab of the truck.

She must've accidentally opened the line on speakerphone.

Was this one of her cousins? A boyfriend?

She moved the phone away from her ear with a wince. Her focus moved to the phone's screen as she tapped rapidly, probably trying to silence it. "Hey, Todd."

"Where are you?'"

"I'm on my way to Austin. You already knew that."

"Then why is your truck sitting on the side of the road?"

She grimaced as she kept punching at the phone, but there must've been some error because she didn't raise it to her ear again, and it remained on speaker.

"McKenna!"

He didn't know her family dynamic, but the person on the other end of the line was pushy. Of course, Pieter'd had his own doubts about her being on her own and broken down on the side of the road. Could he blame the guy for being a little protective?

"The engine finally fizzled," she said as she glanced out the passenger window. "But I caught a ride."

"With who?"

She shot a furtive look at him. "A friend."

"What *friend*? And why didn't you call me?"

She mumbled something beneath her breath. "I didn't call you, or Taylor, or Andy, because I already knew what you would say."

Great diversion. She'd completely ignored the question.

"What, to stop being stupid and just come home?"

Ouch. There was a difference between protective and outright rude.

McKenna's face had turned crimson, and Pieter found himself

wanting to defend her.

Which was crazy, because he didn't have the time or inclination to get involved. It wasn't his problem. *She* wasn't his problem.

"Look," the voice came through the phone. "The rodeo queen thing was a great joke, but you're never going to win at a big rodeo like the one down in Austin. Why don't you just tell me where you are and I'll come get you?"

Pearly white teeth emerged as she worried her bottom lip. Her blush had faded some. Her brows were furrowed, and she looked like she was considering this idiot's words.

"Why don't you tell him to get lost?" Pieter whispered.

"Who was that?" Todd's voice boomed over the speaker.

McKenna shot Pieter a glance. He couldn't tell if it was annoyed or grateful. "I told you, I got a ride."

Before her cousin could demand to know more, she rushed on. "I'm going to Austin, like I planned—"

"You're never going to win—"

"I'll be back in a week." She hung up the phone.

An uncomfortable silence fell.

"You might want to power it off," Pieter offered helpfully. "Your family isn't very supportive, are they?"

———

McKenna stifled a bitter laugh.

*Unsupportive* was an understatement.

"My aunt and uncle are my guardians," she said slowly, not sure how much she really wanted to tell Pieter—a virtual stranger—about her family. On the other hand, everyone around town knew her story, so why not him? It wouldn't change anything.

"They're...fine with me going down to Austin." It was a bit of a stretch. The truth was, they really didn't care as long as she was out of their way. "It's my cousins—three of them, all older—who can be controlling."

*Controlling* was a kind way to put it. They'd bullied her throughout her childhood and teens. Now that she was older, they mostly threatened and teased her.

She desperately wanted to move out of the house, but working a minimum wage job meant she couldn't afford it.

"How'd you end up with your aunt and uncle?" Pieter asked.

She glanced out the window, her hand creeping up to touch her locket beneath her shirt.

"My mom died—I can't even remember her, I was so little. For a while it was just me and my dad. Then he..." The words stuck in her throat, a hard knob of emotion even after almost a decade.

Even if everyone in town knew—or thought they knew—what had happened, she hated talking about it. Her father had been wrongly accused of committing fraud through his financial services business. He'd been jailed and been assigned a court-appointed attorney, who'd botched the case.

Her father hadn't lasted three months in prison.

"He died when I was ten," she said, because she couldn't tell the rest. "My aunt and uncle took me in."

And she'd been thankful, but sometimes it was hard. Sometimes she felt like excess baggage, like they'd be just as happy without her there.

"Sounds like it was hard on you. How old are you, anyway?"

Her chin went up at the slight challenge in his question. "Old enough."

His raised eyebrows told her he wasn't going to let it go. "Seventeen?"

"*Nine*teen," she shot back. Old enough to be on her own, if she could just afford it...

"Nineteen," he muttered under his breath, shaking his head a little.

"Why does it matter?" she asked. "How old are you? Thirty?" She threw out the number because she wanted to irritate him right back, but she pegged him closer to twenty-five.

He smirked a little. "Older than you. Wiser, too. Do I need to be worried about these cousins coming after me with a shotgun?"

"No. Probably not," she amended. Even though Todd had called to berate her, she doubted he or his brothers could be bothered to drive all the way to Austin.

"You don't sound very sure."

She couldn't tell whether he was teasing her or not. She didn't want to talk about her cousins any more. They loved to tell her that her looks were the only thing special about her and that she'd wind up some man's housewife, barefoot and pregnant because she'd never make anything of herself.

Kylie had been the only person in her life who'd told her anything different. Kylie believed McKenna could be criminal defense attorney, something she'd dreamed about since her father's botched trial. She never wanted another family to experience what she had.

Pieter slanted a glance her direction. "So your cousins entered you into the competition but now they don't think you can win?"

"They entered me as a *joke*," she reminded him. "I'm not exactly a fashion icon or anything. Horsemanship is my strongest suit."

Her cousins had hooted and howled from the stands when she'd walked onto the makeshift runway for the fashion portion of the contest back home. She'd visited the attic and found her old gun used for bedazzling clothing from elementary school and gone to town on a boot-length denim skirt she'd found at the nearest Goodwill two years ago. She'd found a sparkly pattern surfing the web at the public library.

She'd also spent hours poring over videos that showed different riding patterns for the horsemanship part of the competition. Not to mention the questions for the interview with the judges.

She wasn't poised. Wasn't confident. Had no idea what she was walking into.

The cash winnings from the small-town rodeo was a windfall she'd never had before, and she'd plugged the money into fancy duds for the fashion part of the Austin competition.

She was betting everything on this. College tuition was expensive, especially if she wanted to make it all the way to law school.

"There's a big difference in our small-town rodeo and what you'll see in Austin. Austin is a regional rodeo that pulls more riders"—and queen contestants—"and the competition will be much tougher."

Another one of those slanted glances. "You're pretty enough to win. What are you so afraid of?"

Her face went hot at his compliment.

Suddenly, there was a loud *pop,* and the steering wheel jerked to the right.

Blowout!

She grabbed the door, her seatbelt locking tight against her chest as the truck bucked, fighting the trailer's weight from behind and the loss of momentum.

Pieter gritted his teeth as he worked to guide the truck toward the shoulder.

Finally, they rolled to a stop. A semi zoomed past, stirring a cloud of gravel dust that swirled past the truck.

She panted, trying to control the racing of her heart.

"Are you all right?" Pieter asked. His face was white.

"Yeah. I've got to check on Maximus."

She could only pray her horse wasn't hurt.

What would she do if she got to the rodeo and didn't have a horse for the contest?

# Chapter Three

MAXIMUS WAS UNHURT BUT AGITATED AS MCKENNA slipped through the trailer beside him. He neighed and bobbed his head, showing his displeasure at the sudden and shaky stop.

"Easy, boy," she said, rubbing one hand against his neck to settle him.

She checked both front legs, but he didn't appear to have lost his balance or kicked any part of the trailer, which might've injured him.

She sighed, tears threatening because of her relief.

"All right," she told the horse. "I'm going to go see how quick we can get back on the road."

Outside the truck, Pieter stared at the blown front tire. It was completely shredded. They weren't driving anywhere on it.

"Know how to change a tire?" she asked, already guessing the answer.

"I know how to ring for a tow," he said, still staring at the tire.

She sighed. "Not necessary. I can do it. Let me unload Maximus, again"—she muttered under her breath—"and I'll change the tire."

"Isn't it dangerous to do that right off the side of the interstate?"

As if to underscore his words, a sports car blared its horn as it passed them, going well over the posted speed limit.

She glanced at her watch. "I'm supposed to check in for my interview with the competition judges in five hours. If we wait for someone else to do it and then have any other delays, I'll miss it completely."

And she couldn't miss her one shot.

"Are you certain?"

She nodded. She couldn't quit now.

She unloaded Maximus, who wasn't happy about the noise coming from the cars passing on the interstate. This particular field that they'd stopped near wasn't fenced, and there were no nearby trees, so there was nowhere to tie him off.

"You're going to have to hold his lead," she told Pieter, who'd stood back to let her work.

Pieter approached her at the horse's head, well back from the interstate.

"I'm not, ah..."

"You don't like horses?" she asked.

"I'd prefer to ride a bicycle," he said. "I'm an avid cyclist."

It figured.

"Well, for right now, you're going to be a real cowboy."

She gave a quick introduction to Maximus, letting the horse get his scent. "Just act confident." Pieter shouldn't have any trouble with that, not with the cocky smiles he'd been delivering. "He'll be able to smell if you're frightened."

And the last thing she needed was for her horse to bolt along this stretch of interstate.

Pieter grudgingly took the lead rope.

She glanced over her shoulder as she trudged toward the truck to see man and horse sizing each other up. "Don't stare straight at him!" she called back.

"Are you sure you won't need help?" Pieter returned.

She only shook her head and kept going.

It took longer than she wanted. She ended up having to unhitch the trailer completely to get at the spare tire connected beneath the truck bed.

It was heavy work that made her arms and back ache and, at one point, she ended up lying on the ground on her back to get the jack positioned correctly.

She got a blister cranking the lug wrench, but at last, after almost forty-five minutes of sweaty work, she had the tire back on and the trailer re-hitched.

She couldn't wait to get back in the air conditioned cab.

She blew hair that had come loose from her braid off her forehead as she walked toward Pieter and Maximus on the slight hill off the side of the highway.

The horse munched on summer grasses while the man sat with legs outstretched. He got to his feet as she approached. He offered her

Max's lead rope, and she took it, grimacing at the black oil on her hand against the white rope.

"Thank you," she said.

"Thank *you*."

She wrinkled her brow at him.

"For fixing the tire."

She waited for more. Waited for him to say something snarky, like one of her cousins would. He just stared at her.

She wiped at her cheek with the back of one hand—the only place that seemed remotely clean—and hoped she hadn't smudged oil on her face. "Aren't you going to ask if it's safe to drive on?"

His brows creased. "Why would I ask that? I just watched you change the tire."

"Yeah but..."

He still seemed puzzled.

"I'm a girl. I'm not as strong as a man..." She heard her cousins' voices, even though the words came from her own mouth.

She shook her head, turning to the truck and trailer. She wanted in that A/C now. Especially with her face flaming so badly. "Never mind. It doesn't matter."

"Hang on." He caught up to her, tugged on her elbow. For once, his gaze was clear and sincere. It stopped her in her tracks.

"Do you let your cousins feed you that load of crap? Because I've just been watching you work your butt off and thinking that you'd never trust your horse to the truck if you didn't feel it was safe."

That was true. So was his assumption that it was her cousins' voices she heard in her head. She'd heard the refrain that she wasn't good enough daily.

———

PIETER GAZED down at the pixie of a woman and her too-wide eyes. She wore a slightly skeptical expression, but he didn't have to look far to see the slight vulnerability revealed beneath.

She really didn't know how impressive it was that she'd just manhandled that truck tire into submission?

"You've got a smudge..." He pointed to the bridge of her nose.

When she lifted her oil-stained hand, the one not holding onto the horse, he caught her wrist. "You'll make it worse."

He reached up himself, carefully brushed away the dust with his thumb.

Nineteen. She was only nineteen.

He repeated the words internally, needing them to cut through the waves of attraction that battered him.

She was practically a baby.

He was only twenty-four, but after dealing with his mother since his childhood, along with the expectations of being nearly royalty, he often felt much older. Hadn't he seen the worst in people over and over again?

She was not his type, he reminded himself, but he seemed to be caught in the laser-beam of her bright-eyed gaze.

His hand moved to cup her cheek.

And then it was knocked away as her horse butted its head between them with a *whuffle* of breath.

"Maximus!" She didn't sound particularly upset, though, as she curled her arm beneath the animal's neck and turned her face into its coat. She'd probably welcomed the intrusion.

Pieter stepped back, exhaling heavily.

He didn't even know where that spike of attraction had come from. She wasn't his type. She was too naive and fresh-faced. He'd destroy her if he let her get too close.

He moved to the front of the truck as she loaded her horse in the trailer. His phone rang. The display showed it was the mental health institution where Mother resided. He let the call roll to voicemail. He'd deal with it later.

As he slid into the cab and cranked the engine, he felt the weight of the ring on his right pinkie.

McKenna's face appeared in the passenger window. She opened the door.

He flipped on the A/C. He'd noticed the fine sheen of sweat across her brow and upper lip—he'd been too close—and she needed to cool off.

They both did.

———

PIETER HAD TALKED McKenna into stopping off at a combination gas station and mom-and-pop diner, even though she'd told him it wasn't necessary.

She was worried about getting to Austin in time, but he was hungry and knew she must be too.

He owed her for fixing the tire, at the very least.

He came out of the washroom to find she'd already cleaned up, removing the last traces of oil from her hands and arms and fixing her braid.

She sat in a small booth, half hidden behind a rack of garish postcards.

He watched for a long moment as she bent over something, reading silently and then mouthing something to herself. Flash cards?

She started to stand when she caught sight of him approaching, but he motioned her to keep her seat.

"We should get something to eat. You might not have time to grab supper before your event tonight."

She started to shake her head, and he couldn't help but wonder if her protest had more to do with her wallet than her appetite. He quickly rushed on. "My treat, since you saved me from paying a tow company."

She still looked like she might protest, so he slid into the booth next to her, effectively trapping her in her seat.

A harried-looking waitress in a stained apron over a worn knee-length uniform rushed over. She stopped short and gave him an assessing gaze. Grinned at him. "What can I get for you, hun?"

He started to order a grilled chicken salad when he caught McKenna's slight shake of her head.

"Always get the special," she whispered to him, then proceeded to order just that—a bacon double cheeseburger with fries and a choco-late shake.

"Roadside diner etiquette?" he asked when the waitress had moved on.

"Common sense. Not many people come to places like this to order a salad, so you can count on their vegetables being old and wilty."

Smart thinking.

He leaned his elbow on the edge of the table, propped his head on it, and craned his neck to get a closer look at the index cards she had spread on the table.

"*Who is the rodeo commissioner?*" he read aloud.

She slapped one palm down over the cards and shuffled them into a pile. "I was just reviewing some questions they might ask me tonight."

He raised one brow at her. "So who is the commissioner?"

She gave a name he didn't recognize, and she must have been right, since she'd been practicing, but with her head ducked down, her voice was just a mumble.

"You'll never make a good impression talking to the table—or to your hands."

Her shoulders straightened. "I was just *practicing answers*."

He shrugged. "Seems if you're going to practice, you should do it right. Hand over the cards."

He moved into the opposite side of the booth, so she was forced to look at him.

She hesitated, her hands covering the cards on the tabletop.

"Come on. I won't poke fun at you."

She looked up, watching his face. For what, he didn't know, but he met her gaze squarely.

Finally, she pushed the stack of cards across the table.

He shuffled through them and chose one at random. "Define *jackpot*."

She explained how the rodeo winnings worked, speaking almost in a monotone.

He looked back down at the cards in his hands. "Do you want the truth?"

She nodded tightly.

"You sound a little...wooden. Rehearsed. You should be more natural when you answer, if you can."

She bit her lip, the third time he'd seen her do that. Was it her nervous tell? "How? If I'm nervous just sitting here with you, how do I pretend that I'm not when I'm in front of a judge?"

He made her nervous. Did she feel the same attraction that had seemed to spark to life between them?

If so, he was in trouble. He had only so much goodness in him, and he'd already used up a lion's share when he hadn't leaned forward and kissed her next to the truck.

"Think about your best friend," he suggested. "Pretend you're talking to her instead of to the judge."

She nodded slowly, a smile dawning across her lips.

And that made his stomach flip.

He returned his gaze to the card and asked her about the current head of the PRCA. This time she was slightly more relaxed.

He watched her for long, silent moments after she finished. Mostly to see what she'd do when she became uncomfortable.

Noise from the patrons around them intruded. Snatches of conversations, clinking silverware, a muffled shout from someone in the kitchen.

She held his gaze steadily, then a slow flush climbed into her cheeks. Her eyes flashed.

"What?" she hissed across the table. "It was the right answer."

He nodded. "I know. I just wanted to see if you'd lose your composure."

Her face mottled again, but he couldn't allow himself to feel sorry for her. "No matter what, you must maintain your composure."

It was a hard lesson. One he'd learned first at his mother's knee, then later when the press speculated on his connection—or lack thereof—to the royal family, sometimes even getting in his face about it.

She looked to the side. She breathed in and out, her shoulders rising and falling. She was so easy to read. Which intrigued him all the more. He was unused to women who showed their every thought and feeling so freely. McKenna was a breath of fresh air.

He glanced at the next card but didn't read from it. "Don't you think it's cruel to the animals they use in the rodeo events? The steers and bulls?"

"That question isn't on the cards."

"Are you going to sass the judge like that if they ask you something you don't want to answer?"

She frowned at him slightly, but he wiggled his eyebrows at her, challenging her. "There will be questions where they aren't looking for your memorized answer. They'll want to know what *you* think."

Her eyes slid past him as she gave the question thought.

"There are a lot of protections for the animals," she said slowly, "both in and out of the arena. And I guess I don't see how it's any different than breeding animals for human consumption. So no, I don't think it's cruel to use the bulls or steers for rodeos."

"That was your best answer yet."

She beamed at him, her obvious joy hitting him low in his stomach. Didn't anyone ever tell her *good job*?

Thankfully, the waitress appeared with their artery-clogging meals, providing a much-needed interruption and another of those looks.

McKenna noticed, raising a brow at him, though she didn't comment.

After the waitress left, McKenna dug in, chomping through the burger and stuffing herself with fries. Another refreshing change from what he was used to, as most women he dated ordered salads and ate daintily. Not this one.

He sipped the chocolate shake, letting the sweet coldness flow over his tongue.

She swallowed. "It's good, isn't it?"

"You were right." He was glad he'd let her change his order.

She beamed again.

How in the heck did this woman let her cousins walk all over her, tell her she was worthless? How could she believe them?

And what was he doing, trying to use her to get close to Alessandra? The next bite of burger tasted like ash in in his mouth.

He'd wanted revenge for so long that he couldn't imagine letting it go. He wanted his cousin to feel some of the same pain he'd felt at being abandoned by his family and left to the manipulations of his mother. It was incredibly difficult dealing with a parent who was mentally unstable on his own.

For so long, revenge had been the only thing he'd wanted. How could he even sit across from someone as pure and sweet as McKenna and not poison her?

Should he just forget about the boon entirely? He could easily drop off McKenna and her horse at the fairgrounds and go on his way. That would be better for her, but he wasn't willing to let her go just yet.

*Chapter Four*

ORANGE LIGHT FROM THE SETTING SUN FILTERED through the open drapes in the hotel suite Alessandra shared with Gideon in a posh Austin hotel. She sat on the sofa in the living area between the two bedrooms, idly paging through a bridal magazine. In the background, the TV flickered as it played a national news station, but she'd muted the volume an hour ago.

The magazine was mostly a guise to hide her nervousness. Most of the wedding preparations had already been put in place. She'd hesitated to even come over to the states with Gideon, as the wedding was only weeks away. And her father's health had declined much in the past months. Now he had trouble eating and speaking. Often when he allowed her to spend time with him, he listened as she read or they sat in companionable silence.

She hadn't been able to stay in Glorvaird knowing that Gideon's people had a strong lead on her missing half sister. Plus, she hadn't wanted to be away from her fiancé, and he had to visit his family's ranch and tie up some loose ends before they returned overseas.

Gideon had agreed that they would remain in Glorvaird after the wedding. Everyone tiptoed around the subject, but her father was not long for this world.

The sound of a keycard being inserted into the door brought her head up from the magazine. The door opened, revealing Gideon.

Alessandra jumped up from the sofa, leaving behind the bridal magazine.

He took off his Stetson and set it on a credenza near the door, giving her his shoulder momentarily. The tense set of his back wasn't a good sign.

She slid her arms around his neck and squeezed, giving him a *welcome home* peck on the lips, hoping to erase some of the tension.

It didn't work. The tight muscles of his shoulders and neck didn't relax at all.

"I ordered room service," she told him. "A nice juicy steak and baked potato for you."

It was one of his favorite meals, but his expression didn't reveal an iota of peace. He nodded. "Thanks, Allie-girl."

She let him go, and he sat in the sofa she'd just vacated. She perched on it next to him.

"Obviously, you have bad news. Why don't you just tell me?"

He flicked a glance at her. "The fairgrounds are a security nightmare. There's no way to control who comes into the venue. On top of that, there will be trucks and trailers in and out all day. Even with a team surrounding you at all times..." He sighed. "I don't like it."

"All right."

His head jerked as he looked at her. "What?"

"I said, *all right*."

He shook his head slightly. "I heard you, but... *All right*, you're fine with the risk, or *all right*, you'll stay at the hotel?"

"I'll stay here."

She shouldn't laugh, but she couldn't help a huff of soft laughter at his stunned expression. "Do you want me to argue?"

"No. I just...thought you would."

She scooted closer to him and put her arm around his broad shoulders. "We're getting married in less than a month. That means I trust you with my life. If you don't think it's safe to be out at the rodeo, then we'll make other arrangements. Find some way to get Cindy"—the barrel racer they'd come to meet with—"to come here."

She wasn't sure that Gideon's hunch that there was still someone after her was right, but she wasn't joking about trusting him with her life. If he didn't want her out in the open, she could respect that.

Some of the tension left him, and he turned to capture her lips in a searing kiss. "Thank you," he whispered against her lips.

She hummed her *you're welcome* back to him without breaking the kiss.

Finally drawing away moments later, he leaned his forehead against hers. "Is it too late to elope, like your sister did?"

She brushed a final kiss against his jaw. "That ship has sailed. You lost your chance when Mia got married."

He groaned low. "I know."

She thought he was mostly joking about calling off the royal wedding. It was too late now anyway, as the cathedral where her mother and father had been married was being prepared. The invitations had gone out weeks ago—to nearly five hundred guests—and her sisters would be her attendants, as was tradition.

She couldn't wait to be married to Gideon, but she also couldn't forget why they'd come here. "Maybe we can patch Mia in on the meeting with a video call. Do you think Cindy will mind?"

A tiny bit of tension returned to his shoulders. "We still aren't sure she's your sister."

She nodded. They hadn't been able to match up financial records, although they could always do a DNA test, though that could take weeks. But she was cautiously optimistic that this was the lead they'd been waiting for.

"When can we set up a meeting?" she asked.

He sighed again. "I'll reach out to her when she arrives tomorrow. If she is your half sister and she knows it, she may not be receptive."

Alessandra couldn't think about that. She had to keep hoping.

And then take her new sister home to say goodbye to their father.

———

TIME HAD BEEN tight when they'd hit traffic in Austin, but they'd made it to the fairgrounds with an hour to spare before McKenna's interview. She'd been here once as a small child and the venue still seemed as huge as it had back then with its stock barn, show barn and outdoor arenas. Could she really win at an event this big?

After the fiasco of her broken down truck, she hadn't had time yet to form a new plan and knew that Pieter planned to check into a hotel later.

She had no funds for that. She'd planned to bunk down at one of the cheap hotels near the fairgrounds—if she could find an available room at this late date—but now she needed to find a way home. She couldn't count on winnings from this rodeo, and who knows how much money it would take to get her horse home. She needed to conserve what little cash she had left.

She didn't have time to worry about where she'd sleep tonight. Right now, she had to face this interview. She found a public restroom and washed up as best she could, dressed in the slim, dark wash jeans and dress boots she'd bought for the occasion. She wetted her hair down in the sink and dried it with her hair dryer, then put it up in rollers and sprayed it with copious amounts of hair spray. Hopefully that would battle through the humidity in the air tonight.

Then she donned the glittery black snap shirt she'd chosen for the occasion. She focused on keeping her breathing even and deep. Ran through the instructions Pieter had given her. *Pretend the judge is Kylie. Breathe deeply. Keep composure. Think.*

She didn't understand him. Pieter had spent nearly an hour, at lunch and then on the road, coaching her. As if he'd had media training himself or at least been in the public eye often. She still didn't know anything about him.

Except that she'd thought he might kiss her back beside the interstate.

And she wasn't sure how she felt about that. Her cousins had often told her that her looks, her body, were the only things men would be interested in.

She'd been very careful not to put herself in a position that would prove her cousins right. She hadn't gone to prom. Hadn't ever been in the backseat of some teenage boy's car.

She'd never even been kissed.

And she had the sense that Pieter was a player. A rogue. That he had experience—a lot of it. Someone like him would probably laugh at someone as inexperienced as she was, thinking that he'd wanted a kiss.

She yearned to be valued for more than just her appearance.

She did the best she could with the makeup—she rarely wore any, and without a mom around, didn't know what she was doing—and took her hair down, spraying it again with the aerosol hairspray.

She'd left her black felt hat in the truck and needed to put her duffel back. The cooling evening air had her taking a deep breath, though it did little to calm her jangling nerves.

When she hit the gravel parking lot, Pieter was there.

He took one look at her and then a double-take. "What'd you do to your makeup?"

Her stomach flipped at his question and the horrified expression on his face.

"What?" Her face went hot, but she hid it as she opened the passenger door and tossed her duffel onto the front seat, then ducked around the open door to lean down and look at her face again in the side-view mirror.

"You've..." He rounded the front of the truck, moving toward her and shaking his head. "You can't go to the interview like that."

Was it that bad? She didn't think she looked like a clown or anything. "I did the best I could."

"Wasn't there any other woman in there who could've helped you?"

She shook her head. She'd been alone in the public restroom and knew that most of the other queen competitors were likely getting ready in hotel rooms or travel trailers. Besides, who would want to help a nobody like her, anyway?

"It's too late—" she started, but he shook his head almost violently.

"Do you have one of those makeup-remover wipes? Maybe we can fix this."

She did, though she had to dig through the duffel to get to the package.

"Where's your makeup bag?"

Seriously? He was going to do her makeup?

She guessed it was no more of a role reversal than her changing the tire on his truck. She motioned to the duffel—there wasn't anything she was ashamed of in there—and he pulled out the gallon-sized plastic zipper bag stuffed with the remnants of makeup she'd collected during her teen years.

She'd never purchased makeup for herself. When you were dirt poor, even the cheap drugstore stuff was out of range.

So when girls at school would leave the ends of their eyeshadow or blush in the bathroom, she'd take it. She wasn't proud of it, and it probably wasn't the most sanitary thing, but it was what it was.

She hardly ever wore it anyway.

But she saw the furrow of his brow as he looked through the odds and ends.

She scrubbed at her face with the wipe and pretended she didn't care.

———

"So you've done this before?"

Shadows fell around them as Pieter fought to keep his focus on the tiny eyeshadow brush he was wielding and not the smooth face beneath his fingertips. From this close, McKenna's lush lips were a distraction he could ill afford. Each breath she took warmed the skin of his chin and jaw.

"No," he admitted. "But I've watched."

He'd smeared plenty of lipstick before and watched as dates had reapplied their makeup. Sometimes on large wall-mounted mirrors. Sometimes on small compact mirrors.

And anything had to be better than the job McKenna had done on herself. The colors hadn't been natural, the base washing out her complexion and the too-dark blush making her look like a vampire or something.

He finished applying the smoky gray color that made her eyes pop and went back to the plastic bag McKenna had given him with her makeup inside.

That had been eye-opening.

"So... This is an interesting collection of makeup for an aspiring rodeo queen."

Her eyes remained closed. "My family doesn't have a lot of money."

He'd guessed as much from the sorry state of her horse trailer and the dilapidated truck, but this was... He didn't purchase makeup obviously, but he didn't think it could cost that much, even for the department store brands. She seriously didn't even have a couple hundred bucks for something so important in a pageant?

He was beginning to think perhaps her aspirations to be a rodeo queen were a long shot. Wouldn't the other girls have the very best?

Not that McKenna didn't look hot in those slender jeans that showed off shapely legs and that black button-up shirt that sparkled with her every movement.

But she was all country girl. They'd be polished.

Unfortunately, there was nothing to be done about it now.

He tried to remind himself why he was here, that he shouldn't care about some waif he'd picked up on the roadside. He'd only given her a lift because he wanted the boon, hadn't he?

What did it matter if she failed in her little mission? He wouldn't see her again after this weekend.

Except it mattered to her. Couldn't forget the pinched expression on her face when she'd hung up on her cousin, or the determination she'd shown when he'd peppered her with questions over lunch.

"So how'd you end up with your horse?" he asked. "If your family isn't well off?"

Pieter didn't know anything about horses, but even he could see that the animal was quality. Tall with strong lines, and that glossy black hair...

"He was my dad's. Dad was a small-time farmer with big dreams of breeding horses."

She'd mentioned her dad briefly before, that he'd passed away, and Pieter couldn't help noticing the little catch in her voice.

"You should see him perform..."

Her voice trailed off, her eyelids fluttered open, and he was distracted by the depths of her eyes. It took him a moment to realize she was still talking about the horse and not her father.

"I mean, if you aren't busy tomorrow, the horsemanship competition is during the early afternoon."

Soft pink rose into her cheeks. He could almost feel the warmth beneath his fingertips as he smoothed out the blusher on her cheeks.

"I'm not sure I'll be around. I'm heading out to find a hotel in a bit." He let his hands fall away from her. Needed the distance. "Finished. You can do the lipstick yourself."

He tossed the blusher back into the plastic bag and held out the softer pink color than what she'd previously been wearing—a bright red that had clashed with her blush.

She bent slightly to see herself in the truck's side mirror. "Huh. You did a good job."

It certainly wasn't perfect, wouldn't stand up to the models he'd dated before, but it was much better than what she'd done.

She pursed her lips slightly, applying the lipstick quickly.

He moved another step back when she straightened, smacking her lips together lightly. "Thank you."

He nodded.

She put the lipstick back and turned away momentarily, then placed a black cowboy hat atop her head, completing her look.

She might not be perfect, but she was stunningly beautiful. If the judge was a male, no matter what age, he would have trouble concentrating on the event and not the woman.

"Okay," she said on a breathy exhale. She shook out her hands, and he couldn't help but notice her trembling.

"You'll be fantastic," he said, because it seemed like the right thing to say. And some small, long unused part of him wanted to comfort her in the face of her nervousness.

But instead of smiling back at him, her head tilted slightly to one side, and she seemed to be searching his face. There was no mistaking the hint of vulnerability in the depths of her eyes.

And, stupid him, he reached out and squeezed her hand briefly, the contact with her ice-cold digits a small shock. "I promise," he said, though he really couldn't promise any such thing.

But the slow smile that dawned across her face made him not care if his words were true. He'd do nearly anything to see that smile again.

*Chapter Five*

It was dark when McKenna returned to the fairgrounds parking area where Maximus's trailer remained, now unhooked from Pieter's truck.

There was movement inside the different RVs parked all around, muted voices from other queen contestants and rodeo competitors.

It made her feel a little lonely, trudging back to her horse trailer all alone. What would it be like if her mom had been alive? If she'd come along on McKenna's adventure? If she'd been waiting, ready to encourage her or mop up tears?

Or if her dad had still been here, cheering from the stands?

It was hard to imagine and a little silly to even think about. McKenna didn't need anyone waiting for her.

Good thing, too, because Pieter's truck was gone, just like he'd said. She hadn't expected him to stay, not really. He'd only come to the rodeo to meet up with his cousin, and somehow he'd taken her on as a little side project along the way.

She had to remember she still owed him a favor. He wasn't being kind to her out of the goodness of his heart.

Hadn't her cousins taught her that men couldn't be trusted?

But even as these thoughts swirled through her mind, a flare of disappointment rose up. She was sorry that Pieter had gone.

She wanted to tell him that she'd aced the interview. She'd passed by two other competitors—both of whom had given her scathing once-overs before turning up their noses at her—on her way into the small room set aside for the interview. She'd seen their designer knee-length denim skirts, seen that their shirts were silk or satin or something much more expensive than hers, but she'd done what Pieter had suggested and pretended they didn't exist.

The judge, an older woman who looked like she'd probably seen pageant days herself, was kind and had seemed receptive to all of McKenna's answers. They talked for nearly an hour, and it had almost been like chatting with a real friend.

So much of McKenna's confidence had been a result of Pieter's parting words.

*He believed in her.*

He didn't even know her, but he believed she could do it.

She knew he was hiding something, knew that some of his motives might not be pure.

But she was drawn to him anyway.

She slipped into the horse trailer, stowed her hat and switched her boots for the sneakers she'd left there. Maximus was settled in the rented stall she'd reserved for him in the stock barn nearby. She'd checked on him on her way out here and found him sleeping peacefully.

She didn't like leaving him alone in an unfamiliar place with different sights and sounds than he'd have at home, but she also couldn't stand leaving him out in the trailer all night, small as it was. She needed him at his best tomorrow.

And what about herself?

She'd found the women's locker room, which did have a shower, so at least she'd present herself clean tomorrow.

If it hadn't died, she could've slept in her truck. It wouldn't have been the most comfortable of places, but...now it looked like it was the trailer floor. And the door didn't lock from the inside, which meant she was unprotected.

Not for the first time did she question if all this was worth it. At least living with her aunt and uncle, she had the security of a roof above her head, if not much else. Maybe she was dreaming too big, thinking she could be an attorney, could really help people.

She remembered those dark moments when she'd realized her father was never coming home. She didn't want that for another little girl. If this didn't work, she'd find another way to fund her education. But for now, she was stuck here.

There was nothing for it. She would have to make the best of it and pray that any dark circles that appeared on her skin wouldn't be too harsh tomorrow. She was purposely avoiding thinking about where she'd spend the night tomorrow. With rain in the forecast, the trailer would be soaked and miserable.

She changed out of the black button shirt, opting for a tank top beneath her sweatshirt—an oversized, beat up old thing that she loved —and curled up in a ball at the front end of the trailer. If no one knew she was in here, she'd be safe. Right?

But then a pair of headlights swept over her with a flash through the trailer slats. She shielded her head with her elbow, working to be as still and small as possible. Probably whoever that was would think she was some tack and wouldn't even look in the trailer.

The headlights cut off, but the truck remained idling.

Her heart sped. Even more so at the sound of a door slamming shut and boots crunching in gravel.

"McKenna?"

That was Pieter's voice. She didn't think she moved, but maybe she'd flinched when he'd said her name.

There was a creak of metal, then a flash of a light in her face. She winced and hid behind her elbow again, but he adjusted the light—his phone. He must be using a flashlight app.

"What are you doing in there?"

There was no use trying to hide now, so she stood and made her way out of the trailer. Her mind scrambled for some way to convince him to go on his merry way.

He took her elbow to help her as she stepped onto the pavement.

"I came back to see if you needed a ride to your hotel. What the heck are you doing curled up in the back of your trailer?"

She didn't have to answer for him to get it, because even in the low glare from the light post several cars away, she saw his eyes go dark.

But she didn't understand what he was angry about. A muscle ticked in his jaw, and he clamped her elbow. When he spoke, his accent seemed to thicken.

"Please tell me you weren't going to try and *sleep* in your *unlocked* trailer in the middle of this fairgrounds."

She heard echoes of her cousins' cruelty. *Stupid. Brainless. You'll never amount to anything.*

She jerked her chin up. "I'm an adult. I can stay here if I like."

"You're an adult. Then perhaps you should start *acting* like one."

His lips curled into a snarl, and she tried to wrench her arm away from his grip, but he held her too tightly.

"Let—" *Go.*

Before she could get the word out, his lips descended on hers with crushing intensity.

———

Pieter hadn't meant to kiss her.

He hadn't meant to let his emotions get the better of him. When was the last time that had happened? When he was thirteen and had gotten into a shouting match with Mother?

But now that he'd kissed McKenna, he found he couldn't stop with just one.

He'd meant the first kiss, not as a punishment, but an expression of the anger and the paralyzing fear he'd felt when he'd seen her and realized what she was doing, or trying to do.

But she'd frozen beneath his touch, both his lips and his hand at her elbow, and instead of continuing the punishing kiss, he softened his lips and pulled away slightly. Just far enough to brush butterfly-light kisses against the shadows of her eyelashes, one across her cheek before he returned to her lips.

This time, he started gently, teasing her lips until she responded, until she opened to him.

He used the hand at her elbow to draw her closer, let his opposite hand come up to cup the nape of her neck.

He didn't know why he found her so tempting. She was too young for him, he was too jaded for her.

But he couldn't stop what was blossoming between them. A big part of him didn't want to.

Then he pulled back slightly, intending to brush his fingers over the softness of her cheek before diving in to her addicting lips again.

But the few inches of distance gave him enough room to see the burning hurt and tears pooling in her eyes.

She pulled away from his hold. This time he let her go, but not without his stomach pitching as if he'd skydived off a skyscraper.

She turned and crossed her arms over her middle. As if to protect herself.

From him.

What had he done?

"Come back to my hotel room with me," he said. His voice emerged rougher than he'd intended. He'd booked the last room at the nearest hotel. The desk clerk had been talkative and told him twice how lucky he was.

McKenna shook her head almost violently. He saw her throat move as she swallowed.

Passion and confusion might be clouding his judgment, but he couldn't bear to see the hurt. He'd certainly not meant to put it there.

He closed his eyes against thoughts of her vulnerable, lying in that unguarded trailer all night. Alone. Defenseless. She was small, slight. Easy prey for someone with evil intentions. He couldn't stand it.

"I'm calling in my boon," he said before he'd really thought it through.

Her eyes flashed and her chin came up. "I already said I wouldn't sleep with you."

"I'll sleep on the floor." This time his voice was tinged with desperation. Something he'd never wanted to feel again. "Or in my truck. Just don't stay out here alone. Please."

He should've known that it would be the *please* that did it, that got her to look at him again. She nodded slightly, quickly turning her face away again, though, before he could do more than see the tears still sparkling, unshed, in her eyes.

At least she'd agreed. Where she'd sleep was one less worry.

———

How exactly had he ended up here?

Pieter was a prince of Glorvaird. He'd never slept on the floor before in his life, except for those few awful nights during his childhood. He didn't like to think about those times. Ever.

But now he shifted on the uncomfortable thin carpet, a T-shirt and his sweatpants his only shield from the itchy fibers. His head rested on his bent elbow, and he stared up at the ceiling and the small red light that shone from the smoke detector. The pillow was missing half its stuffing and did nothing for him. Neither did the light blanket he'd found in the small hotel closet.

McKenna breathed deeply and evenly from the queen bed nearby. She'd wanted to refuse his offer to purchase supper. Maybe she didn't want to accept his charity, or maybe she didn't want to owe him.

He hadn't realized she was in such dire straits, even with the broken-down pickup and secondhand makeup bag. Should he have left her on the side of the road, instead of bringing her here? At least she'd been closer to family there, and surely one of her annoying cousins would've come and picked her up. Probably. Maybe.

He'd had to talk faster than ever before in his life to get her to accept a couple of slices of the pizza he'd bought from a fast food place on the way to the hotel. Surprising him again.

She'd practically inhaled the awful, cardboard tasting stuff, sitting cross-legged on the bedspread with no plate, only a paper towel in hand, watching television.

With her long hair spilling over her shoulders and her makeup all washed off, she looked like a teenager. But she'd kissed like a woman. Maybe an inexperienced woman, but he'd never felt such powerful emotion in a kiss.

Until she'd started *crying*. Had he frightened her? That certainly hadn't been his intention.

And what had been his intention?

No, he didn't want to go there, because he certainly hadn't been thinking, only reacting.

He couldn't tell whether McKenna had actually shed any tears, though, because she'd kept her face turned to the window the entire, silent ride to the hotel. She hadn't sniffled, hadn't wiped at her face, so he didn't *think* she'd cried, but she'd been close.

What had he been thinking, kissing her like that? He hadn't, obviously. He'd been turned upside-down, as if he'd taken a hard tumble from a fast-moving bicycle.

How had things gotten so terribly mixed up?

He'd lost his focus. He'd come to the States for one reason only.

But somehow, from the moment he'd met her, his focus had shifted to McKenna and her troubles. Her innocence and her mission to win the pageant.

He tapped the fingers of his free hand in cadence against his chest. Then just his pinkie. His family crest ring was warm against his skin. Its weight reminded him of his purpose, reminded him that he hadn't checked in with the hospital. Probably his Mother had upset a nurse. It wouldn't be the first time, and he didn't feel a particular urgency to call. It could wait until morning.

Ah, Mother. All the reminder he needed that he couldn't afford to be tied up with McKenna.

He could never forget the little eight-year-old boy he'd once been, an innocent child, locked in the pitch-black closet of his mother's suite of rooms. Just the once, just one night. She'd put him there in a fit of temper.

When she'd let him out the next morning, she'd been all apologies and tears until he said he forgave her. But saying the words aloud didn't necessarily make them true, did it?

Because he still remembered the awful fear of being alone in the dark, remembered screaming until he'd gone hoarse, remembered banging on the closet door, praying she'd come back.

But she didn't come back.

And he remembered curling into a ball, shedding silent tears because he wanted a *normal* mother. Not one who sometimes lived in her own head for weeks at a time. Not one who forgot important dates, like when she was supposed to deliver him to his boarding school. One who forgot his birthday. Not one who cared nothing if he ate or starved.

And not one who maintained delusions of grandeur, imagining that she deserved the crown herself.

All he'd wanted was one person who loved him. Someone to take care of him.

And he'd been so resentful of the cousins that Mother had told him about. The ones who had a mother *and* father. Who never had to fear for their lives.

Where had they been all this time? Living in their Glorvaird castle.

When *he'd* needed someone.

Fury and resentment boiled through his veins, igniting the dormant emotion that had spiked next to McKenna's trailer. He'd stuffed away the desperate fear and anger at her carelessness in his effort to protect her.

He'd make a bank withdrawal tomorrow, that's what he'd do. He'd force McKenna to take some cash—or, if she absolutely refused, he'd hide it on her person. Then he'd wash his hands of her. She wasn't his problem.

And he didn't want to have to see that fear in her eyes.

It was like looking into a mirror from his childhood, one he'd ached to escape for so long.

He couldn't bear it again.

# Chapter Six

McKenna had slept hard and woken with her left arm asleep—a sign she hadn't moved in hours.

The hotel room was empty, sunlight streaming through a crack in the blinds. Pieter had left a short note on the dresser saying he'd had to run an errand and would return shortly.

And she was a little glad. She didn't know how to deal with the crazy emotions that the night before had made her feel as if she'd been bucked from a bull.

Her first kiss. And boy, what a kiss it was. She'd never imagined that kissing someone could feel like that. Like she was competing in a barrel race, adrenaline skyrocketing, galloping horseback flat out, the wind in her face. And how could somebody feel all that and as if they were spinning at the same time? No wonder she was all jumbled up.

She'd felt... like she'd mattered to him.

But she hadn't been able to quiet her thoughts and one important question: *why* had he kissed her?

Because she'd made him angry? Or because he wanted something from her? Because he certainly hadn't kissed her because she mattered to him. How could she when they barely knew each other?

Was he just using her?

All her cousins' voices in her head had frightened her, as had the intensity of her emotions, and she'd pulled back.

She didn't want to be just another notch on Pieter's bedpost. Another one of the women he'd dated.

It would be better if they both went their separate ways today. She knew that.

But she couldn't forget hint of vulnerability he'd shown when he'd persuaded her to stay in his room last night. There had been something behind his eyes, something he wasn't saying that had prompted his actions. It confused her.

She ran through the shower and donned the pale jeans and shirt she'd wear for the horsemanship round midmorning. Tonight would be the fashion show, and she wasn't ready to think about that. To remember Pieter as he'd applied her makeup. Close enough to kiss.

When she emerged from the bathroom, Pieter still hadn't returned, but a local newspaper had been shoved beneath the hotel room door. She carried it to the bed and started reading, her ear half on the door to listen for Pieter's arrival.

The current event headlines were depressing, and she flipped to the local news section, where a picture of a beautiful blonde woman in a fancy ballgown graced the front page of the section.

*Princess Alessandra of Glorvaird rumored to be in Austin for rodeo.*

A real-life princess? Here in town? It seemed ludicrous. McKenna read through the article quickly. It talked about an assassination attempt from months ago, how the princess had met a real Texas cowboy and fallen in love.

There weren't any details about whether the princess would visit the rodeo, only speculation as to why she'd come to Austin and whether the rodeo was the draw.

But niggling questions darted through McKenna's head like minnows in a shallow pond. She didn't know where Glorvaird was—somewhere in Europe, possibly?—but Pieter had an accent. He'd claimed to be attending the rodeo to meet his cousin, but he hadn't said that the meeting was *planned*. His new clothes, the fancy rented truck. How his hands were more manicured than hers.

It was all circumstantial evidence, but... could Pieter be cousin to a princess?

Would that make him a *prince*?

It seemed crazy. Completely crazy.

She heard the electronic lock click as the door unlocked. Pieter pushed the door open slowly, peeking inside.

"Good, you're up." He came into the room and closed the door behind him. He wore a crisp black T-shirt, another pair of pressed, brand-new Wranglers, and those stupid dress boots.

Was he trying to fool someone? Pretending to be something he wasn't?

It was subtle, but he seemed different than he had yesterday. More closed off. Or maybe she was imagining things, trying to make him fit the image of a prince that was now burned into her brain.

She held up the paper for him to see the princess's photo.

"Is this your cousin? The one you're trying to meet?"

His face went white beneath his tan, which was confirmation—sort of.

She jumped to her feet, unable to remain still. "You're a... a prince? Why didn't you want me to know?"

Why was he trying to dress like a cowboy instead of the royalty he was? That behavior—it was suspicious, that's what it was.

He pushed one hand through his hair. "It's complicated."

She let her hands rest on her hips. "I'll bet. And the country girl wouldn't be able to understand it?"

He frowned. "Ha. Look, I didn't want to announce my arrival because I'm not sure she'll see me if she knows I'm here. We're not...close."

His expression might be closed off, but she sensed he wasn't telling the full truth. "So you didn't tell me because...?"

"What does it matter? I didn't tell anyone. It was a lucky guess on your part."

She snorted. "Not likely, not the way you're trying to dress. And your accent gives you away."

He didn't seem to have a response for that. He twisted a ring on his little finger.

"What's so important about you meeting up with her anyway?"

Pieter turned away. He ran one finger over the edge of the dresser across the room, his shoulders tense and set.

There was a small wall-mounted mirror, and she could see the side of his face, the muscle jumping in his jaw again, and the angry set of his lips.

And she couldn't help remembering what she'd just read. Someone had tried to assassinate the princess.

And suddenly her heart was pounding.

"You're not going to...hurt her. Are you?"

She wasn't sure where she got the courage to say the words. Maybe all those arguments with her cousins, trying to prove she could be something they said she never could.

He didn't respond.

Was his silence confirmation?

After the way he'd insisted she not be alone last night, the things he'd done to help her get here to Austin and get through her first interview, she couldn't imagine him trying to physically harm another person.

Had she been that wrong about him this whole time? *Had* she accepted a ride from a criminal?

She took two sidesteps toward the door.

He caught sight of her in the mirror, whirled, his eyes a little wild. "Are you kidding me? You're scared of me *now*? Not of spending the night in the same room with me, but you think I'll what...try to kill you?"

He was angry. Sparks flew from his eyes, but he didn't make a move toward her. And if she wasn't mistaken, there was also a hint of pain there...

She crossed her arms, stuck out her chin, and stood her ground.

"Then what? Tell me what you came to Austin for. Because sneaking around the way you are doesn't exactly seem like the behavior of someone trying to reconcile a broken relationship."

———

Pieter blew out a frustrated breath.

It didn't help.

He'd judged McKenna all wrong. She might be young, and naive, and innocent.

But she wasn't stupid.

She'd figured out his identity from a newspaper article.

"I don't want to *physically* hurt her," he said finally. He felt slimy just admitting this aloud.

Admitting the truth aloud made his plan sound...petty.

"But if I find something that would make her life a little more miserable, I would use it."

It was the least the princess deserved for his pain.

But McKenna looked at him as if she wanted to recoil. As if he'd betrayed *her* somehow.

Which was crazy. He'd saved her from the side of the road yesterday, had provided her food and a safe place to stay. He'd helped her.

He didn't owe her anything.

And he didn't like how he felt when she looked at him like that.

It was a look he'd seen in the mirror, directed at his mother. But he wasn't his mother, and he never would be.

"That's not very...noble," she said finally. Quietly. Like she was resigned that he wasn't going to change his mind.

Why should he?

"I'm afraid my title is more of a formality than anything," he said. He couldn't contain the trace of bitterness in his voice. "My mother was forcibly removed from the kingdom before I was born. I've never met my cousins, never stepped foot in the royal palace. So if I don't act exactly like a prince, perhaps that's why."

Her eyes were shadowed as she looked at him. His words hadn't changed anything. He'd known they wouldn't.

And he couldn't forget the decision he'd come to in the night. It was better to part ways now.

"I'll drive you back to the fairgrounds," he said. "If you want a ride. Or I can call a taxi for you. I've been to the bank and made a withdrawal. I thought...I want you to have it."

He held out the wad of large bills he'd pulled out of the bank earlier. She stared at it as if it was something disgusting.

"I don't want or need your money," she said. "I appreciate all your help, but I can take care of myself."

He'd thought she might say something like that. He shrugged and stuffed the bills in his front pocket—for now. He'd sneak the money into her duffel when he got the chance. Then he'd probably not see her again all weekend.

It was for the best. They both knew it.

But the silence as he drove her back to the fairgrounds was fraught with condemnation, and a boulder that felt suspiciously like guilt settled deep in his gut.

Chapter Seven



At the rodeo grounds later that morning, Pieter didn't think he was doing a horrible job of blending in with the other cowboys, especially since he'd taken McKenna's advice and worn a plain T-shirt instead of the dressy shirt he'd bought.

He couldn't do anything about the boots now.

Rough-and-tumble men were everywhere, traipsing around the dusty outdoor pens near the rodeo arena. A sense of anticipation swelled in the air, or perhaps it was the pressure and humidity building for the coming storm front predicted to arrive later in the day. Whatever the cause, everyone was talkative, especially the bull riders.

Biking as a sport had its inherent risks—such as getting in a crash at nearly forty miles per hour with nothing but a jersey to protect you from the road—but these guys willingly went into the arena against thousand-pound animals that wanted to kill them.

They were crazy.

Of particular note was a handsome blond bloke who didn't seem to talk or brag all that much. Cody Austin. Pieter had heard it rumored that he and Gideon Hale, Alessandra's fiancé, were buddies from elementary school or some such. Pieter kept the man in his peripheral vision but hadn't spoken to him.

Instead, Pieter was talking to two other riders not too far from where Austin sat on the pen railing. That's when he caught the perfect opportunity.

Alessandra's fiancé approached Austin. They exchanged a friendly handshake, and Hale asked whether Austin was still coming to his wedding.

It was rumored that the fiancé was special ops, and Pieter could readily believe it the way the man scanned for danger all around him. He had a stance that said he could kill you easily—probably with his little finger.

Hale's eyes skimmed right over Pieter without taking notice. Lucky for him, the two cowboys he was talking to made him look like he belonged.

Pieter talked with the two men long enough for it not to be suspicious and then pretended to take a call on his cell. He edged closer to Austin and Hale.

With his phone to his ear and his arm partially blocking his face, he hoped they wouldn't be able to see that he was eavesdropping.

"...how well do you know Cindy? Rumor is you dated her."

Austin snorted. "You know how the rumor mill can be, especially on the circuit. We've crossed paths a few times, but that's all."

Hale didn't seem about to hear that. "I hoped you might have her number."

"Stepping out on your princess already?" Austin teased. Brave soul.

That was juicy, but Pieter didn't believe it for a second. Hale was after something else. The question was, what?

One of the bulls in the pen bellowed and butted the fence on the opposite side, snorting and blowing with strings of saliva running down from his mouth.

Hale and Austin were distracted, started talking about bulls and Austin's draw.

Pieter knew he couldn't keep standing here for long without drawing suspicion, so he pretended to hang up the phone and acted as if he were texting instead. His chance to find out anything was dwindling, and he knew it.

And then he got incredibly lucky.

From his peripheral vision, Pieter saw Hale craning his neck to look all around. He spoke in a low voice. "Look, the truth is... Alessandra and I are trying to track down someone, and we think Cindy might be her."

Austin was quiet for a moment. "What, does she owe you money?"

Hale sized up his friend. "You seem awfully protective for someone who's only an acquaintance."

Austin gave a one-shouldered shrug. "Folks on the circuit gotta look out for each other." Nice evasion.

Hale was silent for a long moment, focusing on the other man. Finally, he sighed. When he spoke, his voice was even lower, and Pieter had to strain to hear.

"Alessandra's... half-sister...just found out...trying to locate her..."

A half-sister? Now *that* was the kind of information Pieter had hoped to find. He'd read every biography, newspaper article, and tabloid story about his cousins and the King. Once, he'd even attempted to bribe a royal staffer. There'd never been any hint of a scandal of this proportion.

An illegitimate child. A lost princess.

He turned away, satisfied for now that he had something he could use against the royal family when the timing was right. He definitely didn't want to draw Hale's attention. He ducked behind a stock trailer, pausing for a moment just to digest this new information.

Leaking this to the press would put a dark spot on the royal family's reputations and would likely create a media storm.

And... It sounded as if Alessandra wanted to find her sister. If a media storm blew up, would the sister she didn't know pull back from the relationship?

Now *that* was a punishment fitting for his cousins. But... Was it enough?

He needed to think about this.

He was making his way among the trucks and trailers when he caught a flash of what might be McKenna's hair.

She had her riding event this morning, didn't she?

He shouldn't go anywhere near her. She knew his identity and if she wanted to, could blow any sense of cover he had. Although now that he had this information about a lost princess, he wasn't sure he needed to keep his identity hidden.

And somehow he couldn't keep his feet from taking him in that direction.

He didn't have to talk to her. Didn't have to get close to her. He'd stand in the back somewhere and watch.

Just watch.

———

MCKENNA WAITED on Maximus's back, just outside the arena gate. Another few seconds and she'd be riding the horsemanship pattern in front of judges, contestants and a smattering of onlookers.

*Don't blow it.*

She and the other contestants had received notes on the horse-manship pattern, which was identical for all riders. If she couldn't remember the pattern and direct Maximus around the outdoor arena, she would lose points. If she couldn't get Maximus to obey, she'd lose points. If she was unseated, she could kiss her chances for winning goodbye.

And then, after the first round, she'd have to repeat the pattern on one of her competitors' horses. That might be the worst part, depending on how difficult or cranky an unknown horse could be. And it was luck of the draw.

"We can do this," she whispered to Maximus from her seat in the saddle. The other contestant exited the arena and McKenna nudged her horse forward.

She tried to ignore the judges, who were sitting on the front row of the arena stands. Ignored the building thunderheads above that made it necessary for the arena lights to be switched on.

*Just concentrate on the pattern.*

She raced Max across the dirt-packed arena floor and drew him up short, almost sending him to his haunches.

She nearly slipped her seat on the saddle and had to clamp her thighs tightly around Max to keep from doing so.

She hadn't meant to do *that*.

Face flaming at the amateur mistake, she forced a long exhale through her lips and kept moving. Left turn. Sidestep. Backwards. Tight circle.

Almost there.

She'd barely blinked and then was guiding Maximus out of the arena to a smattering of applause. She released the breath she'd been holding.

She maneuvered Max out of the way of the gates, where the next queen contestant, a young woman wearing bright pink from her hat to her boots, waited to be called inside. McKenna slipped off the horse.

She leaned her face against Max's shoulder. Maybe hiding a little. Distant thunder rolled, and Max's skin flickered, a sign of nerves.

"Good job," a female voice said from nearby.

McKenna looked across Max's back to see a girl in a pair of blue jeans, a purple dress shirt, and a white hat. She realized this girl had gone two ahead of her.

"I could've done better," McKenna said. "But thanks."

The girl winked. "I think that same thing every time I come out of the ring. I'm Danielle."

"McKenna."

"You're better than ninety percent of the other girls," Danielle said. "The rest is how the judges score it. Everyone makes little mistakes. Don't sweat it."

This girl thought McKenna was better than most of the other competitors? Was she for real?

Danielle must've seen the disbelief on McKenna's features because she laughed, a soft trilling sound that had Max's ears flicking, though he remained alert and calm.

"Is this your first contest?" Danielle asked.

"I won my hometown title last summer," McKenna said. "But I'm a total newbie."

"Well, you're a natural. Some of us have been going it awhile, and we don't handle our horses like you just did."

McKenna's face heated again at the unexpected praise. "How many times have you competed?"

"Too many to count. My mom and older sister made it all the way to Miss Rodeo USA, and I've been queening since I was eight."

Wow.

Danielle laughed again, softer this time and a little bitterly. "Yeah. It's a lot of pressure. If I can't get there this year, I'm out."

But at least she had family supporting her. Helping her.

McKenna was all alone, and too conscious of the fact since Pieter and she had parted ways earlier in the day.

"So your beau is a total hunk," Danielle said, breaking McKenna out of her morose thoughts.

"What?" she half-laughed. "I don't have a—"

Danielle pointed to the stands, and McKenna could see Pieter sitting at the highest level, not quite hidden in shadow but obviously trying not to be noticed.

As if someone like him could hide in plain sight. The man commanded attention wherever he went. Like yesterday in the diner, and just this morning he'd turned heads as they'd walked through the hotel lobby.

She couldn't see from this distance, but now that Danielle had pointed him out, McKenna felt Pieter's piercing gaze on her.

"He's been staring at you since before your ride," Danielle said.

"He's not my beau." McKenna averted her eyes.

Maybe she shouldn't have said what she'd said at the hotel, but she'd been blindsided to see another side of the man she'd come to think of as a hero. Which was silly, because she'd barely known him thirty-six hours.

Before she could protest again, the head judge moved to the side of the stands with a piece of paper in hand.

"She's posting the draw for the next round," Danielle said.

McKenna couldn't think about Pieter. All she had left was her dream. She couldn't afford to mess it up now.

———

THERE WAS AN ANNOUNCEMENT—A break due to the severe weather gathering overhead. Sprinkles splattered the metal bleachers even as the voice said they'd reconvene mid-morning tomorrow. The stands around the arena quickly emptied.

Pieter's stomach was gurgling, and he figured he'd tortured himself enough watching McKenna. She rode like a queen, controlling her horse with expert movements and exquisite grace.

She wasn't like anyone he'd ever met before.

Why did she have to appeal to him so very much? He'd dated plenty of women, wealthy, polished women, but there was something about her...

He made his way through the small throng of people huddling beneath a batch of umbrellas, careful to watch ahead and make sure he wasn't going to bump into McKenna.

But once he'd navigated around the largest cluster of people, loud voices drew his attention. There was a scuffle near the trailer lot. And he couldn't help but focus in on the black horse and the woman in the tan hat who seemed to be at the center.

He knew trouble when he saw it, and just the fact that McKenna was in the midst of it had him pushing past a few slow-moving grandmas.

Two men who could pass for taller versions of McKenna with their brown hair and hazel eyes flanked her, one attempting to edge between her and her horse.

"You've humiliated yourself enough."

"And us."

McKenna shook her head. Even from several yards away—and closing—he could see the color rising in her face. "How exactly have I humiliated you?"

"Everybody back home is talking—"

"That's their problem. Not mine."

Good girl.

Pieter was aware of the curious glances from several of the people nearby. And...was that one of the judges standing at a slight distance, watching?

The cousin closest to Pieter reached out and grabbed her elbow. "Look, you had your fun. It's time to go home."

McKenna tried to shake him off, but he was a head taller than she was, obviously much stronger, and he didn't let go.

Her horse neighed and bobbed its head, agitated. Thunder clapped loudly, and the horse's eyes went a little wild, the whites showing.

The girl standing a few feet from Pieter's elbow, the one he'd seen chatting with McKenna outside the ring, looked over at him. "If the judges see this, McKenna might be disqualified for poor behavior."

He didn't know why this girl thought *he* had anything to do with the situation, but her words were like taking a spill off his bike. He knew how much this event meant to McKenna.

He jogged a couple of steps and put himself between McKenna and her cousin, forcing the man to drop his hold on her.

He stepped closer, got into Pieter's face. "Who're you?"

"Todd...' McKenna said.

So this was the cousin who'd belittled her on the phone.

"If you want to talk, let's find somewhere more private," Pieter said, using the same commanding tone he'd affected with his mother when she wasn't in a mood to be reasoned with. "Or better yet, let's meet up after McKenna's next ride tomorrow. She needs to concentrate."

"She needs to come home," the second cousin said, joining his brother in Pieter's space.

Pieter glanced to see that the judge had remained where she was, and her entire focus was on this confrontation.

*She could be disqualified.*

He looked at McKenna, who stood at his elbow, and saw the resignation in her eyes. She was fully expecting her cousins to ruin her chances at being crowned rodeo queen.

He wasn't so accepting.

He smiled at her. "Why don't you take Maximus to his stall, and we'll meet up near your trailer," he suggested. The storms were threatening, but at least they could have a modicum of privacy there, in case her cousins got loud. He suspected they might.

Miraculously, her cousins agreed.

He waited until McKenna had led the horse away, then followed the cousins to the parking lot to make sure they didn't make more trouble for her. The two brothers stood several feet from him, arms crossed and silent. Tension roiled as thick as the humid pre-storm air.

McKenna joined them minutes later, panting and out of breath.

She slanted a glance at him. He couldn't tell whether she was relieved he was still here or wanted him to leave.

"Who's this guy, Kenna?" not-Todd asked, jerking his thumb in Pieter's direction.

Lightning flashed in the distance. The air around them felt electric with the storm about to break.

"A friend," he said

Todd laughed. "Oh, that's rich. Some rich boy like you making friends with our cousin?"

McKenna's face went crimson.

"This the guy who drove you down here?" not-Todd asked.

McKenna nodded.

"How much did you put out to get him to help you? You little—"

"That's enough," Pieter said, hearing the dangerous tone to his voice. He felt on the verge of losing control, his hands shaking as he fought to hold onto it. He couldn't lose his temper like his mother. "You shouldn't speak of McKenna like that."

Not-Todd's eyebrows went up. He took a step into Pieter's personal space but looked at McKenna. "Awful protective for someone you're not sleeping with."

"You should be more respectful of your own flesh and blood." His voice was cold, angry. He didn't back down, though the man had at least an inch and twenty pounds on him. And there were two of them.

"You should mind your own business," not-Todd said. "We've been telling her for years to watch who she sells her body to—"

Before he'd meant to move, he'd thrown the punch. The other man didn't see it coming.

Not-Todd went down, hard, but that left Pieter open to Todd's attack.

———

"I can't believe you did that," McKenna murmured.

She knelt in front of the trailer where Pieter sat holding a paper napkin to his lower lip.

His bleeding lower lip.

"They shouldn't disrespect you like that," he mumbled, but he wasn't quite meeting her eye.

She put both hands on his thighs, and his head came up, though he still held the napkin to his lip.

"No one's ever done something like that for me before," she said softly.

She hadn't believed it when she'd seen Pieter throw the first punch, had stood in shock when Todd responded with one of his own. She thanked God a security guard had arrived—said he'd heard from a gal named Danielle that there might be trouble out here. He'd broken up the fight and told her cousins the police would be called if they didn't get lost.

Her cousins had been escorted from the property and ordered not to come back. Which was a relief, but also had her second guessing herself. Was she doing all of this—and alienating the only family she had left—for nothing? Was it going to be worth it in the end?

She brushed a few strands of her hair out of her eyes. The humidity from the building storm was ruining her carefully-crafted curls. She looked down at the gravel between their knees.

"Maybe they're right," she said softly. "Maybe I *should* go home. I'm not sure I belong here. The other girls..."

"Your aunt and uncle should've taught them better," he said hotly. "They should be supporting you, not belittling you."

Her lips formed a sad smile. "My aunt and uncle might've taken me in, but they never bothered to care."

Pieter touched her chin, tipped her face up. "I know a little something about unfit parents."

"Your mom?" she guessed.

He nodded tightly. "Bi-polar. *And* schizophrenic." He snorted softly. "As if one weren't bad enough. Father's never been in the picture and..."

"I'm sorry." Her cousins weren't the easiest to live with, but his childhood sounded even worse than hers had been.

He clasped her hand and held it loosely between them. "You've worked hard to get here. You can't give up now."

She wrinkled her nose, made a face. "What if it was a fluke—the other contest?"

"It wasn't."

Looking into his confident, clear gaze, she could almost believe him. Wanted to, so very badly.

"You'll hate yourself if you give up now—if you don't even try."

He was right.

"I was a little surprised to see you watching the horsemanship contest," she said. "And you've come to my rescue again."

A hint of color crept into his neck, the only visible reaction to her words.

And so she went for it all. "You're more than this desire for revenge you carry," she whispered. "More than whatever it is your family's done to you." With a schizophrenic mother, she couldn't imagine what he'd been through.

His eyes were wary and watchful as she reached up. She pulled his hand away from his lip, took the napkin from him. There was only a small touch of blood on it, a small swelling at the corner of his mouth. He'd mostly evaded Todd's hit, even when her cousin had had the element of surprise.

"You've been my prince since this whole thing started," she said, looking straight into his face. "There has to be a better way to confront the situation than whatever you're planning. Act like the prince that you are."

She rose up from her crouch, surprising him as she brushed his lips with hers.

She couldn't maintain the kiss for more than a few seconds, which was fine, because her face was flaming now, and she couldn't help but compare herself to all the women he'd probably kissed before.

She stood straight as another growl of thunder ripped through the sky. "I've got to check on Maximus. And get ready for tomorrow."

She didn't look back as she made her way to the stables.

Because she wasn't giving up yet. Not on being rodeo queen.

And not on the prince she'd begun to care for.

*Chapter Eight*

SEQUESTERED IN HIS HOTEL ROOM LATER THAT afternoon, Pieter lay on the bed with his arms folded behind his head and stared at the ceiling again as rain poured down outside.

Turned out the bed wasn't much more comfortable than the floor.

Or maybe it was his own conscience that made it impossible for him to rest.

His mind had been spinning since McKenna had kissed him earlier in the afternoon.

He didn't understand her. How she could be treated so poorly by her family and still be kindhearted. She was driven, but not bitter.

She'd said he could *be better*.

The words had been like a cleansing waterfall, releasing something inside of him.

Or maybe it was her kiss that had felt like absolution. Like forgiveness, which he most certainly didn't deserve.

He didn't have to be like his mother. Seeking revenge, always grieving a crown that wasn't hers to have.

He could take the high road. Keep what he'd learned about the lost princess to himself, though it went against every molecule in his body not to use the information as a bargaining chip to benefit himself.

He could be worthy of McKenna. If he gave up his quest for revenge.

Did he want to do it?

*Could* he do it?

And if he did, what was he doing here in Austin? He'd come all this way. Could he leave empty-handed?

And what about McKenna? She had plans. Was college bound—he believed she'd get there eventually—and law school meant extra years in the classroom.

Was there even room in her life for him?

He didn't know.

But he wanted to find out.

———

IT WAS JUST after lunch the day after Gideon had met with his friend Cody Austin when the knock came at the door of their suite.

Alessandra glanced nervously at her fiancé as he went to the door. Out of habit, she smoothed the long pencil skirt she wore, standing beside the sofa but not moving.

She didn't want to scare her new sister the moment she walked in the door.

"Relax," Gideon said. He nodded to her hands, which she realized she'd twisted in front of her.

She was so nervous. This was a big moment for her. For her entire family.

She heard the murmur of his voice, but not his exact words as he opened the door.

And then a young woman followed him inside the suite, looking around in wide-eyed wonder. She was only a year or so younger than Alessandra. While Alessandra and her two biological sisters Eloise and Mia shared the same almost platinum blonde hair, Cindy's hair was more dirty blonde and was cut around her shoulders. Her eyes were brown instead of the blue Alessandra had expected.

But there was a different mother in the picture, she reminded herself. Of course her half-sister wouldn't be an identical match for the three princesses.

"Hello," Alessandra said, hoping her voice didn't betray her nerves.

"Howdy." Cindy nodded in Alessandra's direction, though her eyes still flicked around the room, taking everything in. "Nice place you got here."

"Won't you sit down?" Alessandra indicated the sofa facing hers, which would put a coffee table between them. "We've ordered refreshments, if you'd like a glass of tea or water."

The other woman sat, so Alessandra did as well. Gideon perched on the arm of the sofa beside her.

"I'm not that thirsty. Just real curious why I got a mysterious summons to meet you here. You really a princess?"

The girl's diction wasn't the best, and her twangy accent was much worse than Gideon's. But Alessandra could overlook that.

"We have a couple of questions for you," Gideon shot Alessandra a look that she interpreted as *don't jump the gun.*

She appreciated her fiancé and his careful approach, but she just really wanted to know if Cindy was her sister.

"Where were you born?" Gideon asked.

"Lubbock, Texas," the girl responded, though she looked a little suspicious.

"Have you ever lived in Kalispell, Montana?" Gideon asked.

Cindy crossed her arms. "For a little while. Why?"

Gideon put a hand to Alessandra's shoulder. "We're looking for someone. We've been keeping things very private, but Alessandra recently found out she has a half sister."

The other woman suddenly pealed with laughter.

Startled, Alessandra looked at Gideon, who appeared as flummoxed as she felt.

Cindy slapped her thigh and even wiped away tears before she quieted. "And you think"—she hiccoughed—"you think *I'm a princess?*"

Alessandra swallowed the unease that rose in her throat. "Yes."

Gideon shot her another look. "Your birthdate matches," Gideon said. "We'd tried to verify your birth certificate, but we've been running into roadblocks."

Cindy shook her head. "I'm not who you're looking for," she said, now serious.

"Our father—" Alessandra started, but Cindy interrupted.

"I know my dad. He's a deadbeat, not a king. Believe me, as a little girl, I wished all the time for someone to come and take me away."

Alessandra shivered.

Now the other woman stood. "This has been fun." Her tone indicated it had been anything *but.* "I'm sorry I'm not who you're looking for."

Gideon stood too, but Alessandra's legs were shaky and felt too weak to hold her.

"Would you consent to letting us do a DNA test, just to make sure?" Gideon asked quickly. "It's just a swab on the inside of your cheek."

Cindy shrugged. "I guess that'd be fine. Won't do you any good, though."

She and Gideon conversed in low tones as he helped her with the test. Just a few minutes had passed when Gideon stuck what looked like a cotton swab in some kind of plastic tube and then sealed it in an envelope.

Thirty seconds later, Cindy ducked out of the suite.

Alessandra remained on the sofa, stunned and inexplicably hurt.

That had gone all wrong.

———

LATER THAT NIGHT, Gideon found Alessandra staring out the hotel room window at the Austin skyline. She'd barely touched her dinner, hadn't wanted to talk after Cindy had left the suite earlier.

He hated seeing her despondent. He'd tried to warn her that things might not go smoothly in this search for the lost princess.

Now he sidled up behind her at the window, set his hands on her waist.

Thankfully, she leaned back against him, settling her head in the hollow of his shoulder.

He watched her reflection as she stared out the window. He search for any sign of tears. Alessandra was good at hiding her feelings, though usually not from him.

"I'm sorry things didn't go the way you wanted," he said softly.

She breathed in deeply. "You told me it wouldn't be simple."

"Doesn't mean I didn't want it to be."

She breathed in again, and it was shaky this time. "Thank you for that. Do you think we'll ever find her?"

"It's hard to stay hidden forever, at least from what I've seen. The DNA test might still come back with a different result than she thinks."

He didn't know whether to hope that could be true or not.

He talked Alessandra into sitting beside him on the couch as the room darkened around them. She curled into his side, and they played a local news station.

And then he was reaching for the remote and turning up the volume as a reporter interviewed a dark-haired man outside the rodeo fairgrounds.

He vaguely recognized the man, maybe had passed by him earlier or in the few days he'd been scouting the venue.

Now the man was dressed in a finely tailored suit. He spoke with the same light, cultured accent similar to Alessandra's.

"...name is Prince Pieter of Glorvaird. My mother was estranged from her family before she was born."

Alessandra sat up and perched on the edge of the couch.

"You know this guy?"

She shook her head. "I've never met my cousin."

"I'm seeking reconciliation with the royal family and have some information concerning recent attempts on the princess's lives that may be of interest."

The camera zoomed in on the guy. Dark hair, blue eyes. He looked very little like Alessandra, but the way he carried himself, the high cheekbones.

"I have no ulterior motives and would welcome a meeting with my cousin and whatever security she deems necessary."

The news moved on to other stories, but Alessandra continued to stare at the screen. Then she turned to him, her face curiously blank. "Do you think he meant it? That he wants reconciliation with our family?"

Gideon shrugged. "I'm more interested in what he said about the attempt on your life. You told me in the beginning you thought your aunt was trying to kill you."

She was quiet for a long moment. "Do you think he's a part of it? That he could be trying to make an attempt of his own?"

"I think that'd be pretty stupid after he just went on TV and announced himself." But of course Gideon was suspicious.

"You should call your sister," he said. "Maybe have Eloise talk to your dad. We need to find out why your aunt was banished and what he thinks about meeting with this Pieter guy."

She nodded slowly. He knew she had a tumultuous relationship with her father, but if the king told her not to meet with this cousin, Alessandra likely wouldn't.

But that didn't mean Gideon couldn't meet with him. He wanted answers about the attempt on Alessandra's life and assurance that it wasn't going to happen again.

He'd do anything to protect the woman he loved.

# *Chapter Nine*

Pieter had gotten the call late last night, but he hadn't been sleeping, as he'd been waiting for it.

He'd agreed to meet Alessandra's fiancé for breakfast in the hotel restaurant.

The firm knock on his door shouldn't have been a surprise. He finished knotting his tie and looked through the peephole. Gideon Hale.

He should have expected this. Didn't his mother love to show up unexpectedly? It was an intimidation technique Pieter was familiar with.

But today he wouldn't be intimidated. He fixed McKenna's kiss in his mind and opened the door. The former Navy SEAL pushed his way inside—Pieter was no match for his honed strength and didn't even try to block Hale's way.

He endured the pat down the other man insisted on and then straightened his tie and jacket as Hale proceeded to open the closet and every drawer in the room, even ducked into the bare washroom. Pieter stood in the center of the room, watching and waiting.

"If I was planning something against Alessandra, do you really think I'd leave evidence in my hotel room?"

He knew it was the wrong thing to say but resented the other man's suspicion. It wasn't as if the assassination attempt had been *his* idea.

"*Are* you planning something against Alessandra?" Hale got in his face. "Because I'll do anything to protect her."

It was a real threat, one that Pieter met head-on. He spoke steadily. "The only thing I want from my cousin is to reconnect with her. Our families have been separated long enough."

Hale continued his stare down, and Pieter met his gaze evenly. For once, he had nothing to hide. It was a feeling he'd rarely experienced.

Finally, Hale stepped back with a slow nod. "She said the same thing."

Pieter experienced a moment of hope. Maybe she was downstairs, waiting in the restaurant, but it was quickly extinguished when Hale said, "She's in talks with her sister and the king."

Whatever hope he'd been feeling disintegrated. The king had been the one to send his mother away, the one to keep both of them away.

"I think you'll find things have changed a lot in Glorvaird," Hale said, still slightly wary. "The king is...not well."

Pieter experienced a pang of sympathy for his cousin, one that would've been foreign to him before McKenna.

"Tell me what happened in New York," Hale demanded.

"Can we at least get breakfast? I'm starving." And ready to be in public instead of this private room with this very large, aggressive man.

Hale agreed grudgingly.

The restaurant in the hotel lobby was bustling with patrons.

As Hale sat across from Pieter, a flash went off from a few yards away.

A hostess rushed over to escort the camera-toting reporter out of the restaurant.

Hale glared at Pieter, who shrugged and smiled a little fiercely. He might be changing his stripes, but that didn't mean he had to give over *every* advantage. If the press saw him with Alessandra's fiancé, they would report favorably about him.

A waitress took their orders and filled their mugs with coffee. The booth in the corner was semi-private, and when she left, Gideon leaned forward. "Start talking."

Pieter told the solider about going on tour with the cyclists and returning home to discover his mother's sinister plot, how she'd gone off her meds and hired an assassin. He also shared what he'd done to fix it, paying off the men his mother had hired and heightening security around her.

He went on to explain how he'd come here to enact revenge on the royal family and even the fact that he'd gotten close enough to discover their secret mission. "But I won't do anything with the information."

Gideon looked skeptical. "Why the change of heart?"

Pieter's gaze was drawn behind his companion to a slender figure standing in the entryway near the hostess stand. McKenna.

What was she doing here? He hadn't seen her since last night.

Gideon turned, following Pieter's gaze.

Pieter half stood, letting McKenna catch sight of him and then enduring Gideon's curious look as he stood to greet her.

She wore a pair of what must be favorite jeans, worn as they were, and a tank top. Her hair was pulled in a ponytail behind her head. She looked just as she was, young and fresh and wholesome.

And she made his heart pound.

"Hey." She bussed his cheek with a kiss.

He was surprised by the confident move and found his hand rested at her waist naturally.

"You look... Princely." She looked him up and down, taking in the suit and tie, his usual apparel. He wasn't sorry to say goodbye to the cowboy-imposter clothes.

She looked delectable. If they were alone, he'd kiss her properly, find out why she'd sought him out this morning. He was brimming with hope.

But he was uncomfortably aware of Hale's gaze on his back. And then the other man said, "Why don't you join us...?"

There was nothing to do but make introductions.

McKenna slipped into the booth where he'd just vacated his seat, leaving him to slide in beside her.

The waitress brought their food, and McKenna declined to order anything, saying she'd eaten with a friend earlier.

He snuck her a piece of bacon anyway and grinned a little when she sipped from his coffee mug.

But his grin faded when Hale said, "I'd like to hear more about your mother."

———

McKenna felt the tension overtake Pieter and couldn't help reaching for him. She'd spent the night with Danielle and her mother in their RV, and they'd all been watching the evening news when she'd seen Pieter's segment.

She was running on instinct, coming to his hotel this morning. She'd only hoped to see him, talk to him after seeing him on TV.

She'd told him he could act the prince, and he had.

And maybe a small part of her wanted to know whether he was

still enacting his plan for revenge or if he was genuine in his desire for reconciliation with his family.

And now Gideon Hale had asked the hardest question of all. Pieter had mentioned his mother's mental illness but not gone into detail.

If he was really changed, if he was moving forward with his life trying to live up to the title nobody seemed to think he deserved, wouldn't he tell Mr. Hale what he wanted to know?

"One of my earliest memories is of my mother going into one of her rages," Pieter said quietly. He set his fork aside. Maybe talking about his mother made his appetite disappear.

She sidled closer on the bench and curled her fingers around the fist in his lap.

"Sometimes hours later, maybe the next day, she'd be apologetic and tearful, begging forgiveness."

He paused, and she saw the bob of his Adams' apple as he swallowed.

"With Mother, it's often impossible to tell whether she's genuine or trying to manipulate. Sometimes her tearful apologies were real, and others, they were simply designed to win me into her good graces once again."

How awful. She'd often longed for the mother she'd never known, but this... To know that your own mother was manipulating you... She couldn't fathom it.

"When I was a teenager, I tried to hide Mother's condition from everyone. I was embarrassed, ashamed. And there was always that part of me that ached for mother's approval—"

He broke off, continued with, "That's neither here nor there."

As if his feelings didn't matter.

"When the press began printing stories about her decline, she would—well, if she saw the newspaper, she would go into a rage. I was able to nudge her out of the public eye and have spent a lot of money hiring caretakers and doctors that would keep quiet."

Gideon nodded solemnly.

"I tell you this so you understand that my mother is not well and that her motives are not always clear. She often disappears in her own head for weeks at a time."

His shoulders steadied. "I don't know what happened between my mother and the king, only that she speaks sometimes of betrayal and plots. Whatever passed between her and your future father-in-law happened before I was born, before Alessandra was born. Whether my mother can be welcomed back into the royal circle, I don't know, but I shouldn't be exiled for something I had no part of."

Gideon sipped his coffee before speaking. "I can't guarantee a meeting," he said. "Alessandra is very careful with fulfilling her family duties. If Eloise or the King decline a meeting, I don't know that she'll go against them."

Pieter's hand tightened in its fist , though he betrayed no other outward sign of emotion. "I understand."

"But..." She started to say something. She didn't know what, but Pieter had come so far, and Gideon couldn't even see it...

Gideon nodded at her, then returned his gaze to Pieter. "Alessandra is very interested in reconnecting the family. I think with her father's condition uncertain and not knowing how much time he might have left, it's been hard on her. I think she's more aware how important family connections are."

Some of Pieter's awful tension eased at that. Enough that he released his fist and threaded their fingers together beneath the table.

It wasn't assurance that he'd get to meet his cousin, but it was a sign, however small, that his cousin hadn't rejected him.

———

ALESSANDRA PACED the unfamiliar suite's living area. She was unaccountably nervous.

What was Pieter like? Would he like her?

After Gideon's rendezvous with Pieter, she and her fiancé had made a video call to speak with her father and Eloise. They'd given tentative approval for a meeting.

And now the meeting time was here.

She'd also spoken to Mia on the phone earlier, and her sister had been just as excited about the meeting as Alessandra and wanted a full report as soon as he left.

Pieter was dark where she was light—Gideon had managed to find a picture of her cousin—and the wariness in his gaze as he entered the small sitting room at a separate hotel from where she and Gideon were staying threatened her composure. Gideon was taking no chances with her safety, even though he believed Pieter's intentions to be good.

"Thank you for taking the meeting with me," her cousin said, reaching forward, probably to give her hand a royal kiss, but she stepped toward him with both arms out.

He accepted her hug, embracing her loosely as Gideon watched.

Pieter's distance, the wary way he held himself, brought tears, and she found herself sniffling as they stepped apart.

"I'm sorry," she said, wiping away the few tears that fell.

Pieter looked as if he had no idea what to do with her tears. His eyes were wide, almost panicked.

Gideon chuckled and motioned the other man to sit down. Pieter took a wingback chair, leaving her and Gideon the sofa.

"I've been curious about you for a long time," she said. "I wanted to know you."

Pieter's expression was shuttered, but she had to believe she saw something like relief pass through his dark eyes.

"I've long wondered about you as well."

Gideon's phone buzzed from his hip pocket, and he excused himself to take the call. She didn't miss the tense lines around his face. She watched Gideon pace back and forth in front of the window on the opposite side of the room. His voice was low, and she couldn't hear what he was saying, but his expression grew more and more concerned.

She forced herself to concentrate on her cousin. "Gideon tells me you've someone special."

He lit up from within, though he remained reserved. It reminded her of her own expression in the mirror when she thought about Gideon and how much she loved him.

"It's very new—" Pieter started.

"We've got a problem," Gideon thundered, rushing back across the room. He reached for Alessandra, and she found herself being pulled to her feet before she even knew what was happening.

Gideon leveled a pointed finger on Pieter. "Your mother is missing. She's escaped the mental institution, and the orderly who helped her says she's bent on destroying the royal family."

Pieter looked as stunned as she felt. "I spoke to her last week. How could she have just left?"

Gideon squeezed Alessandra's elbow. "Perhaps you should've taken more precautions before *you* left the country."

She wanted to shush him, to keep him from wrecking the budding relationship with her cousin with his suspicions and protective nature, but he was already pulling her from the room. She knew he'd be on high alert, and she'd be in lockdown mode until he could pull in enough security to feel a modicum of safety again.

Why this? Why now?

# Chapter Ten

MCKENNA STOOD "BACKSTAGE" JUST BEFORE THE FASHION event of the pageant was about to begin, trying to calm her racing heart.

Each contestant would be called on stage, where she'd have to model her own fashion statement in western wear. The host judge would ask one question, drawn randomly from a pool of questions, and the contestant would have to answer in front of all these people. Then the contestants would line up on the long stage.

They had to wait, in front of everyone, as final scores were tabulated.

And then the new queen would be announced.

This was it.

Everything she'd worked for depended on this event. Although the scores for the horsemanship rounds and private interviews weren't publicized, she knew that without a good score in the fashion round, it would be impossible to win.

She was thankful her cousins hadn't shown back up, though she wondered if they'd returned home or were still waiting to watch her fail.

A cool hand touched her forearm, and she turned to fine Danielle at her elbow.

"I'm so nervous," the young woman whispered.

"But you've done this hundreds of times."

"Doesn't mean it gets any easier to walk out there and be judged on your appearance."

They shared a knowing look.

When the second round of the horsemanship competition had resumed yesterday, Danielle had found her. She'd thought maybe the young woman was looking for gossip, wanting to know what had happened with McKenna's cousins, but she'd been utterly surprised when Danielle had checked to see if she was all right.

Like a friend might.

When Danielle had found out McKenna didn't have any place to stay, she had offered a second bunk in her travel trailer, and McKenna had accepted, knowing she couldn't displace Pieter from his bed again.

Plus, after the kiss she'd delivered to him, she didn't know how to classify their relationship.

She'd been proud to be beside him at breakfast, but she'd had to leave to check on Maximus at the arena. She'd heard too many horror stories of horses injuring themselves because of being in unfamiliar surroundings. She wasn't about to leave him for long.

She didn't know whether she and Pieter could move forward from here. He was a prince. He was reconciling with his royal cousins.

And she had her own mission. First university, then law school.

"He's here," Danielle said, as if she knew who was on McKenna's mind. "About halfway up the stands, left side of the aisle."

McKenna peeked through a crack in the heavy curtain and caught sight of Pieter.

He'd come to see the final event. Because he cared for her, or just to see it through?

She didn't know, and there wasn't time to dwell on it, because the rest of the contestants were lining up behind the curtain. It was time to strut her stuff.

She had no strut, and she barely had any stuff.

But she wore the best charming smile she could muster as she walked onstage.

———

"FIRST RUNNER UP... MCKENNA HASTINGS!"

*First runner up.*

It wasn't what she wanted, but it was something.

Pieter watched as she graciously hugged the winning rodeo queen. Her smile seemed genuine.

Would she be disappointed? Excited? She'd beat out thirty other women, so she should be pleased. He waited in the stands as the other competitors and their families dispersed and the arena began to clear out.

He watched her talking to the young woman who'd called security the day before. They seemed to be friends now, and he knew that McKenna needed one.

Now the question remained...did McKenna need *him*? Did she have room in her life for a reformed prince?

He hung back near the bottom of the stands, and then finally she walked toward him. Her makeup was impeccable. The western-style long denim skirt with all its sparkles and a simple snap shirt accentuated her trim shape.

Her face was alight, though he read the slight disappointment beneath.

"Congratulations," he said, reaching out to take both of her hands in his.

She let him, which was one relief.

"I know it isn't what you wanted, but this could be a start for you."

She smiled, and her lips trembled a little. "Danielle...well, she made me an offer. She said I could travel along with her and her mom, bunk with them. They're hitting nearly every big pageant this season."

His insides squeezed hard. So she could still chase her dream.

He twisted his family crest ring. "That's wonderful."

Her brows crinkled. "What's the matter?"

"I have to visit Glorvaird." It was the last thing he wanted to say.

Her countenance fell. "Oh."

"It's my mother. She's disappeared."

McKenna's eyes widened. "Oh no."

"Oh yes," he said. "From what I can gather, she coerced one of the orderlies to help her, and she just walked out of the institution. I've tried calling her, phoning some of her local friends"—not that there were many—"but she's simply vanished."

"I bet your cousin wasn't happy."

"No." But it hadn't been Alessandra's reaction that bothered him. Gideon was the one he'd been slightly afraid of. After the soldier had told him the news, they'd descended into a shouting match until Alessandra had calmed her husband.

Gideon couldn't possibly blame him any more than Pieter blamed himself. He'd missed calls from the institution, telling him of Mother's escape. If he'd checked his messages sooner, would he have been able to rush home and find her before she'd completely disappeared?

There was a part of him that wanted to let it all go. Why did he have to be responsible for Mother? Wasn't she an adult, responsible for herself? He was so weary of it... Hadn't he suffered long enough? Of course, he knew she wasn't sane. Couldn't be expected to watch over herself.

McKenna seemed to understand his conflicting emotions. Her eyes were soft and compassionate.

Then her lips trembled slightly. "I'll pray for you to find her quickly. And for your peace."

He hated this. "I wish..." He swallowed against the hot knot in his throat that wanted to choke him.

She squeezed his hand, and he couldn't face the innocence in her eyes.

He looked down. "I wish things were different." That *he* was different.

The hall had slowly emptied around them. It was silent now, enough so he heard her soft sigh. "We both know we have to play the hand we're dealt."

He screwed up all his courage and met her eyes. "I'd like to..." Darn, this was hard. "We've only known each other a couple of days, but I think it's safe to say I'm falling in love with you."

Soft color crept into her face. "Me too."

Relief smacked him in the solar plexus and made it hard to breathe. He maneuvered her into a loose embrace, leaning his forehead to hers.

"I should probably try to talk you out of your feelings," he said, "but I'm too selfish for that." He breathed in deeply, trying to memorize her scent. "You've got a bright future—big things ahead. I don't want to take any of that from you. And I've still got to travel to Glovaird. But I'd really like it if you'd wear my ring. As a...promise."

She inhaled sharply as he let go of her to pry the gold ring from his finger. His hands were trembling. He knew he didn't deserve her, but by some miracle, she seemed to want him.

She allowed him to slip the ring on her fourth finger, and he curled her hand in his to admire his family's crest against her skin.

He lifted her hand to kiss her knuckles. "Until I can replace it with another kind of ring."

Her lashes were clumped with tears as she smiled up at him. He was happy—the happiest he'd ever been in his life—and found himself smiling like an idiot.

"Isn't this the part where you kiss me?" she asked.

"I'm trying not to mess anything up," he returned. He would

work harder than he ever had, make whatever sacrifices he had to make, if it meant keeping McKenna for his own.

Her hands curled around his neck, and her fingers threaded into the hair at his nape. "Then I *definitely* think you'd better kiss me."

So he did.

<h1 style="text-align:center">Epilogue</h1>

Three weeks after Alessandra's return to Glorvaird, Crown Princess Eloise sat in the family parlor in the centuries-old castle, listening to her two younger sisters argue. The DNA test for the barrel racer named Cindy had come up negative, leaving them without a lead as to their missing half sister.

But what the two sisters argued about now was of much less importance.

"Lilies are prettier," Mia said.

"But roses are classic," Alessandra returned.

Eloise's future brother-in-law, Gideon, walked in to the room, pocketing his cell phone and frowning fiercely. He'd been particularly intense since the princesses' aunt had gone underground after sneaking out of a mental ward where she'd been held for her own protection.

He moved to stand behind Alessandra, resting one hand on her shoulder, as if she were his touchstone. Alessandra looked up at him briefly, their gazes connecting.

Eloise had to look away, heart pounding uncomfortably against her sternum. She was happy for Alessandra, really she was. But seeing how deeply her sister was loved was a stark reminder of everything Eloise didn't have.

And never would.

She forced herself to concentrate on Gideon's words. "...we'll add a dozen guards for the grounds and another half dozen to check in the guests. Do you think that'll be enough men that it won't slow down traffic into the church?"

"Gideon, is that really necessary?" Alessandra asked. "We don't want the guests to feel as though they are going through security at an airport."

"There haven't been any credible threats, even with Aunty Beatrice on the lam," Mia said.

Gideon shot her a look. "If we let our guard down, we'll be vulnerable."

Eloise tuned them out. Her gaze drifted to the hallway. Father had promised to come down for a bit for family time, but it was already half an hour past his usual time.

Father's nurse stuck her head around the doorway and shook her head slightly.

Father wasn't coming.

The others didn't notice. Mia's husband Ethan had joined her on the sofa, and they spoke together quietly, heads bent close together. Alessandra and Gideon continued to argue, though Eloise knew Gideon was only concerned for his soon-to-be wife. Alessandra would relent, because she knew the same thing.

Eloise couldn't help the jealousy that speared through her.

It was a ridiculous emotion, one she wished she could eradicate.

Father was dying. There was no disguising the way his health had declined in the past few weeks. And while her sisters were wrapped up in their own lives with new husbands, Eloise remained alone and would soon have the pressure of ruling the kingdom on her shoulders entirely.

A kingdom of citizens who despised her. Some refused to look at her when she made public appearances.

Wild, hot emotion welled up inside her, and before she realized what she was doing, Eloise was on her feet.

"Enough," she screamed.

Mia jumped. The room went silent. Gideon's hand closed over Alessandra's shoulder protectively.

"None of your petty problems matter," she fumed. She didn't really mean the words but couldn't stop the audible flow of emotions.

Mia blinked, her eyes now glistening.

Before she could do any more damage, Eloise rushed from the room.

She ran through the castle's stone halls, brushing past a housekeeper before ducking through one of the servant's halls and out into the salty sea breeze on the private beach.

She gulped in breath after breath of the briny air, but it didn't help calm her roiling emotions.

It wouldn't be long now. Alessandra and Mia put up with her outbursts because they wanted to stay close to Father as his health declined. Once he was gone, what reason did they have to stay with their monster of a sister?

Soon she would end up all alone, alone with her beastly temper and what staff she could keep on.

She hated herself. Hated that she couldn't change things. Hated the scars that defined her life and had for years.

She'd wanted what her sisters had. Desperately, throughout her lonely teen years, she wanted someone to love her.

But who could ever love a beastly princess like her?

The Beastly Princess

*Chapter One*

A ROYAL WEDDING WAS A MEDIA CIRCUS.

Eloise hated it, and she wasn't even the bride.

What made it infinitely worse was the criticism the press had spewed continually about the royal family.

She had perhaps ten more minutes of privacy before she would need to face the five hundred pairs of eyes eager to look at her, to judge her.

She used her fingertips to flip through the newspapers that covered the desk in her private office, part of her suite of rooms in the royal palace.

*Royal Family Reveals King's Terminal Diagnosis.*
*Who's Really Been Running the Royal Family?*
*The Beastly Princess Strikes Again.*

Reporters were having the time of their lives criticizing her family and the way they ruled the kingdom, but they didn't understand the inner workings of her family. Not at all.

No one could know how much she feared being in the public eye, how much she detested it. How much she'd wished her father would live forever, instead of succumbing to the multiple sclerosis that kept him bound to his own suite of rooms.

Leaving the crown to her.

Lately, there had been rumblings from the royal council. The small group of men and women who assisted the royal family also advised Glorvaird's parliament. They were sensitive to the criticism in the media, and the council had been suggesting that they might take a proposal to the parliament that would change the laws that had been in place for centuries—and put her sister Alessandra on the throne.

At seventeen, Eloise had read the entire Glorvaird constitution, trying to find a way out. Unless there was a major change—like what the council was proposing—the law did not allow her to abdicate. While her younger sister, Alessandra, was much better suited to the public eye than Eloise was, she hadn't spent years learning the kingdom, like Eloise had.

There were sensitive trade agreements in play. Taxation that if weighted too heavily might crush the small businesses that were the backbone of their kingdom. Relationships with other national leaders that had been cultivated carefully over many years. Alessandra couldn't just step into being the reigning royal.

No, Eloise's people needed her too much.

But how could she rule when she loathed being seen by those very people she had the duty to?

The intercom on her desk phone buzzed. "Your highness? We're ready for you."

She shook away her melancholic thoughts as best she could and pressed another button on the phone. "I'll be right down."

She smoothed the floor-length skirt of the elegant gown her stylist had chosen for her. She'd been plucked, powdered, pulled every direction in the two-hour marathon makeup and hair session. She trusted they'd done what they could to improve her appearance. Nothing helped, nothing ever would.

She avoided the wall-mounted mirror as she exited her rooms into the hallway.

She could only pray that her ugliness wouldn't ruin Alessandra's perfect day. Her sister was deeply in love with her cowboy groom and deserved the very best on this day.

This would be Eloise's longest public appearance since her coronation as crown princess on her eighteenth birthday. She still had the scathing tabloid headlines from that event tucked in an envelope in her bottom desk drawer. They'd called her scars *horribly ugly, nasty,* and one publication had even written *cringe-worthy.*

Today, she wouldn't be standing up for her sister as a bridesmaid, though she'd wanted to.

She must represent the crown in her father's absence, so she'd watch from the first pew in the huge cathedral where her parents and grandparents had been married. Where she, as an innocent little girl, had dreamed of being married.

No longer.

Maybe it was better this way. Most of the five hundred wedding guests would have a view of her back. The only people who would have a good view of her face would be the minister and the bridesmaids and groomsmen—she doubted the bride and groom would have eyes for anyone but each other today.

In the expansive castle foyer, she found the new media specialist whom Father had hired. Jill was supposed to help Eloise navigate the minefield that the media had become.

"Right on time, Your Highness," Jill said. She was maybe a decade older than Eloise's twenty-eight. Perfectly coifed and wearing a professional suit jacket over a matching skirt and heels. She'd stay in the background at the wedding and the other upcoming PR events that Eloise was dreading.

"The car is waiting." Jill looked Eloise up and down. "You look great!"

But Eloise detected the note of false cheer in her voice and couldn't help noticing the way Jill's eyes darted quickly past on the scars across her face and neck.

"Let's go," Eloise growled.

As far as she was concerned, Jill's reaction to her scars was only the first of the thousand tortures she'd face today.

———

Professional bull rider Cody Austin had been to plenty of weddings before. Stood up for his friends a time or two.

But nothing like this. This was crazy.

He wasn't even that close with his buddy Gideon Hale, though they'd been tight back in high school. Gideon had confessed that he'd asked Cody to join the lineup of groomsmen—only one short of a football lineup—because his bride-to-be had such a long list of bridesmaids. Cody was happy to stand up for his buddy. More so because he needed the distraction. He'd had plenty of spills as a bull rider, but a nasty one a couple months before had given him the worst concussion of his career.

The doctors wouldn't clear him to ride again for another month. That is, if they cleared him at all.

He didn't want to think about that, about losing the only career he'd known. He was at the top of his game. The prime of his life, as cliché as that sounded.

If he lost his career, what did he have left?

He pushed the gloomy thoughts away and matched the other

groomsmen's stances—arms hanging loose, hands clasped together. Gideon sure was patient, waiting through the long procession of bridesmaids for the real prize—his princess.

Cody had heard snatches of the story about how Alessandra ended up on the Hale's ranch in north central Texas. She'd been on the run from an assassin and had fallen in love with the Navy SEAL-turned-rancher while laying low there.

He was curious how they were going to make things work, because he knew Gideon intended to keep running the Triple H. It was a nice spread and supported Gideon's sister and brother as well.

Cody honestly hoped they could make it work, but he hadn't seen the best examples in his own life.

As distractions went, this trip was the once-in-a-lifetime kind. He'd been too busy on the circuit to do any international traveling and had had to get his passport expedited. He'd only been in Glorvaird for thirty-six hours, most of them sequestered at an expansive villa near the castle, but he'd enjoyed what he'd seen. And they'd let him bring along his uncle EJ, who'd never been out of the good ol' U.S. of A. before either.

EJ had raised him after Cody's parents had split when he'd been ten. Both of them had just up and left him with his uncle. They'd come sniffing around when he'd started winning big on the circuit, but he'd told them to get lost and they had. He'd lost touch with EJ for a couple of years—his fault for traveling so much—but they'd recently reconnected and he hoped this trip would show EJ he was serious about wanting to maintain a closer relationship.

Flying over the clear blue waters as they'd neared the coastal kingdom had been awesome. They'd driven through the bustling metropolis before entering the sleepier part of the kingdom, which felt more like a village than a city. Gideon had invited the groomsmen to stay for a week or so, make a vacation of the trip, and Cody couldn't wait to explore. Get out on the beach, get some sand beneath his feet, feel the warm water on his toes, even if he couldn't surf. Didn't know how. He wanted to learn, but his doctors would probably kill him if he did something so dangerous when his head hadn't healed to one hundred percent.

His head was throbbing now, but it was probably more from the heat than his injury. The centuries-old cathedral was steeped in history—including a musty scent he'd never smelled anywhere else before—and it felt like the air conditioning unit must be from a century ago. He was pretty sure he'd sweated through his undershirt and the white button-up beneath his tuxedo jacket.

The stained glass windows that soared stories above his head cast colorful patterns across the stone floors and the guests, all decked out in their finest for the royal wedding. Whispers from the past seemed almost audible. It was enough to make a chump like him who'd failed history—had hated nearly every class in school—want to find a library or historian dude to tell him about the building.

Another bridesmaid pranced down the aisle. He'd been around enough women to know that most of them were eating up the limelight. There were a few invited press sitting in the very back, their cameras clicking away.

The one person he was most curious about, though, seemed like she didn't want to be here.

The crown princess.

While Alessandra's younger sister, Mia, and Mia's husband, Ethan, had hung around the villa some and been a big part of the dress rehearsal last night, Cody hadn't seen the older sister until today.

She'd been announced before the procession and made her way down the aisle to sit on the front row. Representing the crown or something. But she was all by herself, and he couldn't say why that bugged him.

Maybe because of the stiff, uncompromising way she held herself.

She was dressed more like a grandma than the woman she was. He guessed her age close to his—just on the edge of thirty. But the pale blue pencil skirt and buttoned up jacket she wore had a ruffled collar that hid everything up to her chin. Her hair was tucked in a bun at the back of her neck, but part of it on the right side—the side facing him —swooped down to cover most of her cheek. It had to be intentional. He didn't imagine her stylist or whoever would let her come to an event like this with a mistake in her appearance.

But it was a pretty unusual hairdo.

She didn't look right or left. Hadn't since she'd walked down the aisle. Only stared straight ahead.

He couldn't say why she intrigued him so much. Maybe the little frown she wore. Was she unhappy about her sister's marriage? Didn't prospective grooms have to be approved when you were a royal? He didn't know for sure. But if she was mad about it, why attend?

From where he stood, he could see perfectly the way the end of her nose tweaked up, just the tiniest bit. And her lashes... They were miles long surrounding her blue eyes.

The combination of those two things slayed him.

Not that he was looking. With his injury and his future career up in the air, he didn't know where he'd land, on his feet or on his butt. With the bull of life chasing him or not.

And anyway, it was unlikely that he—a plain 'ol Joe—was a match for a princess anyway.

Plus, with his injury still fresh, his emotions were as unpredictable as a bull in the arena. How could he ask someone to put up with that? Not knowing when it would end?

Emma Jean hadn't even lasted through his collarbone injury.

He'd been staring at the crown princess for a long time, but with the long procession of bridesmaids—none of whom he really knew— his thoughts had wandered. Probably a coping mechanism to distract him from his pounding head and the twinge of an old knee injury from years ago.

All of a sudden, the crown princess turned her chin slightly, and her gaze fixed on him.

He'd never seen someone so furious. Her face hadn't changed expression, but it was there in her eyes.

What had he done to annoy her?

He'd never even met her before. He would've remembered if he had. He was reasonably sure he hadn't done anything to offend anyone since he'd landed in her kingdom.

He ducked his head, looked down to see whether he'd buttoned the front of his tux wrong or stepped in something unsavory. Nothing was amiss.

When he looked back up, the crown princess had gone back to staring straight ahead.

What was her deal? Why had she given him such a scathing look?

He was curious, but he doubted he'd see her again after this.

He couldn't be sure, not from this distance, but did the crown princess's lips tremble a little?

Gideon shifted, cleared his throat, and Cody's focus was broken.

———

PRINCESS MIA OF GLORVAIRD had never been so glad that she'd eloped as she was right this moment. She proceeded down the smooth stone aisle of the four hundred-year-old cathedral, the tenth in a line of bridesmaids clad in cornflower blue. The slippers Alessandra had chosen barely made a rustle of silk against cool stone and certainly weren't a match for the whispers and rustling of the sanctuary crowded with attendees. Fancy hats with plumed feathers bobbed and nodded as women whispered their opinions and judgments.

She clutched the simple bouquet of three white roses wrapped in ribbon, pressing her fisted hand against her stomach, where nausea roiled.

Of all the times to get a stomach virus. She'd lost her breakfast yesterday. She'd felt better in the afternoon, but now it was five minutes until noon, and her stomach had started bubbling violently. She forced a smile for the five hundred sets of eyes watching her. Tried to breathe shallow pants without anyone noticing.

She was especially careful to smile and look healthy as she neared the front of the cathedral, where her husband Ethan stood in line with the rest of Gideon's groomsmen.

Gideon had vacillated between asking his trusted hands to attend the wedding as his groomsmen or having them stay and watch over the ranch. He'd ended up with two hands here, Chase and Nate, plus his brother, and he'd asked other friends to match Alessandra's ten bridesmaids.

And Gideon had asked Ethan to stand in.

Now she felt her husband's eyes on her as she joined the bridesmaids and groomsmen already flanking the steps that led to the altar.

She saw the warmth in his eyes change to something else. Concern maybe, but he couldn't come to her now, couldn't check on her. And she couldn't reassure him, other than with what turned out to be a tremulous smile, thanks to her still-burbling stomach.

Finally she reached the front of the cathedral, climbed five shallow steps, and turned to face the guests.

As the maid of honor, she had a great view of Gideon, who stood several feet away in a sharp, black tuxedo. She'd gotten to know the man over the last several months as he and Alessandra had alternated between staying here Glorvaird and in Texas. He appeared calm and unaffected, his face turned toward the back of the cathedral where Alessandra would appear momentarily.

But Mia saw his hands fist, then straighten. Saw the slight tremor in his fingers. He was nervous, even if he wasn't showing it.

Alessandra had been flip-flopping between peaceful joy and nerves. Mia didn't think it was marriage to the former Navy SEAL that made her nervous but more the grand event itself that was making her sister worry.

Alessandra and Gideon shared a deep, abiding love that Mia knew would last a lifetime.

Just as she and Ethan did.

Over Gideon's shoulder, Mia met her husband's eyes and tried again for a smile.

A rush of sick rose in her throat, and she swallowed slowly, hoping to stem the tide. They'd done two walk-throughs for the ceremony last night, and it was slated to last forty-five minutes. She could get through that without embarrassing her sister, or herself.

A voluminous rustle of clothing and bodies filled the space as the guests rose. Alessandra appeared in the arched entryway, a vision in white. Her off-the-shoulder dress with its glittering seed-pearled bodice flowed all the way to the floor and, though she couldn't see it from here, she knew the train extended a good six feet behind the dress. Mia knew Alessandra had been worried about tripping on the multiple petticoats, but now she seemed to only have eyes for Gideon. The emotion shining in them made her own tingle with tears.

Gideon's swift intake of air told her what he thought of his bride. She'd look at his reaction, but she couldn't tear her eyes away from the beautiful bride.

Alessandra walked the aisle slowly, as she'd been directed to, but Mia thought her sister looked like she wanted to jog to her groom. She reached him, linked her hands in Gideon's. The two smiled at each other as if they were the only people in the room.

The minister spoke words that Mia remembered from her own, much simpler, wedding eight months ago. She looked past the bride and groom to meet Ethan's eyes again, attempting to send him all the love she felt—and not the rolling in her stomach.

Gideon spoke his vows fervently, face coloring with emotion.

Mia couldn't see Alessandra's face past the veil but heard the tears in her sister's voice.

And then it was over, and the newly married couple faced their guests as man and wife, ready to start the next chapter of their lives.

Chapter Two

"WHAT ARE YOU DOING IN HERE?" CODY HAD SEEN HIS Uncle EJ slip out of the royal wedding reception, back at the castle. He'd followed him because he was concerned.

Cody had reconnected with his uncle about a year ago when EJ had phoned and told him he had a heart condition. Cody had cancelled a contracted appearance at an event that weekend to be there for EJ's consult with a cardiologist, and the news wasn't good. His uncle had maybe two years left. Cody had moved some things into his uncle's small ranch house and been there ever since.

Things were different than when he'd been ten. EJ was different. There'd been a hardness to him that Cody didn't remember.

And Cody'd heard some rumors in town that EJ was suspected in a robbery of the local pharmacy. He hadn't believed them. And nothing had ever come of it, so Cody figured the rumors were unsubstantiated.

They'd settled in to a comfortable routine. EJ had had a couple of spells that had put him in the hospital. Cody figured he was running out of time to spend with his uncle, so it was natural he'd invited EJ as his plus-one for this shindig.

When he'd first followed him out of the ballroom, he'd figured EJ was looking for a restroom. But when EJ had slipped into an empty, darkened room, Cody had started to wonder.

He came up behind the gray-haired figure, who turned, eyes wide. The crystal rose clutched in the older man's hand brought back the memories of those rumors and a twist in his gut.

"Uncle EJ, what are you doing?"

"I was just looking at this," EJ said. But Cody couldn't help but notice that his uncle didn't put the jeweled flower back on the empty pedestal. How much was that thing worth?

The room was cavernous, quiet after the voices and music of the reception in a nearby ballroom. Paintings of what must be royals, judging by their elaborate costumes and the crowns they wore, lined the walls. Pedestals stood at intervals, some of them with glass enclosures. But the hall was shadowed and empty. Dark.

Off-limits.

"How'd you get in here, anyway?" Cody drew a little closer. He needed to get EJ to put the rose back and get them both out of there. There were probably security cameras everywhere, and he really didn't want his uncle to get into trouble.

"How'd you get in here?" EJ countered.

"I followed you."

EJ shrugged as if he hadn't done anything wrong by wandering into the royal family's private quarters. "The door wasn't locked."

"Doesn't mean you're supposed to be in here."

"This hall is off-limits to party guests." A strident female voice rang out in the quiet.

Cody whirled to find the crown princess moving toward them, her heels clicking on the marble floors.

He didn't know the exact protocol, but bent at the waist in hopes that would suffice.

She marched right up to them. Out of some sense of protectiveness, Cody stepped closer to his uncle, angling his body in hopes of shielding what EJ was doing.

It didn't work.

"What are you hiding?" She gasped softly. "Guard!" she called out over her shoulder.

Lights flared, and he blinked against the brightness.

A man in a dark suit—as opposed to a uniform, like Cody had kind of expected—rushed into the room.

All Cody could think about was his uncle's heart issue. "Wait!"

But the guard didn't wait as the crown princess pointed to the treasure in EJ's hands. The guard roughly took the older man's arm.

EJ promptly lost his grip, and the rose slipped from his grip.

Cody reached for it, catching it before it hit the floor. Barely.

It was heavier than he'd thought it would be, though fragile. He straightened and held it out to the crown princess.

She ripped it out of his hands. Color was high in her cheeks, and their eyes met and locked.

The moment seemed suspended in time.

The chignon behind her head had come loose, and the hair that had covered her right cheek had fallen away. A silvery scar snaked down her cheek and jaw, disappearing into the ruffled neck of her jacket.

Her shoulders rose and fell as if she were fighting some high emotion.

"How dare you come into my home and attempt to steal one of my family's heirlooms?"

Cody couldn't believe she'd jump to that conclusion. Never mind that it had crossed his mind as well. This woman didn't know Uncle EJ.

"I want him arrested immediately."

The guard nodded, his grip on EJ's arm tightening.

"Wait a minute." Couldn't they see how white in the face EJ had gone? "He wasn't stealing anything—just looking at it."

The crown princess didn't look him directly in the eye. "I was just sent a digital photo of a man in a dark jacket placing the rose in his pocket."

Then why had it been in EJ's hand? Had EJ had a change of heart?

"Please return to the party. Your uncle will be dealt with—"

"No."

Her eyes flicked to him in surprise. Maybe she wasn't used to being refused.

"He's sick," Cody gestured at his uncle. "He has a bad heart." Even if his uncle had had intentions of doing something he shouldn't he was family, and Cody wouldn't just walk away.

EJ's breaths had started to go shallow, but he still stood upright by his own power, which Cody counted as a good thing.

She looked to EJ and back. "The fact remains that he attempted to steal from the royal family and must be punished."

Seriously? She couldn't give him a break? It wasn't like he'd actually gotten away with anything.

Uncle EJ had gone from white to a pasty gray, and Cody was growing more worried by the second.

"I took it." The words were out before he'd thought anything through. Blame it on his brain injury, maybe or his worry for his uncle. "I was trying to take the rose and Uncle EJ came in here to stop me."

Another guard came in. The first had probably summoned him with that little mic on his lapel.

The crown princess's eyes locked on him, and Cody felt a momentary blip of unease at the lie. One look at his uncle erased it.

"Really? Maybe we should visit the security room and run the tapes back." She didn't believe him. He could see it in her eyes. "Because you're going to have to stay here in Glorvaird until we can resolve the matter. Weeks. Maybe even months. And if you're found guilty of attempted theft against the crown, you'll be imprisoned. You're sure you want to stick with that story?"

"I'm sure. Now can you get my uncle to a doctor?"

The second guard took hold of Cody's upper arm. Firmly. But Cody didn't have any intention of trying to get away, not if they would help his uncle. There was plenty of time to get his lawyers involved later.

He heard the crown princess instruct the first guard to find a doctor among the partygoers—and not to let EJ out of his sight until he was on a plane back to the States.

The second guard spoke into his lapel, asking for a doctor, but before anybody'd moved, a flash went off. Then another.

The crown princess gasped softly and whirled away from the photographer that must've followed his nose to such a juicy story. She bumped into Cody's arm in her haste, close enough now to touch if he dared.

He didn't.

"Don't move." The hulking guard in the suit's voice held enough authority, Cody wasn't dumb enough to disobey. The guard let him go and rushed off toward the man with the high-tech camera.

Dude was still taking pictures. Cody could hear the click of his digital machine over the guard's footsteps and he did the only thing that came natural to him.

He took the princess's elbow, stepped in front of her, and shifted her behind him, out of sight of the cameraman.

For a long moment, he looked down at her, saw the surprise and vulnerability in the depths of her eyes.

Then her expression shuttered, and she jerked her arm away. "Don't touch me," she hissed.

He nodded, raising both hands like he would if he'd frightened a filly he was trying to saddle break. "I'm sorry."

He was sorry for all of it. Sorry Uncle EJ had gotten him into this mess. Sorry a reporter had gotten it all on film. Sorry he'd caused a scene that had put the princess in distress.

He had no idea what was going to happen now, but as he watched the first guard escort EJ out of the hall to meet a doctor, he could at least feel he'd done one thing right. EJ would be okay.

He had to be.

———

THE NEXT MORNING, Eloise braced herself before pushing through the door to her father's suite for their weekly debriefing. Jill bustled along behind her.

Eloise had already seen the morning's headlines, so she anticipated that her father wouldn't be happy.

She wasn't happy either. She'd spent a restless night after the reception had finally wound down in the early hours of the morning. No doubt she looked horrid this morning, thanks to the lack of sleep.

And what foolishness had kept her up all night? Nothing but brooding about the cowboy who was her newest, biggest problem.

Not enough she'd had to have the man—a friend of her new brother-in-law—detained. But to have his face staring back at her from the morning paper, thanks to the awful photographer who'd burst in on what should've been a private issue. By the time the security team had caught up with the photographer, he'd been surrounded by people, and they'd been unable to force him to give up the digital files of the photos he's taken The wily man had apparently been close enough to overhear her unleash her temper, and now the entire country knew she planned to prosecute the cowboy.

When her fit of temper had passed, she knew it would be better to settle things privately. Except now the entire country believed she intended to prosecute him. If she went back on her word, she would look fickle to her subjects.

No, Father would not be happy.

Father had been bedridden for the last several months, but seeing his body swallowed by the hospital bed in his room was still a shock. His blue eyes were cold, and he barely acknowledged her as she entered and nodded to his nurse, who stood in the corner, and his assistant, who was always available with a tablet and paper planner in hand. His breakfast remained uneaten on a side table.

A local news channel blared from a wall-mounted flat screen TV in line with the foot of Father's bed.

"...interrupted a theft of the palace's famed jeweled rose..."

The tinny words, even with the volume turned low, reverberated through Eloise's ears and echoed through her skull.

"Good morning, Father," she said a bit stiffly. "Alessandra is off to her honeymoon, as expected. There's been no sign of Aunty Willow." Outdoor security for the wedding had been incredibly tight, and there'd been a small contingent of men assigned to follow her cousin Pieter around all night.

Father waved at her to be quiet even as he stared at what was unfolding on the television.

"Crown princess Eloise showed her beastly side as she threatened an elderly wedding guest."

Heat flared in her face. She loathed it, because when her cheeks pinked, the scars etched into her skin stood out in stark relief. Oh, how she hated them.

"Please tell me you didn't actually threaten one of our guests?" Her father's voice was raspy from the pneumonia he'd been fighting off for the better part of a week.

"It was a mistake." The whole thing had been one big, herculean mistake. She'd seen the cowboy darting through the hall where he most certainly hadn't been invited. She'd meant to go in and ask him to leave, but her emotions had gotten the better of her.

It was *him*. She hated how he affected her.

He'd stared at her throughout the wedding, making her uncomfortably aware of her ugliness. There had been no escape from his constant focus, and it had driven her crazy. She'd had to fight the impulse to stand up and scream in the middle of it all.

She'd shown an amazing amount of willpower in keeping her seat.

When she'd run across him again, that hot knife of the bottled-up scream had sliced open her insides and made her crueler than normal.

Or perhaps she'd forgotten what it felt like to be normal.

"Mr. Cody Austin, a professional bull rider, has been detained," her father's aide said oh-so-helpfully. "He's currently residing in the castle with strict instructions not to leave. I believe a hearing with the royal council has been set for two weeks from today."

Already? She hadn't meant the threat. Or if she had, she'd known as soon as her anger had burned away that it was foolish, but now that the attempted theft and her threat were public knowledge, the ruling body would have no choice but to respond.

She sighed softly. "It was a mistake," she repeated. "I'm certain we can take care of it. Smooth things over with the council."

"They're saying you're unfit to be queen," he rasped.

It wasn't the first time it had been said, but it stung just as much.

She schooled her features not to show her pain. A crown princess did not show emotion.

"You must learn to control your temper," Father said.

She resisted the urge to curl her lip. She'd inherited her temper from him.

She only nodded tightly.

"Maybe we can turn this around," Jill suggested brightly. "He has a measure of fame in the United States. If we spin it as a simple misunderstanding with one Gideon's American friends, publicly show that there's no animosity on either part... The general public will forget all about it."

Eloise resisted the urge to growl. Her media specialist seemed to look at life through rose-colored glasses. Next to someone like the cowboy, all of Eloise's faults would be glaring.

"And what about the council?" Eloise asked through stiff lips. "Will they forget about it? The rose is a priceless heirloom that has been in the royal family for generations. They could consider his actions a crime against the royal family."

Jill shrugged. "It wasn't as if he made off with the flower, was it? I'll reach out to the council. See if we can't get him off the hook."

Eloise looked over her shoulder, wanting only to escape. She didn't want to do *any* media events. Ever. But she could not shirk her duty, not when she'd been preparing for years to take over the crown's duties.

"You'll be fine," Jill said with a friendly pat on her shoulder.

Eloise glared at her. How dare a commoner touch her? She hated being touched as much as she hated being patronized.

"You must do better than fine." Father coughed, which started a fit that lasted long enough that Eloise clenched her fists to keep from reaching for him, asking whether she could help.

She'd tried it once before, and he'd lost his temper with her, shouting her out of the room.

When his nurse had helped him adjust the bed to a more upright position and his coughing fit had calmed, he aimed his intense gaze at Eloise. "You must convince our people that you're capable. That you'll be a queen they can trust."

"Father, there's still time—"

He waved his hand violently and cut her off. "You must do so *now*. Do not let any question of your suitability grow in their minds. You mustn't."

He was working himself up and began coughing again.

"Yes, Father," she said quickly, hoping to stave off another lengthy episode. He needed to conserve his strength to fight the pneumonia.

He nodded and waved at the door to indicate the meeting was over.

She left the room, Jill trailing, as the nurse moved in to help him again.

In the hallway, Jill flipped open her leather-covered planner, no doubt ready to take on the day. "We have the children's home visit—"

"I'm sorry." Eloise couldn't get the vision of her father, bent and unable to catch his breath, out of her mind. "I need a moment." No, that wasn't enough. "A half hour."

"If we don't leave now, you'll be late for the mayor's breakfast."

Eloise opened her mouth to argue, but then snapped it closed again. Father's words rang in her head. *You've got to prove yourself to the people.*

She had to find a way.

———

IT WAS MUCH LATER, nearly nightfall, by the time Eloise found an escape from her duties. Shaking and near tears, she practically ran down the hall and descended a set of stairs usually reserved for the staff. She ducked through the expansive kitchen, receiving a glare from the on-staff chef and curious but quickly averted looks from two white-aproned helpers.

*Don't stare at the crown princess!*

And then she was outdoors, slipping down the stone stairs that curled around the base of the castle against the beach. She kicked off her shoes, but paused on the last step.

She couldn't breathe through her rioting emotions. The sea air did nothing to clear her thoughts.

She usually loved this beach. It was restricted to those inside the castle by the towering cliffs that curved behind the castle and out onto a small spit of land that disappeared at high tide. The other side of the beach disappeared past the castle itself and was patrolled by guards around the clock. The castle staff was kept too busy to loiter on the beach, and Eloise often had the outdoor space to herself. Usually, it was peaceful and serene unless winds whipped the waves into a frenzy. Like today.

A match for her roiling emotions.

She'd lost her temper again, this time when an impertinent journalist who'd been seated at her table at the mayor's breakfast had slung question after question at her. He'd been trying to upset. *Is the King really dying? Why have you cancelled so many public appearances this year? How many staffers have you fired this year?*

It hadn't mattered that she'd known the man was only trying to get her to lose her temper. Eloise had become so angry that she'd left in the middle of the mayor's speech. A photographer had been stationed outside the building and followed her to the car.

As far as Eloise was concerned, the entire event was another huge failure on her part. Jill had spent the ride home lecturing her and pushing for her to invite the cowboy to one of the upcoming events.

She'd returned to her office to find to a mountain of work: a new bill from the royal council to review and consider, petitions from several small businesses, a meeting with their trade partner to schedule.

In the midst of all that, Father's nurse had interrupted to tell her that Father's fever had spiked.

It was too much. She'd escaped here.

The doctors had been unable to slow the progression of the disease. Watching Father, the man she'd idolized all her life, a man stronger, more powerful, than any other man in the world, succumb to multiple sclerosis, was breaking her heart. And now, something as simple, as common, as pneumonia had him confined to bed, trapped but alert enough to watch his eldest daughter destroy all the public goodwill he'd built.

Their relationship had been more political than personal since she was a teenager. He'd seemed to want it that way, and even still, though she longed to reach out to him, longed for the daddy she'd known as a child, she didn't know how to change it.

Since Alessandra had come home from the States after nearly being assassinated, she'd been intentional about setting aside what little time Father could carve out for her to spend together.

Eloise didn't have that luxury. Father had given her more and more of the tasks relating to governing their people.

And it seemed as if every time she tried to make some overture to reach out to Father, to get more personal with him, he rebuffed her attempts.

And now... He was fading away. There was no other way to describe it.

She stepped off the last stone stair, sinking her bare feet into the cool, dry sand. The wind was high today and blew strands of her hair into her face.

She breathed in deeply of the briny sea air, trying to calm her rioting emotions. Father. The event today. The cowboy. Since she'd felt his stare during the wedding, his very presence had disconcerted her.

Where was peace, when she so desperately needed it?

And then she realized she wasn't alone.

# Chapter Three

CODY COULDN'T SAY WHAT HE'D BEEN EXPECTING, BEING detained by the palace guard, but it certainly wasn't this.

He'd been assigned a suite of rooms, not a dungeon cell.

He hadn't been locked in his rooms either, but had been allowed to roam the castle with one guard who dogged his every move. Right now the man was tucked up against the stone castle wall right now, watching him with arms crossed.

He wasn't used to inactivity, and when he'd seen no one by ten a.m., he had to get out of the rooms, as nice as they were. He'd spent over an hour on the phone with his lawyer, who'd promised to do what he could to get Cody home as quickly as possible. There were international laws in place, and though Cody argued that he and his uncle had only been looking at the jeweled rose, there was the digital picture that the crown princess had threatened EJ with. It was a mess. There were careful rules to follow, even about setting up a trial and getting charges dismissed and Cody's lawyer would have to do some studying on the Glorvaird laws to ensure they did things right. He'd advised Cody sit tight and try not to worry.

Ha.

He still couldn't figure why EJ had done it. For the thrill? Cody paid for most of the man's medical bills, what insurance didn't cover anyway. His winnings were plenty to support the both of them. He couldn't figure it.

In his restless state, he'd wandered through the second floor. Most of the rooms were private suites, but he found a small library and a two different sitting rooms.

By the afternoon, he'd found the kitchen and made friends with some of the staff.

He'd called to check in on Uncle EJ, who'd made it back to the States. His uncle had only changed the subject when Cody had tried to ask about what had happened.

Cody hadn't had contact with Gideon's other friends, the guys staying at the villa outside of the castle. Hadn't tried—he didn't know any of them well. With his attorney's advice in mind, he couldn't go out and see the city like he'd wanted to upon his arrival.

After supper, he found himself restless again.

So he wandered down through a narrow, twisty hallway that landed him on a thin slice of beach.

It was private, backed by the massive castle and lined by cliffs.

An afternoon storm was rolling in. The wind was high and clouds boiled off the horizon.

But the fresh air was a relief after being cooped up all day, and he stood on the sand breathing it in.

He took off his boots and socks, left them on the bottom stair, and walked toward the water.

He was still taking in the beauty of the sunset when movement from behind turned his head.

It was the crown princess.

He was sketching a bow when she reached him. "What are you doing out here?"

He straightened, shoulders tightening at the rude tone of her words. She didn't have to be polite. She thought he and EJ had tried to steal from her family.

His attorney had told him to stay out of trouble. He gritted his teeth, but forced his voice to an even tone.

"I needed some fresh air," he said simply. "I didn't know I was confined indoors."

Her lips pinched, her eyes flicking to his face and then away. "I don't suppose you are."

Her chin jerked as she looked away.

He watched her face as the wind blew strands of hair across her cheek. That pert nose... It frustrated him to still be attracted to someone who'd been so cold toward his uncle.

She frowned, brushed at the hair in her face. She didn't say anything.

"My uncle is fine," Cody said, not that she'd asked. "He had a minor episode but was able to take some meds and get stabilized."

She mumbled something under her breath.

He'd never been under the impression that everyone had to like him. Some guys on the circuit made no secret of their dislike for him. But her distaste seemed personal.

He stuffed his hands in his front jeans pockets. "Do you want me to go inside?" he asked, even though he'd been here first.

"What I'd like is for you to *stop staring at me*." Her words were venom-filled. "Didn't anyone ever tell you it's rude to stare?"

Though her words had started rude, they ended angry, like a sudden burst of thunder.

She moved past him, closer to the water's edge, and wrapped her arms around her middle.

Her shoulders were up, and her anger washed over him, but he couldn't help feeling the emotion behind her words. And with her arms like that...it sure seemed defensive.

Something inside him shifted. Some of his anger and frustration over what had happened falling away.

It bothered her when he looked at her?

He stood two paces behind her, watching the surf roll, not knowing what to say.

———

ELOISE HADN'T MEANT to yell at the cowboy. She definitely hadn't meant to reveal so much through her loaded statement. Now he knew her weakness.

She was feeling especially sensitive because Jill continued to harp on her idea of bringing the bull rider into their media plan to spin his presence here in a positive light. Earlier, she'd produced a full-page magazine spread that proclaimed Cody Austin not only the number one rider on the circuit, but also the number one most attractive man in bull riding.

All Eloise could remember was the way he'd stared at her during the wedding ceremony. She'd been so relieved to sit and turn her face away from the guests only to have his stare on her for almost the entire time.

She'd hated every second of it.

She should leave, before she made things worse. Go back inside.

But the cowboy stepped up next to her. "You know, the scars aren't that bad, if that's what you're worried about."

Her mouth opened in a shocked gasp, but nothing emerged. *No one* mentioned her scars aloud, nor the accident that had caused them.

She turned to berate him, but he was already gone, his broad back disappearing up the winding stone staircase.

How dare he?

But...what had he done, exactly? Gotten close enough to mention her scars? He'd been kind, even if she couldn't believe him. In light of everything that had happened, his gesture was even more surprising. Even if she hated that he'd felt he had to say the words.

Her scars had cost her everything. Had created the ugly creature that she was.

*Not that bad.*

If only he knew how her life had been upended. She'd gone from being beautiful, full of life, the beloved daughter next in line for the throne, to a monster her own father hadn't been able to look at.

She'd retreated from the world, and they'd been content for her to disappear. Until her father's illness had pushed her into the spotlight once again.

And now this cowboy was here, and unlike the rest of the kingdom, he refused to look away.

*Chapter Four*

Two mornings after the wedding, Ethan stood in the small sitting room in the suite he shared with Mia.

He was still getting used to the luxury of having staff. Of having someone else launder his tighty-whities and make his breakfast. Yesterday, Mia had caught him tucking in the bedspread after they'd gotten up for the day.

Now, she emerged from the bathroom and touched up her lipstick using the small mirror in an alcove near the outer door.

She didn't meet his eyes in the mirror. "Would you mind terribly if I don't go with you to tour the university? I'm feeling a bit under the weather."

She sent him a smile over her shoulder. She didn't look sick, though maybe a bit pale.

"That's fine."

He'd wanted the company, but he was an adult. He meant to tour the nearby university and enroll, or at least find out what paperwork he needed to get sent over from the small town Texas high school he'd barely graduated from.

Going for the tour alone wasn't ideal. He was also still getting used to being in the public eye. Being a public figure. Him. A poor kid from Texas.

Sometimes paparazzi followed him and Mia around. What was he supposed to say if they trapped him somewhere and asked hard questions about the royal family? Or his family?

His brothers had been sent to a juvenile detention facility back home and refused contact with him.

He'd gone through several rounds with the palace's media specialist when he and Mia had arrived in Glorvaird after their Vegas wedding. During their early public appearances, most of the journalists seemed to want to ask about Mia's dating life before him. All he had to do was refuse to comment. He could handle that without embarrassing Mia or her family, right?

Mia came close and pressed her cheek against his. "I need to run down to talk to Eloise before she gets going on her days' tasks."

But, once again, she didn't quite meet his eyes before she turned and swept out of the room.

And this was the first time she hadn't kissed him goodbye since they'd declared themselves to each other back in Texas.

Something was wrong.

He had a hunch that something had happened at Alessandra and Gideon's wedding. There was no other explanation for Mia pulling away the past two days. She'd been busy right up to the wedding, helping her sisters with preparations and all that entailed.

But she hadn't held herself back from him.

He knew that two of her former beaus had been in attendance, because of their political connections with the Glorvaird royal family. She'd told him about the guest list well before the wedding, which he'd appreciated.

He hadn't particularly worried about those guys until now.

Mia had spent most of the wedding day at his side, but had there been a time where they'd been apart and one of the beaus had approached her?

Jealousy flared through him, thinking about Mia even sharing a peck on the cheek with someone she'd had feelings for before.

He didn't want to think it, but what if something had happened...?

Because the other choice was that Mia had grown tired of him in the seven months they'd been married.

Maybe the extravagant wedding had upset her, since theirs had been so small, only witnessed by Alessandra and Gideon. Did she regret marrying him that way?

Or maybe it was him.

Did he really know how to keep her interest? A small-town guy like him? He'd been excited to sell the dairy and be out from under its mortgages. Surprisingly, there'd been a small amount of profit from the sale, and Mia had forced him to bank it in a special account.

Should he have bought her an extravagant present, since he hadn't even given her a wedding gift? The wedding rings they'd exchanged had been simple gold bands.

He'd felt incredibly blessed when Mia had declared her love for him, bestowing a kiss on him that had meant she wanted to marry him.

But ever since they'd arrived in Glorvaird, he'd felt uncertain. Out of place. How could someone like him fit in here? Gideon had been something of an ally when he wasn't busy with security or wedding preparations. He was nothing like Gideon, though. Gideon was college educated and well-traveled. If he didn't feel he belonged, the soldier never showed it.

Ethan, though. He was a very different story.

Eloise had welcomed him stiffly—which Mia had warned him about—and while the staff was kind, he still wasn't sure of where he fit around here.

He'd hoped his decision to focus on business, economics, and political courses at the university would help ease his transition into his role as Mia's husband.

But her behavior over the last two days had him questioning everything.

Everything except for how much he loved her.

———

THE NEXT MORNING, Eloise's mood hadn't improved.

Jill had called an early-morning impromptu meeting with Father, surprising Eloise with her new idea for showing the public a softer side of Eloise.

After the fact, it was apparent that she'd blindsided Eloise with the meeting because she never would've agreed to the idiotic idea.

But Eloise had been five minutes late to the hastily-scheduled meeting, and Jill and Father had made the decision for her.

For once, Father had looked bright-eyed and excited.

She couldn't mess this up for him. For the kingdom.

But... A camera crew. Inside the palace walls? Like they were some reality TV show?

Apparently Jill had been contacted by a local news network's producer who wanted to do a week's worth of pieces on life inside the castle.

And Eloise had been nominated to be in many of the shots. It was her chance to show her people how personable she could be.

Except she wasn't. Not personable. Not nice. Not friendly.

She had no idea how she was going to pull this off.

———

ELOISE WAS RIGHT. She'd been slathered in makeup, then blinded all morning by bright lights.

Behind the camera crew, Jill looked more worried than ever.

And her obvious fear about how this was going was just making Eloise tighten up more.

They'd just visited the kitchens where the on-staff chef had been tense and unnatural in front of the cameras.

Now they moved through one of the staff hallways, but the camera guy paused when laughter seeped out between a cracked door.

A laundry room, if she remembered correctly, though it had been ages since she'd explored down here. She and her sisters had played hide and seek—and driven the staff crazy—but that was well before the accident.

The reporter stopped, curiosity crossing her features. And unfortunately, it matched Jill's expression.

Eloise knew Jill would do anything to have this make a positive impression.

"That's just the laundry—" Eloise started, but Jill had already pushed open the door.

It opened to a large, sun-filled room, with washing machines along one wall and electric dryers along the opposite wall. An older maid, Cindy, who'd been on staff since Eloise had been a little girl, worked at folding bundles and bundles of sheets laid out across tables beneath a huge window.

In the center of the room, the bull rider was flipping and parachuting a towel over the head of a young girl Eloise didn't recognize.

As the camera crew and reporter pushed into the large, airy room, the occupants froze.

Cindy bowed quickly. "Your highness."

The cowboy was next to move, nodding his head. "Ma'am."

Cindy put her hand on the little girl's shoulder. Cindy's face had gone white, though the little girl showed only simple curiosity. Of course her gaze went straight to Eloise's scars. When she saw them, she gasped.

"Who's this?" Eloise asked, trying to find a friendly smile and too aware of both the cowboy's gaze and the camera crew filming everything.

The little girl continued to stare, and Eloise felt her face heat. Lovely. Now her scars would stand out more.

"My granddaughter, Christy. Her mother was sick today, and Mrs. Ellison"—the head housekeeper—"said it would be okay if I brought her to work."

Eloise saw the tremble in the older woman's hand and felt the tension throughout the room. As if they were all holding their breath. They were all waiting for her to react.

"Of course it's fine," she said, but that horrid heat remained.

———

CODY DIDN'T KNOW what was going on with the high-tech TV cameras, the dude holding a boom mike, or the princess, but he could see in the fine lines around her eyes and the tense set of her shoulders that whatever was happening, it was important to Eloise.

He'd been bored again this morning and the attorney had nothing new for him. He had met Cindy and Christy in the staff kitchen at breakfast. The little girl had charmed him. He'd had nothing better to do when she'd invited him to "help" her and her grandma, and now found himself here.

And it was obvious that Eloise didn't know how to relate to anyone in the room.

He couldn't say what possessed him, but he shot a wink at Christy. "I think the princess needs a lesson in folding laundry, don't you?"

Eloise's brows crunched together.

The little girl remained frozen, obviously scared of what the princess would do. He'd heard whispers among the staff about the princess's beastly temper, had seen it for himself on the beach, but he also had that split-second memory of Eloise on the shore, the way she'd held herself together, as if she might fall apart.

He grabbed one of the washed sheets from the pile of rumpled, clean laundry. He took a few steps toward Eloise and flipped it up. Air whooshed beneath the light fabric, light refracted for a moment on the princess's luminous eyes as the sheet descended on her. He didn't cover her face, but wrapped the sheet around her shoulders, letting it flow around her like a kid might play dress up as a superhero.

"C'mon, Christy," he encouraged.

For a long moment, the room descended into shocked silence. Everyone seemed to be waiting for the princess to lose her temper, all eyes on her.

But a sudden giggle emerged from her pert pink lips.

And then all bets were off.

Christy grabbed a corner of the sheet and unwound the princess, and the two of them played tug-of-war until he joined Christy's side, and they ripped the sheet out of Eloise's hands. Christy laughed, and he found himself chuckling.

Eloise's eyes flashed, and she turned to the pile of clean linens, snagging a sheet of her own, and then a real battle was on as she whipped it through the air.

It was easy to forget the cameras as the princess, Christy, and he dueled it out, whirling between sheets as they tried to capture each other. Cindy had ducked out of the way, joining Jill behind the cameras.

As he panted and tried not to look like a wimp because he was winded from a little linen fight, Eloise bent and whispered something to Christy. Both girls shot him evil looks and then joined forces and chased after him. He gave it his all, feinting left and then right, imagining he was a steer in the arena, giving his ropers a merry chase.

Of course, he let them catch him, because Christy was all-out belly laughing, and he'd never seen the princess's eyes so filled with light.

The girls laughed as they wrapped both sheets around him, holding his arms to his middle and keeping him from walking. He wobbled across the room and was rewarded by their laughter.

Eloise ended up right in front of him, tucking in the sheet to a fold of linen up against his chest. His chin was about level with her forehead, and he found the little wrinkles of concentration across her brow entirely too distracting.

They'd only been this close once before, in the hall of art when he'd thought to step in between her and the photographer-turned-party-crasher, and that time, she'd shied away from him quickly.

But now she was so focused on what she was doing, maybe she didn't realize exactly how close they were. The warm air from the massive set of electric dryers against the far wall was still swirling from all their running around, but the sweet smell of clean laundry didn't overpower the scent that was distinctly the princess. She smelled like ocean spray and something exotic he couldn't name.

Looking down at her, he barely registered the scars, instead fixated on the sweep of her golden lashes against her cheeks and the way her lips puckered in her concentration.

Then all of a sudden, she looked up. He could see the realization of how close they were as it dawned in her eyes. Color crept up her throat and into her face, and he really wished his hands were free because he wanted to touch her skin to see if it had warmed.

Maybe it was the cameras or the little girl on her knees at their feet, still happily wrapping all the way down to his boots, but Eloise didn't jerk away this time. She patted his chest twice, cleared her throat, and stepped back.

"I think we've saved the kingdom from this rapscallion, Christy," she said. Was he the only one who heard the huskiness in her voice?

"Awesome!" the young girl exclaimed. She jumped up and raised her hand to high-five the princess, who looked surprised, but only for a moment. Then she lifted her own hand and high-fived back.

A woman in a suit he'd seen around the castle but hadn't met herded the camera crew out the door as Cindy collected her granddaughter and also made a quick escape, which left him and the princess standing somewhat alone.

"Well, that was..."

"Fun?" he finished for her when she seemed to stall out.

She glanced at him, and maybe it was the play of sunlight through the dust-motes they'd stirred up, but he once again got a glimpse of that vulnerability he'd seen on the beach.

"I suppose it was," she said softly.

"Been awhile since you've experienced it? You don't sound too sure." He meant the words as a tease, and maybe if the crew and staff was still close enough, they'd have frozen up again, because did anyone really tease this woman?

Her lips pinched a little, but she nodded slightly. Then she looked embarrassed at the silent admission and turned her chin slightly away.

He was a little afraid she was going to bolt out the door. "You aren't going to leave me like this, are you?"

Her lips twitched slightly as she moved toward him again. This time, without the distraction of the faux fight and Christy playing with them, he noticed the hesitation before she reached for the linen at his chest.

"You don't think Cindy and Christy would return and untangle you?" she asked. She didn't look at him this time, kept her chin turned slightly, maybe trying to hide her scars?

"Maybe not if the crown princess left me here."

Her hands shook slightly as she untucked the fabric and then swept against his ribcage as she unwound him.

It tickled, and he jumped.

She jerked back, looking up at him with her face coloring again.

"Ticklish," he admitted.

Something shifted in her eyes, and he thought maybe she'd taken his admission as a challenge.

"Don't even think about it," he warned. Although...what exactly could he do to stop her if she did? His arms were still trapped against his sides and his legs were hog-tied. If he tried to move his feet, he was likely to end up on the floor on his rear.

She hesitated, then continued to unwind the fabric. This time she kept her head down and didn't speak.

What exactly had he expected? For her to descend into a tickle war with him when there were no cameras to witness it? That's something a woman who was interested in a man might do, but the princess hadn't indicated any interest in him. Other than the couple of times he'd thought he caught a flash of attraction in her eyes. Up until now, she'd seemed more suspicious of him than anything.

And anyway, whatever hint of attract he might have seen in her eyes was irrelevant. He wasn't exactly prince material.

But as she ducked out the door and disappeared down the hallway, he couldn't help the stab of disappointment that she'd chosen to return to the icy tundra princess instead of playing with him.

*Chapter Five*

Pregnant.

Mia stared down at the twin pink lines on the home pregnancy test before squeezing her eyes tightly shut.

She couldn't stop shaking. Her heart was flying, sending adrenaline and nerves through her.

What she'd thought was a virus hadn't gone away after twenty-four hours or even forty-eight.

On the third morning, huddled over the toilet bowl, trying to be quiet so Ethan wouldn't hear, she'd begun to suspect. She hadn't wanted him to be worried.

Now what was she going to tell him?

They'd been careful. She'd been *especially* careful because she knew how much of his teenage years and early adulthood Ethan had given up to care for his younger stepbrothers.

He'd even commented once, when they'd been cuddled up late at night talking, that it felt like a weight off his back not to be responsible for his stepbrothers.

What would he say when she told him? She couldn't imagine he would want the responsibility of raising a child *now*, not when he'd just won his freedom, thanks to a judge and his stepbrothers' own irresponsibility.

He'd been looking forward to attending university courses. Would he think he had to give that up because of the baby?

Tears burned her eyes.

She sensed he'd been suspicious when she'd ducked out of going to the university visit him the other day. She'd been too afraid to kiss him goodbye, afraid he'd smell the truth on her breath, even after she'd brushed her teeth.

Beneath her worry, there was the tiniest kernel of joy. She'd longed for someone to love her, really love her, and God had blessed her with Ethan. And now they could have a family of their own.

She just wished she could be sure of her husband's reaction.

If he didn't want the baby, she'd be devastated. She hadn't known how much it would matter to her, how much she could love something so tiny she couldn't even feel movement yet.

But she did love the tiny being growing inside her.

And she desperately wanted Ethan to as well.

———

ELOISE STOOD in the last curve of the stone stairway that led to the sea. From here, she had an unhindered view of a stretch of beach and high cliff walls, but with evening falling, it would be difficult for someone near the water to see her tucked in against the wall.

She anchored herself with one palm against the cool, rough stone, breathing hard as if she'd run down here.

She hadn't. She'd dawdled, walking as slowly as she could get away with.

She'd known what she had to do even before Jill had caught her just after supper with another push for using the bull rider to help their publicity. The media specialist had already spoken to the council about dropping the charges against Cody and they had seemed amenable to it, though nothing had been finalized yet.

Eloise had finally considered the suggestion after leaving the laundry room, breathless and unsure of herself. The cowboy—Cody —had made her forget herself, even if just for a few moments.

It had been years—before the accident, at the very least—since someone had treated her like a regular girl. No one on staff dared do anything that might remotely offend her. They were all afraid of being fired.

She'd thought she preferred it that way, keeping everyone at a distance, but this afternoon, she'd felt a lightness and freedom that had been foreign to her for two decades.

And then he'd challenged her. His words had been a teasing warning, almost an invitation, to get into a tickle fight with him. Though it wouldn't have been much of a fight, not with him all wrapped up like that.

Had he really wanted that? Wanted to spend time with her? Maybe she'd been imagining the light in his eyes. Which she very well could've been. She couldn't figure out *why* he might be attracted to her. She was ugly. And all she'd done was act cruelly toward him. Except for today.

Was it possible that their playtime with Christy had spawned his attraction?

And even if he was attracted to her, she knew it was only a matter of time before she lost her temper again, and whatever he might feel for her evaporated. If it had even been there in the first place, and wasn't a figment of her imagination.

She couldn't afford to allow her heart to get involved. To have any expectation that he might like her or feel friendship for her. She had her people, her kingdom to think about.

She needed the bull rider's help, but she would have to be careful to maintain a distance between them. She'd managed to craft walls between herself and everyone else for all these years. She knew how to do it.

So why was her heart beating so frantically against her breastbone? Her palms were sweating, and she felt as if she couldn't catch her breath. And she hadn't even faced him yet, though she watched him standing at the water's edge.

*She* was attracted to *him* in a way she hadn't ever felt before.

It was frightening, because she knew there was not—couldn't be —any hope. Not as scarred as she was, inside and out.

She forced her feet to carry her forward before she could chicken out. This was for her people. For her Father, even if he wouldn't appreciate the sacrifice she was making.

The sand was soft and warm beneath her feet, and the wind off the bay blew her hair into her face. She pushed it back with one hand as she approached the bull rider.

He didn't seem surprised when she joined him at the water's edge, only turned his head and graced her with a nod. Fine lines fanned from the corners of his eyes. Was he stressed? Missing his family, the uncle she'd had sent away?

How did she even begin? She'd learned early at her father's knee that the diplomatic way required one to make conversation before asking for a favor. She could converse with princes, diplomats, and politicians, but her nerves threatened to overwhelm her for a mere man.

"Are you finding your accommodations to your liking?" she asked finally. Then wanted to slap her own forehead for the idiocy. She curled her hands into fists at her sides instead.

"Everything's fine," he said. "The staff has been taking good care of me." He rolled his shoulders, the movement in her peripheral vision making her notice the muscles of his upper arms. "I just get a little stir-crazy, being inside all day."

Should she apologize for keeping him here? She hadn't forced him to take the blame, but she could have forgiven the old man's attempted theft. If only her temper hadn't gotten the best of her.

She couldn't quite do it. "My assistant is working to get the charges against you dismissed."

This time his face turned entirely toward her. His raised eyebrows showed his surprise. "That's... great. Thank you."

"It may still take some time. Things with the council move slowly."

He nodded, searching her face. It was deeply uncomfortable for her and she stared at the water and focused on simply breathing.

Perhaps he sensed her discomfort, because he went back to watching the waves.

And she still procrastinated, holding back the true question she'd come out here to ask.

"What's a normal day like for you? Back home?" she asked. "Do you have property of your own? Like Gideon?"

"Not me. In between rodeos, I bunk down at Uncle EJ's place, try to help out with his small herd. On the circuit, it's a lot of travel. You travel much?"

She was surprised when he turned the question on her, though maybe she shouldn't have been. "No."

A warm wave came farther up the shore, brushing her toes with foam.

He tilted his head toward her. "Your sisters travel some, though."

It was a statement, but she heard the question behind it. Why didn't she?

Her hair blew against her cheek. She used one finger to pull it down when it caught in her lashes, but she let it remain against her cheek, hiding the scars.

"I prefer to be out of the public eye as much as possible," she said. "And my sisters have helped me by taking over duties for international events."

She felt his gaze on her face but refused to look at him. She couldn't help the hot flush that spread into her cheeks or that it would make the pale scars stand out, but maybe with the wind blowing her hair into her face, he wouldn't be able to see them well.

"If you don't like to be in the public eye, how come you had a camera crew following you around today?"

"It's complicated," she said after too long a pause.

He didn't press for more, but silence lengthened between them until she spoke again.

"My father is not well." Just saying the words aloud threatened to close her throat. "And if he... When he...passes..." She gulped a breath, trying to stem the tide of her tears. "Running the kingdom will fall to me. I don't know if you've seen any local press, but...they have not been kind to me. My father wants me to present a kinder, friendlier image to the public. And my media specialist came up with this idea to allow cameras into the palace. Sort of a behind-the-scenes thing."

His question opened the door for her to ask what she needed to ask. She drew in a deep breath.

———

CODY HAD DEVELOPED A RAGING headache in the early afternoon, and it hadn't abated.

The fading sun's glare off the water had him squinting against the pain.

It was frustrating, because it was a reminder of his injury. All his doubts had boiled to the surface. Would he heal enough to go back on the circuit? If he didn't, what was he going to do next? He wouldn't risk his life to get on a bull again, but he also didn't have anything to fall back on.

All the doubts had driven him out of the castle.

And now, apparently Eloise had sought him out. To tell him she was trying to get him off the hook for the attempted theft. Or for some other reason?

He'd heard whispers about the king's health, but hearing Eloise admit that things were dire had his compassion for her rising.

And that vulnerability that she only seemed to show him. She didn't like to look directly at him, hid behind her hair.

She had more to say. He sensed it, but she'd hesitated. He knew enough to be patient.

"Would you...?" She breathed in deeply. "There's an event tomorrow at the children's hospital, and I was wondering if you'd accompany me. Sort of... act as my buffer." She breathed in as if gathering courage, then went on quickly. "Jill said she'd seen you'd done some similar events as part of your charity work with the rodeo asso-ciation..."

Pain lanced his head. Stupid concussion couldn't let him relax for a minute today.

She must've seen his wince, because she quickly backpedaled. "If you don't wish to, it isn't required or anything."

He turned to face her. Behind her, the blue sky and surf extended to the horizon.

"I don't mind," he said with a shrug. "It's not like I have anything else to do." It would be a chance to see more of the kingdom, which he'd wanted to do. "And if, by chance, I still have to face a trial, it'll probably look good that I tried to help the kingdom, right?"

It was her turn to wince slightly and he felt a little guilty for the teasing. "I never meant for it to get as far as the royal council."

No doubt. In his boredom yesterday, he'd picked up a newspaper and seen how the press skewered her. Reading that had removed most of his residual anger about being detained. Today, hearing that she was going to bat for him and seeing that she sincerely regretted what had happened swept the last vestiges away.

"I really don't mind." And he meant it. He was attracted to the princess, maybe more than he should be considering she'd be ruling the kingdom soon. He wouldn't mind spending time with her.

"Thank you." She still didn't look directly at him, still the wind blow her hair across her face. He itched to tuck her hair behind her ear, get a good look at her, but he couldn't help remembering her sensitivity when he'd touched her elbow to help shield her from the photographer on that very first day.

"What kind of event is it?" he asked, imagining having to pull out the rented tuxedo again. "Some fancy dinner?"

"It's an on-site visit to the children's hospital. The crown has an annual fundraiser, and recently there's been a wing of the Glorvaird hospital dedicated to my father."

He nodded. "Doesn't sound so bad."

But she frowned. "Perhaps." Then she forced a small smile. "I suppose you're anxious to get back to the States and your rodeos."

And that was the rub, wasn't it?

"I'm not in a rush." He started walking again, sand sticking to his feet. He was relieved when she rejoined him, though he couldn't say exactly why. "About six weeks ago, I was in a pretty bad wreck off the back of a bull, and I haven't been medically cleared to get back on yet."

"You were injured?"

He nodded slowly. "Nasty concussion. Doctors were afraid there was some bleeding on my brain."

He saw the twist of her lips. "And you do this willingly?"

He shrugged. "I didn't have many prospects coming out of high school. I'd rodeoed off and on as a kid. And I was good at it. But now..."

"You'll retire?"

He wasn't ready to think about that. "It depends on what the docs say when I get back. Rodeo is a young man's game, but I'm not done yet." At least he hoped so.

Something buzzed, and she pulled a slim, silver phone from her pocket. Sighed softly. "I must return to the palace. I still have work to do tonight."

He settled in next to her. He couldn't imagine how difficult it must be to run an entire kingdom.

Her face turned to the castle, her expression almost wistful as she gazed at the massive building built into the cliff walls.

"Thanks for walking with me," he said. "It was nice to have the company."

Her eyes slid to meet his gaze, surprise evident in their depths. Did no one tell the princess they enjoyed being around her? Had her temper alienated her from everyone? Or did the staff just remain distant out of necessity?

It must make for a lonely existence, especially with her father fading away. Who did the princess confide in? Share her secrets with?

"I'll probably be out here tomorrow," he said, "if you want to join me again." Maybe it was presumptuous to ask, but he did it anyway.

Her glance skipped away at his words, color leeching into her face. "Good evening," was her soft spoken response.

"Good night."

*Chapter Six*

ELOISE THOUGHT SHE WAS PREPARED FOR THE CRUSH OF reporters and flashing cameras, but her heart was flying against her ribs, and she couldn't breathe. And she was still inside the limousine.

She couldn't let them see weakness. Nor could she let her father down.

And above the nerves, she was acutely aware of Cody's knee pressing into hers. After greeting her good morning, he'd been mostly silent through the car ride through Glorvaird's quaint downtown to the newly constructed hospital.

She'd glanced his way once to see him avidly taking in the buildings with their sconces and decorative sandstone. Jill had spent much of the ride telling him interesting tidbits about certain shops that had been in operation for generations, about their nation's growing wine trade, and about how things had changed just in Eloise's lifetime.

How long had it been since Eloise had gone out into the city on her own? Enjoyed the people and the uniqueness of Glorvaird?

She'd never done it. As a child, she'd always been accompanied by her nanny and scores of security personnel. And since the accident, she'd never dared.

It was another thing the scars had ripped away from her. Another long-buried pang of grief.

Now the driver rounded the car, and Eloise had no more time for her worries. Jill clambered out of the front passenger seat and stood next to the rear door as the driver opened it for Eloise.

She gulped in a breath. *Stay calm. Breathe. Smile.*

But she was having trouble doing all of those things as the door opened in front of her. All she wanted to do was shrink into the leather upholstery and demand to be returned to the castle.

The cowboy shifted behind her, reminding her that she *had* to get out. She had to do this for the kingdom.

And maybe, to some degree, for herself.

Her knees shook as she planted her feet on the pavement outside the car and straightened to her full height. Her lips trembled when she tried to stretch them into a smile, so she did what she always did and firmed them into a straight line, nodding regally at the press. Jill had told her that only a couple of trusted reporters would be allowed inside to document the tour.

Eloise could ignore the shouted questions of the rest of them. She took a few steps away from the limo and stood beside Jill.

Cody got out of the car, his imposing height throwing a shadow across her face and shoulder.

She was intensely aware of the click of camera shutters. Had Jill prepared the cowboy for what being photographed next to her would mean?

"You okay?" he asked quietly. His hand came beneath her elbow, warm and solid.

The cameras clicked away, faster now. Whispers rustled through the crowd of media.

His support was surprisingly welcome, but also documented for all time.

She didn't know whether she nodded, but somehow she got her feet moving.

Two of her security detail flanked them as they made their way through the multitude toward the glass doors of the hospital. Voices shouted questions at them, but Jill had already warned Eloise not to stop and answer them.

But that didn't mean she was rendered temporarily deaf.

"Who dressed you for this outing?"

"How is your father's health today?"

"Princess, who's your new beau?"

Her face burned, and she knew her scars were highlighted in stark relief. She wished she could duck her head and hide.

But didn't. She stared straight ahead. *Just keep walking.*

The voices faded into a jumbled cacophony as they moved beneath the overhang and neared the doors.

And one last question rang out, loud in the silence as the automatic doors closed behind them.

"Do you really believe a monster like you is capable of running the kingdom?"

She meant to let the words flow over her like rain, bounce against thick skin and disintegrate into nothing. The trick had worked before.

But this time, the words sank into a soft place in her heart and took hold.

———

CODY WAS USED to being in the spotlight, but he'd never had media interest like this.

Reporters asking questions about Eloise and a possible relationship didn't bug him.

But that last question, shouted into the quiet...

He was watching her face closely enough that he saw the minute tremble of her lower lip. Her lashes swept low against her cheeks, hiding her eyes.

Jill glanced back, her gaze dark with concern, but there was no help coming from her as she greeted a group of what must be hospital administrators.

"Do you need a minute?" he asked quietly. "Nobody would say a word if you duck into a restroom or something."

"I'm fine," she said stiffly.

Sure she was. Her nerves had been obvious the entire car ride. She hadn't smiled once. He could feel her practically vibrating with tension.

She'd brought him along for a reason, to help ease her through this the way he had in the laundry room the day before, but he felt helpless. Had no idea what to do.

Jill turned toward them with a wide smile and introduced two hospital administrators and two approved photographers.

Cody was introduced as a friend of the royal family, here for Gideon's wedding—which was technically true. No mention of being detained by castle guards. He couldn't help noticing the curious looks he got from the press and administrators, but at least they had the decency not to say anything in front of the princess.

He followed the group down a long, light-filled hallway. Childish artwork was framed along the walls, and he couldn't help smiling.

The administrators leading the way turned into some kind of open sitting room, smiling and holding out one hand to usher the princess forward.

He followed her in, nodded at the people within, a mix of doctors and nurses in scrubs, patients—some heavily bandaged—and what must have been patients' families and friends.

"This is our brand-new burn trauma wing," the chief administrator said, "which is dedicated to your father. We are so grateful for the royal family's significant contributions."

Cody was two feet behind her, but he couldn't miss the moment when Eloise froze. She went absolutely still, probably not even breathing.

Applause erupted. Only then did the words the man had said to her register.

*Burn trauma.*

He didn't know how Eloise had gotten her scars, but he could guess that this was the last thing she'd expected to face today. Had she not known what the dedication was for? How had her media advisor not warned her?

Jill looked panicked. He started forward and reached out to touch the princess, pull her away from what had the potential to be a real spectacle.

He stepped up beside the princess, not caring that the photographers were snapping away, not caring who was watching. He turned toward her, ignoring everyone and everything else.

"Breathe," he said, quiet enough that no one could hear him above the applause.

He saw the color had leeched out of her face entirely. She was shaking badly.

And he couldn't just leave her like that. No matter if she would hate him later.

He reached out and clasped her hand in his. Her skin was ice cold.

He leaned down, whispered in her ear. "Somebody's told you that you've got to be brave, keep your chin up. Smile." He had to imagine it was her father, though he couldn't know for sure. "But I'm telling you that it's okay to feel what you feel right now. It's okay to show your people that what's happening right now is affecting you."

Her gaze darted to his, the first movement she'd made since she'd frozen.

He could see the sheen of moisture glazing her eyes, the tears gathering at the corners.

She squeezed his hand as tightly as he tied his gloved hand to his bull rope when he was going into the arena.

"You don't have to show them a happy face," he said. The applause had turned to a smattering now. She was going to have to do something. "You know what these people are going through. Show them you care."

———

*SHOW THEM YOU CARE.*

Cody's words rang in Eloise's head as the lingering applause died down and then stopped completely.

She didn't know how to do that. Didn't know how to be vulnerable to the public when she hated so many things about herself—especially the scars.

They felt like they were physically on fire, like her skin was burning as it had that horrible night. She'd been fourteen and for days afterward, she'd mourned the loss of her beauty. She'd desperately wanted her father—her only living parent—there, but he'd been in the middle of an important negotiation and she'd faced those dark days alone.

Right now she couldn't let go of Cody.

One of the doctors stepped forward, one she recognized. She'd seen him every day for weeks after the accident.

He bowed from the waist and then extended one hand to her.

"D-Doctor Mendoza."

She still didn't let go of Cody, but accepted the doctor's handshake.

"Your Highness. We're honored to have your presence here today."

He nodded to Cody, but didn't make a move to shake the other man's hand. No doubt he could see how close to the edge she was, that she was barely holding on to her composure.

"Might I introduce you to one of my patients? She's talked of nothing but meeting you all morning."

He turned, expecting her to follow him.

And somehow, amazingly, her wooden legs carried her in that direction. Cody was a warm, solid presence at her side as she crossed the room, following the doctor toward a person in a wheelchair at the edge of the crowd.

It wasn't until they were only feet away that Eloise realized it was a young woman. A teenager, really. Her face was half-hidden by stark white bandages, one eye completely covered, and her forehead and hair were hidden by the bandages. Both hands were covered, too.

It was an image near to what Eloise had seen in the mirror for those agonizing weeks. Doctor Mendoza must remember it.

But he acted casual as he made introductions. "Princess Eloise, I'd like you to meet Miss Melinda Winters."

A part of her wanted to recoil from the memories, from the pain and loss they still carried. But hadn't she seen others do that to her? It was a vivid, painful memory still, the way people turned from her ugliness. She refused to do that to an impressionable young woman, to anybody. She was aware of the cameras, of the crowd, and of the many people who watched nearby to see what she would do.

"Hello." She bent to the girl's eye level, still clinging to Cody's hand as if it were her lifeline.

The girl bobbed her head, not speaking. Maybe too shy—or too scared—to meet the beastly princess, though the doctor had claimed differently.

Doctor Mendoza put a hand to the girl's shoulder. "Melinda was trapped in her bedroom when her family's apartment caught fire. She suffered burns and smoke inhalation."

Eloise's throat was closed off, and she couldn't find words.

Cody was there to rescue her again. "I'm real sorry to hear that happened to you. Seems like you've got a good team of doctors here to take care of you."

Eloise didn't have to look at the man beside her to know the warm, genuine smile he wore as he talked to the girl.

Melinda nodded, her gaze lingering on the cowboy.

Doctor Mendoza said something to Cody about the medical team, but it passed over Eloise's head. She couldn't take her focus off the girl.

"Your boyfriend is really cute," Melinda whispered as Cody answered the doctor.

Heat flamed worse in Eloise's face. "He's not...we're not..." She shrugged helplessly, aware of the curious eyes all around.

The girl tilted her head, considering Eloise. When Cody's attention shifted back to Melinda, she asked with an innocent curiosity, "Don't you think the princess is lovely?"

They were still connected, palm-to-palm, and instantly she wanted to distance herself from him.

But he didn't let go.

Prickles climbed the back of her neck, awareness that everyone was listening and watching.

She half-turned to him, and he to her, so they were nearly face-to-face. She couldn't look him in the eye, but stared at the collar of his shirt.

"Please," she whispered, and she didn't know whether she was asking him to lie—and say he found her lovely—or to put her out of her misery.

He didn't rush to answer, which left her heart beating anxiously in her throat and the desire to close her eyes and disappear into the floor. Or run away.

"As a matter of fact," he said in his careful cowboy drawl, "I think the princess's scars enhance her beauty. They show how courageous she is."

He shook her hand where he held it, jogging her out of her misery and making her raise her eyes to his. He looked sincere, his eyes holding hers steadily, but how could he mean what he said? He wasn't smiling, wasn't teasing or joking. He seemed...serious.

There was an audible hum of appreciation from the nearby guests, reminding Eloise that they were in a very public setting.

Then Cody turned to Melinda. "In my profession—bull riding— we happen to think scars give us a story to tell. My best one is right here."

He lifted one lapel of his shirt, revealing a slab of flat stomach roped with muscles. He pointed to a jagged pink scar just beneath his left rib.

Melinda smiled widely. Cameras snapped away.

He was telling the story about how he'd gotten the scar, but Eloise was distracted by one of the other doctors approaching to talk to her.

While her emotions were still close to the surface, she was able to converse with the guests and even pose for some pictures.

But the entire time, she couldn't forget Cody's words. They burned in her stomach like acid.

How could he act like her scars didn't matter?

# Chapter Seven

She had come.

When he arrived on the beach to find her already there, Cody could barely believe the princess had come out to the beach. She stood with her back to him, looking out on the setting sun.

He'd seen her upset during the hospital visit. Saw how hard it had been on her. She'd been quiet and attentive during the short tour of the new facility.

On the drive back to the palace, she'd been silent, stared out the window the entire time. With Jill and the driver in the front, he hadn't wanted to try to mention the conversation they'd had with Melinda.

He'd worried that the princess had been more upset than she'd let on, that the few things he'd been able to say had made things worse for her.

But here she was.

"Evening," he said easily as he joined her.

She continued to stare out at the rolling waves. A storm was brewing off the coast. He could see lightning flashes in the distance, near the horizon. The wind was high, too, whipping her hair against her cheek and rifling through his too.

The princess's arms were wrapped around her middle, like they had been that very first day.

Her lips moved, but in the high winds and with the surf breaking loudly at their feet, he couldn't make out her words.

"What's that?"

She turned to him, her arms coming away from her body and her hands flailing.

"I want you to explain yourself," she said. Her eyes flashed, or maybe it was a reflection of the far-off lightning. "I demand it."

She was furious.

So much for her not being upset after what had happened earlier.

"Which part?" he asked, honestly curious.

She poked her index finger into his chest, her fury boiling. "You said...you said..." She took a breath, seemed to stall out.

Her eyes were wild, her hair blowing in her face.

"I said you were beautiful," he said calmly.

"You lied." She poked him in the chest again. Her voice was almost a shriek.

"I didn't lie." He took hold of her wrist, because that finger was starting to hurt his pec.

She didn't jerk away from him, didn't distance herself like she had before. He held her wrist loosely between them.

"It was kind of you to try and help the girl, but you *lied*. There's nothing about me that's beautiful." She gulped, her shoulders rising and falling with each breath.

It was as if the rising storm was contained within her. He wanted to protect her from it.

"Your scars don't define you," he said.

She shook her head violently. Her hair blew across her face. He desperately wanted to see her eyes.

So this time, he did what he'd wanted to do before. He reached up with his free hand and brushed the hair away, tucking the long strands behind her ear. He cupped her jaw with his hand, the side of her face that was smooth and unblemished.

"You're beautiful," he said, holding her gaze steadily. "Including your scars."

Her eyes closed. She shook her head again, her cheek rubbing against his palm. He didn't let go of her.

"You are beautiful," he whispered.

Two silver tears slipped from beneath her lashes and down her cheeks.

He let go of her wrist to raise his other hand. He gently ran the pad of his index finger over the pale scars that marred her skin.

"You are beautiful," he whispered again.

Her face crumpled as if the weight of the emotions bombarding her was too much to bear. She squeezed her eyes closed.

He ran his finger along her scars until he touched the corner of her mouth.

He couldn't resist. He cupped her jaw with both hands and leaned down to kiss her.

At the first brush of his mouth against hers, she jumped. Maybe she hadn't been kissed in a long time.

She didn't pull away. He focused on that and the tiny tremble of her lips against his.

He feathered kissed against the corners of her lips, the bow of her upper lip, then slanted his mouth fully over hers.

Her hands, uninvolved until now, came to rest at his waist. Not quite clinging to him, but close.

And then a nearby rumble of thunder startled them both, and he stepped away.

———

ELOISE STARED AT CODY, who was still standing close enough that she could feel the warmth emanating from his body, such a contrast to the chill of the cold front that had swept in.

*You are beautiful.* His words whispered through her mind, bouncing off her loss and the truth of her disfigurement.

His intense eyes held her captive. Only inches separated their bodies.

"Don't hide from me," he said, his words punctuated by another flash of lightning, another roll of thunder. "Not now."

How did he know that was her instinct? That his words had frightened her with the intensity of how desperately she wanted to believe him.

How could she believe his word, when her past had pummeled the truth of her hideousness into her? When so many had shied away from her, turned away in disgust?

When she knew the ugliness she carried whenever she unleashed her horrible temper?

She wanted to believe him.

He reached for her, but a wall of icy rain descended on them.

Lightning struck again, and thunder boomed, dangerously close now.

They needed to take cover.

She met his outstretched hand, and they ran for the steps. As soon as they were sheltered in the curve of the outdoor stairwell, Cody pressed her against the stone wall. He brushed wet hair off her face, away from her scars. She thought to insist they continue upstairs and into the shelter of the castle.

But she didn't, because the last thing she wanted was for this moment to be over.

All her life, she'd longed for this, a man who looked at her as if she were beautiful. A man to hold her and touch her as if she were a priceless treasure. She hadn't even known the ache was there until the look in his eyes massaged it away.

He leaned closer, seemed to waiting for her to protest. She opened her lips, thinking she should. But the words lodged somewhere between her fear and her aching desire.

He took her hesitation for permission and kissed her again.

In the curve of stone, the rain only reached them when it was carried on a gust of wind. His skin was warm, his lips both hot and gentle against her rain-chilled skin.

This time she clung to him, her hands linking behind his neck, his resting respectfully at her waist.

Perhaps she couldn't believe his words, but could she believe his kiss, just for these moments?

*Chapter Eight*

M IA OPENED THE DOOR TO ELOISE'S SUITE, QUIETLY SO AS not to disturb her sister if was on a phone call for official business.

But as Mia looked into the room, Eloise stood near the window, watching the downpour that had begun late yesterday and continued through this morning.

Eloise didn't seem to be looking at the beach. She seemed to be staring at her reflection in the weeping glass. As Mia watched, her sister lifted one hand to touch the scars on her chin, at the corner of her lips.

In ten years, Mia had never seen her sister glance in a mirror, never seen her consider her appearance.

Eloise wasn't smiling, but she wasn't frowning or furious either.

What happened that had caused Mia's sister to be able to look at her reflection?

Eloise must've sensed Mia's presence, because she turned away from the window.

"Good morning," Eloise said briskly. "Thank you for coming down."

Eloise started toward her credenza but slowed when she caught sight of Mia. "Are you all right?"

Mia knew she was pale, had spent several minutes in the loo earlier giving up her breakfast. She'd hoped to mention the pregnancy to Eloise, enlist her sister's advice on how best to broach the subject with Ethan, but now the words lodged in her throat.

"Fine," she mumbled, feeling a twinge guilt. She was usually completely honest with her sister.

"Alessandra texted and said she needed to speak to both of us. My assistant is keying her up on the screen." Eloise motioned to the digital screen along one wall.

"From her honeymoon?" Mia asked with a little laugh.

Eloise wrinkled her nose, sharing a look with her sister. "I assumed it must be important."

Mia cherished the moment of intimacy with her sister. For years, there'd been a wall between them, one of Eloise's making. But since the assassination attempts last year, their family had come together in ways that had seemed impossible before.

But there was still a small part of her that wished for Alessandra's presence. She was closer to her middle sister and wouldn't have hesitated to bring up the pregnancy and her fears.

The dark screen lightened, and Alessandra's image appeared against a wood-paneled wall in what must be her hotel room.

"You'd better have a good excuse for taking time away from your brand new husband," Mia teased.

"It was his idea to call," Alessandra said with a wry smile. "How's Father?"

"The pneumonia is taking a lot out of him," Eloise said.

In the video screen, Alessandra's gaze shifted to Mia. "What's wrong with you?"

Mia's face heated, but she did her best to keep anything from crossing her face. "Nothing that can't wait. I might call you later." She was aware of Eloise's sideways glance but ignored it. "What's going on?"

"We've found the missing princess. Gideon's inside man came through. We think her name is Kylie Winters. She's the right age, and everything matches up."

Mia's heart pounded. Their sister was found. But Alessandra wasn't done.

"There's a problem, though. We know where she was up until last year, but she seems to have dropped off the face of the earth. She quit her job, vacated her apartment, and disappeared. Gideon's friend is working to track her down, but she's essentially off the grid, so it's difficult."

Eloise nodded. "At least we're closer."

There was a moment where Alessandra focused off screen. Mia heard Gideon's voice, though she couldn't make out the words.

Alessandra turned back to the camera. "Gideon wants to know if you've heard any news from Pieter."

Eloise shook her head. "I've met with him twice, but he hasn't been able to locate his mother."

That wasn't good. If their aunt learned of their half sister, if she somehow found this Kylie before they did, what would she do?

Mia's stomach gurgled all over again, this time not because of the baby.

———

CODY HADN'T KNOWN what to expect from the crown princess after they'd shared those kisses, but it surely hadn't been an invitation to join her shopping. Not that he minded. He'd wanted to visit the downtown area, get a look around, so a trip to the shops seemed a good enough excuse to him.

Yesterday, they'd spent hours dawdling along the quaint streets in the historic downtown area.

There had been no camera crew, no media lady, only one unobtrusive security guy following a few paces behind.

The car had dropped them off on the sidewalk, and other than a few curious glances, no one seemed to pay them much attention.

"I haven't done this... ever," she'd admitted with a glance at him.

He'd taken her hand in his, let his gaze roam the quaint two-story buildings, the stone sidewalks, the hand-lettered signs. "Then let's explore together."

Today, it seemed he was in for a repeat, and he was glad for it.

The morning was half over as they ducked out of the misty rain and into a bakery. Sugar and cinnamon smells permeated the air. There were only a couple of patrons inside. A man in a white apron, stained with chocolate across the middle as if he'd swiped his hand there, stood behind a glass counter. His eyes widened almost comically when he took in the princess.

But they'd visited different businesses for the past two days, and apparently word had gotten out, because he didn't show the shock and fear the other proprietors had but welcomed them with a smile, albeit a hesitant one.

Cody and Eloise weaved their way among small, round tables for two and toward the counter and the delectable treats there.

"I already ate breakfast," he confessed, letting his hand rest at her waist.

She glanced over her shoulder at him, eyes open and warm. "Me too, but everything smells so...heavenly."

Pain pierced behind his right eye, but the princess was leaning forward, peering into the glass case and didn't notice.

He'd gone forty-eight hours without a headache. He'd even let himself hope they were gone for good.

The baker was finishing up with one customer as they perused the baked goods when suddenly, a small head and shoulders popped up from behind the counter.

"Hiya!" a high voice said.

He had to smile as he looked over the top of the counter to the wooden stool that a little girl—who couldn't be more than four or five—stood on.

"Hey, you're the princess!"

He couldn't help smiling at the little girl's excitement, though he felt Eloise tense beside him.

"What's your name?" he asked.

"Cecily," came the instant answer. "That's my grandpa." She pointed to the aproned man. "You never been to our bakery before, have ya? Whatcha gonna have?"

"Does your grandpa bake everything here?" he asked. There was a wide selection, from donuts to pastries to cookies and cakes.

"My dad helps too, before he goes to his other job at the cannery." The words were said proudly. "Dad and grandpa get up at three in the morning to start the baking."

He wanted to groan, thinking about early mornings like that.

"What's your favorite thing your grandpa makes?" Eloise asked.

He glanced at her, proud of the way she'd jumped in.

"The chocolate twists," Cecily said immediately. "If I'm a real good helper, Papaw lets me have one before nap time."

*Papaw* joined them, wiping his hands on his apron. "Cecily-girl. You're not bothering the princess, are you?" Now the man's glance darted to Eloise, and a twitch of his mustache betrayed his nerves.

Eloise could have tightened up—probably would've before—but she shook her head slightly, and he caught the smile from his peripheral vision. "She's talked me into a chocolate twist. If there's enough to hold one back for her naptime treat."

The older man smiled. "Of course, Your Highness."

"How long have you been in business, sir?" Cody asked as the man wrapped a donut in tissue for Eloise and did the same for a slice of coffee cake that Cody had been eyeing.

"I helped my granddad with the shop when I was Cecily's age," the older man said, and his pride in the legacy was unmistakable.

They'd experienced the same sense of pride at the shops they'd visited over past two days. Eloise had a large load of responsibilities, and it was hard for her to take time away from the palace, but she'd done it, and it seemed to be paying off.

They took their pastries and the coffees that *Papaw* provided and settled in a corner table in the nearly-empty bakery.

It had been good for Eloise to be out among her people. While the press might call her unflattering names, her work in the palace had paid off. Glorvaird was prospering, the tourism providing income for small business owners, and the trade partnerships the palace had created and maintained helping the large import/export businesses.

The Glorvaird people held a clear respect for Eloise and her family, and being out in public, she'd been able to experience it first-hand. The papers had exaggerated what people thought of her. The palace had thought to protect her from it, but being out with her people had shown her the truth.

And Cody was proud to have been a part of that, no matter how small.

The Eloise who sat across from him now, a smear of chocolate on the bow of her upper lip, was not the same woman who'd glared at him during her sister's wedding.

He was starting to fall for her, no matter that it had only been a few days, no matter the difference in their stations, or that she'd initially thought him a crook. He knew it was as dangerous as being on the back of a bull—maybe more so, because when he rode, he wore a helmet and protective vest. Right now, his heart was totally unguarded. But he couldn't seem to help himself.

"It's good, huh?" he asked, after sinking his teeth into the coffee cake. Some of the best he'd ever tasted.

All he got was a hum of acknowledgement, because her mouth was full.

Beneath the table, he slid his booted foot next to hers, nudged her sandal. When they were in public, he was always careful with what affection he showed.

But privately... Just this morning, they'd shared a searing kiss before they'd been ushered into the palace limo.

Soft pink color crept into Eloise's cheeks, but she didn't dismiss his gesture.

One of the bakery's customers left, and a little bell tinkled over the door, sending a new shaft of pain pulsing against the bass drum that Cody was experiencing.

Eloise noticed this time. Her hand moved to touch his wrist. "Another headache?"

———

A NIGGLE of worry bloomed in Eloise's gut when Cody nodded. "It's not that bad."

Except for the wince he hadn't been able to hide.

"I can get one of our physicians to meet you in your suite later, if you'd like." He'd told her about his concussion and recovery, about how the doctors hadn't released him to ride bulls again.

It worried her. More than it should, probably. They'd made no commitments to each other. When he returned to the States—which, inevitably, he would—they likely would never see each other again.

But she'd begun to feel so close to him that it was impossible not to worry about his health. If the doctors released him to ride again, what if he re-injured himself?

What if he died?

She couldn't bear to think it.

"I'll be fine," he said. "It's nothing an ibuprofen won't fix. And I've got an appointment with my head docs when I get back..." *Home.*

Her chest tightened at the thought.

She tried to force a smile, tried to speak naturally, even though her throat closed off and the words didn't want to come. "I spoke to Jill early this morning, and she's cleared things with the royal council. They've dismissed the charges against you, and there won't be a trial."

So there was no real reason for him to stay in Glorvaird.

She'd received the news with both touches of relief and grief. Cody had changed her for the better. Had dared get close enough to her, climb her walls to show her that she still had value, scars and all.

He'd made her feel beautiful again.

And she was afraid she was in love with him.

His eyebrows crunched together, but before he could respond to what she'd said, Cecily popped up next to their table.

"Didja like the donut?" the girl asked with a winsome smile.

Eloise pulled her hand back across the table, aware that perhaps she shouldn't be touching him. "It was excellent." She welcomed the chance to focus on the girl instead of on the cowboy who might be leaving Glorvaird. Maybe even today. "The best I've had in a long time."

Cecily's chest puffed with pride. "I knew'd it. Are ya gonna come back some other time?"

Cody chuckled at the girl's bluntness, and Eloise couldn't help smiling. "Of course. Now I'll be craving a chocolate twist donut."

Although it would be a bittersweet visit without Cody at her side.

Cecily tilted her head to one side, considering Eloise. "My Papaw said you got those scars in a bad car accident. Do they still hurt?"

It was a loaded question, one that would've ignited her temper before.

She caught Cody's concerned gaze but quickly turned her attention back to the girl.

"Not anymore." The words were truer than she'd expected them to be as she spoke them aloud.

Her scars hadn't hurt physically in years, but she'd felt the pain of having them, felt as if being physically scarred had destroyed all her dreams.

Until now. Until Cody.

They finished their bakery snacks and loaded up in the limousine to return to the palace.

Eloise had her gaze fixed out the window when Cody's hand closed over hers on the seat between them.

She glanced over to him.

"I was thinking I might stay in Glorvaird awhile longer," he said. "I'm not in a rush to get back."

His words sent joy spiraling through her. He wanted to stay? He wanted to stay!

She tried to temper it, tried not to let it get out of control.

"Maybe you should check in with your uncle," she suggested.

Cody nodded. "You mind if I call now?"

She shook her head, and he pulled his smartphone from his jeans' pocket. Their hands remained linked on the seat between them.

He tapped and swiped across the screen until the video chat app kicked on, and then his uncle's image appeared in the screen. She tried not to watch, tried to let Cody have his conversation as privately as possible.

But it wasn't his uncle as she'd last seen him. This version of EJ was pale, almost gray in coloring. And he seemed to be...oh, my. Was he lying in a hospital bed?

"Uncle EJ, what's wrong? What's going on?"

"Nothing much, boy." But even from across the bench seat, Eloise could hear he was lying. She could hear the shallow pants of his breathing, hear beeps from a machine. "Just had a little episode, that's all."

"Have you seen the cardiologist yet? What are they saying?" Cody fired off questions at his uncle, but Eloise turned her face to the window.

She gently extricated her hand from Cody's, and he didn't seem to notice, now clutching his phone with both hands.

The joy from moments ago was replaced with both worry for Cody's uncle and the knowledge that she couldn't ask him to stay, not now. Not when his uncle was sick, could even be dying.

He rang off just as they pulled beneath the portico at the castle. She turned to him in the back of the car, their knees brushing.

"You have to go to him," she said earnestly. "He needs you."

He ran his hand through his hair, agitated. "But..."

She reached for him, let her palm rest on his thigh just for a moment. If she held on any longer, she'd beg him to stay.

"It's all right," she said, holding his gaze steadily, keeping her emotions at bay by a thread. "EJ needs you. I'll have my assistant book you a flight out as soon as possible."

*She* needed him. She hadn't realized how much until just this moment.

She needed him, because she'd fallen in love with him.

And because she loved him, she had to let him go.

———

LATE THAT NIGHT, Eloise stood in one of the upper towers, standing beside a window overlooking the beach. It was a clear night, and she'd just seen the lights from the last plane flying out of Glorvaird.

Cody was on that plane.

She missed him with a visceral hurt, and he'd only been gone a few hours.

She'd spent so long keeping up her barriers, the walls that kept everyone from getting close enough to hurt her, that she didn't know what to do with this pain.

She loved Cody, and she'd had to let him go.

His life was across an entire ocean. He had sponsorships and his uncle and possibly even a return to the rodeo circuit to attend to.

And who would want to give up all of that for a princess who was just learning how to live again?

Chapter Nine

CODY STARED AT THE ONLINE NEWSPAPER HEADLINE HE'D pulled up on his uncle's tablet. *King of Glorvaird Passes Away.*

Oh no.

He immediately reached for his phone to dial Eloise, though she hadn't answered any of his calls since he'd left her a week ago.

She didn't answer now either.

"What's the matter, son?"

Cody looked up to see EJ's curious gaze from where he reclined in his La-Z-Boy. EJ's ranch house was small but functional, the place Cody had spent his teenage years.

The TV was old school, thick and heavy. The furniture was more than fifteen years old, and it showed.

It still felt like home, and EJ was still his closest kin. But something had changed inside Cody. Everything was the same, but not. Texas chafed.

Part of it was EJ. He wasn't the man Cody remembered from years past. He was flawed. He'd apologized to Cody and written a letter to Eloise at Cody's behest. But Cody wasn't sure what to believe about EJ's intentions the night of the wedding reception.

He could forgive his uncle, because without EJ's interference, Cody never would've gotten close to the princess. Although his uncle's episode had passed, he was still sick, still dying. And he'd promised no more shenanigans.

Another consideration was his injury. He'd met with his doctors to talk about his ongoing headaches and they'd recommended he end his rodeo career. They couldn't definitively say he'd kill himself if he rode again, but it was a risk. If he didn't compete, didn't win, his sponsorships would dry up. He'd invested enough of his winnings along the way that he had a small cushion in the bank. He didn't have to choose a new profession immediately. But no longer having a career meant he was at loose ends.

The bigger part of why Texas no longer fit was a princess—now a queen, he realized—half a world away.

"Eloise's dad died." Just saying the words hit him low in the gut. She must be devastated.

He knew things had been difficult with her father, with the pressure the king had put on her and her duties running the kingdom.

Was she taking care of herself? Allowing her sisters in or drowning in grief all alone?

"You should go to her," EJ said. "I've got all those church ladies to look in on me."

It was true. EJ had made international news, photographed with a princess and his semi-famous nephew, even though the press hadn't been exactly kind to his uncle either. Some of the busybodies from their local church had got it in their heads that EJ could be set on the straight and narrow if they plied him with casseroles. There was a parade of old, single women through his home nearly every other day, something Cody couldn't help but chuckle about when he thought of it.

Cody imagined returning to Glorvaird as he dialed again and held the phone to his ear. Would Eloise be happy to see him?

The phone rang but he still got her voicemail. He left a message this time. "It's Cody. I just heard the news. Wondering if you're okay. I wanted..." To be there with her. "To check on you. Call me." He hung up.

After a week of silence, somehow he knew she wouldn't.

If Cody did go back to Glorvaird, would Eloise welcome him? Or would her protective walls have come back up, reinforced and stronger than ever, since he'd gone?

He missed her with an ache that rivaled the stupid headaches. With the distance between them, he'd come to realize that he wasn't falling in love with her. He'd already fallen. Hard.

He loved her resilience. That she hadn't given up on life, even though she'd guarded herself so carefully.

He loved her devotion to her family and her kingdom.

He loved the little wrinkle that appeared at the bridge of her nose when she was lost in thought.

He also knew she wasn't going to invite him back. She'd been careful in her goodbyes, wishing him luck and asking about EJ's health. She was so used to keeping everyone at a distance, he couldn't imagine her making herself vulnerable enough to ask him to return.

If he loved her, he needed to go back and prove it. See if they could have a future together.

# Chapter Ten

ETHAN HAD HAD ENOUGH. ENOUGH OF HIS WIFE AVOIDING him. Enough of fearing the moment when she'd tell him she didn't love him anymore.

If she was done with him, he wanted to know it.

He took a deep breath and pushed open the door to their bedroom. He found her sitting on the edge of the bed, hunched over with her face in her hands. She was crying quietly.

Maybe confronting Mia wasn't the best idea, not in the dark days after her father's death.

She looked up, her face tear-streaked, and he couldn't stay away. Even if things didn't end up the way he wanted.

He held out his arms. She came into his embrace easily, like it was the most natural thing for her. He tucked her head beneath his chin as he sat with her on the bed, holding her through her grief.

He loved her so much. He honestly didn't know how he would survive without her.

When her tears seemed to be spent, he pulled her back to lie on top of the coverlet next to him, her head tucked against his shoulder.

He stared up at the ceiling. Desperation crawled up his throat.

"You've been distracted lately," he said into the stillness of the room. "Even before...your dad..."

She took a shaky breath.

"If you want me to go back to the States after the funeral... take some time for yourself, I will."

The words cut his throat like glass, but he didn't call them back, no matter how much he wanted to.

Her head moved slightly, the crown of her head brushing his jaw. "I don't want that."

He swallowed, throat tight and hot. Couldn't help his eyes from closing in thankfulness. She didn't want him to go.

Her legs tensed, shifted. "I need to tell you something, and I'm not sure how you're going to react."

What could be so bad that she'd fear telling him?

"I'm pregnant."

Everything in him—all the whirling thoughts, the beat of his heart, everything—went still. *A baby?*

"We're having a baby?" The words came from deep inside, passed through a mouth gone desert dry.

He rose on his elbow, jostling her slightly, but he had to see her face.

Her eyes were still tear-filled as she nodded slightly.

He didn't know how to read her at this moment. She looked... miserable.

"And you're... upset?" he asked tentatively, afraid to make things worse.

"No!" she exclaimed fiercely. "Aren't you upset? I thought after everything with your brothers that you'd want some time without... without the burden."

He tucked some loose strands of her hair behind her ear, brushed a kiss on her cheek. "Our baby won't be a burden. She'll be a little bundle of joy."

Mia's face brightened, and she threw her arms around his neck.

He laughed, some of the tension of the past days seeping from him. A baby. They were having a baby.

He cupped Mia's jaw, kissed her passionately as tears fell on both their cheeks.

———

It took Cody two days to get there, between scheduling flights out of the U.S. and coordinating with Jill, who would only tell him the princess "wasn't herself."

Of course she wasn't. She was grieving.

The staff pointed him to the beach, and he found her at the farthest edge. He'd hiked the sand plenty enough times to know the spot where the sand met stone walls.

She was lying prone on the sand amidst jagged black boulders that jutted out of the sand.

The tide had come in and was lapping at her bare feet. Was she hurt? Had she fallen and hit her head?

Facedown, he could only see part of her pale cheek not obscured by her hair. She was as pale and still as death.

"Eloise!" he shouted when he was still yards away, loping toward her at top speed.

He fell to his knees beside her with a spray of sand and reached for her with trembling hands.

She rolled over, her shoulders shaking in his hands. She took a ragged breath.

She was covered in sand, damp from being in the sea air for who knew how long, but she was alive.

He brushed at the sand on her face, trying to get her hair out of the way so he could get a proper look at her. Was she injured? Why was she just lying there?

"Don't," she mumbled, batting at his hand.

He ignored her protest. "It's all right, honey, I'm here."

Her eyes flashed open, and she rewarded him with the first glimpse of her devastated blue depths. "Cody?"

"In the flesh." He used his thumb to swipe the last few grains of sand from her jaw, examining her face from close up. She seemed unharmed.

She looked worn clear through. Lines of sadness fanned from the corners of her eyes, and dark circles drooped beneath.

He still thought she was beautiful. And back in his arms, just where she belonged.

Maybe not lying in the sand with the surf licking at their feet.

He helped her sit up.

"You scared me," he said, one hand at her back. And then, because latent fear and adrenaline were still spiraling through him, he crushed her to him. He held her tightly to his chest, just breathing in the sand and salt and Eloise's own unique scent.

Her hands clutched his T-shirt, fisted tightly in the material.

She was still shaking, and it took him a moment to realize she was crying. Her tears were hot where her face pressed against his neck. He cupped the back of her head, content to hold her as long as she needed.

Eventually, she quieted to soft hiccups and then to the occasional sniffle.

His left leg had gone to sleep, and he had to shift. She let go of his shirt and wiped her face with her palms.

When she sat up, and her shoulders straightened, the signs of the grieving woman were gone, save the blotches of color that remained in her face.

"What are you doing here?" she asked.

———

ELOISE WAS afraid of the massive outpouring of hope that had risen in her breast when she'd realized Cody was real—really here—and not an apparition she'd dreamed up in her haze of grief and pain.

It was entirely possible he'd come for the funeral and that was it. She had to tame the wild hope swirling in her like a typhoon.

He brushed wet strands of hair out of her eyes, then cupped her cheek, his palm covering her scars.

"I would've been here sooner, but it took three connecting planes and too long..."

She shook her head, unable to find words. She still couldn't fathom it. He'd come.

"I called."

She hadn't been able to listen to his voice, knowing she would never see him again.

"You're here, but...why?" she dared to ask.

He tilted his head slightly to one side, his eyes warm as they focused on her face. "Because I love you."

Joy and hope rose up inside her, bubbling out in a strangled half sob. "*Why?*"

He didn't lose his smile, didn't stop touching her face. "For a million reasons. I think I started falling for you during the wedding, wondering what it was about me that you hated so much that you glared at me the whole way through."

Her face flushed with heat and she raised one hand to cover her embarrassment from him, but he wouldn't let her hide. He linked their fingers together and pulled her hand away.

"I know I'm no prince, but my intuition tells me you might feel the same way," he continued.

Her face was on fire now, but she nodded minutely. "I do. I love you."

He lost the slight edge of tension that had tightened his shoulders. His smile softened, and he leaned in to brush his lips across hers.

She laid her palm against his chest, content to lean her head against his chin and bask in his embrace.

How had it come to this? She'd been so sure they'd never see each other again.

She cleared her throat. "Your uncle?"

"Ornery as ever," he said, pressing another kiss against her temple. "He pushed me to come to you." His arms squeezed tight around her. "I'm sorry about your father."

So was she.

She'd been shocked and surprised at the dedication of the hospital's burn center. She hadn't realized how deeply Father's passion for the project had run until she'd seen it in person. The dedication had opened the door for her to finally reach out to her Father one last time, realizing that he loved her in his own way, even when he hadn't been able to say the words.

Her grief over his death was all-encompassing, still pounding her heart like ocean waves even beneath the joy of being with Cody again.

"Can you stay through the funeral?" She whispered the question. "We're having a family service tomorrow, but the state funeral won't be for another week."

"I can stay longer than that," he said. "And if I have to go again, I promise I'll come back." He used one hand to turn her jaw, so she was looking right at him. "I'll always come back to you."

# Epilogue

"DO YOU REALLY BELIEVE SHE'S FIT TO RULE? SHE HAD AN outburst in public just three months ago."

Eloise overheard the question from where she stood outside the door to one of the castle's meeting rooms. She knew the identity of the speaker—one of her father's top advisors and a member of the royal council—and his words stung.

But not like they would've before Cody had come into her life.

Now...well, she didn't exactly feel pretty, but somehow Cody thought she was beautiful. And by seeing herself through his eyes, she was able to ignore people's snide comments and appreciate the friends and citizens who supported her.

She'd stopped expecting everyone to hate her for her looks, stopped reading the tabloids altogether, and started listening to what her people really had to say. She believed she could run the country, provide for her people, make the world a better place.

She was changed, and it was all thanks to the man she loved. Because of Cody, she could face this meeting. It was important, because of the question Cody had told her he wanted to ask her.

He wanted to marry her. And because she was the crown princess, the royal council had to approve of him before the marriage would be allowed. It was an archaic law, and probably she could get it changed if she really, really wanted to—although that process could take years— but she'd rather do things the traditional way. It was in her own small way a tribute to her father.

And the sooner she got this over with, the sooner she could return to Cody, who was waiting in the palace gardens.

"Good afternoon," she said as she walked into the meeting with a smile.

The men and one woman of the council seemed completely baffled by Eloise's poise and demeanor.

And that was the moment when she knew she'd be able to convince them that Cody was the best thing that had ever happened to her.

———

*SHUSH WHUSH, shush whush.*

"That's her," Ethan said, his voice soft with awe.

Mia couldn't take her eyes off of the ultrasound monitor, where the tiny blip of their baby's heart beat like hummingbird wings. Ethan's hand clutched hers, or maybe they clutched each other.

Mia's heart was flying, too.

She sniffled. "It could be a boy."

The ultrasound tech locked the baby's image on the screen and faded into the background as their gentle, teasing argument continued.

Finally, Mia's tears wouldn't be stemmed, and several ran down her cheeks.

"Hey," Ethan whispered, cupping her cheek in his big, warm hand. "What's the matter?"

"We're really going to do this. Have a baby."

"Little late to change our minds now." He nodded to the ultrasound screen and the little body curled in the fetal position. "You scared?"

"A little," she admitted. "What if I'm not a good mom? I don't even remember my own mother."

And he'd lost his mom at such a young age, and his stepmother had been horrible to him. A tiny sob hiccupped out.

He didn't seem fazed. He pulled her in so her face was tucked into his shoulder and allowed her to vent the overwhelming emotions. Stupid hormones.

When her tears had descended to mere sniffles again, he sat next to her on the examination table. "We'll both have a lot to learn about being good parents," he said softly. "But we can do it together. There's nothing to be scared of as long as we've got each other."

His words were a balm to her, reassurance of what she already knew. Cody was strong where she was weak, and when he was vulnerable, she could be his rock. They were a good match, a perfect fit. Their baby would be loved, endlessly, and she couldn't wait to meet him or her.

———

## Two months later

*WELCOME TO OKLAHOMA!* the roadside sign proclaimed.

Kylie Winters curled her hands around the steering wheel, tensing until her knuckles were white.

She was really doing this.

Four states, fifteen hundred miles, one grieving heart.

This was her last stop on a year-long road trip, her last chance to connect with a deceased mother. Kylie had wanted this trip to be about discovery, but she hadn't found what she'd been looking for.

Maybe it didn't exist.

Autumn was turning the landscape into a kaleidoscope of color. Kylie turned off the interstate and onto a meandering two-lane road. It would be another hour of driving before she reached her destination, and she knew to watch out for speed traps as she drove through small towns along the way.

She wasn't in any hurry, not really. Facing these memories would be painful.

So she rolled down the windows in her beater of a car and let her foot ease off the gas a little.

Her road trip buddy, a white shepherd mix named Snow, stretched from where she'd been dozing across the backseat. The dog stuck first its nose and then entire head out the open window, barking with joy as the wind ruffled the fur on her face.

Kylie laughed. And then she was pierced with grief, because Mom would've laughed and tried to take a photo even as she drove.

Snow had been Mom's dog. Kylie had rescued her when she'd arrived at mom's apartment two days after she'd received the phone call from her mom's neighbor telling her of mom's sudden passing.

Kylie and her mom hadn't agreed on much in the last six years, but Kylie could see why her mom had loved the dog. Snow was kind-hearted and sensitive, often coming near to put her chin on Kylie's knee when a wave of sadness hit, as they did so often and so unexpectedly.

Another roadside sign showed that Bear Lake was only forty-five more miles.

Forty-five miles to the last place where she'd really felt safe. The last moments of her childhood had taken place in Bear Lake.

Would she be able to face the last untarnished memories of Mom?

# The Lost Princess

<h1 style="text-align:center;font-style:italic">Chapter One</h1>

KYLIE WINTERS LIFTED HER FOOT FROM THE ACCELERATOR and let her old beater slow as she took in the grandeur of the changing colors. She knew Oklahoma had its share of plains and wheat fields, but this eastern part of the state was hilly and covered in trees. The autumn season was performing its magic as it turned the leaves a rainbow of yellows, oranges, and reds.

Cool evening wind from the open passenger window whipped her hair into her eyes, but Snow—her white shepherd mix—had her nose out the window, and Kylie couldn't bear to ruin the animal's enjoyment.

Her memory didn't do the tree-covered hills justice. Had it always been a kaleidoscope of color like this?

The two lane road wound through the hills, inviting a leisurely pace, and Kylie went with it. Shadows fell as the evening lengthened, and she flipped on her headlights.

But simple enjoyment of the scenery felt out of her reach. She wanted to slow her journey, to try and grasp the peace that was so elusive, even after a spring and summer of searching. Bear Lake was her last stop. If she couldn't find what she was looking for here, maybe it didn't exist.

Right now, she felt more chaotic than she had just after Mom had died.

And the small town nestled beside the lake that was its namesake was only another mile ahead.

Apparently, her dawdling had attracted attention, and not the good kind. Blue and red lights flashed, and a siren gave a short *whoop, whoop* from behind.

Biting her lip, she put on her blinker and pulled off the shoulder, tires crunching in the gravel.

She was cranking down her window by hand when the officer approached. He was clean-shaven with a military-precision haircut and metallic reflective sunglasses that hid his eyes. It was really too late in the day for glasses like that.

No matter that he was handsome, like a young Tom Cruise. His expression revealed nothing as he halted next to her open window. That blankness gave her a little shiver.

Snow barked once, and Kylie shushed her.

"Is everything all right, Officer?" she asked.

"You've got a brake light out. You aware of that?"

She ground her back teeth together. "No, sir."

He waited as if he were expecting her to say more, but years of experience living with her mother had taught her when to keep silent.

Finally, he spoke again. "You've got out-of-state tags. What brings you to town?"

An inquisition was the last thing she needed. She forced her lips into a semblance of a smile. "I remember this highway being a speed trap, but I didn't realize it was a free-for-all to pull people over."

Shoot. She hadn't meant to mouth off like that. Her hands trembled but, she clutched the bottom of the steering wheel with both hands until her knuckles turned white.

He looked down his nose at her, mouth twisting slightly. "See your license and insurance, please?"

Snow panted in Kylie's ear as she reached over to pop the dash console and flipped through the tire and oil change receipts to find the insurance paper. Why did they make them so tiny? *Expired. Expired.* There it was. *Current.*

Her hand still had a little tremble as she passed the paper and her license to the cop. Prayed he wouldn't notice.

He took the documents. "Keep your car parked."

———

OFFICER NICK HARRIS tapped the woman's license and papers against his opposite hand as he strode back to his police cruiser.

He hated being assigned to the speed trap. The one-mile stretch leading into Bear Lake was the worst assignment on the small-town force, and everybody knew it. A lot of sitting in the patrol car and not much else. He'd been stuck on ticket duty for months. And he deserved it, but when was penance enough?

When would it be enough to absolve him of the guilt that chased him at every turn?

The little gal was pretty enough, and it irritated him to have to pull her over. The attitude should have been a turn-off, but something about her called to him. Beneath the sarcasm, there was a hint of vulnerability in her eyes. The car gave off clues. An older model, not in very good shape. But the dog was well-cared for. White and clean—when it would be so easy to let it get dirty. The backseat had been littered with fast food bags. Where was she coming from?

She'd said she remembered the speed trap. So she'd been here before?

He glanced at her photo on the Illinois license. Dark blonde hair, pale blue eyes, and pixie features—the photo was attractive but didn't do justice to the woman in person.

Then he read her name.

Kylie Winters.

*His* Kylie?

His hands shook as adrenaline rushed through him, heating his face.

By rote, he typed the license number into his dashboard computer. Even if this was the girl who'd haunted him for twenty years, he couldn't afford another mistake.

Her record was clean, insurance current. Thank God, because his curiosity was about to kill him.

He went back to her car and extended her license and insurance through the window.

Her delicate eyebrows went up. "That's it? No ticket, no warning?"

"Do you want me to write you a ticket?" he asked with a smile.

She was quick to shake her head. "No, thank you."

He put his palm on her open window. "You said you remembered the speed trap. I don't suppose you're the Kylie who used to beat up her next door neighbor."

Her eyes widened slightly, and then she squinted at him, tilting her head to look more closely.

She bit her lip, color creeping into her cheeks. "I do remember an annoying brat who followed me around constantly."

She paused, probably searching her memory for his name.

"It's Nick," he said. "Nick Harris."

*I've searched online for you. I've missed you. Where have you been all these years?*

Words pressed against the back of his throat, but he knew better than to let them out. All that would accomplish would be to overwhelm her or scare her off.

Her gaze slanted forward through the windshield. He remembered that micro-second of vulnerability he'd seen in her face earlier.

"If you want to get that taillight fixed, I know a guy who can help." He didn't say it was himself.

"Oh, um... Thanks."

Her hand flexed on the wheel. She was impatient to get away.

His heart was still thundering in his chest, and he dared one more question. "Where are you staying? Need directions?" There. Make it sound like he was only interested in helping her, instead of just plain interested.

Her lips pinched, and his gut sank like a fishing weight on the line.

After an extended pause, she said, "I'll be at the campground."

Camping? By herself? A fission of unease shot through him, but she was a grown woman. Capable of making her own decisions.

The state park was two miles out of town, directly on the lake. It was usually quiet, but occasionally, the department caught drug deals going down up there.

Maybe he could make a sweep or two of the area after his shift was over.

And if he happened to run into Kylie, maybe share a s'more and a campfire...that would be a bonus.

The thought buoyed his spirits. "Welcome back to Bear Lake."

———

GIDEON HALE, former Navy SEAL and now an official prince of Glorvaird, thanks to his recent marriage to Princess Alessandra, stepped off the charter plane onto Oklahoma soil. The tiny airport was surrounded by wheat fields and not much else. It also appeared empty, save a small steel hangar and the guy approaching the pilot. Near the hangar, an older model pickup truck waited. Their ride.

He took a deep breath of the rich autumn air. It was hotter than he'd expected.

It was good to be back in the States, but he hated being away from his wife. He let his thumb rub over the gold ring on his finger. Life was...different being married now. Having someone depending on him—someone who wasn't his brother or sister or niece. Having someone to lean on.

Normally, he and Alessandra would travel together, but her father, the king of Glorvaird, had recently died after a long battle with MS, and they'd both agreed she needed to stay with her two sisters in their kingdom.

Gideon hoped to bring home their missing half sister—the lost princess. They'd been searching for her for almost a year, ever since the king had revealed her existence.

Gideon felt so impotent to comfort Alessandra. She'd had a difficult relationship with her father, which made her grief more poignant, wishing for things that could have been. He didn't know what to say to her, how to ease her grief. All he could do was hold her when she needed a shoulder.

But he could do this. His former career as a SEAL gave him the skills he needed to track and find the missing girl.

Pieter followed him off the plane. "*That's* our rental?"

Gideon shot a look at the guy. Pieter was the princesses' cousin and a prince in his own right, though he was not in line for the throne. He'd been reunited with the family after decades of estrangement.

But the guy's mom had tried to kill Alessandra, and that wasn't something Gideon found easy to forgive. So far, Pieter had proved himself trustworthy, but Gideon preferred to keep him close. Having a thousand miles between the prince and Alessandra seemed about right.

Gideon didn't trust easy. That was part and parcel from his SEAL days.

Pieter would just have to live with it. Hopefully, it wouldn't be long until they found the missing princess.

———

Kylie's insomnia kicked in hard, and she tossed and turned in the sleeping bag and bivouac through the darkest part of night. Beside her, Snow snored softly, oblivious to the whippoorwill calling out, the crickets chirping all around.

She'd always had trouble sleeping, even as a child. It had only grown worse after her mom's death a year ago.

Mom's passing had been a wakeup call of sorts—shown Kylie that she was unhappy with her normal life. She'd taken a leave of absence and gone on a road trip. Something she'd never considered, not since she'd broken ties with Mom years ago.

She hadn't really planned to return to Bear Lake. It was the first place in her memories living with her mom. She never would have planned to run into Nick. He'd been an ornery runt of a boy back then, shorter than her with freckled cheeks and bright eyes.

Now he was all grown up. She hadn't recognized him with the military-style haircut and sunglasses. And that uniform that hinted at his physique.

She wasn't sure what to make of the encounter. He'd seemed...interested in her. Curious, or more than that? She didn't know what to think.

Sleep remained elusive... What was she really doing here?

# Chapter Two

THE DAY AFTER HE'D PULLED HER OVER AT THE SPEED TRAP, Nick got lucky during his patrol and saw Kylie and her white dog eating lunch at Pops, a local cafe with an outdoor patio shaded by a large elm tree, now turning colors.

His own stomach rumbled, and he pulled over his patrol car to park on Main Street, parallel to the brick-paved sidewalk. He'd been busy with a fender bender late into the evening last night and hadn't wanted to seem like a stalker, so he hadn't headed out to the park after all to look for Kylie.

If there was an emergency, he'd get a call on his shoulder-mounted radio and be able to get moving quickly, which was what mattered.

Of course, they rarely had real emergencies in Bear Lake. Mrs. Hannaman's lost cat was the most excitement he'd seen last week.

Kylie being here was excitement enough. He hadn't been able to sleep last night thinking about her. Why was she here? Why now?

And why did it feel like the second chance he'd been waiting for?

The cafe had a front entrance, but he chose to use the wrought-iron gate that separated the outdoor seating from the sidewalk.

There were a few other patrons enjoying the brisk mid-morning sunshine, and he nodded to the local florist sipping her coffee and eating a cinnamon bun.

The dog noticed him first, its ears perking and its chin coming up off its paws. Then Kylie lifted her eyes from the paperback she had spread next to her menu. Which one was she focused on?

"Hey." He pretended casual. She didn't need to know his heart was beating up in his throat.

"Hey." She didn't seem *unhappy* to see him, even if her greeting was quiet.

"I thought I might grab a quick bite for lunch. Do you mind if I join you?"

"Um, okay."

He took the seat caddy-corner instead of the one across from her, and her eyes widened infinitesimally, but she didn't frown or say anything to discourage him.

Her dog sat up between their knees and nosed into his pant leg.

"Snow," she cautioned, but Nick smiled.

"It's all right." He reached out and let the dog have a good sniff of his hand before he ruffled its ear. It leaned against him, and he spared a thought of the white fur that was now adhering to his uniform. It was worth it. "Snow?"

Kylie shrugged slightly. "She used to belong to my mom. Mom named her. Not very original, but it fits."

The dog was obviously well cared-for, its fur almost blinding white. Maybe this wasn't one of those animals that loved to get dirty.

The waitress appeared with a familiar, if subdued, hello for Nick and a glass of iced tea for Kylie. She ordered the Reuben—a good choice—and he ordered the same with a Coke. The waitress disappeared again, but not before she'd raised one penciled eyebrow in Nick's direction.

He did his best to ignore it. Still felt the hot sting. Ironic how the people he'd tried so hard to protect didn't trust him.

"How is your mom, anyway?" he asked, trying to brush off the feeling of being watched. The florist could probably hear everything they said.

Kylie's expression shuttered, her expressive blue eyes darkening before her lowered lashes hid them completely.

She picked at a rust spot on the wrought iron tabletop. "She passed away." Her throat worked as she swallowed. "Just over a year ago."

She blinked rapidly, and he instantly felt like a heel, even though there was no way he could've known. Instinctively, he reached for her, letting his hand close over hers on the tabletop. Her skin was cool and dry.

She jumped slightly at the contact, her eyes flicking to his before she looked away. The tears that shimmered there reached a long dormant corner of his heart. He thought maybe that image would be lodged there forever.

"I'm sorry." He wouldn't leave his hand on hers too long, was too afraid of making her uncomfortable, considering they hadn't seen each other in such a long time, but he couldn't excuse himself from making the contact, not when it was obvious her grief was still potent. He squeezed her hand and let go.

She went back to playing with that rusty spot, running the pad of her finger over it again and again. She didn't look up at him as she said, "It was...really unexpected. She was healthy, but... A brain aneurism. That's what the doctors said."

He resisted the urge to reach for her again. Barely. "That must've been really tough on you. I remember how close you guys were."

A shadow passed over her face, some hidden hurt that made her expression crumple for the briefest moment.

When she looked up, he saw the brittleness, glimpsed the hurt behind her shored-up smile. "What about you?" She motioned with one hand to his uniform. "You're a cop now? Seems like you always wanted to play spies, not cops and robbers."

He leaned back in his chair, allowing the subject change. "That was kid stuff." Sort of. When he'd been ten, an only child, he'd been lonely and obsessed with Kylie, his next door neighbor and best friend. He'd spied on her more than she'd known, watching between their backyard fences when his parents had been home, and he'd been ordered to stay in the yard.

She'd caught him a couple of times, and he'd made something up about wanting to grow up and be a spy.

He *had* had dreams of something bigger than being a traffic cop in their small town, but since Farah, those doors were closed to him. His chief wouldn't recommend him for much beyond writing tickets.

"I bet your parents are proud of you."

She couldn't know how much those words punched like a bullet against his flak jacket. He'd let them—and everyone else—down, and sometimes it was still hard for his dad to look him in the eye. "I guess. They still live over on Maple. You should come over and say hi before you leave town. Oh! You should definitely visit your old house. Ella Mae Jenks teaches third grade at the elementary and lives there now, but I'm sure she wouldn't mind."

Kylie smiled that fragile smile again and shrugged her slight shoulders. "We'll see."

———

THEIR SANDWICHES ARRIVED, along with a basket of fries and bottle of ketchup to share, and Kylie was grateful for the reprieve, even if it was only momentary.

She knew Nick was just trying to be friendly, but his innocent questions were hitting her in soft places.

Bear Lake was her last stop, and until she'd hit town, she'd fully intended to visit her childhood home. But now that she was here, even with his encouragement to do so, she wasn't sure she could.

Everything was too sharp, too painful, like bright colors behind your eyelids when you'd been lying in the sun too long.

It *hurt* to remember being with her mom here. How they'd been before everything had begun to unravel.

She didn't know what she was doing. Wandering, when that was one of the things she'd hated most about her flighty mother.

Nick seemed oblivious to her discomfort, or maybe he was really good at pretending, because he popped a bite of French fries into his mouth.

"You know what I do," he said when he'd finished. "What are you up to these days? Did you ever become a veterinarian like you wanted?"

She couldn't help an absent smile at the decades-old childhood dream. "Once I realized I wouldn't be able to save all of the animals, the shine wore off that idea. I'm an accountant—an auditor for a CPA firm."

At least she had been, up until a year ago. Her boss had graciously allowed her a leave of absence to grieve her mother's death, but no one—especially Kylie—had planned for it to carry on this long.

It was as if she'd dived beneath the water and couldn't find her way back to the surface. Grief and indecision still clung to her like seaweed, trying to trap her in the depths.

And she didn't know how to escape it, any of it.

She couldn't continue in this state forever. She knew it. Her boss had begun calling her twice a week, though she'd avoided the calls and ignored the voicemails. Surely her time was up, but she couldn't think about that, not now.

Or about Michael, who'd been so quick to let her go.

"That sounds..."

"Boring?" she finished for Nick, because that was what most people held back, behind their *"nice"* or *"interesting"* or *"safe"* comments. She'd fielded them enough times to shrug it off. "It's steady work. I like it."

She'd learned to stop apologizing for the choices she'd made. She couldn't please everyone, and CPAs would always be in demand.

She didn't *have* to apologize for enjoying the stability and steadiness of a career, no matter if some people thought it was boring.

He tilted his head slightly, holding his sandwich between strong, capable fingers. Considering her, maybe, and what she wasn't saying. "I wasn't going to say boring."

She took a bite of her sandwich, letting the flavors burst over her tongue. Saving herself from having to make conversation, at least for the moment.

"What's your favorite thing about the job?" he asked.

"Meeting new people," she said. "Even if we're working with a company we've worked with for years, there's always something new to learn, someone new to meet."

A smile crossed his lips. He pointed a fry in her direction. "I remember you always liked to sit next to the new kid when school started. How many kids did you welcome to Bear Lake Elementary? There was Ginny, Aiden...what was the scrawny kid's name? The one with the glasses? Eli? E.J.?"

"Elijah," she said softly.

She'd forgotten about that in the flurry of moves that had come after Bear Lake. After the first two back-to-back moves, she'd found it harder and harder to connect with children her own age, knowing she and Mom might have to move again, probably in the middle of the night.

"You always loved making new friends," he said. "Just like your mom."

She started to tremble. Had she stopped reaching out before she'd even recognized she was doing it? In some effort *not* to be like her mom, when things had first started being difficult...?

She didn't know. She'd spent so long trying to block out some of those difficult times in the years where her childhood had ended so abruptly.

Nick's radio squawked, and she saw the instant shift as he answered the dispatcher. He listened and then pushed a button and responded.

He swiped the last bite of sandwich off his plate but didn't stuff it in his mouth. "I'm sorry to rush off, but—"

"Duty calls." She found a smile for him. At least with him gone, she could ruminate without having to pretend that everything was okay.

But he didn't instantly turn away. His eyes considered her for a long moment. "It was good to catch up. If you need anything... I hope you'll call. Me."

She smiled tightly and nodded, because it was all the promise she could make.

She watched him walk away, stopping to say something to the waitress and then pressing cash into her hands before he let himself out of the wrought iron gate and striding purposefully toward the parking in front of the restaurant.

How could it be both unnerving and peaceful to be with someone? Nick had been a figment of her childhood memories... Someone she hadn't seen in fifteen years. And yet, he could make her smile with his recollections of their shared past.

Which also...hurt. Because of Mom, and everything that had changed after they'd left Bear Lake.

She didn't know if she should see him again. She should pack up her bivouac and car and return to Chicago. Staying could reopen wounds from the past.

But she still didn't have the closure she'd sought after Mom's death. How could she both love and hate someone so much? How could she let go of Mom when she'd died with so many things unresolved between them?

She couldn't leave. Not yet.

*Chapter Three*

AFTER A SECOND NEARLY SLEEPLESS NIGHT, KYLIE FOUND herself on the lake, just down from her campsite, as dawn broke. Her feet dangled from the end of a small, wooden dock, her toes inches above the water.

A soft fog rolled over the water's calm surface. It was so early that, for now, most of the animals must still sleep. There was no croak of a bullfrog, no cricket singing. Not even the splash of a fish to break the silence.

It was cool enough that Snow laid beside her without panting, only their soft breaths breaking the silence.

What was so wrong with her?

She'd felt it since her childhood, a disconnect between her and the world around her. Though yesterday at lunch, Nick had mentioned how easily she could make friends, it was rare for them to stick.

She couldn't blame everything on her mom, either, and on the way she'd moved them from place to place, the way she'd been unable to hold down a real job. Kylie would like to blame her problems on her mom's flightiness, but the reality was that Kylie hadn't had an easy time of it since she'd made the decision to settle down. First, in college, waiting tables and buying her first apartment. She'd had acquaintances from class, from work, but she hadn't had a best friend. Hadn't had someone to call when her apartment flooded in the middle of the night.

She'd hoped for more when she'd begun working with the CPA firm, and for a while, it seemed maybe she'd found it. She liked her job, did well at it, even if she sometimes found her clients challenging. She'd met Michael at a singles event through her church, and they'd settled into an easy, steady relationship. Until the end, at least.

Her mom was absent for most of that, moving six times in the seven years between when Kylie started college and Mom's death.

It really felt as if she didn't fit *anywhere*.

Maybe part of the disconnect Kylie felt was the insomnia she'd battled her entire life. She often woke uncomfortable in the night, no matter the comfort of the bed—or the bare ground, as was the case right now. She'd tried softer beds, firmer ones, even done a sleep study once. The doctors had been unable to diagnose any reason she should wake and be unable to go back to sleep.

She didn't know what she'd hoped to find coming back here, the place where most of her earliest and most treasured memories had come from. The place she'd felt the closest to her mom, before things had started to fall apart.

Maybe she was as bad as her mom, always searching for something that was never to be found.

She tried to pray, tried listening for an answer as the sky slowly brightened, as fish started splashing and sounds from the two older couples on the other side of the campsite started their morning routines.

And then the sound of an approaching engine cut through the morning stillness. Two car doors closed.

And then voices. "I thought I told you to stay in the car."

That sounded like Nick. But why in the world would he be here this early?

It had seemed he'd come upon her by chance while she'd been having lunch yesterday. Was he seeking her out now?

Why?

A second voice joined his. A younger, female voice. "Like you thought that was going to happen."

There was a loud sigh, and then Nick's voice again. "Well, at least make yourself useful and hold this."

Footsteps crunched, and she could tell they'd stopped near her campsite, but as she looked away from the still lake and over her shoulder, woodsy trees and brush hid her from their sight.

"She's not here," came Nick's voice again, sounding disappointed.

And from the other side of the campsite, an older male voice shouted too loud in the silent morning, "Try down by the water!"

Should she be disturbed that her neighbors were keeping tabs on her? She'd only been here two nights, but whichever one had spoken seemed to know where she was. At least someone was looking out for her. When was the last time anyone kept tabs on her, cared about her comings and goings?

The two older couples seemed to be friends, both with fifth wheels parked in spots next to each other. The only other campers in the state park. They played cards on the picnic table between their two RVs late into the night. They seemed nice enough that she shrugged off any concern.

Footsteps crunched again, and she looked over her shoulder to see a uniformed Nick round an orange-leafed bush and come into sight. He was followed by a petite figure in jeans and a hooded sweatshirt with the same chestnut hair Nick had, hers pulled into a ponytail behind her head.

"Hey." Nick greeted Kylie with his trademark easygoing greeting and a smile that made her stomach flip over.

He held up a medium-sized paper bag. "Brought some breakfast from Pat's Doughnut Shop."

Her mouth instantly watered, and she patted the planks beside her. "Join me in my breakfast nook."

Snow's tail thumped against the planks as Nick stepped onto the small dock, sending it swaying slightly.

Behind him, the girl hesitated at the end of the plank. She held a cup holder with three paper mugs tucked in it. She looked to be about eleven, so... Not his daughter, surely?

He nodded to the girl. "My kid sister, Gentry."

———

NICK KNEW it was a risk bringing his kid sister along on this visit, but he had a twelve-hour shift ahead of him, and his mom had begged him to drive Gentry to school.

He couldn't wait to see Kylie again, not after glimpsing the vulnerability she'd shown yesterday at lunch. Last night had seemed interminable. Hours and hours of watching cars putter by at the speed trap, all with no action.

He looked over his shoulder to Gentry and jerked his chin to get her to join them on the short dock.

"No fishing pole?" he asked. "The bass are probably biting this time of day. Perch for sure."

He rustled in the brown bag and pulled out a donut covered in chocolate and sprinkles. He handed it over to Kylie, along with a paper napkin.

Her instant smile was worth the early morning rushing around.

"I used to have one of these every Saturday morning,' she said with a wistful smile.

He rustled in the bag again. "In case your tastes have changed, I also got some plain chocolate and a couple of jelly-filled."

She shook her head slightly. "Give me the sprinkles."

He handed it over and sat next to her as Gentry leaned down and reached over his shoulder for the bag.

"Filled donuts are gross," his sister muttered.

"Are not." He tried to pull the bag out of Gentry's reach, but he didn't try too hard, and she pulled out a plain glazed, giving a triumphant, "ha!"

"Watch it, twerp," he said.

"Thirty minutes until drop off," his sister reminded him with a nudge to the back of his shoulder.

"I know." He scooted the drink container closer and nudged Kylie's knee, pointing to the coffee and sugar packets stashed in the middle. She took one gratefully and sipped the brew black, her eyes closing in apparent joy.

"That's good," she whispered. "Thanks."

He'd do it every morning if it got this reaction. There was something viscerally satisfying in making her happy.

"What grade are you in?" Kylie asked Gentry, then stuffed a bite of donut into her mouth.

"Fifth," Gentry said through a mouth full of donut.

He tapped her foot with his boot as a reminder to watch her manners, but she just rolled her eyes.

Kylie's eyes cut to him. "So you must've had a fun time in high school with a baby sister."

He could vividly remember the horror he'd felt when his mom had told him she and Dad were expecting. He'd been sixteen and self-absorbed enough to think mostly about how the new baby would affects his last two years of high school.

Plus, it had been weird for all his friends to realize his parents were still intimate at their old age! Like he'd needed all those jokes.

"It definitely killed my social life," he agreed. "I missed the homecoming basketball game because mom needed me to babysit."

Gentry shoved his shoulder. "You said chicks loved it that you took such good care of your baby sister."

He grinned. "Did I? I don't remember that." Of course being good with a baby had gotten him some looks, but he'd been too immature back then to do anything about it.

"I'll bet your friends think he's pretty cool," Kylie said to Gentry.

Gentry's face clouded, and she shot a look in his direction. "They used to."

His heart beat fast. He'd purposely avoided any mention of last year's scandal yesterday when he'd been with Kylie.

Not that she wouldn't hear about it around town. Folks in Bear Lake had big mouths.

He shook his head slightly, donut turning to sawdust in his mouth, but Gentry responded with a quiet, "She's gonna hear about it anyway."

Maybe, but he'd hoped to have a little more time for Kylie to get to know him again before her opinion took a dive.

"Last year, Nick's girlfriend Farah skipped town after she scammed a bunch of people out of their retirement funds."

He winced.

"Ex-girlfriend," he responded automatically. He hated the flush that heated his neck and face.

He hated how it sounded. Hated even more that it was true.

He could still remember the piercing ache in his stomach when he'd discovered what she'd done. The sense of betrayal and the heart-rending grief at knowing she wasn't who she'd said she was, that she'd tricked him, that their entire relationship had been a lie. At least on her side.

Fool that he was, he'd fallen for the lying scammer.

He slanted a glance to Kylie, wondering if Gentry's revelation would erase the friendly warmth in her eyes.

But all he saw was compassion in their blue depths.

"That sucks," she said softly.

He nodded. More than she knew. He'd been thinking of ring shopping while all Farah had thought about was stealing as much as she could before she skipped town. Then, he'd been the one to suffer when folks from town lost their trust in him, somehow believing he should've known better. He'd been investigated by the FBI. And even now, the captain gave him all the suckiest jobs on the squad.

He checked his watch as Kylie fed her dog the last bite of donut. "We've got to get going." He stood, and Kylie craned her neck to look up at him.

"Thanks for breakfast. That was...really nice."

Nice? He didn't want to be *nice*. Didn't want to be lumped in the Friend Zone, though if that was all she could give him, he'd accept it.

Gentry bent to pet the white dog.

"You get that taillight fixed yet?" he asked.

"Not yet."

"My shift lasts all day, but I'll come back tonight and fix it for you." It was presumptive, and he saw the flash of Gentry's eyebrow raise behind Kylie.

But he also saw Kylie's soft smile. "You don't have to do that."

"I don't mind." He let himself be presumptive again and reached out to cup her shoulder. A friendly gesture. He wished he could do more.

He forced himself to let go, to follow Gentry off the dock. He'd be in trouble with his mom if his sister was tardy. "See ya later," he called back to Kylie, who waved him off with a smile.

"Thanks for breakfast," she called after him.

———

GIDEON AND PIETER had hit town late last night. Gideon had done some reconnaissance while checking in to the one hotel in town. No one named Kylie was checked in. He'd asked about a B&B and discovered there were several that he'd have to visit today.

There'd been no late-night coffee shop on the small Main Street, no sign of her through the window of the one, nearly empty, cafe where he'd witnesses a high school kid mopping floors. The town apparently rolled up its sidewalks at nine p.m. Just like home.

Not that that helped him in his mission...

Now, mid-morning, and he'd come to the tiny police station where his contacts said the ping on her driver's license had originated two days ago. Pieter stayed outside, playing with his phone. Maybe texting his girlfriend.

The station was tiny too, tinier even than the one back home.

Behind a tall counter, four empty desks were separated into cubicles, but someone sitting at any of the desks could see to the front counter. The desks and counter sported piles of paperwork that looked very familiar from his SEAL days.

A uniformed cop—one who looked a few years younger than Gideon—looked up from his desk, then rose and came to meet Gideon at the counter.

Desk duty. Must be a rookie.

"How can I help you?"

Gideon scanned the guy's metallic, badge-shaped name tag. Officer Harris.

Gideon put a photo of the lost princess on the counter facing the young officer and slid it across. "I'm looking for someone, hoping she might be staying here in town."

He didn't mention that his sources had showed her license had been dinged in the state system, that she'd been here two days ago. She could've been passing through, but Gideon hoped differently. He needed to finish this for Alessandra.

The cop's eyes flicked to the photo and held for a fraction of a second too long.

"She in trouble?" he asked coolly. A little too casual.

"She's a friend of my wife's." It was only a little stretch of the truth. He wasn't ready to divulge more, not about Alessandra or his purpose here. He didn't want to tip his hand too early, didn't have feet on the ground here and couldn't risk spooking her and sending her running again.

The cop's steady gaze didn't flicker as he held Gideon's gaze. "I pulled her over for a broken taillight a couple days ago."

He already knew she'd been pulled over. What he didn't know was where she was staying. Did she have family here? He hadn't been able to find any connections with his computer searching other than a decades-old address, one that had been dark and silent when he'd driven by last night.

"Do you know if she's still in town? Where she might be staying?"

The other man shrugged, his face as neutral as any professional poker player.

But Gideon had an itch behind his shoulder blades that told him the other man was fudging.

And his gut told him that no matter how he spun it, the cop wasn't going to divulge what he knew about Kylie to Gideon, even if Gideon told him about Alessandra and her family.

———

PIETER STOOD on the sidewalk next to the quaint Main Street, phone to his ear as he watched the passersby.

"Gideon's team turned up a report of Mother's passport going through customs at DFW yesterday. Gideon believes she might be coming here." Dallas was too close for comfort. If Mother had a hired driver waiting, she'd be here in several hours.

"What do *you* think?"

McKenna's voice never failed to soothe him. It had been a month since he'd seen her in person. He'd attended one of her rodeo queen pageants in Wyoming. A month was too long. He missed the feel of her hand in his, the kisses that belonged to him alone.

"I think there's a chance he's right. Hopefully if Mother sees me out in the open, she'll come to me." With Gideon along, that choice would be as good as turning herself in. And slightly less risky for Pieter. He'd been on the wrong side of her wrath too often, and she'd apparently become more dangerous as of late.

He hadn't spoken to his mother in months, not since she'd coerced an orderly to help her escape the mental health ward he'd admitted her to. He had no idea whether she was on her stabilizing meds for her schizophrenia, or if she was harboring an agenda toward him. There was no telling.

But he couldn't just stand by and let her continue to threaten his royal cousins.

# Chapter Four

He hadn't come.

Kylie knew it was silly to be so disappointed by it. The sun had gone down hours ago, and she'd tucked herself into her sleeping bag early, but she couldn't sleep, shifting on the ground that felt harder than it must be. Her breath wasn't quite fogging in front of her face, but there was a definite autumn chill.

The two older couples that still shared the campground with her had had some kind of party tonight. They'd had the outdoor lights on and had settled in with a campfire near their picnic table, playing cards or something for hours past sunset.

Kylie could have blamed her sleeplessness on their noise, but that wasn't it.

It was her *life* that was bothering her.

Even after things quieted at the other campsites, she couldn't sleep. There was no moon out tonight, but she slipped from her tent and woke Snow with a poke.

Her feet found the familiar path around the lake, one that she and Mom had hiked often when they'd lived here. Apparently, even a decade and a half of being away didn't erase those childhood muscle memories.

Stars lit the sky and reflected off the dark water that lapped off to one side as she stepped almost silently, Snow tracking just behind her.

It took a while, longer than she remembered from her childhood, to find the little offshoot path. It was more overgrown than she remembered but led right to the huge, flat rock that jutted out over the lake. With it being dark, she didn't go all the way to the edge but perched in the middle, folding her legs up and putting her arms around them. Snow settled next to her, a comforting weight, leaning against her side.

She and Mom had come out here once, late in the night, and watched a meteor shower. Mom had whispered about God's power. Kylie had thought the whole experience magical.

Tonight, she shivered with loneliness.

Even after a year of searching, of backtracking through her life with Mom, she couldn't reconcile things.

How did you love someone but resent them as well?

How could she forgive her mother when Mom had died without resolving anything between the two of them?

She'd hoped to find something among her mom's things. Maybe a journal or even a painting that would explain why Mom had been such a wanderer.

Because if she could figure out why Mom had been like that, maybe she could figure out how to *belong* somewhere.

Reconnecting with Nick had given her a false sense of hope. She knew better than to trust that such an old friendship would hold up.

He'd forgotten her, or avoided her. It hurt more than it should've.

Something shifted in the quiet night.

A shiver of unease slithered through her. She didn't register a noise that didn't fit with the night, but her senses heightened, and the hair at her nape rose.

She'd felt it before, sensed it in the last two cities she'd visited. A sense that someone was watching her. It made her infinitely uncomfortable. As if she were in danger.

What was it? Someone after her? Something more innocent, or her imagination?

Beneath the arm curled over the dog's back, Snow tensed. A low growl came from the dog's throat.

That was enough for Kylie. She reached in her pocket for her phone. It wasn't there. It must have fallen out somewhere between the campsite and her rock. She was sure it had been in her pocket when she'd started her hike.

She let go of Snow and scrabbled around on the rock face to see if she could feel it, but only rock scraped her palms.

Breath caught in her throat. If someone was out there, she had no way to call for help. Would the older couples even hear her if she screamed? They would have no way of knowing where she was.

What should she do?

————

THE NEXT MORNING, Nick braked his pickup truck behind two patrol cars in the early-morning brightness. He slammed the truck into park and jumped out, not caring that the door didn't fully latch behind him.

He was off-duty today, which meant he didn't *have* to be here.

But the moment the police scanner in his apartment had burst out with a report of vandalism at the state park, he hadn't had a choice.

Everything else had shut off, and his entire being had cried out *Kylie!* He had to see for himself if she was all right.

The park was nearly empty, just two RVs and a ransacked campsite. Two police cruisers parked in front of the tent site. The familiar woods were still and silent. Barely visible across the lake stood some cabins on the opposite shore.

He nodded to the other officers, his brothers in arms, but didn't approach them in his hurry to get to Kylie. He couldn't help noticing her stuff was trashed. The tires of her car were slashed, all four windows broken. Her tent was slashed through, her clothes and food scattered across the grass.

He averted his eyes, heart pounding.

He found her huddled in the backseat of one of the patrol cars, the door open and her dog lying on the grass at her feet. She had her arms wrapped around herself as if she was holding herself together by sheer will.

She was whole.

She was safe.

Relief crashed through him, culminating in a huge huff of breath that pushed out of his chest.

She'd been staring at the ground, or the dog, but at his noise, she looked up. And her face crumpled.

He didn't have a right, not after he'd abandoned her last night, but he reached for her anyway. She came out of the squad car and into his arms, tucking her face into his chest.

He was such an idiot. When military-man had come in to the precinct looking for her, Nick had gotten spooked. She was from out of town. Staying in the state park, not at a hotel. And with his history with Farah, he'd decided it might be better to keep his distance, at least for the moment.

Obviously, he was a jerk. Look what had happened to her campsite.

She was shivering, or he was shaking, or both. He tried to calm his galloping heartbeat as he held her and let relief barreled through him.

He touched the back of her head, felt the silkiness of her hair slip through his fingers. Moved his hand to touch her back.

She seemed content to let him hold her, burrowed into his embrace. He wasn't arguing, not while he still felt the terror of knowing she'd been involved in a violent crime.

His chin nudged her temple as he raised his head enough to watch Officer Stokes, who'd graduated the academy two years ahead of him, lift the corner of what must've once been her tent and peer inside the ripped canvas. It was completely shredded, as if someone had taken a knife and sliced it.

He had to close his eyes against the thought of what such an action could do to the human body.

She was here, in the circle of his arms. She was whole.

He forced his eyes open again, trying not to focus on the shards of glass that glittered in the grass around her car.

The second officer, Boortz, was across the campground, speaking to an older man with salt-and-pepper hair standing outside a fifth wheel.

And all Nick could think about was the man—former military, he was sure of it—who'd visited the station yesterday, asking about Kylie.

He let her go slightly, enough to look into her face even as he used one hand to cup her cheek.

He needed to look at her.

Her eyes were red-rimmed and bright, and he had to clear his throat before he could speak. "What happened?"

She took a shaky breath. "I couldn't sleep, so Snow and I took a walk. A hike, I guess. I got spooked by something—we were far enough I wouldn't have been able to hear anything happening here at the campsite...and..."

She bit her lip, her words cutting off abruptly as sobs shook her.

"If you thought something was wrong, why didn't you call it in?" *Or call me?* His number was in the public phone directory. He held back the second part, because really, how could he expect that after he hadn't shown up last night like he'd promised.

"I lost my phone."

He exhaled hard. She was safe. It could've been so much worse.

But he had to know. Especially after yesterday.

He held her gaze. "Are you in some kind of trouble?"

*Chapter Five*

KYLIE HUDDLED ON NICK'S COUCH IN THE SMALL efficiency apartment. It was mostly clean—she'd seen him quickly swipe several balls of laundered socks off the couch and into an empty laundry basket when she'd first come inside. It was less bachelor-like than she'd expected, with tasteful framed prints on the walls, pictures of Nick and his sister on a side table, even colorful pillows on the neutral sofa.

He'd brought her inside and then excused himself to take a phone call on the upstairs balcony outside the second-floor apartment.

Snow lay across her feet, the dog sensitive enough to know there was still something very wrong with her master.

Kylie had been through the gamut of emotions when dealing with her mother and the situations they'd found themselves in.

But she'd never felt as vulnerable as she did right now. Violated, broken.

Someone had slashed her tent, her tires. Had gone through her things. Had touched her stuff, maybe stolen from her.

She couldn't think about what might've happened if she'd been in her tent.

Nor could she think about Nick's question. *Are you in some kind of trouble?*

She'd told him no, but the shadows in his eyes hadn't cleared. One of his coworkers, another officer, had interrupted, telling her she could leave the scene for now. All her belongings, her car, were part of the crime scene until they finished searching for clues.

Nick had taken pity on her, had brought her here, but she still wasn't sure she could call him a friend. Where did she go from here?

Where would she stay tonight?

How could she find enough peace to sleep, after what had happened last night?

Snow's head came off her paws as Nick came back inside, the balcony door closing with a soft *snick* behind him.

"You okay?"

She ran a shaky hand through her bangs, tucked back the strands of hair that wanted to fall into her eyes. "Not really."

He went to the small kitchenette and flicked on a Keurig single-cup coffee maker. "I mostly have dark roast, but I might be able to scrounge up something else..." His voice trailed off as his head and one shoulder practically disappeared into an upper cabinet. "Aha!" he cried triumphantly, coming out with a small box. "My mom gave me a mixed basket last Christmas. There's...hazelnut, a lighter roast, pumpkin spice..."

He looked up expectantly, waiting for her answer.

She was so cold, still shivering, she wouldn't mind anything to try and get warm. "Surprise me."

He plugged the coffee canister in to the coffee maker, opened the fridge, and bent to peer inside.

Snow nudged Kylie's foot with her chin, and she let herself relax enough to lean down and scratch the dog's head and ears. If she just focused on that, on keeping everything else at bay in her mind, then maybe she could get through the next few minutes.

The next day. The next year?

It didn't work as her thoughts spiraled and emotions crashed over her like waves battering a rock at the seashore. Problem was, she didn't feel like a rock. She felt like a sandcastle, eroding more with every attack.

Minutes later—hours?—Nick entered her tunnel vision as he knelt next to her knees, nudging Snow out of the way.

He set a white plate with two pieces of toast and a scramble of eggs next to the matching white coffee mug.

The scents of food and coffee roused her slightly from her panic. Maybe more so was his hand on her knee, warm and steady even through the fabric of her jeans.

"I'm guessing you hadn't thought about breakfast."

The sunlight outside was bright now, edging closer to midmorning. It had been dawn when she'd discovered what had happened and run to the nearest camper, pounding on her neighbor's door.

But she didn't reach for the food. "If you need to get to work, maybe I can find a room at the motel."

"Today's my day off. I'm not going anywhere."

And then he picked up the coffee mug and pushed it into her hands, where it almost, but not quite, burned her chilled skin. He settled onto the sofa next to her, casually draping an arm across the back and using a remote to turn on the wall-mounted flat-screen television across the room.

She sipped the coffee, and a slight amount of tension seeped from her shoulders.

"Cooking competitions?" she asked when he'd settled on the channel.

He tilted a sideways glance at her. "I've been bacching it since I left for the police academy. Sometimes I pick up tips watching these."

She smirked a little at this secret side. Had he done it to distract her?

She kept the coffee and picked up the plate, slouching into the couch and criss-crossing her legs to make a table for it. With her coffee in one hand and her fork in the other, she ate.

The toast and eggs were simple enough, and he'd been right that having the food settled her a bit.

They sat shoulder to shoulder through two episodes of a crazy timed chef competition. By the end of the second episode, she'd scraped her plate clean, and she'd stopped shaking.

And then she knew the small reprieve was over when Nick turned to her.

Whatever happened, friends or not, she was grateful that he'd taken the time to take care of her this morning.

———

NICK HATED to break the fragile peace that had settled over Kylie, but they weren't done yet. There were too many unanswered questions.

He'd called in to the precinct and asked Boortz to hold off on filing the paperwork into their system. There had been a very long silence, one in which Nick read all the skepticism Boortz didn't say aloud. His coworker had agreed not to create the official report until Nick had spoken to their captain about the man who'd been in asking about Kylie. Likely they had his image recorded from the surveillance camera, and maybe they could figure out who he was and what he wanted from her.

Of course, if Kylie could give them the info, it would save some time.

He cleared away her plate and mug. She used the restroom while he puttered in the kitchenette, then she met him at the high bar.

"At lunch you mentioned you'd been traveling. Is there a reason...something you've been running from?"

Her eyes clouded. "Not exactly."

"If there's something you can tell me, some reason someone might be following you or want to hurt you?"

She shook her head. Perched on the barstool. "It's nothing like that." She blew out a huge sigh. "My mother and I... After we left here, things got a lot more difficult for us. Or maybe they were difficult here too, and I was just too young to notice."

"What do you mean?"

She idly traced a water ring on the counter. "Mom... She was such a dreamer. I think." Her brow furrowed. "She wanted to take pictures, but you know, freelancing doesn't pay that well, and..." She swallowed hard. "She wasn't all that great at holding down steady jobs. At paying rent. Keeping us fed."

He'd had no idea. He let his hand cover hers on the counter, stilling her nervous motion for the moment. "I'm sorry."

She shrugged slightly, her head down. "Things started unraveling when I was a freshman in high school. I started working what jobs I could find to try and supplement our income. So maybe *this time* we wouldn't have to move in the middle of the night or be evicted. It didn't help that much."

He hated thinking about a teenaged Kylie going through that. In all his imaginings, all the wondering he'd done about where she'd ended up and what she'd been doing, he'd never thought of *that*.

"We had a falling out my freshman year of college. I'd managed to wrangle some scholarships and had a somewhat steady waitressing job. She was ready to move on. And I wasn't. So I got a crappy apartment in a not-so-nice part of town, and she left. I'd only seen her once since our split before she died." She shrugged again, trying to play off her emotions, but he saw the tears sparkling on her lower lashes. "I took a leave of absence, and I've been revisiting the places we lived, trying to find...her, I guess. Find some piece of the connection we must've once had."

His heart ached for Kylie. Sure, he and his parents didn't always get along perfectly, but he'd never felt unsafe during his adolescence. Never wondered where his next meal was coming from.

He also couldn't forget Military-Guy who'd been looking for her.

He wanted to believe her story, but the memory of Farah and everything that had happened made him cautious. He'd give her the benefit of the doubt...for now.

He squeezed her hand beneath his. "When she died, did she leave anything to you? Anything valuable, anything someone might have a reason to come after?"

A near-hysterical laugh burbled out of her, not one that had any trace of humor. "She was dead broke. Her apartment was full of junk."

He didn't tell her about the man who' been asking about her. Not yet. She was safe enough here and after her story, after how shaken she'd been this morning, there was no reason to throw gas on the fire. He could do some quiet checking, make sure her story panned out. Later. All that could wait.

But the hug he wanted to give her couldn't. He rounded the counter and went to her, intending to offer a friendly shoulder-hug from the side, but she turned into his chest.

And he was more than happy to give her the comfort she obviously craved. The sense of protectiveness that had risen in him this morning when he'd seen her destroyed campsite, when he'd glimpsed her, hadn't diminished. If anything, he felt more protective now after hearing her story and getting a glimpse of what she'd been through.

He allowed himself to bury his nose in her hair.

But he didn't want to be a creeper. Didn't want to hold onto her too tightly when what she most needed was a friend.

So he let his arms loosen around her.

She moved back slightly, her chin lifted, and their eyes met and gazes held.

Heat sparked between them. She inhaled, and he was so close that he felt it.

He wasn't the only one feeling the attraction between them.

Relief and want crashed through him, and he lowered his head to capture her lips with his.

He meant the kiss to be a gentle brush of lips, but she raised on tiptoe to meet him, and he fell deeper into it. His hands tightened on her waist. He wanted her closer.

But he also knew that her emotions had to be seesawing wildly today. And he desperately didn't want to take advantage.

He set her away gently, brushing one last kiss at her temple. "Unless you want to eat eggs and toast again for lunch and supper, I'd better make a run to the store. What do you need?"

He left with a short list of supplies for her, since all her things were still evidence.

He headed for the precinct to talk to the captain. This might be his day off, but he wasn't going to let anything hurt Kylie, not when she'd come back into his life. She'd be safe enough in his apartment, and hopefully, he'd have some answers when he returned.

———

"YOU SEE THAT?"

Pieter followed Gideon's nod to a guy gassing up a dark sedan at the gas station across the street.

Evening was falling, and the two Glorvaird men were seated at an outdoor table at the small cafe along Main Street. The gas station was caddy corner across the street.

Pieter didn't see anything amiss. He shrugged.

"He did something to the license plate on his car," Gideon said. He'd tensed beneath the brown jacket he wore.

"Are you certain he wasn't just cleaning off some dirt?"

Gideon turned a stone-set face to Pieter. "I'm going to track them." He slipped from the chair and disappeared before Pieter could respond. The man was uptight, though nothing much had happened in town—at least as far as Pieter knew—since their arrival.

What was he doing here? It was a long shot that Mother was nearby. She could be anywhere in the States by now.

Gideon was never going to trust him, not really. Why was he doing this to himself when he could be with McKenna? She was up in Montana right now, preparing for a pageant next weekend. He knew she had to be careful of her reputation while on the pageant circuit. Rodeo queens were supposed to be unattached young women. So their relationship needed to remain a secret.

She'd put off her enrollment to university until the spring semester. When it began, she'd be in one place. He could... Well, he didn't have any marketable skills, but he could rent an apartment close to her and *try*, couldn't he? It wasn't as if he had real royal duties.

But what about Mother? She shouldn't be on her own, not with her mental challenges. He needed to find her, settle her, get things figured out. He couldn't move forward in his relationship with McKenna until that happened. And he couldn't expect her to wait forever.

*Chapter Six*

Twilight was falling when Nick parked in front of his apartment and headed up the outside stairwell. He'd spent too long researching on his computer at the precinct and the day had slipped away.

He had several bags of groceries in the bed of his pickup. He'd come back for them next, but with his arms full of a garbage bag filled with Kylie's possessions, those that the PD had released anyway, he knew she'd want her things first.

He could provide at least one good thing, since the rest was bad news.

He used his key then pushed the door open. His apartment was dim and quiet inside. His stomach pitched.

"Kylie?"

No answer.

A chill went down his spine. Had she left? Why?

He kicked the door closed, then set her bag beside it. He reached for the small handgun in his ankle holster, the weapon he carried when off-duty.

"Kylie? Snowball?"

There. A soft noise from the laundry room—really a small alcove behind the kitchen.

"Kylie?" he tried once more. "It's Nick. Are you okay?"

There was a muffled bark, and his heart leapt.

He lowered the gun to his side as he strode across the linoleum, flipping on the kitchen light as he went.

He rounded the corner to find Kylie and Snow crouched beside the top-and-bottom washer-dryer combo. She was clutching a small wooden mallet that he used to tenderize meat and blinking against the bright light, her pupils large and unfocused.

And panting. Like she was caught in a panic that wouldn't let her go. Worry ratcheted up in his throat.

He squatted in front of her, mindful of the mallet. He also kept his weapon out of sight behind his thigh. No reason to scare her more. "Kylie?"

She blinked again and seemed to come back to herself. "Nick?"

"What happened?"

She was shaking, and he reached out to take the mallet from her trembling hands.

"S-somebody was here."

His hackles went up.

She wasn't finished. "They knocked, but when I looked out the peephole they must've"—she sniffled—"must've covered it up, because I couldn't see anything at all."

He drew her up, intending to have her sit on the couch while he poked his head out the door and looked into the parking lot. He hadn't noticed anything amiss when he'd pulled in. If there were bad guys out there, they were good at hiding.

"Then—then someone started shining a flashlight in the window."

His pulse beat in his temple, adrenaline rushing through him. His hand tightened slightly on his weapon. "How long ago was that?"

She shook her head, eyes a little wild. "I don't know. A few minutes?"

There was a crash of glass, and Nick turned and pushed her behind him, back into the alcove. He pointed his weapon at the window, but didn't fire. Snow barked but went silent when Nick make a slashing motion next to his thigh with one hand.

He flipped the light off. No reason to give whoever was out there an easy target. The outdoor fire escape attached to the balcony was difficult to access from the ground floor. Who was out there? He felt naked without the bulletproof vest that was a part of his uniform.

"Stay here," he whispered to Kylie. "I'm a police officer," he shouted.

He pulled his cell phone from his hip pocket and dialed dispatch even as he stepped forward to see beyond the kitchen bar to the window.

The fire escape was empty.

Was it Military-Guy? Nick had thought upon meeting him that he had the look of Special Forces. Somebody like that could probably scale the wall like Spiderman.

Which meant Nick had to keep them from climbing inside.

"Dispatch," came Aibgail's voice in his ear.

"This is Nick," he said, voice low to try and keep the possible intruder from hearing. "Someone's vandalized my apartment, broke the window. They might be trying to come inside."

She told him the nearest on-duty officer had been called to an injury accident on the opposite end of town. Not good.

Nick didn't know if they had time, not if whoever was after Kylie was Special Ops.

There was no one visible in the window, not a shadow. But the hairs on the back of Nick's neck remained raised.

The glass had shattered on the floor around a large rock or brick. Had someone thrown it from downstairs? To what end? To flush Kylie out of the apartment? Were they waiting for her to run outside?

He approached the window slowly, from the side, trying to get a glimpse of anybody who might be hanging on the wall or maybe standing on a ladder beneath the window. There was no one there, but he thought he caught motion on the ground.

"Kylie!" he whispered. He motioned her to join him, but as she padded softly across the floor, he realized she was barefoot. "Wait! There's glass everywhere. Here, let me lift you."

She shook her head. "Snow first."

He figured they could argue long enough to get themselves in trouble, so he tucked the gun in his waistband before he quickly reached down and scooped up the dog with both hands under its belly. His shoes crunched on the glass as he crossed, moving the animal quickly through the living room and leaving it beside the couch with a quick order to "Stay!"

Then he went back for Kylie. Having her in his arms should have been a long-fulfilled dream, not this nightmare he'd walked into.

There were shouts from below.

"Where are your shoes?" he asked as he set her next to the dog. "Get them on. We're getting out of here."

He ran into his room and grabbed a second ammo clip from the top shelf of the closet. He shoved it into his pocket and grabbed his vest. His spare was at the precinct. He wished it were here.

Kylie was frozen where he'd left her, but thankfully she'd donned her shoes. He was a little apprehensive about running onto the upstairs balcony. It would be quicker than climbing down the fire escape. But had someone noticed his arrival? If so, they might be waiting near his truck.

The iron-railed balcony offered no protection. But they were sitting ducks in here.

Options ran through Nick's mind at warp speed, and he finally came to a decision.

They had to go.

———

KYLIE STARED up at Nick as he pulled the bulky vest over her head and snugged it around her middle.

His focus was completely on his task, his eyes glued to what he was doing. It was dark in the apartment, and shadows flickered across his face, the dim light illuminating his intent expression. His jaw was locked, his focus completely on his task.

Shivers of fear still ran through her, but she was no longer locked in the dark place she'd gone into when she'd realized someone was attempting to break into Nick's apartment.

Because he was here now.

"What about you?" she whispered, realizing that he wasn't wearing a vest.

"It's not me they're after," he said grimly.

Well, that was scary, but it was hard to be afraid with him looking so close.

He pulled a ball cap down over her forehead and then looked at Snow. She thought she heard him mutter that he wanted some shoe polish, but she couldn't imagine what for. To paint the dog? "Stay close and move fast."

He put his back to the door, and she stood at his left side. And tried not to shiver when she saw he held a gun.

She hadn't had time to leash Snow, so she looped her fingers beneath the dog's collar. Her nerves were jangling, but she wouldn't focus on the fear. She's just follow Nick. Trust Nick.

He opened the door more quickly than she'd expected and stuck his head outside, looking both directions.

It seemed quiet, but that didn't erase her fear.

With his empty hand, Nick motioned her to follow as he crept onto the landing and looked over the railing.

The parking lot was well-lit, with lights at intervals, but shadows remained between the vehicles big enough for someone to hide in.

"You sure that's the right apartment?" a male voice she didn't recognize rang out, and footsteps approached from around the corner where the landing continued on to more apartments.

"C'mon," Nick whispered. He clasped her hand in his free one and pulled her with him toward the nearby staircase.

Snow's claws clicked on the cement as they ran.

"Hey, you!" The same voice shouted as Nick's feet hit the first stair.

He never outpaced her, even steadied her when she tripped on one of the stairs.

Heavy footsteps clattered on the cement above them. The man yelled, "Is that her?"

She didn't hear an answer, didn't want to think about where the man's companion was.

Nick said, "Run to the truck!"

He'd only parked a couple of spaces away from the bottom of the stairs, and she did as he told her, passing him as he turned to confront their pursuers.

"C'mon, Snow!" she panted. Thankfully, the dog seemed to understand Kylie's urgency and followed at her heels.

"Stop right there!" Nick's voice rang out strong and sure. "I'm a police officer, and I'm armed."

A glance over her shoulder showed Nick with feet spread and gun pointed at the two bulky bodies in dark clothing mid-way down the stairwell.

She didn't wait to see what happened next. Instead she focused on the truck and kept moving.

A shot rang out. She ducked her head, feet stumbling as fear spiked. Had they shot at Nick? He at them? *She had his vest!*

She was half afraid someone would have guessed their escape plan and waited at Nick's truck, but the parking spaces on either side of it were empty, and a glance didn't reveal any moving shadows on either side of the pickup or in the truck bed.

Kylie yanked open the driver's side door. "Snow, in!"

The dog jumped in, and Kylie slid in just behind, bumping her knee on the steering wheel in her haste to slide across the seat. "Nick!"

He was already there, jamming his key into the ignition before he'd gotten his door closed. Where had his gun gone?

Another shot rang out and the passenger window splintered into cracks.

"Get on the floor," Nick ordered. He gassed the truck, and it reversed quickly, making it hard for her to maneuver.

Then he hit the brakes hard, and she was thrown back against the seat.

"Now!" he cried out, shoving her shoulder before throwing the car into drive.

She was knocked forward and banged her elbow on the dash as she crumpled awkwardly into the floorboards on the passenger side. Snow remained on the seat, lying down. But Nick had to see to be able to drive. What about him?

Something pinged against metal. Another shot?

Nick swerved once and accelerated. Illumination from streetlights flashed through the cab as they sped along the streets.

Nick held onto the wheel with his left hand and reached into his hip pocket with the right. She saw the dark stain down his forearm.

Blood.

"Nick! Did you get shot?"

He wedged the phone between his shoulder and ear. "It's not bad. Stay down, will you? I want to make sure we aren't followed."

It wasn't bad, just bleeding? Was there such a thing as *a little bit shot*?

"Abigail, it's Nick. There were three perps at my apartment, armed. Shots fired. Miss Winters and I are in route to a safe location." He glanced at her but quickly looked back at the road.

He didn't seem shaken at all as he related the facts about people shooting at them—shooting! And he seemed unconcerned about being shot.

While she couldn't seem to hold back the tears that blurred her vision.

She gave a valiant sniff, but a tear escaped anyway.

Nick said something into his phone that she didn't catch, then ended the call and dropped the device on the seat next to him. He reached down for her, clasping her hand again.

And she hung on for dear life.

———

NICK HAD NEVER BEEN SO SHAKEN in all his life. Someone had taken shots at Kylie.

They'd nearly succeeded too. He'd run into one of them with the rear fender of his truck. Somehow, luckily, the man hadn't been able to grab onto the truck bed and get in.

He hadn't been able to identify Military-Guy. Because it had been dark and he'd been focused on getting Kylie into the truck, he hadn't gotten a good look at the guys shooting at them.

It was clear Kylie was in trouble. The problem was, he didn't know where that trouble was coming from. He'd spent the afternoon verifying different pieces of Kylie's story. He'd looked up her mom's death certificate. Spoken on the phone to her mom's former landlord, who confirmed that Kylie had cleaned out the apartment all those months ago. And he'd spoken to her boss, who said Kylie was welcome back to the Chicago firm when her leave of absence was over.

Now, he could only hope they'd left all of their assailants behind as he turned onto a back road outside of town. The dirt road needed tending badly, and his truck bounced and jostled before the tires caught traction.

Maybe he should slow down, but the residual fear had his foot pressing on the accelerator.

"Where are we going?" Kylie asked, still on the floor.

He flashed another look in the rearview mirror. No headlights shone from behind.

"I think it's safe for you to come up here now."

She shoved Snow's hind leg out of the way and crawled into the middle seat, knocking into his thigh before she settled.

"My uncle's wife has a cabin on the east side of Bear Lake. It's not much, but it will be hard for someone to connect it to me. So as long as we're not being followed, we should be safe there."

Her leg jangled up and down. "I don't get it. Why is someone targeting me? Nobody even knew I was coming to town. Who...who were those guys anyway?"

She sounded sincere, but...there were still chunks missing in her story. Where had she been during the months between cleaning out her mom's apartment and now? Was she hiding something? He wanted to believe she was simply traveling and trying to work through her grief, but his former relationship with Farah made him wary.

He slanted a glance at her, her face shadowed in the darkened cab. "You don't know anyone who might be targeting you? Anybody you might've run across in your travels...? Maybe you witnessed something...?"

"No. Nothing."

Nothing? Or maybe she hadn't realized she'd seen something. A shooting in Bear Lake was unprecedented and he was going to have to work to remember the training he'd gone through at the academy on how to deal with it. Or maybe the captain would call in the OSBI for help with a scene this big...

When Nick was sure they were safe, maybe after they'd slept for a few hours, he'd ask her about every place she'd been in the past few months.

Didn't mean he couldn't probe now.

"I didn't mention it before, but someone came into the precinct looking for you yesterday. I didn't tell him where you were, but obviously he had skills enough to track you to the state park and then to my apartment."

She was sitting close enough that he felt the shiver go through her. "Who was it?"

"I don't know. I checked the video cameras at the precinct, and I've got a photo of him tucked in my pocket to show you. A bigger issue is that there were two guys back at the apartment complex." Two, not one.

The photo was a long shot. It was grainy and only showed Military-Man in profile, as if he'd been aware of the cameras in the parking lot and interior.

Nick turned down another side road. He was taking enough detours that even if someone were following—and they'd have to be far behind for him not to see them, even with headlights off—they'd be lost on these back roads.

He'd be better prepared this time, too. His uncle kept the cabin stocked with hunting rifles. Nick would be vigilant. No one was going to hurt Kylie on his watch.

Another half hour of driving, including a couple of switchbacks, and Nick pulled onto the winding quarter-mile drive to the cabin.

The sliver of moonlight reflected off the midnight blue lake, visible even through the birch and oak trees that wooded the area all around.

He cut the lights as he pulled in front of the single story cabin. The wooden siding was worn, paint peeling in places. A small deck off the side of the house faced the water, a perfect place to watch the sunrise over the lake and enjoy a cup of coffee. Maybe if you weren't on the run from men with guns.

Kylie followed him out of the truck, Snow jumping down behind her.

He rested one hand on the side of the truck bed. "At least I hadn't unloaded the groceries. We'll have eats, even if you don't have a spare change of clothes. Maybe my aunt left some things behind."

Kylie glanced around, and he had to wonder if the trepidation he saw on her features was because of the shadows surrounding the dark landscape or because of what she'd been through in the past twenty-four hours.

"I'm not that worried about my clothes," she admitted. "More that someone is out there, after me, and I don't even know why."

He reached for her, now able to take the time to comfort her. She came into his arms, and he felt the trembles going through her body.

"I'm sorry I left you alone," he murmured, burying his nose in her hair. "I promise I won't let anything happen to you."

He only hoped it was a promise he could keep.

———

IT WAS late as Gideon surveyed the apartment complex's parking lot.

Huge temporary lights had been set up to illuminate the area. Yellow crime scene tape blocked it off from the public.

Skid marks on the pavement showed where a vehicle had reversed quickly and then burned rubber to escape. He'd heard the call on the police scanner about an attempted shooting at the complex and guessed it was the same hired guns that had tried to kill Alessandra last year. Bear Lake was small enough that he doubted they'd seen this kind of crime before.

The crime scene looked like a disaster area.

Pieter stood beside him on the sidewalk, arms crossed, feet spread. The pose was almost belligerent, but Gideon knew the man had to be feeling defensive about what had happened.

Gideon didn't blame him. It was Pieter's mother's fault. Maybe Pieter should've kept better tabs on her or had her in a more secure location, but he couldn't have known she'd escape the mental hospital.

He didn't want to get too close to the officer taking pictures of the scene, though he and Pieter weren't the only curious faces standing around. He figured a small town like this hadn't seen excitement like a shooting in years, if ever.

He knew, or at least hoped, that the lost princess hadn't been hurt. He'd called the local hospital, and no one had been admitted tonight. On the other hand, if it were he protecting the princess, he'd stay off the radar, too.

He and Alessandra had made the decision to keep their search for Kylie out of the media, not wanting the King's indiscretion made public.

But maybe that had been the wrong choice. Maybe if they went public with the search for the princess, she'd come to them. It was worth a shot, wasn't it?

But he couldn't air Alessandra's family's dirty laundry without talking to her first. He took out his phone and hit the first saved contact. His wife.

———

THE BATHROOM LIGHT seemed sunshine bright after the darkness and terror of the past hour. Kylie closed her eyes against it and against the knowledge that Nick was walking the perimeter of the cabin with a flashlight and probably his weapon drawn. He knew what he was doing. She had to keep reminding herself of that.

He seemed certain they were safe here, on this remote lakeside cabin.

Kylie rummaged beneath the sink and came up with a faded white first-aid box. Judging by the layer of dust, the box had been there a long time. She hoped it was stocked enough to help Nick. He'd sworn the bullet wound wasn't bad, but she hadn't seen it yet for herself.

The bathroom was tiny, and he'd told her he'd wait in the kitchenette after he carried in the groceries. It had taken him several minutes to turn on outdoor levers for the electricity and water. Her stomach was grumbling by now, but his wound was a higher priority than eating.

When she exited the bathroom, he was coming through the front door, a brown grocery bag in one arm. The other—the one with the gunshot wound—wasn't exactly held limp, but obviously the wound bothered him.

Their eyes connected from across the room. She paused on the threshold, or maybe he did, but they both ended up staring at each other from across the room, long enough that heat rushed into her cheeks. A vivid, visceral memory of those moments where he'd tugged his bulletproof vest over her head, making her feel protected, almost cherished, popped into her mind.

He was the first to move forward, and she felt a little foolish as she moved into the living area. He passed her and set the groceries on a round kitchen table for four, one that overlooked a large corner window that would have a nice view of the lake in the morning. Snow's toenails snicked on the floor as the dog followed Nick to the kitchen.

The dog snuffled its way into the living area and laid down at Kylie's feet.

Kylie perched on the awful plaid couch, popped open the first-aid kit, and set its contents on the low coffee table. Surprisingly, there were antibiotic ointment, sterile bandages, and antiseptic wipes. As long as Nick didn't need a butterfly bandage or stitches, they should be good.

What if he did need stitches? What did she really know about tending gunshot wounds anyway? Could he get infected from the gunpowder residue or something? She should send him to the local hospital.

She should, but she wouldn't. She could still taste the fear from earlier. He'd survive without a hospital, but she didn't think she'd survive being here without him.

He approached, and she looked up at him, forcing a smile. "Let's get a look at that wound, mister."

"It's not bad." But maybe he knew she was stubborn, because he sat on the coffee table beside her supplies. Their knees bumped.

He used his opposite hand to roll up the sleeve of his T-shirt, revealing blood dried to a dark brown and then a two-inch furrow where red still oozed from the wound where his bicep met his shoulder.

Seeing the blood made her slightly nauseated, and she swallowed hard, willing her stomach to stay strong.

Six inches to the right, and the bullet would've pierced his chest, possibly hitting his heart or lungs. And he wasn't wearing a vest, because he'd given it to her.

Thinking about what could've happened made her dizzy.

"See? Not bad at all."

His words jarred her out of the stifling fear, but not before he'd tilted his chin up and caught her staring.

"Hey." He touched her knee, his skin warm against her chilled flesh. "It's not a big deal."

"It could've been, if that shot had..." She swallowed hard again, unable to voice the awful thought. She raised one hand to touch his chest lightly, just above where his heart would be.

He clasped her hand, pressing her wrist firmly against his chest. Even through the thin barrier of his T-shirt, she could feel the steady thump of his heart.

"You can't live in the *could have beens*," he said softly. You'll drive yourself crazy. And you can't change the past anyway."

The words resonated back, beyond the situation she faced today to the previous year, this journey to find pieces of her mom.

Emotion swamped her, bringing tears to her eyes all over again.

She ducked her head. She was a mess. Whether the emotion was because of her lingering grief or a barrage of relief at what they'd just survived, she didn't know. But it was overpowering.

Nick seemed to know how fragile she felt, because he didn't push, didn't fold her close. He just kept hold of her hand against his sternum. How did he know that if he held her, she'd break?

He was here. He was whole. And he was mostly unhurt.

That was enough for now.

*Chapter Seven*

ON THEIR THIRD MORNING AT THE CABIN, KYLIE WOKE TO the muffled slam of a car door. Sunlight streamed through the window, which was bracketed by gingham blinds. If Kylie sat up in bed, she had a view of the lake through a canopy of red and orange leaves. Right now she'd trade the view to see who'd parked outside.

The bright sunlight told Kylie she'd slept later than she'd intended. She was still having trouble sleeping, even though Nick insisted they were safe at the cabin.

Another car door slammed. From where she lay at the end of the bed, Snow lifted her head. Her ears perked. She didn't bark.

The cabin only had one bedroom, and Nick had insisted she take it. He'd been camping out in a sleeping bag on the living room sofa. With the door closed, she didn't hear any of the familiar sounds she'd grown accustomed to in the mornings. Nick shuffling around, the outdated coffee machine percolating, the sound of pans and plates shifting.

Was something wrong?

Heart pounding, she kicked her legs out of the sheets and padded across the floor barefoot. She wore a T-shirt that Nick had loaned her and a pair of his drawstring shorts cinched tight enough that they wouldn't fall.

She opened the bedroom door a crack and peered out into the main room. It was empty. Where was Nick?

Maybe he'd left a note or something. He'd stuck close the past two days, but perhaps he'd needed to go somewhere. She crept out into the kitchen, Snow following, her nails clicking on the rough wood floors.

There was no note, but through the living room windows, she saw movement outside.

Relief swamped her. It was Nick bending over the bed of his truck.

She let herself out on the step, the cool morning air invigorating her. Snow rushed past and disappeared in the woods to do her morning business.

Nick looked up, a smile spreading across his lips. "You aren't ready, sleepyhead."

His words made no sense. She shrugged, probably looking as baffled as she felt.

"We're going fishing. You aren't dressed for it."

"We are?"

He nodded, looking almost giddy about his surprise. "Here, you'll need this."

He took something out of the bed of the truck, a plastic shopping bag it looked like, and brought it to her.

"What is it?" she asked.

"Couple of changes of clothes. I had a buddy in town pick up some things at the store. I hope they fit."

She'd been making do with the clothes she'd worn when they'd escaped from Nick's apartment.

"You shouldn't have..."

His gaze was steady. "It wasn't a big risk. I've been checking in with the precinct and other friends in town, It's been quiet since the other night. And my buddy Ryan and I were careful. Plus, he brought the bait." He jerked his thumb over his shoulder, indicating the pickup again. "I'll get the poles and tackle box while you run in to change."

Snow bounded out of the woods and right up to Nick, sniffing his boots and jeans.

"Thank you," Kylie said, emotion choking her up slightly.

Nick nodded.

She turned and traipsed inside.

A surge of excitement went through her at the thought of getting out of the cabin. It'd been a quiet couple of days, mornings spent on the porch, sharing coffee and enjoying the birdsong; evenings spent playing cards with one of the decks they'd found in a drawer. Nick had lit a fire last night in the outdoor pit, and they'd pulled up the Adirondack chairs and curled up to enjoy the heat.

They'd talked a lot. Nick had told her about the police academy and the best and worst small-town calls he'd answered. He'd also shared some wild stories about his younger sister.

She'd told him about her favorite college courses and Michael, the boyfriend who hadn't understood why she'd needed to search for her mother's memory. He'd been patient for about a month, then ended their relationship in search of someone available.

She'd found an unexpected friend in Nick. Maybe more, if she considered the way her heart raced when he was near.

But what would happen when she left to go back to Chicago? Nick was firmly entrenched in his life here. His family was here, as was the job that he seemed devoted to.

She dumped the contents of the plastic bag on the bed, blushing a little when she saw the underthings in their package. At least Nick hadn't done the shopping. She hadn't met the friend, and now she sort of hoped she never would. Beyond the intimates, she found sweatpants, jeans, several colorful T-shirts, and a light jacket.

It was simple clothing, but the gesture touched Kylie. The same way his care over these last days had. Every time he proved that he was thinking about her, putting her first, her heart opened to him a little bit more.

She threw on the sweats and a deep green T-shirt and tugged on her running shoes.

Back outside, she stood on the step and called to Nick as he jogged up a thin path through the woods that must lead to the lake. "Should I pack something to eat?"

He shook his head. "Jerry owed me one more favor." He popped the driver's side door, reached inside the cab, and pulled out a brown paper bag.

He wiggled it side to side.

She stepped off the stoop. "Is that from the bakery?"

He nodded. "Fresh from the oven. You can grab the coffee. It's in the console."

She brushed past him and grabbed two paper cups, bringing one to her lips as she bumped the truck door closed with her hip.

Nick was watching her with one brow raised. "I guess that's a reflection on my coffee-making skills."

She grinned sheepishly. "No, no...."

His eyebrow twitched, but he stayed silent. Was this his interrogation technique?

"Okay, yes!" she admitted.

He kept the serious look. How long could he keep it up?

"I'm sorry! I don't mean anything by it, it's just that you brew it so strong!"

He crossed his arms over his chest, still holding the paper bag in one hand. It swung as he settled in to the defiant posture. She really hadn't meant to offend him.

And then he eased out of his stance, a smile widening over his tanned face. "I'm just messing with you. My mom says the same thing."

She wanted to give him a friendly punch, but with both hands full, all she could do was elbow him.

"C'mon," he said, "we're wasting prime fishing time."

———

NICK COULD GET USED to having Kylie close. He knew the past two idyllic days weren't the norm and that life would have to go back to the way things had been before, but the time with her had shown him how much he still liked her. Cared about her.

Was maybe even falling in love with her.

She followed him down the faint deer trail toward the lake. The silvery water reflected the early morning sunlight. A breeze cooled his cheeks.

The dock came into focus, a smudge of dark brown against the blue water. Beside it rested a slender canoe where he'd already loaded the paddles, poles, and tackle box.

Kylie slowed her stride behind him. "A canoe?"

He half-turned, paused near the foot of the trail. "What's the matter? You can swim, can't you?"

"I'd rather not."

He grinned. "Then I guess we'd better not turn it over."

"I'm not sure..."

He jerked his elbow toward the boat. "I'm an experienced canoeist. I won't send you into the water."

She wrinkled her nose but followed him to the water's edge and they juggled coffee cups and laughed a little as he tried to hold the bow steady while she stepped in. He invited Snow to jump in, and the dog settled at Kylie's feet.

Nick waded through the mossy water, the tall rubber boots he'd donned earlier keeping his socks dry. He stepped into the canoe, sitting smoothly on the small bench in the rear seat, barely rippling the water around them.

He picked up a paddle and dipped it in the water, careful not to splash her.

She sipped her coffee, her eyes scanning the shoreline as they began to drift slowly.

It *was* pretty. The leafy birches hung over the water in some places, interspersed with oaks and the occasional elm. The ground was carpeted with decayed leaves in shades of brown. The sunlight broke through the trees overhead, dappling them with light and shadow. A hidden chickadee sang from somewhere overhead.

It was peaceful.

Kylie seemed lost in thought, staring down—maybe at her reflection in the rippling water.

He rested the paddle in the floor and let the canoe float. It took a few moments to attach a hook and sinker to one of the poles and bait it up with a live minnow from the bucket he'd stowed beneath his seat. He let Snow have a sniff of the tiny live fish before he hooked it. The dog was peaceful, resting in the canoe. Impressive.

He cast the line out into the water, the bait and hook sinking with a soft *ploop*. Then he nudged Kylie and pressed the pole into her hands.

She settled her coffee cup between her knees and tested the weight of the pole in her hands. "I haven't done this since... I guess since Mom and I moved away from here."

"Then I bet you're due some beginner's luck," he said. "You'll probably reel in a three- or four-pounder. My dad said the crappie have really been biting this year. Although I remember coming away with the biggest catch the time we fished together."

She sent him a lingering glance over her shoulder. "When we were ten? I'm sure I don't remember it going that way."

He shrugged. "Unless you can provide photographic evidence to the contrary, I guess we'll have to agree to disagree."

She squinted. "Is that a challenge? Because I'm not sure whether you remember how competitive I am."

He grinned as he threaded fishing line through the loops on his pole. "Oh, after playing rummy with you last night, I've got a good idea. I know a few tricks. I'm sure I can take you."

Once the line had been secured, he tied off a hook and sinker on the end.

She wrinkled her nose. "What was that about beginner's luck? Were you just buttering me up?"

"No, no. Of course not."

From behind her, he saw her red-and-white bobber sink beneath the water's surface. He nodded to where it had last been. "You've got a bite."

Kylie whirled and gave a tiny shriek.

"Don't pull too wildly, or you'll—"

She jerked her pole back, sending their canoe wobbling. She shrieked all over again. Snow barked.

He stayed in his seat, trying to offset her movement by his stillness. He clamped a hand on her shoulder and the crazy rocking of the canoe settled slightly. "Easy, Tiger."

She shot a wild look over her shoulder, shaking slightly. "I forgot."

"It's okay. We're not that far from shore. I assume both you and Snowball can doggie paddle."

She shot him a scathing look.

"Of course, we'd lose the donuts..."

"Oooh, I forgot about the donuts."

She'd been tugging against the tension on her line but now her bobber popped back above the water's surface.

"Looks like you lost your fish."

She sighed and twirled the reel, pulling in her line.

He finished tying off the hook on his pole and reached for a minnow as her line crested the edge of the canoe. The hook and sinker were completely gone, snapped off the line.

"Here, you can take mine while I bait you back up," he offered.

"No way. You got me all excited for a donut."

He laughed and cast his line into the water, aiming for a dark spot —maybe a submerged log?—near the shoreline. The gunshot wound in his arm pulled at the motion, but he ignored it.

The paper bag rattled as she dug out a chocolate and sprinkle-covered confection. Snow's head came up off her paws, and Kylie pinched off a tiny piece of the donut and shared it with the dog.

He had a view of the side of her face but tried not to stare as Kylie took a bite, the chocolate disappearing between white teeth and pink lips.

They hadn't repeated the kiss they'd shared the afternoon before their wild flight to the cabin, but not for lack of wanting to, at least on his part.

He was afraid he'd scare her off with the intensity of his feelings. His mom had challenged him the last time they'd spoken on the phone, demanded that he not get in over his head again and brought up Farah. Jerry had done the same this morning, although not as pushy as his mother, edging up to the subject but ultimately just asking whether Nick knew what he was doing.

Their concern only solidified his feelings for Kylie. He'd had plenty of down time the past three days to think. Kylie hadn't asked for his help, even when she'd been at her most upset. She wasn't taking advantage of him.

They'd spent hours upon hours talking. He felt reasonably certain that she'd done what she'd claimed after her mom died. Lots of wandering. Soul searching. He couldn't find anything suspicious in her past, so it was scary that he had no idea where the threat against her originated.

The precinct had been busy cataloguing the crime scene. They hadn't turned up any clues other than a couple of bullets that had been sent off for ballistics testing that could take weeks. His captain had a lead on Military-Guy, and was supposed to hunt him down at the local hotel today. If that didn't pan out... Nick didn't know where the next attack could come from.

Meanwhile, he was falling for Kylie. She was funny, and smart, and maybe a little lost since her mother's death. After spending so much time together, Kylie had sowed seeds of the idea that maybe it was time for him to forgive himself for what had happened with Farah. Her tender heart was another thing to admire.

No doubt about it. He was falling head over heels.

He was certain about his feelings, but it felt quick, which made him hold back. He was afraid that if he declared himself, she'd tell him things were moving too fast. He was afraid she'd disappear, move back to Chicago.

But he'd also determined to at least broach the subject of his feelings with her. Find out if there was a chance she'd consider a long-distance relationship. Or maybe he'd think about leaving his job here and joining the force there to be close to her. Maybe getting away from Bear Lake's long memory would be a good thing.

As Kylie enjoyed her breakfast, Nick reeled in a small crappie and tossed it back. By that time, Kylie had finished her donut, so he tied her off another hook and sinker and baited her hook.

She nearly hooked *him* with a wild cast, sending them both laughing.

Jerry had provided a newspaper along with the donuts, and Nick picked it up now, figuring he'd give Kylie a few minutes to catch up to his fish count. She didn't need any excuses when she lost.

He shook the newspaper slightly as he opened it to the second and third page, but then froze as a familiar picture—two familiar pictures—caught his eye.

The first was Military-Man himself. In the photo, he was dressed in a smart black tux and standing next to a good-looking blonde in a cascading wedding dress. The second picture, below the first, was Kylie, or a sketch of a woman who could've been Kylie. The resemblance was so close.

*ROYAL FAMILY SEARCHES FOR LOST PRINCESS.*

Nick's stomach pitched. Part of him wanted to whip the newspaper closed, ignore this—whatever *this* was. Instinctively, he knew that whatever it was, it could change Kylie's life—and maybe his part in her life—in an instant.

But he had to know. He quickly scanned the article. Military-Man wasn't an enemy after all. He was married to a princess from a small European country Nick had never heard of before. And he was here in Bear Lake searching, on his wife's behalf, for her half-sister.

Kylie.

He reached to his pocket for his phone, only to realize he must've left it in the truck. He'd bet it was blowing up with calls from his captain and maybe even from the local newspaper reporter.

He'd known real life was going to intrude, but not like this.

———

KYLIE FELT Nick's sudden stillness. She glanced over her shoulder, ready to tease him about his fishing prowess. The words died on her lips when she saw how white his face had gone.

Her heart pounded with sudden panic. "What's the matter?"

He folded the newspaper, opening it to a specific page, and then held it out for her. She exchanged her fishing pole for the paper. It crinkled beneath her hand.

Her own face looked back at her.

"What is this?"

He didn't answer. Instead, he paddled toward the shore. His movements were economical and quick, much more so than they'd been during the leisurely float out on the water. Something was wrong, and it had to do with her picture in the paper. She bent her head to read the accompanying article.

"This is impossible," she said with a little laugh. "It's crazy."

The bottom of the boat scraped against the mud and moss as it came ashore. Nick grunted as he hopped over the side and waded through the water to pull the canoe all the way onto the bank, muscles rippling, though he favored his left arm.

Snow jumped out of the canoe, splashing in the mossy water.

Kylie clutched the edge of the canoe, trying to ground herself. "Nick…" she whispered. "This is crazy, right?"

But his eyes were dark when he finally looked at her. "Not *that* impossible. You never knew your dad's identity."

It wasn't a question. She'd admitted that tidbit to him during one of their deeper conversations. That, and how she'd always felt like something was missing from her family because of it.

Nick moved to clasp her waist with his big hands. He easily lifted her from the canoe, transferring her to dry ground with only two steps. He set her away from him and turned back to the canoe to gather up the remains of their breakfast. He stowed the oars and pulled the boat fully onto the bank.

She glanced again at her likeness in pen and ink. "It could be someone else."

"It's you. The paper would've done its research before they ran an article like that." He straightened and brushed one hand through his hair, his agitation clear. He left his tackle box and the two fishing poles in the canoe. "I'll come back for those later. My phone's at the truck and I'm guessing my captain is trying to get in touch with me."

She swallowed against the sudden emotion in her throat. This was a lot to take in. The fact that someone out there—a princess— thought Kylie was royalty. Or at least halfway so. She might have a sister that she'd never known about.

Was this why she'd been targeted by the men who'd shot at her and Nick? Because she might be royalty? But why?

Her swirling thoughts steadied when Nick's hand closed over hers. He tugged her up the path toward the cabin. "We've got to get back."

He whistled for Snow as they moved through the woods together. The dog rustled through the underbrush, hunting squirrels and probably coating her wet fur with dirt and leaves. Although Nick's hand was warm against Kylie's skin, the contact didn't bring the comfort it had for the past two days. She could feel the tension coiled in him.

If she was really a princess, it would change everything.

# Chapter Eight

THEY ARRIVED AT THE PRECINCT SEVERAL HOURS LATER, AS the sun was going down. After reading the newspaper article, Nick had wanted to go right in, but his captain had ordered him to stay in the secluded cabin until nightfall. Apparently, the former Navy SEAL and a prince of Glorvaird was coordinating things now.

Nick itched under the forced inactivity. And didn't particularly care for being told what to do about Kylie's safety. Gideon Hale had claimed the attacks on Kylie were hired killers hired by the Glorvaird princess's aunt and that the men were still out there somewhere. Nick wasn't willing to take chances with Kylie's life, so he'd agreed to wait.

Most of all, he hated that she was leaving. She hadn't come out and said so—she'd been quiet and reserved all afternoon—but he knew it would only be a matter of time.

Now Military-Guy—Gideon Hale—stood on the sidewalk near the front door, a pair of reflective sunglasses similar to the ones Nick owned hiding his eyes. His arms were crossed over his chest and he scanned his surroundings. Nick knew to drive right up to the curb. He waited for the ex-soldier to nod to him before he spoke to Kylie. "It's okay. Go on in."

She glanced at him, worrying her lower lip between her teeth. "Aren't you coming?"

"I've got to park the truck."

She looked at Hale and back to Nick. "Can't I wait and go in with you?"

Hale didn't like the delay and approached the passenger door.

"It's safer if you go in now. I'll be right behind you."

He didn't mention snipers or hired guns, just shooed her out of the truck with a motion of his hand. "I'll be right there."

She stepped out of the car, Hale quickly moving to shield her with his body. Guy looked to be wearing a flak jacket and Nick appreciated the care he was taking with Kylie.

After pulling his truck into one of the open spots, Nick sat with his hands clenched on the wheel. How was he supposed to pull this off? He needed fortitude to walk into the precinct and tell Kylie he was happy that she was flying off to some tiny European country. Was he supposed to pull it out of thin air?

He wanted her to stay.

He snorted.

What exactly could he offer a *princess* to entice her to stay? He was ready to leave his job behind and move to Chicago for her—even if he'd never won over the people of Bear Lake after the disaster with Farah—but Kylie was walking into something neither of them could truly understand. She was a royal now.

And he couldn't begrudge her the family she would have. He hoped that the sisters he'd learned about would welcome her. He knew Kylie deeply desired a family connection, and now she'd have it.

He needed to move before she got curious and tried to come find him. He shored up what smile he could find and pushed out of the truck. Everything was quiet. Maybe Hale was wrong and the hired guns had left.

But just in case, Nick would be on his guard until Kylie got on that plane to Glorvaird.

———

KYLIE SAT in a tiny conference room—an interrogation room?—in the Bear Lake police station, Nick at her side. It was nearly bare with only a scratched table and a few chairs taking up space on the linoleum floor.

She couldn't stop shaking.

She'd just been officially introduced to Gideon Hale. Her sister's husband. A brother-in-law she would have never imagined. His story seemed so farfetched that she could barely believe it. She'd known her mom had gone on a European backpacking trip when she'd been nineteen. But Kylie had no idea how her mother had run across a king, nor how she'd managed a secret affair, even a short one. Gideon was fuzzy on how the king of Glorvaird had kept tabs on her all these years—until Mom had died and Kylie had gone off the grid during her long cross-country trip.

After revealing all of that, Gideon'd handed her his cell phone with one number highlighted. All she had to do was dial the phone and she could speak to her sister.

Fingers trembling, she managed to swipe the screen.

She was peripherally aware of Gideon slipping from the room. Nick started to stand up and she was afraid he would walk out too. She grabbed his hand, anchoring him to his seat. Or maybe he was her anchor.

The call connected.

"Gideon? Did you meet her?" The women's voice was pleasant and cultured, with a slight accent.

"H-hello? This is Kylie."

There was a pause on the other end of the line. Then a tremulous, "Kylie? Is it really you?"

She'd been holding back any hope that this was real. Now it was like a fissure in a dam breaking. Emotion pulsed through her chest and heat flushed her face. "Yes."

"Oh my goodness. I can't believe it. I'm—this is Alessandra. We've been looking for you for such a long time!"

Kylie had to close her eyes against the sting of tears. Someone had been searching for her. Someone wanted her.

She cleared her throat. "Who's 'we'?"

"There are three of us. My—our younger sister Mia. Myself. And our older sister, Eloise, is the crown pr—well, she's the queen now. It's still an adjustment."

Something fierce and hot pierced Kylie's heart. "So the king is—" She gulped.

Another pause. "Father passed away just last month. Multiple sclerosis. Well, complications from pneumonia combined with his disease. We've been looking for you since last spring—over a year now. When he realized he wouldn't be much longer for the world, he told Eloise to find you. Unfortunately..."

It was too late. Sorrow rose for a man that Kylie hadn't even known existed. How she would have loved to have met him, known him.

"Can you come home to Glorvaird? Gideon can make all the arrangements. Eloise won't travel and Mia is—well, she probably won't want to fly internationally. We'll want to talk before we make a formal announcement to the kingdom—" Alessandra cut herself off with a laugh. "I'm sorry. I'm getting ahead of myself. I'm just so thrilled to have finally found you."

Kylie glanced at Nick. She knew her heart must show in her eyes. *She had family. They wanted her to come.*

Home to Glorvaird. It sounded so foreign. And yet...it felt right.

Chapter Nine

THE NEXT MORNING, GIDEON STOOD ON THE TARMAC AT the small rural airport. The Glorvaird royal plane stood nearby, the plane's stairs deployed and its pilot standing at the bottom, conversing with a uniformed flight attendant.

Pieter stood beside him, arms crossed and eyes hidden by metallic shades. Though the man's stance didn't betray anything, Gideon knew Pieter was hyper-vigilant, watching behind those shades for any sign of his mother or one of her hired assassins.

Between Gideon and Pieter was a rented black sedan with dark tinted windows that they'd traded for the truck. Inside were the lost princess, Kylie, and her maybe-boyfriend, Nick. The cop.

She'd introduced him as a friend, but it was clear to see there was something between the two of them.

Last night, after they'd arrived at the police station, Gideon had had the princess do a DNA test that they'd mailed off, just for confirmation, but after the information from Gideon's SEAL hacker friend, it was just a formality at this point. She'd agreed to come to Glorvaird to meet her half sisters. Then she and the cop had spent the night at the precinct, the princess holed up in one of the offices while Gideon and Pieter and one of the other cops stood watch. Nick had bunked down on a sofa in the lobby, but he hadn't slept much. Gideon had come across him once in the break room, hand at the back of his neck and staring into space.

Nick didn't need to worry. There was no way Gideon was letting anybody take out the princess. He owed Alessandra that much.

His wife had been emotional when he'd spoken to her yesterday. Joy and nerves had come through the phone line, and then he'd given his phone to Kylie to let the two sisters talk for the first time. He'd given up waiting on getting his phone back when the conversation had stretched toward an hour.

Now he glanced over to Pieter, who'd been surprisingly steady during this whole ordeal.

"You sure you want to stay?" he asked.

Pieter turned his chin, though the shades hid his eyes.

"If Mother is here, I'd like a chance to find her. Try and convince her to return to the treatment center. Well, to a more secure one," he amended.

Gideon got it. If it were someone related to him causing that much trouble, he'd want first dibs at clearing it up.

For himself, all he wanted was to see his wife.

———

EVERYTHING HAD HAPPENED SO QUICKLY that Kylie couldn't catch her breath. She sat in a sedan with dark-tinted windows, Snow lying across her feet and Nick silent beside her.

She hadn't even known this tiny rural airport existed. It was basically a strip of pavement and a single steel hanger in the middle of two wheat fields.

She still felt as if she was living in a state of suspended disbelief. The fun, quiet morning fishing had turned into a day of questions, some answers, and more questions

She was meeting her three half sisters today. Pieter, the dark-haired prince in his finely tailored suit, was her cousin, though he'd been somewhat distant since they'd met yesterday.

Because his mother was apparently crazy and had hired someone to kill Kylie. That news had been unwelcome, and for a moment, she'd thought Nick would take a swing at the other man. But he hadn't. At least knowing who their enemy was had seemed to unite the men and give Nick a purpose.

But they'd spent their last night apart, and she was confused about where that left their blossoming relationship.

Nick had insisted that she sleep in the captain's office on a lumpy couch. He'd stayed in the main lobby and bullpen area of the precinct building.

It was all too much. Too fast. She had a family. Sisters. She wasn't alone in the world.

She'd wanted to talk about what was happening with Nick, but he'd been distant since everything had gone down yesterday.

Maybe... maybe he didn't return her feelings.

Or maybe he was ready for her to be gone. Ready to be finished babysitting her. Ready to clean up the mess in town from where his apartment building had been shot up. She knew about the rumors and speculation that still followed him around town from his former relationship with Farah. Had Kylie, had their friendship made the rumors worse for him?

Last night, the press had shown up at the precinct. Nick had allowed Gideon to take point and refuse their questions. She guessed Nick didn't want to be caught in their lenses.

Which meant he should probably stay away from her. Alessandra had spoken of making Kylie's place in the Glorvaird royal family public knowledge. No doubt that would bring some crazy media attention, at least for awhile.

She should let Nick go.

She just didn't know how she could.

———

NICK COULDN'T BREATHE. He'd never had a panic attack in his life, but as the pilot came away from the plane to talk to Hale, his chest seized and cut off his air supply.

Kylie was leaving.

Since he'd seen that article, he hadn't had the guts to confess his feelings. When she'd left so abruptly when he'd been twelve, he'd been infatuated with her. But now, after discovering who the grown-up Kylie was, he was in love.

And she was a princess. If he'd thought her out of his league before, it was nothing compared to what he felt now.

He knew how desperate she was for family. Hadn't she told him how disconnected she'd felt from her mom, even before her mom's death? This was her chance to be a part of a real family, a royal family. There was no way he could ask her to give that up.

But once she got on that plane, would he ever see her again?

Gideon turned toward the sedan, and Nick's heart jumped into his throat.

Kylie grabbed his hand and squeezed so hard, her knuckles were white. For one crazy moment, he fought against the urge to beg her to stay.

"Nick," she gasp-whispered his name, and he had second and third and fifteenth thoughts, but he simply held on.

"You've got my number," he said. "In a few days, when you've met your sisters and you're wearing a real diamond tiara and eating caviar, if you have a few minutes, call and let me know how it's going."

She was still trembling, but now her eyes were lit from within. This was exciting for her, even if he was getting left behind.

He popped his door open and gave a tug on her hand. "C'mon. You can't miss your royal flight."

# Chapter Ten

KYLIE'S HEART WAS IN HER THROAT AS THE PLANE descended to a small airstrip in a country she hadn't heard of until yesterday. The jewel-blue ocean water stretched to the horizon. Dark stone cliffs broke up the shore as they approached.

Her leg jittered up and down, and from her knee Snow looked up at her.

"I know," she muttered to the dog. But admitting she knew she was unraveling didn't change it.

Gideon glanced back over his shoulder from his seat two rows ahead, and she attempted a smile in the face of his obvious concern. He'd sat next to her for a while, until she'd run out of things to say and begun to stare out her window.

She still felt a little slack-jawed at the luxury of the private plane. It seated twelve plus the uniformed flight attendant, though most of the seats were empty.

Her derriere had never felt anything like the buttery luxury of the reclining seat, and the attendant had been attentive and even brought Snow a small bowl of water.

Kylie had been too anxious to eat or drink anything.

It was too late to turn back now.

And then her stomach gave a swoop as the plane touched down. Her leg jittered double-time as they taxied for a few short moments.

And then before she was ready, the flight attendant pushed down the steps so they could deplane onto the tarmac.

Kylie paused to take in the sea-soaked breeze and the rocky cliffs that made up the landscape behind the city that seemed tucked into them.

It was breathtakingly beautiful, and her stomach swooped again, this time with a feeling of recognition. Maybe belonging, even. Was this meant to be home?

She was aware of Gideon waiting for her at the bottom of the steps, though he wore a patient smile and didn't seem irritated that she was taking her time.

Snow followed her down the steps and into another of those black sedans. Gideon tucked her into the back seat and then took the passenger seat for himself.

Both the driver and Gideon were quiet as they drove through the cobblestone streets of the city. Kylie couldn't help staring at the buildings that were older than anything she'd ever seen in the U.S. She wanted to ask them to stop, to wander through the streets and dawdle to her heart's content, discover every hidden thing about this magical place.

It almost seemed as if the very beat of the blood in her veins sung for Glorvaird. Was this place really a part of her already? It seemed surreal.

There would be time for exploring later. Right now, she had to meet her sisters. Sisters!

And then, again before she was ready, the sedan crossed beneath a portico and through an imposing gate. They circled behind a stone castle so vast it took her breath away.

Outside a garage that had been an obvious addition to the centuries-old structure, the sedan rolled to a stop. Gideon had told her because of the continued threats to the royal family, security demanded they use the castle's private family entrance.

She'd arrived.

Kylie's knees were suddenly weak.

Snow's head rested in her lap, offering what comfort she could.

Gideon and the driver got out of the car, but a sudden bout of nervousness had Kylie frozen.

Gideon opened her door, and she forced her shaky legs to support her as she climbed out of the car. Snow followed, sniffing the ground and giving a slow wag of her tail.

A door with a curved top built into the modern garage door flew open, and two blonde women tumbled out.

Gideon sighed.

A third woman, also with blonde hair, exited at a more sedate pace. This one was scarred across one side of her face. Eloise. Gideon had warned Kylie of the scars she gotten from an auto accident when she was a teenager, and that Kylie's oldest half-sister was sensitive about them. Now she jerked her gaze away, focusing on the two younger women who'd rushed outside.

"You couldn't wait until we got inside to one of the parlors?" Gideon asked.

Unsure what was the right thing to do here, Kylie looked to Gideon, as he was her one link, the one constant since they'd left the U.S.

He nodded to the slightly taller woman wearing slacks and a soft sweater. "My wife, Alessandra."

"And I'm Mia," the second woman chirped. She was almost bouncing on her toes, eyes dancing. She had the cutest baby bump beneath her pink blouse.

Though their hair was lighter than the blond Kylie had seen in the mirror all her life, all three women had the same bright blue eyes.

Kylie realized she hadn't said anything. Her mouth suddenly dry, she cleared her throat, swallowed.

"H—hi," she stammered. Throat hot, sudden tears pricked her eyes.

But it was okay, because Alessandra wiped her cheeks, where tears rolled down.

Mia gave a watery laugh, and then both younger women moved forward, embracing Kylie.

Her heart banged against her chest as she fought back tears and overwhelming emotions.

She blinked through her tears and saw Eloise holding back, though her eyes were shiny and her lower lip trembled. Did she want to be a part of the embrace as well?

"Eloise," Kylie whispered. She held out one hand to her oldest sister. And Eloise joined in their group hug.

Sisters. Hers. Unbelievable.

———

"YOU THINK this is gonna go on all night?"

Gideon grunted. He glanced at Cody Austin, Eloise's fiancé and his future brother-in-law, as the other man rested one elbow casually on the chest-high bar along one side of the wall and nodded to the four women gathered around one end of the oblong wooden dining table. They hadn't stopped chattering since he and Kylie had arrived.

He'd made a stop in the security office and touched base with

Pieter by phone while the princesses had showed Kylie to a suite off the royal hallway.

The princesses had opted to have supper in the castle's smaller formal dining room. The kitchen had outdone itself, cooking an array of Glorvaird favorites, so much that the leftovers had been enough for the staff to feast after the food had been removed from the royal table.

That had been two hours ago. The chatter had been a bit much and he'd had to get up from the table a bit ago.

The women didn't appear to be slowing down, still talking in rapid-fire tones, often interrupting and talking over each other, as if they could learn everything about each other in one night. Even Eloise had shed most of her usual diffidence and was lively as she participated in the conversation. But it was getting late, and Gideon was two time zones past his bedtime.

He eyed his wife and wondered if he dared interrupt.

From Gideon's other side, Ethan chimed in. "I'm about to pull rank. Mia's been more exhausted than usual this week."

His brother-in-law was particularly protective of his wife. Mia's pregnancy was showing now, and she usually had one or two of the long-time staff following her around the castle. Seemed everyone was protective of their princess and the first royal of the next generation.

If Ethan was going to interrupt the princess's tete-a-tete, Gideon wouldn't have to be the bad guy.

"Any news on the crazy aunt?" Cody asked.

Gideon shook his head, eyes on the women.

"Pieter stayed. I think he was hoping she'd see him around town and come out into the open."

"You still think he's trustworthy?" Ethan asked.

Gideon shrugged. "He hasn't proved otherwise. I believe he's really in love with his McKenna, and she's not going to put up with any shenanigans."

He liked Pieter, even if he was content to wait and make sure the other man proved his mettle.

The women stood, and all Gideon could think was, *thank goodness*! He just wanted his wife and his bed.

Alessandra was still bubbly after they'd said their goodnights and retired to their suite.

"Did you see how much she looked like Mia? It was in her chin, I think."

Her attention was on her hands as she idly flipped through a pile of papers on the entry credenza. Gideon enveloped her in his arms, wrapping around her shoulders from behind and tucking his chin into the curve of her neck. "All I could see today was you. I've missed you."

He knew her neck was a ticklish spot, and she gave a gasping giggle as he breathed the words into the soft skin just below her hairline. "You were only gone a few days this time."

"Too long. I've been thinking..." He took a deep breath and said it. "I might sign over my share of the Triple H to Matt and Carrie."

"What?" She turned to face him, her eyes searching his. "Why?"

"It's too hard being away from you, and the ranch needs managing that I can't do from here. Even with Dan as foreman."

Her brow wrinkled. "But you've worked so hard. Won't you regret just giving it up?"

He shrugged. "I did the work for their benefit. There's a lot I can do from here for the royal family. Maybe it's time to let my little brother grow up, grow into running the ranch."

It hurt a little to say the words, but he knew it was the right thing to do. Was his brother Matt ready for that much responsibility?

---

NEARLY A WEEK LATER, Kylie wandered down one of the vast hallways of the Glorvard palace, letting her hand trail against the cool, smooth stone walls.

Snow following, nails clicking on the cold floor.

She'd been hoping to find—there! She ducked through a door in an alcove and was suddenly outside in the salt-soaked sea air.

A winding stone staircase led down to a white sand beach that was totally private, thanks to the cliffs surrounding it and the castle behind.

The sky and water were unbelievably blue, and Kylie breathed in deeply.

Eloise had told her about the private retreat, but Kylie had been so distracted by touring the capital city and learning as much as possible about her sisters and her deceased father that today was her first chance to escape.

Safe inside the castle walls, she'd slept better each night than she had in ages. But it was those moments in the night, just before she dropped off to sleep, that troubled her.

That was when she thought of Nick.

She stepped off the last stair and headed for the water, Snow following.

The warm, soft sand against her bare toes was a comfort. At the water line, she stopped to pick up a half-buried white shell the size of a golf ball. She stepped into the water up to her ankles, bent down, and let the waves wash sand and muck off the treasure, revealing a bright and smooth shell. Perfect.

Snow barked at the cresting waves, running after an approaching one and attempting to bite it, but her muzzle just went through the water.

Kylie couldn't help laughing as the dog did it again and again, getting completely soaked. Finally, Snow returned to Kylie, panting and happy. The dog shook herself, water spraying everywhere.

Kylie sat down several feet from the water line and wrapped her arms around bent knees. Snow lay in the sand next to her. Maybe letting the dog out hadn't been such a great idea, now that she was soaked with salt water and sandy all over. Kylie would have to give the dog a bath later. Or maybe if she mentioned it in the right company, a staff member would appear and take care of it for her.

She still couldn't get used to the luxury of having staff assigned to see to her personal needs. It was unreal.

She flipped the shell in her hand, staring at the minute details God had etched into the surface, but not really seeing them.

The truth was, she missed Nick with a fierce ache. It never really went away, even when she slept, even when she was pleasantly distracted by her sisters.

She'd fallen in love with him. It was unplanned.

Loving someone meant giving him the opportunity to hurt you. To let you down. Kylie's mom had proved that over and over, until Kylie had built high walls around her heart. Even Michael hadn't been able to scale them.

Somehow Nick had found a way over, or through, when no one else had been able to.

Maybe it was because he'd been willing to lay down his life for her, protecting her with everything in him.

Or maybe it was the way he listened to her with a singular intensity.

Or maybe it was just Nick.

So...she loved him. What was she supposed to do about it?

Eloise, Alessandra, and Mia were pushing her to make her permanent home in Glorvaird. They had scheduled a press conference for early next week to introduce her as the king's offspring and their half sister. They'd assured her they would have a media consultant coach her on how to answer questions that might arise about her parentage.

She'd committed to stay through the press conference, but after that she could do whatever she wished. The princesses had promised that her suite would be permanently hers, or if she preferred, they could give her a stipend if she wished to find housing elsewhere in Glorvaird.

She'd spoken to her old boss at the CPA firm briefly. He'd told her he would always have a job for her if she wanted it.

Or possibly she could find work here. Eloise had already asked if she'd take on some of the royal committees. She thought that with Kylie's business acumen and knowledge of accounting principles, she could be an asset to the palace. Kylie hadn't answered yet. Because she had no idea what the answer should be.

What if she returned to the States to find out Nick didn't feel the same way about her?

He'd asked her to call when she'd settled in, but with the realization of her feelings over the past few days, and the crazy-busy business of getting to know her sisters and her home country, she'd put it off.

What if he'd already forgotten all about her?

$$Chapter\ Eleven$$

She hadn't called.

Nick stared at the pile of file folders strewn across his messy desk at the precinct. The building was quiet with only one other officer inside. Boortz was at the front desk, leaning back in an office chair with his feet propped up. He spoke softly into the phone, no doubt telling his wife or kids goodnight before he worked an overnight shift.

Nick was off duty, but his butt was glued to his chair anyway.

Better to clear some of the mountains of paperwork that always seemed to accumulate than to return to his empty apartment and stare at the ceiling, unable to sleep for thinking about Kylie.

*Princess* Kylie.

Gideon had sent him a brief text when they'd arrived safely in Glorvaird. Somehow the man had known that Nick wanted—*needed* —to know at least that much.

No doubt she'd been swept up into the life of a royal. Fancy parties, caviar and champagne, eligible dudes, like dukes or whatever.

Stomach roiling at the thought, Nick thumped his fist on his desk.

Boortz looked over, but Nick waved him off. He could use a good sparring session to burn off some pent-up energy, but the other man didn't look like he was getting off the phone anytime soon.

Nick stood, checked the weapon at his hip, and reached for the duffel beneath his desk. If he couldn't even count on his work to distract him, he might as well head home and make an attempt at sleep. And try to duck any of his mother's friends who might be staking out his apartment.

It seemed that all of Nick's stupidity with Farah had been forgotten by the Bear Lake residents. Because some newspaper report had romanticized the night that Nick had saved Kylie's life. Although nothing formal had been announced by the house of Glorvaird, speculation was abundant around town that she *was* a princess and that she and Nick were connected.

He wished the rumors were true.

Nick had rounded the counter when a man stepped inside the front door. Nick knew a moment of uncertainty when he recognized the man—Pieter, the guy who'd accompanied Gideon into town and whose mom was loony enough to send bad guys after Kylie.

But Pieter didn't look concerned, so Nick felt enough relief to breathe. He nodded to the other man.

"I thought I'd pop in to see if there's been any sighting of my mother," Pieter said.

Nick shook his head. "I've been checking reports daily. Nothing so far."

The other man didn't change expression, but Nick got the idea that he was frustrated by the lack of action. Nick wasn't sure why he'd stuck around—did he really think the hired guns would still be here even though Kylie had left?

Too tired to think on it more, Nick made a move to the door and followed the other man out.

At the curb, a Corvette was parked across two parking spots.

Nick looked at Pieter with a raised eyebrow.

Pieter apparently didn't do sheepish. He shrugged. "It's late. There aren't any other cars in the lot. And it's a rental. My insurance will skyrocket if I ding it."

Because Pieter was the kind of guy who could afford high-end rentals. A kind of guy that Kylie might be interested in now that she had choices.

Nick's voice went a little sharp. "You know, you could just call the precinct for an update."

"Yes, I'm aware of that." He shrugged again. "I've gotten bored of the hotel's four walls. I needed to stretch my legs for a bit."

Nick nodded. There wasn't anything more to say, so he headed for his truck, which was parked at the back corner of the lot.

"You don't look so good, you know," Pieter called out after him.

Nick raised one hand, acknowledging the man without turning

around or even slowing his pace. It wasn't Pieter's business. He wasn't even Nick's friend.

"You could go after her, if she matters that much to you."

Nick turned at that, but the other man was already sliding in to the sports car.

Nick got into his truck, mulling over the words. It wasn't like he hadn't thought about it before. Hopping a plane and flying overseas to claim Kylie, to tell her everything he'd kept inside before she'd left.

And maybe get shot down.

But what if...what if she felt the same? Wasn't it worth the risk?

He'd been shying away from anything remotely risky since Farah. He'd been burned, and bad, but was he going to avoid taking risks his whole life?

――――

THIS WAS A BUST.

Pieter knew it, but he'd hoped, really hoped, that his mother would come out of hiding if she saw him in one place long enough. Especially after all the messages he'd left on her voicemail.

He pulled into the hotel parking lot after his brief conversation with the police officer. He remained in the vehicle and dug his phone out of his slacks' pocket. McKenna was programmed to be the first number he saw, and he dialed her.

"No luck?" she asked after a sweet greeting.

"None."

He took a deep breath, but the pressure behind his sternum didn't ease.

"It's not your fault," she said softly.

She was a doll to say so, but he'd been the one to commit Mother to the hospital. He'd left her there, trusting they'd take care of her. He'd left the country, left her vulnerable to escape.

He desperately wanted to be able to make it right. Maybe if he did, he'd feel more accepted by his cousins. Feel like a real part of the family.

At least with McKenna, he didn't feel the awkwardness of not-quite-fitting in.

"I've been thinking," she said now, "about withdrawing from my last two pageants and going back to Glorvaird with you until school starts in January."

His heart leapt up into his throat.

"With you," she repeated when he couldn't find words fast enough.

"Yes," he said quickly, lest she think he didn't want her near. The opposite, in fact. "I would love that. But—?"

"With the two wins I had earlier this year, I'll have scholarships enough for tuition, books, and room and board for a year. That's enough of a start for me, and I'll find a job once the semester starts. So we can have the rest of the autumn together."

He'd take it, and work at convincing her that a scholarship from the royal family of Glorvaird wasn't charity.

"You know I'd love to spend as much time as possible showing you all my country has to offer."

Before she could respond, the passenger door opened, and a slender figure slipped inside.

His jaw dropped. "Mother?"

McKenna gasped on the other end of the open line. "What's happening? Do you need the police?"

He looked his mother up and down. There was no sign of any weapon, though she had on a cardigan and slacks and could possibly have something hidden away. Her eyes were clear and alert, which sent a slight frisson of relief through him.

"My mother is here," he said into the phone. "I think everything is all right. I'm going to ring off and speak to her."

"If you don't call me back in ten minutes, I'm calling the police," McKenna warned.

Her concern warmed him, and he was smiling as he hung up, even though he had to face the most manipulative person he knew.

"Who was that?" she demanded haughtily.

"My future wife." Maybe it was a bit presumptuous, since they weren't technically engaged, but she had accepted his family crest ring as a promise. And he was determined to win her forever.

Mother's eyes widened.

But he didn't want to give her a chance to trick him into giving her information about McKenna. He didn't want McKenna to be a target and didn't want his mother trying to turn him away from the best thing in his life.

"What do you think you're doing?" he demanded. "I've been worried sick about you, and you've hired a killer?"

Her eyes clouded slightly. "I've told you before—the House of Glorvaird betrayed us—"

"I've met them," he interrupted her. "The princesses. They aren't evil. And we've been able to reconcile."

She tapped her fingers on her knee, a sign of agitation. "The King betrayed me—"

"The King is dead."

Her mouth fell open slightly. Had she been so sequestered that she'd missed the news entirely?

He dared to reach out and let his hand rest over hers.

"Your brother is gone," he said, more softly now. "and it's time for old wounds to be healed. The princesses are willing to forgive what's happened with the killers—but you must call them off."

Her eyes clouded. "Pieter?" she asked. "Where are we? What's going on?"

Was she faking? He'd seen her lose chunks of the present before, as if waking up and restarting. But he wouldn't put it past her to try and put him off his guard.

He sighed. "Do you want to go back to Glovaird, Mother? I can make it happen, but you've got to help me."

———

KYLIE CHECKED the overnight bag stashed next to the door leading out from her suite. She'd agreed to wait until after the press conference before she headed back to the States. To Nick.

She checked her reflection in the wall-mounted mirror, still surprised to see the tailored silk blouse and elegant slacks she wore. Mia had insisted on several shopping excursions in the days after Kylie's arrival. Kylie had never worn such expensive clothing before and the quality fabrics still felt foreign to her. A nice kind of foreign. She darted a glance to the tattered cardboard box tucked in one corner of the room. Nick had shipped a box of her things to her, items recovered from the campsite crime scene. She didn't have time to think about Nick right now.

Eloise's media assistant, Jill, was coming to retrieve her any second to escort her downstairs, where a small stage and rows of folding chairs had been assembled in an empty ballroom.

And there was the knock she'd been expecting.

"I'll be back soon," she said, blowing a kiss to Snow, who raised her head from where she lay on one of the overstuffed sofas. The staff would care for Kylie's dog, and Mia had promised to check in and visit with the dog often until Kylie returned.

The big question was, would Nick return with her?

Kylie let her mind focus on that question, instead of the nerves bubbling in her stomach like a geyser getting ready to erupt. What if the people of Glorvaird rejected her? The King's indiscretion with her mom was a scandal. Though it had happened years ago and been kept a secret for so long, Eloise didn't believe the majority of Glorvaird citizens would hold it against Kylie or anyone in this generation of royals. Or so she'd said when they'd discussed it a couple of days ago.

She loved her sisters, even though she hadn't known them for long. They each had totally different personalities and related to each other differently, but it was obvious they loved each other. They'd caught her up on recent happenings, like when Alessandra had almost been killed and the search for their crazy aunt.

Days after Gideon had escorted Kylie home, Pieter had located his mother and settled her in a high-security mental hospital. Pieter and Gideon had coordinated with the FBI in an attempt to locate the hired assassins with the contact information Pieter's mother had, but the two men had seemed to vanish without a trace. Gideon believed that with Pieter's mother under a constant watch, without a way for the assassins to be paid for completing the job, and with the media attention all of it had drawn, they would give up and never return.

Things were safe for the princesses again.

And her sisters had made a special effort to include Kylie, to make her feel welcome in the castle. She'd finally found the home she'd been looking for all her life. She'd made peace with her mother, as much as she could with a deceased woman. She might never know why her mother had suffered from so much wanderlust, but maybe that was all right. Things were lovely in Kylie's life.

But one thing was still missing.

Jill paused in front of the ballroom door, and Kylie knew a moment of blinding panic. She had to go in.

Jill pushed open the door and held it.

The lights were almost blinding.

Dozens of cameras clicked as she crossed the threshold. There was a hushed, almost expectant silence as she took the handful of steps to join Eloise at the podium.

"I'd like to introduce you to my sister, Kylie Winters." Eloise extended her arm to welcome Kylie to the podium.

She felt slightly faint as she stood behind the wooden box, and she gripped it tightly with both hands. Staring out over the group of unfamiliar faces, many with cameras or phones raised in front of them, she froze.

"Um, hi."

There was a moment of chaos as voices erupted. Jill moved to the edge of the stage to act as moderator.

The crowd quieted somewhat, though they still bustled with murmurs.

"Were you surprised to learn of your parentage?" The first question rang out, and she fell into the rhythm of questions and answers. It wasn't so bad with Eloise beside her and with the prep work they'd done with Jill.

Jill gave her the sign that they were about to wrap things up when a familiar voice sent her pulse tumbling. "Is there a special someone in your life?"

*Nick!*

He stood at the back of the crowd, hair rumpled and wearing a button-up shirt and jeans. One hand rested in his pocket, the other held a duffel bag slung over his shoulder, but his posture was more nervous than relaxed. Gideon stood slightly behind him, grinning.

"Do you mean other than my dog, Snow?"

The press chuckled at her silly answer—as she'd meant them to—but Nick's hopeful expression faltered.

"Yes," she said quickly, lest he get the wrong idea. "Yes, there was someone I left behind in the States."

His smile grew slightly bigger. He began edging around the back of the crowd, slowly making his way toward the stage by taking the unobstructed—but longer—route. A few of the reporters began to catch on that something was happening, and two cameramen turned their cameras toward Nick and snapped photos.

"If this special someone was to show up in Glorvaird today, would he be welcome?"

She felt her own smile growing, unable to hold in the joy that was pounding through her with every beat of her heart. "Very welcome."

She didn't want to mess this up, didn't want to do anything that would tarnish the crown. Kylie glanced at Eloise and Jill, who were conversing in hushed whispers. Eloise gave her a regal nod, and Kylie stepped away from the podium and walked across the stage to the steps.

Nick was closer now, and reporters were stepping out of his way, keeping their gazes—and cameras—on him.

She went down the steps, and two security guards materialized, nudging back the press and allowing Nick a clear path for those last few feet. How did they know Nick was welcome? Had Gideon been in on the whole thing?

He looked right at her, still approaching. "And if this special someone wanted to *stay* in Glorvaird—stay with you...?"

Tears pricked her eyes as he crossed the last step. She held out both hands, and he dropped his bag to clasp them in his.

"I'd say *yes, please*," she whispered.

The crowd murmured as the lucky few who were close enough to hear shared her answer with everyone else. More photos were snapped, flashing going off in her peripheral vision.

She didn't care.

"I was coming back," she said with a sniffle and a smile. "My bags are packed upstairs. I'll have to cancel my plane ticket."

Relief flashed in his eyes, and he pulled her into his embrace, looking into her eyes. "I love you, Kylie. Have since I beat you climbing to the top of Mrs. Chin's pear tree. After this long, I'm pretty sure it's a forever kind of love."

She beamed up at him. "I love you, too. But I'm pretty sure I won the race to the top of that tree."

"No evidence," he argued softly as he bent his head toward hers.

His kiss was full of promises for the future, and she didn't need his *evidence* to know he'd be a rock at her side for everything that was to come. He'd proved his love over and over, by protecting her life—and her heart.

The lost princess had finally found her way home. She'd inherited a family. She'd fallen in love.

She'd finally found her way home.